New Era Publishing

I0692846

PRESENTS

LOYALTY REIGNS

In Family and Factions
Where Honors Rules

By: Jap Cureton

Published by: **New Era Books**
1211 Atlantic Ave, Suite 303
Brooklyn, New York 11208
347-651-6366

This is a work of fiction. Names, characters, places and incidents are either a product of the author's imagination or are fictitious, and any resemblance to actual persons, living or dead, business establishments, events, or locales is entirely coincidental.

ISBN: 978-0-9844071-8-7

Cover Design: Bryan Vallejo

First Print: December 2014

Printed in the United States

Web site: www.newerabooks.net
          www.newerapublication@aol.com

In this break through novel "LOYALTY REIGNS" Jap Cureton takes you on a perilous ride through a neighborhood few outsider's ever see or want to see, a world most would describe as a living hell. It's a world Jap, like his main character Jacob Malone Jr., was born into, a world they call home: a world of neighborhoods that have become a war zone patrolled by kids who should've been in school but instead were recruited to be drug addicted street soldiers in a war fueled by the ravages of poverty and four hundred years of repression resulting in a demand for respect no matter who you had to kill to get it. It's a world where few expect to see old age surprised if they seen the next day.

"LOYALTY REIGNS" exposes the raw and often ugly truth about survival in a world tainted by jealousy, rivalry, violence, drama, and mayhem, disagreements settled only by bullets and blood.

The question that determines who lives or dies that day is determined by "Will Loyalty Reign or will the storms of betrayal make it hail? Be forewarned, it's not a fairy tale or a story for the squeamish or the faint-hearted, but if you are unafraid to be inoculated with a dose of reality, join Jap Cureton's "adult-only" tour through the unforgiving world where only Loyalty Reigns and Honor rules.

Jap Cureton is presently at work on the second book of the LOYALTY REIGNS TRILOGY.

AND HE COMMANDED THEM SAYING "THUS SHALL ACT IN FEAR, FAITHFULLY AND WITH A LOYAL HEART."

2 CHRONICLES 19:9

New Era Publishing

PRESENTS

LOYALTY REIGNS

**In Family and Factions
Where Honors Rules**

By: Jap Cureton

PROLOGUE

And he commanded them, saying, "Thus you shall act in fear ...
faithfully, and with a loyal heart"

Place: Albermarle Middle School - **1996 - 3:26** P.M.

Eleven-year-old Jacob Malone looked up at the large wall calendar hanging just above the old metal filing cabinet. It showed there were only two days before school let out for summer break and here he found himself sitting once again in the principal's office, his teacher, Ms. Greene, and the principal, Mr. Garaston, staring at him harshly. In unison, all three sets of eyes returned to the medium-sized wad of neatly folded currency of various denomination displayed in the middle of the principal's desk. In the silence of the room, Jacob heard the ticketing of the large clock on the wall over the principal's desk and Ms.Green's impatient tapping of her yellow No. 2 pencil against the cover of a file which he assumed was his.

After several students complained all through the '95-'96 school year about Jacob's coming to school loaded with money, the staff at Albermarle Middle School began a daily scrutiny of the 5'5", 140 lb kid who had earned the nickname Bealz Pockets, the name "Bealz" referencing the ten-twenty-fifty and sometimes even hundred-dollar bills Jacob always had in his pocket. To

1

assure themselves that Bealz wasn't dealing drugs in school, or perhaps to prove that he was so they could expel him, the staff made it their mission to hassle him to no end, including constant locker and clothing searches. To the staff, Bealz's small plats, baggy clothes and high-priced Air Jordan sneakers could mean only one thing: drug pusher. Substantiating their suspicions, Bealz had black skin and his parents never showed up for Parent-Teacher conferences.

The educators had been sternly addressing the boyish-looking kid he was paying less attention to what they were saying than to the scuff mark on his white sneakers. Whatever was being said was going in one ear and out the other. Besides, he's heard it all before.

When the school bell rang at 3:30 P.M. indicating the end of the school day, Jacob calmly reached over the principal's desk, snatched his money, and bolted towards the door.

"Wait just a minute, young man!" gray-haired Ms. Greene shouted, placing a white withered hand on Bealz's shoulder. Batting her wrinkled eyelids while looking into his eyes, she asked, "Do you wanna be a hoodlum or make something out of yourself?" showing a green-toothed grin.

"Well, Ms. Greene, I don't want to miss my school bus so I'll have to get back to you on that one", he replied sarcastically, his smile revealing straight white teeth. "Now please take your hands off me."

In their usual frustration, the principal and the teacher could do nothing but watch Bealz exit the office, rattling the window of the door that he slammed behind him. They didn't believe Bealz's explanation that the money came from his Uncle Jake for doing chores around the house. But because no drugs were ever found on Bealz or in his locker, there was nothing anybody could do.

IT wasn't as if anybody really cared. Seventy-five percent of the school's faculty members were white and showed little compassion for the school's sixty-five percent Black student body. So when a parent of a student from a Projects household showed no concern for their child's behavior in school, it was all too easy for the teachers to give up on the student as well.

Bealz took his seat on the half-empty school bus, number Zero Fourty One, trying to tune out the shrieks and shouts of the other kids which were generously laced with curse words and obscenities. The bus driver, a sexy female who moonlighted as a stripper and went by the name "Sugar" remained oblivious to the ruckus, totally absorbed with a chat on her cell phone while she drove the bus. Even as a quarrel between two boys intensified, Sugar kept her eyes on the road and her mouth on the phone. The only thing she was aware of was that she was finally nearing the neighborhoods of her twenty-one young passengers and all that concerned her was clearing her bus.

The school bus made a left onto Oaklawn Avenue, stopping between a church and a ball field. After eleven of the passengers rowdily made their exit, Sugar drove onto her final stop by a store called "Pasos".

Bealz joined the other students who exited the bus by Pasos, staying close to his little friend to protect her from the local wine-heads who congregated around the convenience store, hassling them for spare change. A Laundromat connected to the store served as a spot for a few dealers to either make a drug sales or duck inside whenever police were spotted.

Her name was Coneka and Bealz had the biggest crush on her. At thirteen she had reached puberty faster than most girls her age and could easily pass for sixteen. As was his custom, Bealz escorted her into Pasos for snacks and whatever else she desired.

After spending six dollars on wings, sodas and chips, Coneka rewarded Bealz with a peck on the cheek. Although she loved to spend Bealz's money, she would never accept him as a boyfriend.

Bealz's watched Coneka's impressive hips sway in her denim mini skirt as she headed back to the somewhat upscale Greenville neighborhood behind the store where the kids were raised mostly with both parents working. He then turned in the opposite direction and took a swig of his cold Pepsi as he waited for a break in the busy traffic of Oaklawn Avenue. He pumped his fist to a flip –flop colored four-door Cadillac's booming sound system as it slowly passed him. He checked both ways then dodged a slow moving station wagon to make his way across the street. After passing a small brick church, he headed down Edwin Street.

Edwin Street was one of the only three into the Fairview Homes Apartment Complex, one of Charlotte's most notorious housing projects. Known for practically any illicit activity, this neighborhood was a priority for the city's demolition plan. The size of the complex made it difficult for local authorities to police the drug traffic and violence. There were several escape routes for the drug dealers and gang-bangers to use. Ironically, the neighborhood streets were always crowded with kids playing and fighting with each other.

Bealz stopped by one of the dumpsters, referred to as "holes", meaning a dumpster, located in a square parking lot, to watch a dude named Loosey gaming cats out of their money. He looked over Loosey's shoulder to figure how the cord game "Skins" was being played.

"I got 'cho over here!" Bealz heard another cat named "Butter" shout to a slim female. Bealz took notice of Butter spitting something from his mouth into his hand and exchange whatever it was for the slender female's money. It was nothing new to Bealz; he had seen the same of transaction many times in the living room of his parents' apartment.

Jacob Malone Sr., Bealz's father, never hid his drug addiction from his son. An addiction so serious that his slim, brown-skinned father often urged his wife, Yolanda aka "Londa" to go trick with local dope boys to help support his habit, he made more love to the needles than he ever did to Yolanda.

Jap

Eighty percent of the time, Jacob Sr. had his best friend, Jake Wilson look out for Bealz. Looking out for Bealz included shopping, taking him to the movies and keeping money in his pockets. At his partner's encouragement Jake had no problem assuming the role of father figure in the Bealz's life. As long as Jacob Sr. had that boy flowing through his veins in his desperate and relentless pursuit of euphoria, nothing else mattered. When he couldn't shake the sickness, when the euphoria for whatever reason eluded him, as soon as he was able he'd entertain his demons by beating Yolanda viciously.

The police would often be called by their next door neighbor, Ms. Tam who'd report hearing fighting, cursing and other noises from the Malone residence. Ms. Tam always sat outside in one of her favorite long flowered dresses, bright blue rollers in her hair and fuzzy house slippers adorning her feet. Drug dealers made every effort not to zpeddle their drugs around Ms. Tam knowing she wouldn't hesitate to drop a dime and call the cops on them. Everybody else on Edwin Street was afraid to open their mouths and would turn a blind eye to any criminal activity, but not Ms. Tam.

4:54 P.M.

Bealz was within two apartment units from where he lived when he noticed a broken down two-toned sliver van that had been backed into a parking space. Noticing it rocking from side-side, he was curious and upon investigation discovered that

6

it was two men simultaneously having hot, nasty sex with a woman whose identity he couldn't make out except to note that she was wearing a hideous bright pink top. He snickered and kept moving. Approaching his home, sure enough he could see Ms. Tam at her usual observation post, swinging her orange tipped fly swatter by her ankles.

Suddenly he was almost knocked off his feet by a known drug dealer named "Vic" who sprinted from between a couple of buildings, pursued vigorously by several police officers on foot. At 6'3 and still retaining his former track star's speed, the police were no match for Vic and he quickly outdistanced them. When Vin cut behind a row of apartments, the cops came to a standstill, scratching their heads in frustration. They barked into their radios signaling for back-up cruisers to box up the complex.

Bealz was within fifty feet of his front door when he heard someone whisper his name. He turned around and only saw a hand waving at him from beneath a parked car. Figuring it had to be Vin, he crept up to the car. When Bealz leaned down to greet him, Vin handed him a fat sack of crack rocks.

"Hey Lil Malone...if they catch me, I'ma be gone for a long time," he whispered and started trembling when the barking of what he assumed were police K-9's echoed in the distance. "Hey, you can make three hundred and fifty dollars if you sell each one of dose for ten dollars." He paused and the bark of the dogs sounded closer. "Go 'head now...I'll catch up with you later if I get away. GO!"

Stashing the sack, Bealz skipped away from Vin and out of the parking lot just as several officers and their dogs descended upon the car that was shielding Vin. Bealz could hear the police shouts for Vin to come out with his hands up admist threats of siccing the K-9's on him.

"Mmh-mmh-mmh," Ms. Tam uttered, lowering her thick glasses "Tha's what that Nigga gets." Tilting her head in Bealz's direction she asked, "That boy didn't give you shit, did he?" Seeing Bealz shake his head in response, she continued, "Mmh-mmh, yo mammy ain't home but yo junkie Daddy is"

Bealz stepped through the missing screen of the front door of their apartment, fanning his hand through accumulated smoke and putrid air. He made his way to the stove and removed the pot of long-forgotten popcorn burned almost beyond recognition and stuck the mess in the sink beneath some running water. In the trashy living room he stepped over some clothes and broken glass then noticed the missing television set and love seat and assumed that his father had sold them.

"Dad," he cried out as he tan up the staircase. At the top, directly in front of him was Malone propped up on his toilet seat, his pants around his ankles. Bealz registered his father's protruding unblinking eyes, the thick mucous oozing from his nose and the dried vomit trailing from his mouth to his bare chest.

Bealz covered his nose from the unbearable stench of his father's bowel movement. The scene was not novel to Bealz; he'd seen his father through this many times before. But what paralyzed young Bealz with fear this time was the spectacle of the needle that dangled obscenely from the head of his father's penis.

Bealz instinctively knew that from this moment on, his life would never be the same. He had never allowed himself to cry, but suddenly he unable to stem the tears as he felt himself slide down the frame of the bathroom's door onto the floor.

Bealz had no idea how long he sat there. All he knew was that when he finally opened his eyes, he had no tears left and it was dark outside. When he heard the voices of Jake and his Mom he could barely make his voice work. "Up here," he choked, "up here" as the sounds of the footsteps could be heard stomping up the staircase.

Bealz let Jake pick him up from the floor. "Don't look son – don't look," Jake kept repeating, holding his hands over Bealz's eyes. "Everything's gonna be all right." With his free hand, Jake used his cell to call for an ambulance.

Surprisingly, Londa acted like she didn't have a care in the world. She kneeled down and casually extracted whatever money she could find from Malone' s pockets. "I'll be right back," she said. Over Jake's wide shoulders, Bealz recognized the hideous bright pink top as being his mother's as she disappeared down the stairs and the slamming of the door with the missing screen.

When the ambulance arrived, when all was said and done, Malone's dead body was finally covered with a sheet. Jake told the authorities that he would keep his nephew.

Jap

Two days later, dirt was shoveled over Malone's mahogany casket. Maybe two dozen people showed up for his funeral, including Bealz's teachers who saw the scene on the newscasts. Londa wasn't one of the attendees. She hadn't been seen since that fateful day.

A couple of weeks after Malone's death, Bealz began catching a bus to Fariview Homes and blended in with other kids. He ended up hustling what Vic had given him, soon he became the new drug connect in the projects. Out of respect for Jake, the older drug dealers looked out for Bealz. Before long he had built up a respectable clientele and crack fiends would look for the youngster first to do handle their drug transactions.

Bealz thought Jake didn't know about his small time dealings but Bealz had no idea the connections that Jake had in the heroin and cocaine game. Bealz assumed Jake just made a lot of money driving a cab; what he didn't know was that Jake owned Destination Cab Company.

It didn't take long for the bond between Bealz and Jake to become as strong as that of a father and son. Jake didn't stop Bealz from doing pretty much whatever he wanted as long as Bealz used common sense.

By the time he was twelve, street experience had catapulted Bealz into manhood and he never looked back.

CHAPTER ONE

As he stared into the wrong end of the barrel of Angelo's pistol, 22-year old Bealz ignored the incessant ringing of his cell phone, wisely choosing to keep his hands held steady at his side. Instead of wondering who was calling, or what the fool with the pistol was going to do next, Bealz worried about what Karma was thinking as she sat waiting for him in the car right around the corner in the parking lot of a strip club called "Players" that sat facing Statesville Avenue. Bealz was thinking, "If I make a run for it, dis nigga might just shoot me in the back." Bealz's slanted eyes and flaring nose displayed his frustration and anger.

It was the second meeting Bealz was having with this dude who he had met two weeks earlier while they waited in line to purchase baggies at a convenience store in a plaza on Beatties Ford Road. Now Bealz wished that he would have ignored the stocky, brown-skinned dude who had also purchased a fourty-ounce Bull which happened to be the favorite drink of The Alliance leader.

Bealz flinched when Angelo fired his fourty-five caliber over his head. Bealz reached into his denim jeans for the eighteen hundred dollars that he was going to use to purchase the two ounces. He stalled, hoping that the gunman would find a change of heart. Bealz was staring directly into the gunman's dark eyes when an unexpected chunk of Angelo's forehead opened up from the impact of a bullet. Bealz instinctively jumped back and shielded his eyes from the blood and brain fragments that

Jap

exploded onto his face. When he opened his eyes, he first cued in on the smoke smoldering from the barrel of The Alliance's only pistol which Karma was holding steady, pointed at Angelo's downed body. Bealz looked down and saw the thick flow of blood pumping from Angelo's head and backed further away. He looked up at Karma as a gust of night wind blew her sultry hair over the left side of her face.

Bealz grabbed her hand and they both took off running arouto their car. Luckily the music from the club had masked the sound of the gunshots. The patrons of the club were so engrossed in their own business, either going inside, sitting in their vehicles, or standing outside talking, enabling Bealz and Karma to make their exit unnoticed.

In the passing decade, Bealz had matured, grown even wiser, more sophisticated and street-wise, and managed to carry with dignity the inevitable baggage that came with street experience.

At twenty-two, Bealz stood 5'8 and weighed a trim and toned one-hundred and eighty pounds. His skin was smooth and his complexion the color of barely creamed coffee. He sported braids that rested on his shoulders. Artwork covered both his arms and a tattoo of two dogs facing each other was etched on his chiseled chest. In very large letters, the words "SKID ROW" stretched in blue ink across his stomach. His full lips, goatee and narrow nose accentuated his beady, slanted and dark brown eyes. His appearance, carriage and demeanor made him irrestestible to women and feared by men. Intimidated by nothing except his personal demons left Bealz questioning the loyalty of even his closest associates, but that caution had not only saved his life on many occasions over the years, it projected a countenance that silently demanded from everyone who crossed his path the one thing he treasured most in life: respect for him and his organization, THE ALLIANCE.

Driving through the night, both Bealz and Karma were quiet as they let the adrenaline rush subside. Bealz cut his eyes admiringly at this rescuer, the glamorous Sharelle/Relle, or as Bealz had named her "Karma". She had developed into 5'6 140 lbs of hotness, with silky jet black hair that hung to just above her waistline and a caramel complexion that was the envy of any woman. Her breasts were naturally perky and she didn't like wearing bras. Plump lips and cantaloupe green eyes and perfect teeth offered up a beautiful smile, and her thick thighs only complimented her forty-two inch hips and ass. Behind that disarming, alluring smile hid a temperament that would kill at the blink of an eye...especially if Bealz gave her the go-ahead. She was not only The Alliance's sexiest member, but it's deadliest.

It should have been no surprise that during the whole ride Karma remained calm since it wasn't the first time that she'd killed someone. She was known for her sassy attitude, suggestive clothing, and slick footwear, but most importantly for her unquestioned and unrelenting loyalty to Bealz, and for backing his every word. There was no doubt she would kill for him.

Jap

Down the street from Johnson C. Smith University and Beatties Ford Road was a group of upstairs brick apartments known as the Belvedere Apartments. Bealz's apartment 140 on West Trade sat directly across from the Boy's Club.

There was a mutual respect amongst the dealers that operated in the projects. One's hustle and turf would not be disrespected without serious consequences. If an outsider ventured into the area, the outsider was automatically considered a FORGEIGNER and all sides would unite like an army to eliminate the intruder. These were the unwritten rules, the code which was the only law respected in the Belvedere Housing Projects.

The fan and air conditioner kept Bealz's apartment at a tolerable temperature, but above the hum of them both the unmistakable tapping and scrapping of a razor blade against a plate could be heard. Seated on an old couch in the living room, Bealz was so involved with rolling up a blunt that he barely noticed Karma walk in and turn on the television. She watched the screen for a moment, dissatisfied with what she saw and tried to find another channel. The aging floor model TV had difficulty with reception, often receiving the signal of just one local channel. Karma angrily twisted the antenna around but to no avail.

"Fuckin' TV," she complained. "Can't get nothin' but the news and that dickhead DA always saying how he's gonna get rid of gangs and drugs. What a joke!" She fiddled with the antenna again but it did no good. Pumping her fist she complained, "I hate this fuckin TV! When we gonna get a new one?"

Meanwhile, Bealz, paying little mind to her rant, licked the Dutch Master to perfection. He cut his eyes at her, got her attention, then tossed her the blunt. He reached for the universal remote on the couch next to him, punched a button which turned off the TV, and pushed another to switch on the power of a small CD player, pushing the volume wide open. 50 Cent's "Many Men" blasted throughout the confines of the small living room.

Bealz looked up when the funniest member of The Alliance clique entered from the kitchen. Bealz was seldom seen when not accompanied by this dark-skinned, five-foot ten soldier who went by name of Shellz. He was Bealz's right hand man, was bug eyed and had a medium build and wavy hair.

Following Shellz Crip walking out of the kitchen was the soldier next up in the organization and who happened to be its latest recruit. His name was Bizzo and he resembled the rapper, The Game. The two had been cutting up Bealz's biggest purchase of his career, a Big Eight.

A knock at the door made Bealz cut the music down. He gestured at Bizzo who went to the door and discreetly looked to see who was there. "It's Trips." Bizzo opened the door and unlocked the glass screen door for Trips who was a slim junkie the group had doing some running for them. Trips entered smiling widely, his mouth twitching and fanning some wrinkled bills around.

"Yo Bealz, can I get six for fifty?" Trips pleaded licking his white chapped lips. Bizzo interceded with, "HELL NO, NIGGA – you can get FIVE for fifty!" Bealz silenced Bizzo with one finger and granted Trips not with just the six he requested, but with eight dimes instead, promising him that for every fifty, he'd give him the same deal. Trips examined the pieces, then bumped fist with Bealz. Before making his exit, he shoved a couple of bags into his mouth, then bolted out the door.

Bizzo sat on the orange milk crate by the window. He peeled back a corner piece of the off-red curtain as he watched Trips sitting in a black Toyota. It appeared to him that the male driver and Trips were going back and forth like in some kind of dispute.

"Man...Bealz, how we gone come up givin' doze crackheads deals," Bizzo questioned with his arms stretched out. Bealz answered, "That's how we come up, by looking out for those that bring us money." Bizzo dropped his head in resignation when Karma and Shellz agreed with Bealz. Bizzo leaped to his feet and went into the cooler and popped the top off a 40 ounce Bull.

Bealz sat down, enjoying the regular grade of chronic that they were smoking. For the last three days he and Shellz had worn the same attire. Both Shellz and Bealz had lost their parents to the struggle of the streets and reverie induced by the smoke turned to distant thoughts of their family. In fact they laid their heads where they made their bread.

Karma was an only child who had been spoiled by her well-off parents. She fell under Bealz's spell when she, Bealz and Shellz all attended East Mecklenburg High School. Karma ended up being the only one of them who graduated.

With Trips' loose tongue working overtime, business really started to pick up. Customers of all shapes, sizes and colors wanted a taste of The Alliance's product. As the apartment's living room overflowed with eager, sometimes unruly customers Karma stood watch over the activity from her perch on the wooden staircase, strapped with a Ruger 9mm. It was the organization's only pistol and it stayed with them at all times.

For the next six and a half hours, the package had dwindled down to two ounces and a quarter. Including shake, Bizzo and Shellz would easily split twenty-two hundred dollars. Mathematically, minus the shorts, they'd already made four thousand dollars and counting.

When the flow of customers had slowed, the foursome nearly always went out together. Bizzo, however decided that he'd stay behind to make a little more money. Bealz called his connect who told him it would be around 2 A.M.

"What about the pistol?" Karma asked.

"Leave it with ---"

Nah, yall take it," Bizzo insisted, interrupting Bealz.

After Bealz, Shellz and Karma rolled up some blunts, they adjourned to Bealz's prized '79 midnight blue Cutlass Supreme. The car was pristine, free from dents, no rims, nor rust and the engine was kept so fine-tuned that it purred like a sewing machine. Shellz positioned himself in the driver's seat waiting for Bealz to finish his conversation with a couple of hustlers.

Before long the trio was cruising through the city streets. The Sony CD player had a pair of factory 6x9's popping like they were blown. Karma was riding shotgun checking out the many whips that were shining like the stars in the sky.

"Where we going?" Shellz questioned. He passed Karma the blunt and brushed of some ashes that had fallen onto his black t-shirt.

"Hit Sixteen... we'll see what's going on down at Club Sa'joy"

"I'm wit that," Karma said excitedly, peering down at her pink neatly painted toenails that showed through her open toed sandals. As they rode they listed to DMX's CD "Flesh of My Flesh, Blood of My Blood."

"WHAT THESE BITCHES WANT FROM A NIGGA" DMX rapped, followed by Cisco singing on the hook. Smoke billowed from Bealz's mouth and nose as he passed the blunt and lit up another one. All three heads were nodding in time to the base line.

After a quick stop at a convenience store, the Cutlass then slowly approached the packed Club. Sa'joy's was at one time a Shoney's Restaurant. When Shoney's moved on, the owner of the building gutted it out, replaced the tables with long cushioned seats that lined the walls and a dance floor in the middle. He installed a bar where the kitchen once was and eight pool tables in the rear.

The Club sat between an ABC liquor store and a Burger King.

At the entrance to the Club, the doorman ruled that Karma could enter but denied Shellz and Bealz's entry because of what he described to be "inappropriate attire."

Incensed, Karma gave the doorman a look that could kill and announced, "Then let's get outta this dump." She grabbed Bealz's hand and waltzed of, exaggerating the sexiness in her stride as the rear of her beige form-fitting capris rocked from the jiggle of her soft ass cheeks.

Shellz nudged the doorman's arm, "Damn, Dawg...you played your cards right, you might could have got... ..." he paused and pointed at Karma's luscious hips retreating, then added... ... "some of dat pussy."

Shellz laughed at him. The doorman just looked annoyed, folded his arms and watched Shellz run to catch up with his friends.

Back at the car, Shellz yelled out over the roof, "What now, my nigga?" holding his arms up and spread.

Before responding, Bealz stuck his finger inside the hold that once housed the locking mechanism which had been removed. Unlocking the door he folded the passenger seat up, giving Karma access to the backseat. Bealz then caught Shellz's gaze over the car's roof, suggesting, "Let's check out Lovely's Lounge."

Shellz jumped into the car before Bealz changed his mind. There were plenty of entertainment venues in Charlotte, and abundance of places to go, but with the gang activity escalating, The Alliance had to be careful of the places they frequented.

When the Cricket tone on Bealz's cell phone sounded, he checked the caller ID. Bizzo's name appeared on the display.

"Yo," Bealz answered on the second ring.

"Man, Trips beat me out of twenty bags," Bizzo lamented, sounding panicked.

"Calm down bra... ..."

"Whassup?" Karma inquired, straightening her pink halter top that had the word "SEXY" emblazoned across her chest. Bealz covered the receiver with his hand.

"Bizzo said that Trips beat him for some bags," he whispered.

Karma and Shellz uttered a sigh because this wasn't the first time that this had happened. Bealz continued to calm Bizzo down before the call finally ended. A foreboding silence ensued...

CHAPTER TWO

Just before one thirty a.m., right when Lovely's Lounge had begun to fill up with more lovely ladies, Bealz received a call.

"Big Sake, whattup?" he answered on the second ring after checking Caller ID.

"Where are you?" Jake responded in his usual Barry White voice.

"As L——--—"

"I'll be there in a minute," Jake said, cuttin: Bealz off. Bealz stuck his cell phone into his front pants pocket. It was normal for Jake to finish his sentence then hang up before any response.

As the DJ slowed things down with the Isley Brothers"Choosey Lover,' Bealz lowered his head and nodded to the beat of the song.

"Come dance with me," Karma insisted, offering her killer smile while grabbing his hand. Bealz looked up at her and, unable to resist the sparkle in her eyes, allowed himself to be dragged out onto the dance floor. With her seductive dancing, he almost forgot one of the crew's unwritten rules that no one is supposed to sleep with Karma. Truth be known, that was Bealz's rule. Even though he'd seen her ass naked before and he'd been naked in front of her as well, the two had never engaged in any sexual activity.

Bealz eyed Shellz over Karma's shoulder and smiled when he saw him grope some tall chick. "Look at Shellz," he whispered. In one fluid motion, Karma spun around to grab a discreet look at Shellz's risque antics and the roaming of his hands over the chick's body.

Bealz stared down at the seductive sway of Karma's soft hips, realizing that his dick had begun to harden. Just when he was about to put some distance between his crotch and her ass, she reached back and grabbed the pockets of his pants, pulling him back up against her butt.

"A'ight, now . . a Nigga's dick's gettin' bard," Bealz said playfully. She turned back to face him, clutched his wrist and forced his hands to cuff her ass. The softness was intoxicating. "Hey . . ." he started to say before her tongue entered his mouth. His eyes closed as they continued to swap spit. "What the fuck we doin'?" both thought silently.

Suddenly Bealz felt a hot breath whisper in his ear, "You mean kissin' ain't against the code?" Shellz mocked.

Their liplock ended with both wiping their mouths. Karma gave Shellz a look of pure menace. Shellz shrugged with a sly smile, then told Beazl that Jake was outside waiting for him.

A stupid grin stole across Bealz's face. He peered through the huge window of the lounge and saw an Orange cab double— parked near the entrance. "I'll see y'all at the crib," he said confidently. He threw his head up, eyed Karma lustfully, then exited the lounge.

Shellz and Karma watched Bealz climb into the back seat of Jake's cab. Grinning from ear to ear, Shellz inquired, "Hey, uh, can I get in on some o'dat kissin', too?"

Sarcasm dripped from her voice as Karma responded, "Nigga, please," rolling her eyes.

Outside, the cab pulled slowly away from the lounge. Like clock work, Jake started the meter. Bealz kept silent as Jake spoke on the CB with the dispatcher who was his wife. Bealz looked over admiringly at his mentor. Each street light or the beam of a passing car's headlights served to highlight Jake's salt and pepper hair.

Jake was in his mid—fifties, stood over six feet tall, weighed two hundred and forty pounds, had dark chocolate skin. He'd been in the dope game since the seventies and had been to prison only one time. It was alleged that he and Malone, Bealz's father, had robbed a bank but no money was ever: found. While Bealz's father was getting himself hooked on heroin and letting his life get flushed down the toilet, Jake had been selling weed and accumulated enough cash to invest in a taxi company called Destinations Cab. He started out with two Chevy's but now the company had a fleet of cars including Presidential Lincolns for the wealthy and an orange Navigator for visitors and tourists.

Jake always maintained that crack dealing was slow money but that heroin was constant, fast money and always in great demand. Regardless of whatever money that he had, one thing about Jake was that he was never flashy. All he ever wore was Farmer John suits and plain black boots. Dismissing claims to any family, he'd always insisted that his only son, Junior, accidently shot himself to death many years back.

"What's up, Son?" Jake spoke, placing the CB "to its holder.

Staring out at the bright lights of the city, Bealz responded, "Ain't shit, man. Just thinkin' bout buying some new furniture."

Pulling up to a red light, Jake glanced at Bealz in the rear view mirror. He had always regarded Bealz as his sons replacement. Pulling away from the light, they trailed a slow—moving pick—up truck as they headed towards Billy Graham Parkway.

"So how many chicks have you slept with?" Jake inquired stroking his naked chin.

Responding to the coded question in his mind Bealz flipped through the money that he'd made, plus what he had saved, before responding.

"I on' know, maybe about forty—two," Bealz answered happily.

When Jake turned up the volume on his radio, the smile on Bealz's face disappeared, aware that it was getting serious time.

Jake never took a chance that anybody night have bugged his car. It's only normal procedures, Bealz reminded himself. He had to react quickly to catch the package that Jake had tossed back to him. He handed his payment to Jake. Before he could examine the package, another smaller package bounced off his chest. Retrieving the package and removing the rubber band, whatever was wrapped in what seemed to be coin bags remained a mystery.

Bealz looked up and noticed that Jake had turned down into Belvedere from the back way, gliding down a street where apartments lined both sides, a few abandoned, all looking like crap. In spite of the late hour, some people still sat on sagging porches in their never—ending struggle to avoid the heat, both kinds.

Bealz rewrapped the last packet and stuck it into his pocket as Jake pulled the cab along side of the first unit of apartments, parked and killed the engine. He then turned and handed Bealz a piece of paper folded several times. Making eye contact with Eealz, he placed a finger over his lips.

"Sir, that '11 be twelve dollars and seventy—five cents."

Bealz handed Jake fifteen dollars, thanked him, then opened the door of the cab and stepped out into the night. Taking a deep breath, Bealz stood for a moment assessing his surroundings. Most of the streetlights were dead but the few that had survived the neighborhood blight lit the street enough to reveal a few dudes still out grinding. In a show of respect Bealz spoke but kept it moving.

Approaching his apartment he saw that the Cutlass was parked in front. Before he could reach his front door, a notorious female crack—head who had known him since he was a kid flashed her boobs at him.

"Hey, Lii Malone," she said with her mouth twitching. "When you gonna let me suck that dick?" she inquired, rubbing beneath her armpits; the top row of her teeth were missing and her eyes were bulging. Her body trembled and she was barefoot.

"Lorraine, go 'head on wit' that bullshit," he threw back at her. Bealz slipped into his apartment so quietly that his entrance went unnoticed by Shellz and Bizzo who uwere consumed in serious competition against each other on a Playstation 2 game console. Karma sat demurely on the couch with her legs folded under her, smoking a blunt, her head back, her eyes closed.

In the quiet of the semi—darkness, instead of immediately making his presence known, he leaned back against the door, thinking hard to himself. The scene before him caused the demon inside him to stir. Looking around at his two associates involved in the video game, the sexy woman on the tired old couch, he realized how tired he was of the old furniture, going through the same motions day after day wearing the same old clothes and driving the same old car. Okay, so he loved the car, but still. His wardrobe consisted of five pair of good pants and three designer shirts. What did he really have? If it wasn't for Jake having some chick he knew renting this apartment in her name, he and Shellz would be homeless.

His eyes cut to Karma. As he looked at her admiringly, he thought about the fact that she could have easily gotten with a Nigga that's balling but instead she'd been sticking with him and Shellz since their school days. That's one of the many things he dug about Karma — her loyalty, but he hadn't been able to show her much in return. Karma had been there even in the leanest of times, when Bealz and Shellz couldn't get off a quarter ounce, long before Bizzo joined The Alliance. As hot as she was, she seemed to be content just hanging around with the boys, smoking weed, drinking liquor and whatever nonsense they night come up with.

Looking around at them, it dawned on him why he was feeling restless. She deserved better. They all did. Well, at least Karma, Shellz, and himself did.

As if connecting on some invisible wave length, Karma suddenly sensed his presence, looked up and smiled brightly at him. He returned the smile, crossed the room and took his place beside her on the couch. Shellz and Bizzo were so involved in the game that they didn't even acknowledge his passing "How'd it go?" Karma asked quietly.

"Better than I expected," he replied, closing his eyes momentarily and leaning his head back. Remembering the folded paper Jake had given him, he pulled it out of his pocket. "... at least I think so." He unfolded the paper and held it closer to the light to read it for the first time.

"HERE IS THREE BUNDLES OF TEN OF LIGHT SCRAMBLED, BOY — HEROIN.

I KNOW YOU SAID THAT YOU DON'T WANNA FUCK WITH THE STUFF. TRUST ME, TELL ONE PERSON AND

AFTER THEY SNORT OR SHOOT THIS SHIT AND SEE HOW
FAST THE MONEY COMES, YOU'LL CHANGE YOUR MIND.

ON THAT OTHER THANG, YOU OWE ME THREE
HUNDRED DOLLARS. I COULD'VE TAXED YO ASS BUT
SINCE YOUR FATHER HELPED ME OUT SO MANY TIMES,
I'LL DO MY BEST TO RETURN THE FAVOR. NOW
INDIVIDUALLY EACH ONE OF THE BAGS GOES FOR $25. I'M
TALKING ABOUT THE BUNDLES. THAT'S JUST A GIFT.
HOLLA AT ME LATER.

PS — BURN THIS PAPER."

Bealz finally exhaled, not realizing that he was holding his breath as he read the note. He nodded his head once as if in silent confirmation then immediately picked up Karma's lighter from the coffee table, lit the paper and watched it burn to a crisp in the ashtray.

The stench and smoke was enough to get Shellz to pause the Ultimate Fighter game that he and Bizzo were playing. Frowning, he complained, "Damn, Nigga, you tryin' to burn down the crib?"

Bealz gave no response but instead got busy unwrapping the second package, pulling off the black electrical tape until he could see a Big Grab potato chip bag. He carefully poured the contents onto the table.

"Oh, shit," Karma blurted, sitting up straight.

Her outburst got Bizzo and Shellz to lose interest in the game. All four gathered closely around the table and stared, stunned. Bealz removed the small digital scale from its hiding placc, a hole in the couch's pillow. One by one he weighed each cookie—shaped ounce of crack. All were white with a crystal look, solid with no holes.

"Finally, nine ounces," he muttered to himself.

Shellz emitted a low, soft whistle of astonishment. "What now?" he finally questioned of Bealz who had just been standing there staring at the drugs, overwhelmed momentarily by unspoken fears that he might blow this golden opportunity that he'd been working towards for so long. The demon inside his head was growling.

Shaking off his trance, Bealz snapped, "Let's bag this shit up!" Turning to his confederates, he rattled off his orders. "Bizzo, go get the blades, bags, and two plates. Karma, roll up."
It didn't take long for word to spread on the street that The Alliance was home and doing business. Although The Alliance was on the edge of a gigantic escalation in their business, for the crackheads it was just business as usual. While Shellz and Bizzo were in the kitchen cutting up what was destined to be their future, Bealz kept the usual junkies happy taking shorts while displaying a rare willingness to offer bargains and hand out deals.

Apartment 140 was just one of the two hustling spots on Bealz's unit. Their apartment was the second to the left. At the opposite end, a light—skinned weed dealer named Tuson hustled as well. He was from Arizona but his baby moms grew up in the hood. That was the only reason that no one treated him like a Klan member.

Bealz noticed Tuson as he stepped out into the a.m. hours when the traffic through his crib thinned out. With his typical close observation of all his surroundings, he noticed Trips emerging from behind the Boys Club. Bealz called out to him and Trips trotted across the road. Bealz did not fail to notice the crowd of hustlers lingering further up the block.

Out of breath, Trips asked, "Wha's up, Bealz? You call me?"

"Yeah ... you seen Bad? I need to see him pronto."

Trips looked at Bealz like he was crazy. He sucked his teeth and pulled a cigarette from behind his ear.

"Damn, baby — you call me over here to ask 'bout that muh—fucka Too Bad? You know I don' like that Nigga," he proclaimed, sticking the cigarette into his mouth.

"I got you three dimes," Bealz promised, interrupting Trips going through the motion of lighting his smoke.

"Three dimes!" he shot back with excitement. "Ohhh, that's Too Bad! That's my boy! Give me five minutes.

Bealz watched Trips dart out in front of a slow moving car barely avoiding being hit. Before going back into the apartment, Bealz peeped through the window of the vacant adjacent apartment, Number 141. He had seen the workers touching up the place like someone was expected to be moving in. All he hoped for was that his new neighbor wouldn't be some old church—going people who were going to cramp his style.

Just as Bealz entered his apartment, two unmarked police cruisers approached the seven hustlers up the block. When five of the dudes took off running, the sounds of screeching tires penetrating the stillness of the night followed shortly by the wailing sirens which never failed to create panic for the inhabitants of Apartment 140.

"Lock the door!" Bizzo yelled, trying frantically to dispose of what he'd bagged.

"Chill the fuck out, nigga," Shellz interjected with a stone stare. Bealz rushed into the kitchen, a sour look on his face. Re walked over and snatched the plastic bag from Bizzo and carefully emptied the contents back onto the table. Five—and—a—half ounces plus about a quarter of shake spilled onto the round table. Karma entered to check out the commotion, startled to see the venom in Bealz's eyes.

Through clenched teeth Bealz demanded of Bizzo, "Fuck was you gonna do wit'"dis dope?" staring at him with curved eyebrows.

Nervously Bizzo responded, "Nuttin ... uh, I uh ... thought Five—0 was comm'...!'t

"Somebody's scared," Karma mocked indirectly in sing—song fashion.

Taking instant offense to her insinuation, Bizzo knocked over a chair charging at her, but a quick—thinking Shellz intervened and tackled him to the floor. Bizzo was struggling to get free when suddenly, at the back door

KNOCK-KNOCK-KNOCK!

Jap

Silence as everyone looked at each other. Shellz shrugged. No one was expected at the door.

CHAPTER THREE

Unarmed and defenseless, Bealz stared into the business end of the barrel of a loaded pistol aimed directly between his eyes, and the fidgety gloved finger caressing its trigger. As his gaze move up into the evil eyes of the assailant, he found himself wondering why his connect's middle man wanted to rob him, and that Jake would be disappointed at how his protege, who was supposed to be so street—smart, mat his end like a stupid dope—boy.

KNOCK-KNOCK-KNOCK

"BEALZ..."

The intensity in Karma's whisper from across the room jolted Bealz from his momentary stupor. He blinked rapidly a few times to clear his head of the images that would occasionally invade his consciousness, like an uninvited guest prophesying some kind of misstep that could prove lethal.

Again the knock, this time even louder. KNOCK—KNOCK! Bealz looked at the three members of The Alliance who were frozen in place, staring back at Bealz expectantly. Karma nodded her head in a questioning gesture as if to say, "Well..."

Trancelike, Bealz moved cautiously to the door and asked, "Who is it?"

"It's me," a familiar voice replied.

Bealz exhaled. "It's Trips."

Shellz and Bizzo scrambled to their feet and they all hustled to stash the drugs inside cabinets before Bealz opened the door.

Trips entered first, followed by Too Bad. Too Bad always wore long sleeves but nevertheless stayed neatly dressed.

"Sup, baby?" Too Bad spoke quickly, scratching his arm through the sleeve. Making eye contact with Karma, Bealz gestured with a head nod for her to leave the kitchen. She folded her arms and poked her lips out in rebellion.

"Okay, den ..." Bealz said, removing the heroin from his pants pocket. "Too Bad, you got ya outfit on ya?" Bealz asked as he slid one packet across the table.

Too Bad smiled his acknowledgment. "Just like "'Merican Express — never leave home wit' out it," he assured.
Sitting down, Too Bad quickly displayed his works on the table. arranging his equipment like a formal silverware setting, telling Trips, "Give me your belt' When Trips pulled his belt through the last loop, his pants dropped around his ankles. Even with the chuckles at his Superman underwear on display, he wasn't embarrassed in the least.

Too Bad ignored the laughter and got down to business wrapping the belt around his arm. After going through all the proper procedures and drawing the drug into the needle, he tightened the belt around his arm. To hold the belt taut, he clamped his teeth into the black leather. Finding a nice vein, he stuck the needle in the vein, drew back on the plunger until he saw his blood, then slowly pushed the potent drug into his system.

Instantly the belt fell from his mouth. His legs stretched out and he began rubbing himself between his legs. Too Bad's body appeared to be going through an out—of—this—world stimulating experience. His head slowly drifted backwards as if he was dead.

The Alliance looked on with mixed feelings. Witnessing this ritual was a first—time experience for everyone except Trips and Bealz. They stood mesmerized by the sight of Too Bad looking like he had drifted into some kind of no—man's land.

"Fuck that Boy shit," Trips blurted, holding his hand out to Bealz. "Lenme get me—me," he said.

"Hold up," Bealz contested, tapping on Too Bad's shoulder.

-

"Man, dat Nigga is a'ight," Trips defended. "I got a glass dick to suck on."

His comments drew chuckles from everyone except Bealz and Too Bad. It was nothing new to Bealz since from a very young age he saw his father go through the same faze. At that time in his younger years, his mother always told him that Malone was just sleepy. As for Too Bad, he and Malone used to get high together.

It wasn't long before the edge of Too Bad's high wore off. Wiping his mouth, "That's some good shit. That bitch gonna get you paid," he assessed.

"Okay, den ..." Bealz said, removing the heroin from his pants pocket.

Jap

5 A.M.

Bealz was awakened by some repeated knocking at the front door. He tenderly removed Karma's head from his lap, rose from the couch, stretched, and answered the door. He was surprised to see Too Bad with eight well—dressed strangers. Bealz stepped out onto the porch.

"'Sup, Too Bad?" Bealz questioned, giving the strangers an ice cold stare.

Too Bad introduced the strangers, explaining, "They my friends; all together they, got eight hundred dollars.

Bealz countered, "I only have twenty—nine bags at twenty—five apiece."

The strangers all but forced their money on Bealz. The slim white doctor—looking dude spent two hundred; a stubby black dude in a suit spent one—fifty. In less than fifteen minutes Bealz had made over seven hundred dollars. Life was good. Bealz handed Too Bad fifty dollars then stepped back into his crib.

Back inside, once again the oldness, the decay of his makeshift quarters, the sameness of his life assaulted his senses with a deja—vu moment. He fingered the roll of bills in his pocket as he assessed what had been his home for the past fifty— three months, and experienced a silent epiphany. The demon inside his head roared, "Stop being cheap, Nigga. You got Jake backing you. The Alliance is strong ... well, aside from Bizzo, that is the point being, get this chedda, make Bealz a household name to deez bitches. Heroin! China White! Mexican Mud! Think big, Nigga get rich!" The demon in his head smiled devilishly.

By 8 am. Bizzo had gone home, Shellz was in the shower. Acting upon his decision to upgrade their lifestyle, Bealz had Karma set herself up an appointment at Unique Designs, the hot new hair salon just off North Tryon Street. As Karma rolled up blunts from the ounce of Arizona Red that Bealz had copped from Tuson, Bealz called around to places that rented furniture. When everyone had their business taken care of, they headed out to greet the day.

About forty minutes away, in the downtown municipal building, another organization was gearing up for the day. The police captain hung up the phone and downed what was left of his coffee which had grown cold. He made a face which disappeared when he looked up and saw through the blinds Detective Sharon Buccannon making her way briskly through the morning chaos of a police precinct towards his office. She knocked lightly then opened the door.

"Detective," the Captain acknowledged her, nodding.

"Good morning, Captain ... I just wanted to drop off those reports you wanted." She walked to his desk and handed him a file marked "Confidential."

"Like you didn't have enough on your plate. The D.A. has a bug up his butt ..,"

"No problem. It's part of our job to make him look good, isn't it?" She turned and headed back towards the door. "I think I remember reading that somewhere when I transferred in."

As she started to open the door, the Captain's voice stopped her. "Any regrets, Detective?"

She turned to face him across the room. "Regrets, sir?"

"You've taken on quite a load. How's it going?"

"It's what I signed on for, Captain. The three agents we've had on the streets under deep cover should be showing results anytime now."

"If they don't get killed first."

"Listen to you — the mother hen. Does everyone know what a softie you are, or is that classified?"

Blushing, he waves his dismissal. "Get outta here — don't you have some crimes to solve?"

"I'm on it .,. sir!" She gave a mock salute and was out the door.

Watching her stride away, out of habit he picked up his coffee cup to take a drink and scowled when he remembered it was empty.

Detective Buccannon had worked her way up through the ranks to earn a gold shield in Metro Homicide Division. When word got out that the D.A. was forming a special tactical squad consisting of agents from DEA, ATF, and Homicide working in concert to combat the out—of—control rise in deadly violence related to the drug scene in the Queen City, Detective Buccannon was first to volunteer and was appointed head agent of the task force. She took the assignment seriously, in fact too seriously it was thought by some; it had practically become her whole life. She had her reasons.

Unique Designs Hair Salon sat between a Kinko's Copy store and the Trust—Me Tax Company. Bealz's Cutlass pulled right up in front of the salon's glass door. Shellz parked the car in an empty space marked "Reserved" between a gray Chevy Tahoe and mint blue LS 600. Bealz held the seat up for Karma and followed her into the establishment, their entrance attracting curious but admiring looks from the customers and the workers.

As was his custom, Bealz immediately assessed the surroundings: the short gum—chewing mixed girl talking on a phone at the receptionist's desk, the burgundy with gold trim of the rug and walls, the huge mirrors that lined the walls behind the stations of eight hair dressers, Ice Cube's movie 'Friday' played on a fifty—two inch Plasma TV that was built into the wall which evoked a burst of envy in him. And what no one could miss was the two wall paintings that greeted people when they walked through the door.

"Excuse me, sir ... please tell your man to move that car," the receptionist begged with fearful eyes, holding the phone away from her ear. Bealz glanced briefly over his shoulder like he didn't hear her. From the corner of his eye he caught a nicely built woman making a beeline in his direction. She was walking so fast and hard that he could hear her abundance of jewelry clanging against each other. Bealz licked his lips and slowly stroked his goatee.

She confronted him, hands on her hips. "Can I help you?" she asked.

The receptionist spoke up first. "I—I told him to move his car, Tracks," she fearfully whined.

Karma spoke up. "I have an appointment," she announced, matching the gaze of the woman the receptionist had called "Tracks."

Tracks was two inches from six feet, two shades from being white, and weighed about 150 pounds. She grinned politely at Karma and introduced herself, showing off her bottom teeth full of baguettes and diamonds. Upon being given Karma's birth name, Tracks checked the log book, scrolling down the page with her long, colorful designer fingernails.

"Here it is," she said joyfully. "Sharelle Robinson. Follow me, please?"

"Sir, your car," the receptionist uttered with the same frightened stare.

Bealz read her name from the small badge pinned to the front of her blouse. "Carrie, is it? Patience, Carrie. Patience," Bealz admonished, awarding her with his best smile.
Carrie sighed and her face turned crimson as she watched Bealz follow behind Karma and Tracks.

Attention was drawn to the hair dresser with the caramel complexion working in Booth Six. She appeared to be about five feet four, about a hundred and thirty pounds, and boasted breasts the size of oranges. She had a Wilma Flintstone waist but an ass as succulent as Janet in "Poetic Justice," complemented by the dark green Apple Bottom short—set that hugged her every curve. Her hair was dark and naturally curly which accented her almond eyes. Although she had to stand on some device to be seen over her client's head, she appeared to be everything that a man could want, and more.

Bealz passed the station where Karma had gotten situated; He took slow steps until he came face to face with MS LIKE THAT. As her head swiveled in his direction, he noticed the dimple in her grin. She looked at him like she was waiting for him to speak. He licked his lips, then made sure she saw that his eyes were seductively studying every part of her body.

She asked Bealz with a hint of irritation, "What? Is something crawling on me?" Her face showed no emotion.

"Nah ... It ain't that, Ms ... um ..." -

She didn't answer but instead just poked out her lips.

"Hey, Tiff, who's your friend?" a feminine—sounding male hair dresser yelled at her from Booth Four.

"Thanks a lot, Vanilla," Tiff muttered under her breath. The female client in Tiff's chair burst into laughter. Tiff nudged her shoulder, "Girl, stop laughing!"

Bealz locked his fingers behind his back. "Tiff, huh? I would guess then that your real name is Tiffany?"

"Ooo, a display of remarkable intelligence — I like that rare quality in a man," she said, her voice dripping with sarcasm as she continued styling her client's hair.

"Well, I'd sure be less than intelligent if I hesitated to speak to someone that I really wanted to know," he said. When he saw Tiff's eyes cut back at him, he continued. "To be honest, I'm just a single guy hoping to meet a single lady. I couldn't help but notice your Gucci sandals ... impressive, if I do say so. I ain't no clothing expert but I know class when I see it. That's my Cutlass outside an————"

"Boy, you better moo' that car before San shows up," Vanilla blurted, cutting Bealz off, snapping his finger twice in a circle.

"Anyway," Bealz countered, ignoring Vanilla's intrusion, "Ms. Tiff, here's my cell number, If you're ever wanting good conversation or a good meal, no strings ... call me."

Tiff kept combing through her client's hair in the same spot, distracted. She stared at his hand holding the paper. She looked into his eyes and saw something she liked so she took the paper from him. As Bealz turned to walk off, she glanced at the number.

"Excuse me ... what's your name?"
He turned back to her. "Jacob Malone, call me Jacob." He grinned and was elated to see her match his smile. She was thinking that his name had a nice ring to it.

"Girl, if you don't want him, I be happy to see wha' his daddy gave 'him," Vanilla's statement causing snickers throughout the place.

Tiff retorted jokingly. "Vanilla, would you shut up before I tell Marve on your scandalous ass." More chuckles and muttered chides.

"Ew, girl! You wouldn't!" Vanilla replied in mock horror, firmly holding his hands over his scrawny chest.

Karma sat quietly in Booth Three, aware of the sexual energy in the establishment and was mad at herself £ or being unable to contain jealousy.

Upon exiting the salon, Bealz returned to the Cutlass to discover Shellz dozing, slumped over the steering wheel. Without making a sound, Bealz entered the car then slammed the door shut and yelling, "Shellz!"

Shellz nearly hurt himself reacting. "Nigga ... stop playin'! I damned near pissed my pants!" Shellz admitted, wiping the corner of his mouth. Reaching for the ignition, "So ... where to?"

"Rent—A—Center." Then to himself, "Wonder if they have Plasma TVs."

When Shellz started the engine and put the car in reverse, he noticed that a late model cream—colored Cadillac Escalade had mysteriously pulled up to the Cutlass's bumper, blocking their way. The Escalade's sound system had been cranked up to such a deaf—defying volume that its decibels activated the security alarms in all the cars parked nearby.

Shellz eye—balled the Escalade in the rearview mirror, keeping the car in reverse but with his foot firmly on the brake pedal. Bealz stared back over his shoulder at the passenger exiting the SUV, closely monitoring the dramatic removal of the passenger's dark gold—framed designer sunglasses that had been hiding dark eyes.

The demon in Bealz's head roared silently, instantly on alert.

CHAPTER FOUR

Rising to about six feet and weighing in just shy of two hundred pounds, the dark--skinned passenger who alighted from the Escalade boasted a walk that legitimately shouted, "I own the world." Bealz immediately assessed the passenger's small blond neatly shaved afro, with neck, wrists and hands adorned with platinum jewels, and gear that consisted of a yellow LaCoste shirt with a green emblem, hue blue Coogi cargo shorts, and some yellow Forces. Striding towards the Cutlass, the passenger took a deep drag of a cigar that had been gutted and stuffed with Purple Haze.

Bending over to eyeball Shellz through the window of the Cutlass, the passenger exhaled a cloud of smok into Shellz's face and protested, "Wha's happening, Playa ... your car in my spot. She cracked a sly grin at a surprised Shellz, displaying a grill like Lil Wayne.

Shellz was about to respond but Bealz noticed the Escalade's driver and back seat passenger exit the SUV clutching their chrome rachettes. Grabbing Shellz's shoulder, Bealz quickly offered, "My fault," ducking his head and staring at them across Shellz's person.

"All right, 'den. Don't let this shit happen again." This time a drag of the blunt drew a deep cough. Dabbing her runny nose with a linen cloth, she turned to her light—skinned cohort with the long dreads, "Gramz, let deze Niggas out,"

"I got you, San," Gramz replied as he shuffled his six—four, medium built frame back into the driver's seat of the SUV. "Milky, let's go," San demanded, unhurriedly moving in the direction of Unique's entrance, looking over her shoulders after every second step first at the Cutlass and then at Milky who was the color of chocolate milk, 5'10", chubby and a face that looked like he always had a bad attitude.

The fact that all three wore the latest and best urban gear available and add to that the twenty—six inch chrome D'Vincis the SUV rolled on and, simply put, their showmanship shouted heavy money but their attitudes certified them as a go—hard crew.

Shellz backed out, waited for Gramz to park, then drove off. "That muh—fuckà didn't scare me, dawg," he claimed, checking in the rear view mirror. "I wonder who dat bitch was."

Bealz did some brainstorming. "Excuse me, Sir," Bealz remembered Carrie saying while he was staring at the paintings, one being Tracks and the other being what he knew now to be San. Bealz removed a blunt from the ash tray and fired up the ass—end of the green Dutch. Smoke rose from his mouth and nostril. "That bull—dagging bitch must co—own that hair salon," he said, nodding knowingly as he passed the L to Shellz.

As he took a deep drag, Shellz remarked, "Well ... that lil titty dyke got some bread wit' her lil titties." The two shared a laugh.

Back in the salon, San waved a greeting at Tracks but stopped at Tiff's booth and started making annoying circles around her. Tiff had been working there for nearly ninety days and San hadn't let up on her from day one. San stopped right on Tiff's heels, her hot breath on her neck causing Tiff to squirm.

"When you gonna let me lick your candy?" San whispered.

"San, girl — you crazy," Tiff said jokingly and flinched when San patted her ass before walking away. She glanced up at the clock on the wall thinking that she could leave at three and she couldn't wait to get to her third shift later on.

San entered the office that she shared with Tracks and quickly closed the door when she saw Tracks inside the safe. Tracks already had the hundred and fifty thousand counted and ready, plus the two bricks of powder. San showed her appreciation with some passionate kisses here and little fondling there.

San was a major player in the Charlotte drug trade, selling more coke than most of her male counterparts. Her territory included the South, West, and parts of the North side. She'd managed to get plugged in with her Spanish connection when San had been Aveely Gonzalez Ruiz's cellmate in State Prison and had helped her fight off other prisoners. Aveely's brothers Ortiz, began hitting San off with the best coke available in North Carolina.

Sandra Tillman a.k.a San, had an organization calling itself Major League which consisted of the negotiator Grams and slickster, Milky. But Pug, her twenty—one year old boyish—looking hitman, hailed from Greenville, North Carolina, who she summoned only when a wipeout was needed. Sandra put money behind her ex—girlfriend and hair dresser, Diana (Tracks') Hicks.

San was unaware of the fact for sixteen months she'd been under investigation but they could never get anything concrete on her. San had cleverly been stashing dope in several spots, some of which was right underneath the nose of the police. But with Track's degrees in technology, psychology, and A—i credit, they'd managed to keep Unique Designs off the radar.

Meanwhile, after a short ride, the Cutlass pulled into a parking lot on Graham Street which was shared by Rent—A—Center, a grocery store and a Family Dollar store as well as other small businesses which kept the huge parking lot almost jammed to capacity. Bealz told Shellz to go on inside while he placed a call.

"Sup," he spoke when Karma answered on the first ring. He could hardly hear her response with a dryer blowing next to her. "I can't hear you," he spoke loudly into the phone. Karma gave her hair designer a time-out gesture, rose from the chair and stepped out of the cubicle.

"Can you hear me now?"

Jap

"Yeah ... peep game. Is that bulldagger--lookin bitch still there?"

Karma looked back to the closed office door. "Yeah, her and that girl Tracks are back in the office," she whispered. "I want you to-"

"I am already on it," she said, cutting him off in midsentence. She added "I seen what happened outside when they had y'all blocked in.

I was 'bout to pull that' foe—fifth from my purse and handle my B—I,"

Karma let it be known, putting a big grin on Bealz's face.

"All right, 'den. See ya."

Click.

When Bealz entered the rental store, he saw how a white service man was cautiously shadowing Shellz. He shook his head and from behind approached Shellz who was standing in front of the Plasma TVs.

"Dis TV here is nasty and it's only three hundred a month or seventy—five a week," Shellz said with excitement.

Bealz had to explain that it was all a gimmick. He left Shellz standing alone and motioned for the service man named Terry to meet him in the furniture section. Bealz was definitely going to pick out a powerful system as well. Not only did Apartment 140 need furniture downstairs, the two upstairs bedrooms also needed beds.

Not wanting to spend an arm and leg on a dope spot, Bealz declined Terry's offer of the money—green Italian leather couch and love seat, opting instead for a black leather living room set and a king size bed for his bedroom. Shellz ended up having to buy his own bed but they went in together on the living room furniture and a 42—inch Plasma TV. Terry promised that the furniture would be delivered to their apartment by two o'clock. Since it was a little past 11 A.M. and Bealz was dealing with a nagging thought that there was something they had forgot to purchase, they decided to do some more shopping.

In the meantime, drama was escalating in the Orchard Park Apartments off Fifth Street. With only eight apartments to five different units, the complex was small enough that anything above a whisper would bring out all of the nosey neighbors. There were three people who hustled out of those roach—infested apartments: two males, one of whom snorted more coke than he sold, and Chrissie Noles, mother of two, who was moving a big eighth a week.

Inside Apartment 35, Bizzo was doing his best to ignore his baby— mama Nicolette who was dark as tar but had a cute little round face. Although only 5' 3" and 145 pounds, she was aggressive. Her breasts were so huge that she never wore a bra. Although she couldnt get rid of her small gut, her ass made up for the negative. Lette, as Bizzo called; was straight GHETTO.

"I'm sick of you not spending time with me," Lette loudly complained, standing over Bizzo sprawled on the couch. He turned towards the back of the plaid couch hoping she'd leave him alone. Instead she leaned down and mushed the back of his head. "Get—cho ass up!" she screamed.

"Go 'head on now, woman ... I'm sleepy," he muttered.

Lette couldn't say he wasn't a good father because he did make sure that bills were paid, food was always abundant and he had copped Lette a silver '98 Taurus from the auction. Most importantly, he bathed, fed, and took his nine—month--old son, Future, to the daycare himself when he was a home. To top it off, Bizzo loved and cared for Lette's seven— year—old son, Adam, the same, even though he wasn't his biological son.

As Lette's annoying voice ceased, Bizzo emitted a grateful sigh and folded his arm behind his head. Bizzo didn't even hear it coming until Lette made her move with a pitcher of ice—cold water splashed on Bizzo's face. He yelled like someone had scared him, rolled and fell hard to the cold floor below. He jumped to his feet clearing water from his eyes, fully aware of what had to be done to get her off his back.

He gave Lette a cold stare. Knowing what was in store for her, she held her hand outward as if in a plea for mercy. He lunged for her throat, gripping it tightly, cutting off her air supply. Tightening his grip, Lette struggled helplessly, bracing her hands on his shoulder as her feet left the floor. Tears began to pour from her brown eyes, the sounds of her being choked slowed to a hush. As suddenly as he gripped her, he let her go. Her legs had no strength and she crashed to the floor luckily the kids were with their grandmother.

Bizzo leaned down and began to rip Lette's pink boy—shorts and halter top from her body. Her breasts bobbled. Bizzo grabbed a handful of her micro braids and dragged her into the small kitchen. Offering no resistance, she allowed him to make her bend over the square wooden table. Bizzo took off his wet boxers and guided his hard dick into Lette's pussy. He began to pound away at her, causing her ass cheeks to shudder.

"Oh, Biz," she moaned, looking back at him over her shoulder. He gripped her hips, spreading them as far as they would stretch. He withdrew slowly, then surged forward with powerful thrusts.

Lette came in a rush. The built—up sweat on the small of her back made her skin look like bronze chocolate.

"I'ma bo—bout to c—cum," he murmured, slowing his strokes down. Lette started backing her hips against his forward thrust

Shortly, he roared like a tiger and Lette enjoyed the feeling of his love juices gushing inside of her love canal.

"Thanks, baby," she said while trying to catch her breath.

"You're very welcome," gasped his reply.

CHAPTER FIVE

It was well after two p.m. when the Cutlass rolled up. Bealz apologized to the awaiting rental center workers that were seated in the delivery truck outside their apartment. The two young white workers were all smiles as they exited their delivery truck. Bealz headed to unlock the front door. At the same time a group of onlookers were staring from both ends of the unit. There were hustlers, junkies, and a few young girls who were smoking weed with the dealers. They all engaged in small talk about the furniture and appliances that were being unloaded from the truck.

Hey Bealz," one of the females yelled, waving her hand.

Bealz nodded, going on to help the delivery boys.

It took several trips and junkie Trips, but everything was finally in place in about two hours. While the oldest and most knowledgeable mover, Winky, mounted the plasma, Shellz hooked up the system and Bealz rolled up two fat blunts. Bobby, the other mover, who thought he was black, bobbed his head on beat to the sounds of The Game and 50 "This Is How We do." The huge house speakers could clearly be heard inside neighbors' apartments and on up the block.

Bealz felt on top of the world as the soft leather seemed to absorb his body into relaxation. He fired up one of the blunts and through the cloud of smoke he saw a petite figure of a girl standing at his door. He passed Bobby the blunt, then headed in her direction to see if he could assist her.

Her skin tone was smooth and creamy like peanut butter. She was three inches shorter than Bealz. Her hair was wavy and cut into a bob. She reminded you of a young Toni Braxton, lips and body.

"Do I know you?" Bealz asked, staring over her head at the UHaul truck that was parked against the curb directly behind the Rent—A—Center truck.

She folded her arms. "NO, you don't. I'm new to the neighborhood. Me and my sister was hoping that you'd move that truck." She paused and stepped to the side, then continued with a pleasant smile, "... so we can pull up in front of our apartment."

Bealz enjoyed her light tone. "Okay, Mrs.," he said, extending his hand in a friendly gesture. His eyes cut deep into hers then back at his hand. After she shook his hand he let out a silent sigh. He turned his head back into his apartment, demanding, "Bobby, move the truck for the Mrs. here."

"It's not Mrs.; it's Tarisa and everybody calls me Pudding."

"What flavor? Vanilla or chocolate?" he responded, catching her agitated gaze. Pudding gave Bealz a "you so silly" look, rolled her eyes, then walked out to a beige four—door Toyota. Bealz stepped out onto the porch, watching Pudding's Capris hugging her hips. He saw that Pudding's sister was struggling to carry a box. In a ditched effort to impress, he ran over and took the heavy box from the older petite sister.

Smiling, Tonya expressed her gratitude with a "Thank you" to Bealz while cutting her eyes at Pudding.

In seconds Bealz was back out to help remove more boxes, this time from the u-Haul while peeking inside he saw that there were at least a set of bunk beds and two other beds not including the dressers, TV set and other furniture. Immediately Bealz knew what needed to be done before the sun faded into darkness.

"Yo, Trips! Go get Shellz and the white dudes ... tell 'em I said to come here," Bealz yelled. Unexpectedly, his ears, along with Tonya's daughters, heard the wailing sound of an ice cream truck. Bealz leaped down from the back of the truck's cab. He looked up the street and saw the white ice cream truck serving a small crowd of kids.

Yall want some ice cream?" he asked. Seeing the faces of the kids light up warmed his heart as he remembered Jake doing him the same way when he was a kid.

"Yeeaahh." the girls yelled, pumping their fists in the air.

Bealz looked at Tonya. "Mama, can we have some ice cream?" he asked in a playful kid's tone.

Tonya liked what she saw in Bealz. "Go ahead."
"Sup, Bealz," Shellz inquired when he finally emerged from the crib.

"Yo ... let's help them move in," Bealz recognized the "we must be going" look on Winky's face.

"I would...."

"I'ma pay you a bone twenty five," Bealz assured, interrupting Winky's complaint.

"Would love to help," Winky finished. Immediately he started, telling Bobby, "I'ma give you fifty."

Pudding turned down Bealz's invitation to hit the blunt, but Tonya didn't. During the process of moving the ladies' furniture in, Too Bad showed up with three hundred dollars. Bealz told him that he hadn't gotten straight yet. Too Bad pulled him to the side telling him. "Between five, six, and seven, a.m. and p.m., that's when people needed their fixes."

"Is that right," Bealz said, looking into Too Bad's eyes.

"Man, you'll be caked the fuck up in a month if you be straight at those hours every day."

He watched Too Bad walk over and climb into a black Lincoln that was followed by a van of junkies. To assure that Pudding couldn't overhear him, Bealz walked a short ways near the small black—owned store that sat at the edge of the Smallwood neighborhood and called Jake.

"Hey, son," Jake spoke on the first ring.

"I got your three dollars that I lost on our best."

"Okay ... we can bet again, if you don't mind losing."

Chuckling. "Man, you crazy ... I'm hoping to go out with this girl that's twenty—eight for the first time," Bealz spoke in code.

"A'ight, a cab will be there to get you in a minute. Then we'll go pick her up."

Jap

When talking on the phone, Jake always hung up first, especially (when the point had been made.

When the sky had become lightly tinted, Bealz ordered four pizzas from Pizza Hut in a show of being neighbor—friendly. Karma had finally made it back from her hair appointment. The Alliance, with the exception of Bizzo, was playing Spades inside the apartment of Tonya and Pudding.

Outside a car horn blared twice. Pudding looked out and asked, "Who called a cab?"

"That's my ride," Bealz said. He handed Shellz forty dollars and added, "I'll be back in a little bit." he made a face that cracked everyone up before he bolted out the door.

Once inside the cab, he looked back to see Pudding's attentive stare. "Independence, buddy," he told Jake.

Bright red lights lit up from the small gray meter that sat on top of the dashboard. As the cab pulled away from the curb, Jake blasted the car's radio. In seventeen minutes flat, the cab pulled into a driveway of a small brown house. Bealz was lost. All he knew was that he was near the borderline of Pineville. On Jake's hand gesture he exited the car's backseat.

The house was surrounded by a dense area of huge oak trees. The six houses on this lonely road were separated by a few yards. All that could be heard were two howling dogs, an owl, and crickets.

Bealz stood behind Jake on the two—step staircase. Jake knocked hard once on the black door with the chipping paint. The once-dark house's living room's light lit up. Once the door opened up, Bealz stared at a dark—skinned stubby gray—haired man, smoking a fat cigar.

"Hey, nephew," the man spoke to Jake flashing a huge grin that revealed missing teeth.

"Uncle Ed ... what's up?"

Bealz watched the two embrace.

"Come on in, boy, 'to dam mosquitos eat 'cha ass up."
Inside the home smelled like moth balls. Vintage furniture and an eight—track slash record player filled the tiny living room. A picture of Martin Luther King was above the bricked—in fireplace on the wall. No TV was in sight; quietly Marvin Gaye's "What's Going On" played at a volume so low it was barely audible.

At Jake's request, Bealz sat at the small kitchen table. Bealz stared at the two strainers and block of Banita. Bealz took notice of Uncle Ed pulling out two masks and one set of gloves.

"What're these for," Bealz questioned, staring at the items that Ed was reaching across the table to him. He gazed at Ed's disappointing stare.

Seriously speaking, "Look, son, don't ask no questions. Look and learn because this will be the only time that we'll be present with you during this process." Jake spoke with no sorrow in his eyes. Just after Bealz slipped on one of the masks and the gloves; Jake too slipped on a mask, giving Ed a nod for the go—ahead.

Bealz carefully watched Ed strain the Banita and dope separately; he then watched him repeat that step ten times. Thereafter, he watched Ed mix up the dope and cut together an astounding twenty times, give or take a mix. Lastly, he watched Ed, the old man, snort the product. And just like Too Bad, Uncle Ed entered a deep nod, but to Bealz's surprise, Uncle Ed was still coherent.

"What now,?" Bealz asked Jake.

"Give me thirty two hundred dollars." Jake quickly flipped through the wad of bills. "Go 'head and bag up your dope."

Bealz had a confused stare.

"Sit down, boy. Let me show you how it's done. I'm glad I didn't have to teach you to hold your talley—wacker, 'cause I'd be dammed if you came to me saying 'Unc Ed'," Uncle Ed teased, imitating someone who had to piss.

All the men chuckled.

"Wha' you selling, boy?" Ed questioned.

"Each bag for twenty—five dollars," Bealz answered up as his cell phone started an incessant ringing.

"What wrong wit' dat contraption? Cut dat t'ang off," Ed commanded.

"It's just my cell phone," Bealz explained, eyeing Karma's name displayed on the Caller ID screen.

"What'd he say . . ." Jake barked in support of Ed.
Bealz thought to himself, Nigga, you ain't my daddy.

"Okay, Jake." Bealz turned his cell phone completely off.

"Dis wha' ya do, boy . .

Bealz watched intently how much dope Ed put in one bag. He only had to see it done once before he started to do the bagging himself.

A good thing about Bealz was that he had a vivid memory. So it usually required him being shown something no more than once for him to pick it up; it was that way with riding a bike, cooking and cutting up Cocaine, and now mixing and bagging up Boy. All it took was once.

So Bealz was on his way to Big Boy status if he could manage to keep a level head.

CHAPTER SIX

It was thirty minutes past midnight when Bealz rolled back to his crib. He parked his car and made his way to the front door. He had just turned the knob and was inching the door open when an unidentified sound made him freeze. He closed his eyes. He had just about decided that at this paint it no longer mattered what happened and was prepared for the inevitable. He opened his eyes and caught a sudden movement over the gunman's shoulder and his gaze shifted slightly to barely discern what appeared to be a the silhouette of a person which crept silently out of the shadows. He flinched when he thought he heard the metallic sound a trigger being cocked.

But the sound had been Bizzo opening the door from the inside of the apartment. The paranoiac images in Bealz's mind instantly disappeared at the sound of Bizzo's voice.

"I thought that was you," Bizzo said, throwing the door open. "Karma and Shellz went out to the strip club."

Bealz shook off an imaginary chill as he entered and glanced around before easing onto the couch. "Any problems?"

"Naw — it's all good," Bizzo replied. "Hey, I like what y'all did wit' the crib."

"Have you moved what's left of that quarter?"

"That's what I was doing here tonight, hustlin' what's left of it. But like I said, business has been good."

"Must be good if Shellz and Karma out partyin'."

Members of The Alliance were making eight hundred off of every two thousand pack, so they were making bank. They were doing well enough that Bealz wasn't about to cut the others in on his heroin money; not yet anyway. Shellz could've been on his own but he loved to spend what he made on women as fast as he made it. All of Bizzo's money went to Lette and the kids. At least that's what he claimed.

All in all, things were looking bright for The Alliance. As Bizzo went on with his hustle, Bealz sat there momentarily, staring at nothing, wondering why this sense of dread and foreboding kept creeping into his consciousness. What were his instincts telling him that he should fear?

He checked his watch, still time to hustle a few fiends before he called it a night. He had an idea.

Four days, two ounces of Boy, and a big eighth of crack later, The Alliance had elevated themselves in the dope game. The hood was aware of it but so were the pigs and rats. Because of the heat from both factions, Bealz had decided it was time to relocate and worked out a deal with a junkie named Phil for his house at 2235 Crestview. Before The Alliance moved in, 2235 had no lights or hot water. Bealz took it upon himself to pay all the unpaid utility bills to get power restored. Although the house had two bedrooms, only the living room, kitchen, and bathroom were furnished, but The Alliance was determined to make it work.

The transformation took place smoothly, especially since their new neighborhood was already a safe haven for crack and Boy users. Only a handful of struggling low—level drug dealers worked the only corner of the Crestview cul de sac of small brick homes, they welcomed The Alliance with open arms especially since they now didn't have to go far to cop an 8 ball or quarter. The Alliance knew it wouldn't take long before they would have the naive youngsters working for them. For the time being they didn't mind sharing sells because in the end the money still bounced back to The Alliance.

It was a week later and Bealz was standing outside a rim shop on South Tryon when his cell phone rang. His Caller ID displayed, PRIVATE CALLER. On the third ring he finally answered, "Hello."

A soft voice spoke, "Is this Jacob Malone?"

Quickly checking his surroundings, "This is. Who 'dis?"

"Tiffany."

"Tiffany ... oh what a surprise, It's been awhile since I gave you my number. What's wrong? You need someone to talk to I——"

Interrupting, "I was hoping that we could hook up this weekend."

It was music to Bealz's ears. Even though he and Pudding had been kicking it hard lately, he was still very single. "What'd you have in mind?" he calmly inquired, hiding his excitement.

"How 'bout a movie?" she suggested.

Distracted watching the chrome 24—inch Zenettis fitted to his Cutlass appear from the garage doors of the rim shop further excited him.

Confused by his silence, "Jacob?"

"Oh, yeah, I'm here. How about grabbing a bite to eat today?"

"I'm down wit' that. I'll be leaving the salon in about an hour."

"A'ight, how's about meeting up at Applebee's out by UNCC?"

"Sounds good."

"All right then ... see you there."

Bealz and Karma were all smiles as they gathered around the Cutlass. Bealz had already installed a booming system in the car. He had High— Jacker Air Shocks put in place around the whip so that the rims would fit, and they fit perfectly. The car now sat up about as high as an SUV.

"It's ready," the white dude told Bealz, handing him the keys.

"Karma, you drive," Bealz suggested, climbing into the passenger seat, noticing how far his foot dangled above the ground.

The car earned the stares from other commuters as Karma merged into the sunny midday traffic. He had her cruise a neighborhood called Wilmore, then uptown Charlotte. Passengers on city busses craned their necks to get a glimpse of the Queen City's newest hoop—ride.

Bealz stuck 2Pac's 'All Eyes on Me' into the CD player and that's just what it was. He sparked up a blunt of Kush. The deep base from the woofers had the cloud of smoke changing directions.

Although Bealz was doing better in the dope game, he didn't spend money on jewelry. He did upgrade his gear but still nothing ridiculous. On the other hand, Shellz thought nothing about standing out on the block which Bealz had given the nickname The View with no shirt on showing off his platinum chain and medallion that hung above his navel. He had put encrusted diamond fronts over his fangs. He copped himself a candy apple red '98 Cadillac STS, complete with a system, factory chrome rims, and TVs in the headrests. Bealz didn't like him spending all that money, especially when rumors of Shellz's spending hundreds at strip clubs began showing up on the jackboy's sensors. Bealz knew that it was just a matter of time before some jackboy made a house call.

"Shellz, how much money you paid that stripper last night," a fifteen—year—old hustler named Flip asked, turning his oversized white fitted to the side.

"I shot the bitch two hundred, but when she wasn't paying attention, I took one hundred and fifty back," Shellz bragged, giggling.

Flip, who was present to hear Shellz's lies, hustled every day. His moms didn't care what he done as long as he gave her a hit.

Next up a light—skinned sixteen—year—old lanky kid who was named Duck because after he'd sell a couple of bags, he'd always duck off.

The only female was named Lynx who was twenty and built like Shawanna from DTP and sexy with her brown eyes. Lastly, Banga at only nineteen years old, had already seen many hardships of the streets and loved gunplay. Banga was pencil—lead black with pink lips and had three tear drops beneath his cold beady eyes. He was an astounding 6'2" and was built like Lebron James. Ever since meeting Bealz, he would stop at nothing to impress the Captain of The Alliance. He always told Bealz that "Loyalty Reigns," which made Bealz take a special liking to him. Bealz called them, The Associates.

Inside a packed restaurant called Tacos Mexico. San was seated at a table in the rear of the Mexican eatery, no food on her table, just two shots of Tequila. Unannounced, in came the chubby Ortiz by himself yelling in Spanish at the new waitress Consetta Tonzale. He motioned for San to follow him. Ortiz proudly strutted in his blue jeans, big hat and cowboy boots.

Once inside a huge office in the back, San held her arms out allowing Ortiz to search her. As soon as he believed everything was safe, his broken English broke the silence.

"How are dangs dojin, mommie?" he asked Sandra, offering her a seat as he took up refuge behind the black desk.

San's sparkling grill could've answered his question. "Life's good, Papi," She responded, slouching down in the seat, sitting like a man does, legs apart, placing a Fendi duffle bag between them on the floor.

Ortiz nodded as he leaned up, interlocking his fingers on top of the desk. "Well, what did ju have in mind?" he asked.
San leaned over and unzipped the duffle bag and for the next several minutes, Ortiz anxiously watched her stack bundles of cash on his desk.

"I wanna cop five bricks and I want two from you on consignment." she said, straightening up her chain and medallion.

Holding them inches from his ear, Ortiz flipped through each stack of money like he could hear how much each stack was. He reached over to San and firmly shook her hand. "I got ju, Mommie," he said.

San thanked her connect, rose from her seated position, then used the rear exit door. Just outside, a chubby Hispanic man was waiting by a Dumpster. Neither of them cracked a smile or uttered a word. He motioned her with his head and San walked over to a yellow Toyota and recovered a black bag from the unlocked trunk. She smiled her appreciation, waved, and slung the straps of the bag over her shoulders. And that fast, the transaction was completed San went unnoticed as she carefully crossed East Harris Boulevard. The rear—passenger door to a dark colored mini—van flew open which allowed San easy entry. "Let's roll," she demanded, tossing the bag onto the seat beside her, adding "Turn that shit up," when she recognized the Cameo's song 'Single Life' playing at a low volume.

As the traffic thickened and finally came to a standstill, the mini— van's air conditioning kept San and her Major League brethren protected from the blistering heat of the day.

Milky waited for the song to come near a close before he spoke. "Is we on deck?" he asked in a deep tone.

"What's my name, Nigga," San conceitedly responded.

"Well, how's about going to check on that bread in Barrington Oaks," Gramz brought up, looking back at San from the passenger seat.

San rubbed her right knee. "Dat Nigga Marley should of been finished," she said, furiously dialing his number on her cell phone.

On the third ring, Marley answered, "What it is?"

"Yo, Marl, dis San ... you ready yet?"

Marley went on to tell San that the police found five of the nine ounces in the bushes. San went ballistic pointing at her phone, shouting what would happen if she didn't get her money in two days.

Scared, but feeling safe since he and Milky were cousins, "Calm down, San. I got you. Just give me a wee———San——— hello? The bitch hung up on me," he told his boys.

Bobbing her head like she was hearing musical tunes in her head, San was making plans for Marley.

CHAPTER SEVEN

Around four—thirty, Tiff approached Bealz's table wearing a huge smile. The two briefly embraced as if they were old friends. "Ladies first," Bealz said as he motioned for her to take her seat before he sat down across from her.

"Well .., well, Mr. Jacob," she said with lustful eyes. She leaned back, confused by his stare. "What? Do I have a booger in my nose or something," she inquired, covering her nose.

He cracked a mischievous grin. "Nah, it ain't that. Even though you've been at work all day, you're still breathtakingly beautiful," he explained.

She poked her lips out. "What?"

"You tryin' to make me blush Jacob?"

"Nah ... but did it work?"

A smile slowly appeared on her face as she reached over the table and placed her well—manicured hands over his.
"I don't like nobody playin' wit' my feelings," she warned.

He tilted his head and with his free hand stroked his goatee. "Ms. Tiff, if I wanted to play a game. I have a Playstation 2 at the crib," he explained sincerely.

She removed her hand. "Either you know how to lie, or you are good at keeping a straight face," she teased, causing both to share a giggle.

They placed their order with the fat redheaded waitress. While waiting for their food, they enjoyed their drinks while using the time to share some details about each other's family backgrounds. Bealz wasn't surprised to learn that her father taught drama classes at Johnson C. Smith University and that her mother was a homemaker who also did in—house telemarketing.

"Enough about me, what does your father do?" she inquired, smiling at Bealz through the rising steam of the food that the waitress was setting in front of her.

Before answering, Bealz waited until she finished laying her napkin in her lap, then snickered.

"Wha's so funny?"

"Oh .. nothing. I just never been out with a well—mannered woman."

"That's bullshit," she whispered, then bowed her head in a silent prayer. When her eyes fluttered back open, to her surprise Bealz's mouth was stuffed with food. "Uh . . ." she hesitated, "please chew your food before you speak," she suggested worriedly.

After chewing his food and taking a swig of his lemon iced tea, he answered her previous question. "My father over—dosed on heroin and my mother's mind was the next to go." Bealz looked up just in time to see a tear roll down Tiff's watery eyes.

"I'm so sorry." she said very apologetically, dabbing her eyes with a napkin.

"No worries; it's all gravy. I have an uncle named Jake that watched after me. He owns Destination Cab Company. Besides, I do well at laying sheet rock," he lied, hoping she wouldn't dig any farther into his occupation.

Jap

Following their meal and a few drinks, the two stood outside of the restaurant watching the skies fade into darkness. She accepted his invitation to walk her to her vehicle. Their stroll was slow and very flirtatious.

Arriving in front of her car she said, "Well, this is me. Where's your car?"

Making note of the 22—inch rims sticking out of her two—door Beamer, Bealz was quick to assume that she was a gold digger or a rich kid like Karma spoiled rotten. So he frantically studied a few parked cars until his eyes fixated on an old and beat up junker. Bingo, he thought to himself.

"That's me over there," he said with a sly grin while pointing at the junker.

"Oh, that's a nice Navigator."

"No, not the Navi ... the gray Ford Escort." By the way she was laughing and carrying on, Bealz knew that he had her. "What's so funny? I can drive on a tank of gas for a month!"

"Bye, boy," she said, pressing a button on her key chain that made the Beamer's lights blink twice while making a chirping sound. She opened the driver's door and tossed her purse onto the passenger seat. Peering through her windshield, she caught Bealz's sorrowful gaze from the light on the poles that surrounded the parking lot. Leaving her car door open, she walked up to him and gave him a peck on the cheek.

"Call me," she said, slowly returning to her car.

Staring at her hips as she walked away, "Damn," Bealz mumbled. He waited until the Beamer drove off at a comfortable parking lot speed before scurrying to his own car. Once inside he searched the floor board until he found his lighter. When he sat back up, to his surprise

Tiff's smile could be seen through her downed window. "Damn, you must got some magical powers," she said loudly. Before he could respond, she stepped on the gas pedal.

He knew he'd been busted but he wasn't going to chase after her. He fired up the powerful 350 engine of the Cutlass when he heard his cell phone ring over the low volume baseline. Bealz checked the Caller Id which read: "Ms. Tiff)'

"Ahhh ... 'sup Tiff?" he spoke into his phone.

"You ain't got to lie to kick it. Jacob." Her voice radiated with seduction.

"You right. Imma call you tomorrow, if that's okay."

"That's fine. Bye," she sang.

A'ight.

As Shellz and Karma were watching The Associates running to cars and serving crack to people on foot, they traded blunts back and forth. Both were seated on the concrete steps of 2235. Respectively, they took turns to determine who could blow the biggest and most smoke—rings out of their mouths. Bizzo then rushed outside talking about the two crack heads who Phil had in his back bedroom. Bizzo looked up and just happened to make out the headlights of his favorite customer's Jetta that approached the entry road to The View.

"I got to get this sell," he said, leaping to the ground over the porch's banister.

Both Shellz and Karma watched Bizzo sprint up to the Jetta and bogard Banga from getting the crack sell. They knew from Banga's body language that he was furious.

"What the fuck wrong wit' Bizzo?" Shellz asked, pulling out his cell phone.

Happily Karma responded, "I don' know, but he fuckin' wit' the right one."

"What's up my Nigga," Shellz spoke into his phone.

"Ain't shit. I'm on my way to The Dere."

"Well, when you get a chance, come holla at Bizzo's lame ass."

"What's wrong?"

"You told us to sit back and let the Associates drain the water from the well, but ya boy keeps jumping them, taking sips."

Bealz read Shellz's code like a book.

"Gotcha."

"What did he say?"

"He'll be here ..."Shellz glanced up at the blunt that Karma had stuck in her ear. "Spark something up." He watched how Karma had positioned the blunt between her lips and immediately his mind manufactured naughty thoughts.

Hidden Valley, a huge neighborhood surrounded by Sugar Creek Road and North Tryon Street, was a very family orientated type of neighborhood. Multiple homes on each side of the street gave the appearance that no drugs were sold in this all—black community. But that all changed with the new generation of young kids that were raised into cold—blooded killers. The once very low murder rate in The Valley changed in the mid— to late—nineties. The murder rate in the new century had sky—rocketed to astronomical numbers. To put it best, the neighborhood had become a war zone, especially for any visitors.

1312 Snow White Drive, a modest one—story brick home that sported a well—manicured lawn and a two—car garage, housed a lab for a cocaine chemist. Soft beige carpet led throughout the home; black furniture blended perfectly with the burgandy painted walls. A single portrait of Scarface neatly overlooked a 42—inch Plasma TV screen. The three bedroom, one—and—a—half bathroom home produced a mixed smell. Thick clouds of weed smoke floated around in the living room while three naked ladies were busy cooking, weighing and bagging up kilos of cocaine in the kitchen. A fourth naked girl laid comfortably before the boss on a coffee table.

"I'll take you all to fuckin hell," San mimicked Al Pacino as Scarface, the most hood—loved flick, played on the pricey oversized screen. She passed Milky the blunt, then snorted more coke from between the girl's exposed breasts.

Gramz sat on a black whoopy cushion by the fireplace recounting the money that they had picked up earlier. "Same thang," he said, trying to shake the cramp put of his fingers. "Twenty—four five." he sighed at San's request of him to count it again. Taking note of her expressionless but cold stare, he said nothing, just licked his thumb end began to count.

'Ewww, I'm A Traffic King... Ewww, I'm A Traffic King,' San's musical ring tone sang on her cell phone.

San cut her eyes over Monica's breasts then raised up, grabbing her phone. "Hello," she breathed into the phone, cocaine covering the tip of her nose.

"It's all good," the deep—voiced caller said before disconnecting.

Happy to hear from the caller, San leaned over and inhaled as much coke that her nose could possibly handle, sending a gratifying rush to her already weakened brain cells. Momentarily subdued by the powerful Peruvian Coke, San clenched her fist, closed her eyes, then shook her head, In seconds she was back to normal, took another snort, then licked her tongue around Monica's areolas, making the sexy Italian—mixed with— Spanish mommie giggle.

"That tickles," the curvy petite mixed breed spoke to San in her soft mostly Spanish accented voice. But she was able to hold her passionate gaze.

It was always a normal routine to have naked girls inside of 1312 handling business for San's Major League crew. This was just one of a slew of homes in the Queen City where San held court to prepare her product. Her other homes or apartments included the Hampshire Hills, South Side Apartment, Garden City, The New Earle Village, and North Charlotte neighborhoods.

"Twenty—five fifty," Gramz said gladly, rolling his neck around. He hadn't counted all of the money. After he'd found a C—note beneath his foot, he'd taken a wild guess and just hoped that the count was accurate and passed by unnoticed by San's high imagination.

San showed her gratitude by commanding Monica to spread her legs. Without hesitation San's long tongue skimmed around the rims of Monica's hairless pussy. Then as San's tongue and teeth tugged at Monica's clit, her pants and squeals sounded like a porn flick was being made. Eagerly, one of the other ladies, a stripper named BlueBerry, rushed away from the cutting table to be licked by San's tongue as well. But Milky blocked her attempt by telling San that their worker, Lil Gas, from Lake View, had complaints about a crew that hustled from the Belvedere, Smallwood area. San gave Milky a sinister glance.

"We gon' handle it," San assured, gradually lowering her head, allowing her tongue to flicker like a snake's against Monica's welcoming clitoris.

CHAPTER EIGHT

10:15 P.M.

Bealz approached the 2200 block on a three hundred dollar dirt bike. The View was only a few blocks away from Belvedere Apartment's so he'd decided not to drive.

He stopped briefly on the corner just long enough to get the lowdown from Banga. He assured Banga that he was going to take care of Bizzo's disrespectful actions. Pulling up in front of 2235, he parked the bike and walked towards the house, bumping fist with Flip and Duck and hugging Lynx. Bealz brushed off a crackhead's sexual advance and pointed three customers into The Associates' position.

When Bealz entered the house he nodded at Phil, suggesting that he take his crack pipe and go smoke in his room. Bealz fanned the crack smoke from his face, ignoring the stench, all the while staring at Bizzo's fidgeting hands as he sat on the floor gazing out of the window at the sky.

"Where's Shellz and Karma?" Bealz asked, but only got a shrug from Bizzo. Bizzo's demeanor was familiar; Bealz had see it before in so many other people.

"Biz, you gettin' high," Bealz stated emphatically as he walked through the dark living room. Up close he could see his face clearly from the street light that partially shined through the cracked window pane. "How long you been gettin' high?" Refusing to be ignored by Bizzo, Bealz shouted, "HOW LONG?"

"THREE YEARS!" Bizzo responded in frustration, his eyes misting. He rose slowly to his feet and stood in front of Bealz with flaring jaws.

Bealz embraced his comrade of six—and—a—half months. As Bizzo's tears began to seep through Bealz's moca—colored Iceberg Tee, Bealz took notice of Banga standing in the breezeway of the front door clutching a nickle—plated 45 caliber Bealz freed up his right hand to wave off Banga who had just one thing on his mind — KILL BIZZO. But fortunately for Bizzo, Banga respected Bealz's every word.

"It's all right, Bro," Bealz assured Bizzo in a friendly tone. Hoping to ease Bizzo's guilt about his shameful actions he added, "We gonna get you some help. Lette and the babies need you, Dawg. So tomorrow I'ma personally take you to rehab and make sure your family's straight."

12:15 a.m. — 3500 Wilkerson Boulevard almost a hundred horny males packed themselves beneath the roof of Deluxe Tails Strip Club. Nestled only thirty feet from the Gaston County Line, the club was going into its third week of being open. With the naked barmaids serving hustlers from Charlotte, Gastonia, and the Belmont Mount Holly area, it was just a matter of time before violence broke out. But one thing about the club: all the strippers had incredible asses.

At least ten dudes were tossing dollars at the three strippers who where shaking their asses on the boomerang—

shaped stage to the song 'Shake What Ya Momma Gave You' that blasted from the eight huge speakers. Dudes were packed together throughout the club but sitting at a round table near the bar against the wall, Karma was sipping a Long Island Tea while Shellz was seated opposite her enjoying a lap dance from a white stripper named Candy Cane.

Karma had been ready to go when a drunk dude approached her, stumbling into the table nearly knocking the drinks off.

"Excuse you," Karma said, staring up at him with hateful eyes.

He slurred, " My bad, baby ... let me get the next dance." He managed to get out fifteen ones and waved them in Karma's face with his extended left while with his right he touched her titty.

Karma angrily shoved his hand away. Shellz quickly stepped between her and the stranger and Karma had to stop the dude from pushing Shellz around.

"Man — she isn't a stripper and don't want to be bothered," Shellz explained, returning the stranger's shove as his aggressive actions began to pick up.

"Nigga, do you know who I am? I'm Low Ball Slim," the dark—skinned skinny drunken dude introduced himself as. Even as two of the club's bouncers approached to remove Low Ball from the club, he became more uncontrollable with his struggles and blaspheme. "Get 'cho fuckin' dick beaters off of me. I'm Low Ball, da best to ever do it. I'm going in the first round, Nigga," he shouted. He spat on the guards, kicked and struggled but Low Ball was no match for the size of the guards as they escorted him outside.

Shellz gave the stripper a tip for her troubles. Meanwhile, Karma kept a close eye on other patrons to see if anybody would exit behind Low Ball, but evidently no one had paid any attention. She figured that Low Ball might not be alone and maybe his friends were too busy paying attention to the live entertainment to witness the altercation. Once she saw the two bouncers emerge from the door they'd exited moments before, Karma grabbed Shellz by the arm.

"Let's bounce," she urged, speaking earnestly into Shellz ear.

Moments later as they slowly exited the parking lot in Shellz's car, Karma shouted, "Hold up, let me out!" Shellz stopped, wondering what was up. "Keep the car running," she said as she threw open her car door and exited in a big hurry. With her arms folded, she had to concentrate on not falling as she had trouble navigating through the gravelled parking lot balancing on her stilettos.

The building's structure and its parking lot was rather small, about the size of a McDonald's. Cars had to park so close together that to avoid bumping doors into other cars, some of the larger people had to get out before the cars they rode in eased into a parking space. Even the smaller dudes had room only to climb out of one side of the vehicle. Whichever side had the most room, that's where they'd exit.

Jap

The silhouette of a lone figure slouched down with his face propped up on his right hand could be seen inside a purple boxed Chevy. Drunk and half asleep, he didn't even hear the footsteps making awkward sounds on the parking lot's white rocks. Even if he'd been sitting up with his eyes open it would have been hard for him to see the imminent figure approaching because of how dark the area was in his semi—conscious state he did hear a soft voice filter through calling his name.

"Hey, Low Ball." As he forced open his eyes, putting his tongue in gear to speak - BOOM! The kick from the handgun sent her hand upwards. A single bullet ripped through Low Ball's forehead, splattering half of his brain matter all over the Chevy's purple and white leather interior.

Karma strolled calmly away from the gruesome scene as she discreetly checked to see if anybody had witnessed the one—second execution. Karma had seven more wig splitters in the clip and her rule was never to let anyone live to identify her. This was her fourth killing since Bealz had formed The Alliance. To be proactive, she never failed to carry a pair of latex gloves in her purse and Bealz had drilled it into her head never to load a pistol with her bare hands.

Shellz looked at her gravely as she re—entered the STS. She didn't say a word and Shellz didn't ask. He just put the car in gear and eased out of the parking lot. He didn't even comment once they were several miles away. Karma burned the latex gloves and tossed them out onto Wilkerson Boulevard. Their next stop was the burial place of the other three murder weapons: The Catawba River.

Returning to a less remote part of Wilkerson Boulevard, Shellz steered the STS into a somewhat crowded Texaco to get some gas and some chicken wings. Pulling to a stop adjacent to a gas pump Shellz glanced over at Karma. Obvious under the bright overhead fluorescents beneath the high square shed that covered the gas pumps were specs of blood and gore on Karma's nose, chin, and left cheek.

"Check ya self," Shellz suggested before he exited the car.

Lowering the visor, sure enough the illumination around the mirror revealed her latest victim's bloody phlegm decorating her face. Studying the gore, she smiled as if she was in a desert enduring 120 degree temperature and the blood droppings were like cold water that splashed on her from the sky.

She retrieved a white hanky from her purse and licked the soft material several times. Once she felt that the cloth was damp enough, she began to wipe her face in small circular motions.

Another rule that The Alliance members, Bealz, Shellz, and Karma, lived by was: those present at the time of a slaying were to keep the details amongst themselves. If anyone broke that rule it meant that it was likely they would end up being a SNITCH!

Deep down a dirt road was parked a stolen black Buick Skylark, surrounded by huge trees, thick brushes, and high grass. The car was occupied by one lone dude smoking on a hyped Black N Mile. The engine was shut off but he'd turned the ignition back on to be able to listen to the radio which was playing at a low volume.

The man looked out at an owl that was perched on a branch that hung over the car from a tree he had parked under. He managed to ignore the muffled sounds of someone locked in the trunk. He took another puff of his cigar when the owl suddenly took wing. Although the night was dark, the stars in the sky gave off enough light to enable him to see the dust rising from an approaching vehicle.

When the vehicle was close enough, thumping ashes between his legs onto the floor board, the man in the Buick flicked its headlights once enabling the approaching vehicle to pinpoint the Buick's location. Watching the car approach, he secured his gloves around his hands and then climbed out with gun in hand.

Stopping fifteen feet from the Buick, two passengers exited a crack— head's charcoal gray Astro van. Not a word was spoken, only head nods as they cautiously approached the trunk of the Buick.

When the Buick's driver popped open the trunk, the terrified captive was blinded by the bright beam of light from the flashlight that the passenger from the van shone in his face. With his hands and feet bound tightly with duct tape and what looked to be a scarf wrapped around his mouth, all the captive could do was mumble and groan, struggling to free his entangled limbs from the binding of the relentless tape.

"Be still, Nigga," the passenger from the van commanded.

The van's driver removed the tight cloth from around his mouth, enabling the captive to work his jaw open and closed several times to get feeling back which had been numbed by the gag.

"Damn, man! Y'all quit playin!" he demanded. Realizing who it was who held him captive, he continued, "Go 'head now and untie me," pausing, breathing heavily, "This shit ain't cool," he complained.

"You right, lil' Nigga," San replied, looking down at him dispassionately. "Oops, I forgot like those five ounces the police will find you in the bushes."

Looking around to the victim's cousin through marriage, San order quietly, "Milky. Chest shot."

Without hesitation ... BOOM!
Marley screamed so loudly that every bird and bat, those silent onlookers in the tree tops, took wing into the night, most likely convinced that the owl had the right idea after all: this was a scene they wanted no part of.

Marley's screams finally started to fade. Tired of hearing it, San once again looked over into the trunk to see Marley choking on his own blood. "See you in hell, Nigga," she said.

Backing away while sharing an evil gaze with Milky, San ordered, "Lil Pug. Head shot."

BOOM! BOOM! BOOM! BOOM! BOOM! BOOM! Click. Click. Click.

Marley's body finally quit jerking. The powerful 357 Magnum had dismantled his entire face.

Like the trunk was a casket, Lil Pug slowly lowered its lid until it sealed. He then retrieved a gallon of gasoline and doused the flammable liquid throughout the interior and around the car, making a trail of gas to the awaiting van. He relit his Black N Mild, took a pull and climbed into the van through the rear passenger slide door. Just as Milky cranked the van and put it into drive, Lil Pug thumped the cigar into the gas—saturated grass.

The van sped of f as the trail of fire quickly overtook the Buick, engulfing the car and grass in flames and even igniting the tree limbs above the car. The van didn't even clear the woods when a loud explosion set a tremor through the ground, the concussion managing to rock the van.

"You feel that," San said gleefully, sticking her nose into an 8— ball of powder.

"Yeah, that's my lil' cousin ... he done blew the fuck up," Milky stated, totally insensitive to the fact that he and Marley had been raised in the same home together as kids. Fact is, if it had not been for Milky baiting up Marley to believe that Pug has two grand to spend, Marley wouldn't have met Pug in a closed park where he had been kidnapped at gunpoint and taken on his last ride.

CHAPTER NINE

8:00 A.M. the following morning two of the five murders that had taken place the previous night earned lead—in spots on all the local news stations. They reported that two older white gentlemen going fishing had discovered a burned and charred vehicle in the woods, and phoned 911. When the police and emergency crews arrived, they had to cut through a burnt tree trunk that had apparently burned and crashed on top of the flattered car's roof.

After a thorough search, they found the body. The medical examiners and the Coroner determined at the scene that the body was a man who apparently been bound and shot multiple times.

The murder of LaMontavious Ballings managed to get the most press coverage, however. It was reported that the former Gaston County High School basketball star was planning to forego his second year at UNC and enter the NBA draft, rumored as a first round pick. The broadcasters went on to mention that LeMon (known mostly, on and off court, by his nickname "Low Bali Slim") had a drinking problem. They went so far as to say that almost every time Mr. Ballings went out he'd be arrested for disorderly conduct. They concluded with mention of the fact that as of Friday morning, July second, Meclenburg County's murder rate had lapped last years, stating that although it was barely through the midway point of it would get much worse.

But neither The Alliance nor Major League watches cared about the news.

Bealz raised his head as the smell of bacon, eggs, grits and sausage disturbed his nasal passage. He hopped off his king size bed and stuck his feet into his black fluffy house slippers. He yawned and stretched, went into the bathroom and got himself together before flying down the stairs wearing only some pajama bottoms over his boxers.

Entering the small kitchen, the song "Gangster White Walls" was playing as Karma grooved quietly to the beat as she organized the food. Bealz never ceased to be amazed at how Karma's white boy shorts accentuated her plump ass. When he noticed there was no bra strap showing through her wife beater, he vigorously rubbed his palms together.

"G'morning," he spoke, gasping at her hardened nipples when she turned from the stove she was cooking over. He stared at her from head to toe in a lustful manner.

"Morning ... I figured you'd be hungry," she replied, flipping the eggs over in the pan,

"Sho' is," he responded, kissing her cheek on his way to the refrigerator to pour himself a glass of orange juice. He decided to ask her whose money he had seen on the glass coffee table, but she answered before he could ask.

"That's your money on the table from the heroin sells I made early this morning. It's twenty two hundred dollars," she said.

About three weeks before, Bealz had let Karma and Shellz know that he would be selling the Boy and Shellz and Bizzo would he selling the Girl. But with Bizzo going into rehab around 10 a.m., Bealz realizing he might have to start back dealing crack. He didn't figure there was any way that Shellz would be able to move a Bird of coke that would be mostly chopped up into dimes especially with Shellz always wanting to go hangout at strip clubs. Even with the help of The Associates, it would still be too much work for Shellz considering his had spending habits. The worst part, Bealz thought, was that Shellz gave up his room in apartment 140 to Karma so he could get the bedroom in 2235 to be hands—on with the money hole. But through it all, Shellz doesn't save any money.

By 10:30 a.m., Bealz and Karma were leaving from the rehab off of Remount Road- They both felt that it was the best thing for Bizzo and his family.

From doing their duty at the rehab, Bealz told Karma to stop at Freedom Mall. After purchasing the newest Jordans for The Alliance and The Associates, they drove down to The View. Bealz enjoyed the looks on the faces of The Associates as he handed each one a gray and black Jordan shoe box.

"Thanks, Bealz," Lynx said, giving him a kiss on the cheek through the downed window.

"Man down!" someone shouted up the block.

The Associates quickly scrambled behind some apartments that Jed to a basketball court that sat atop a hill on the next street.

Karma and Bealz weren't so lucky as six police cars had them trapped.

"Let me see your hands!" several shouted, crouched down behind their opened squad car doors, their service weapons drawn.

With no way to escape, Karma and Bealz raised their hands and were ordered to press their palms firmly on the roof of the car. The officers approached cautiously, shouting every curse word known to man. They made Bealz get out first and ordered him to lay on his belly with his palms stretched out to his side.

Meanwhile, in 2235, Phil had luckily witnessed what was happening outside. He rushed to Shellz's bedroom and started pounding on the door shouting, "POLICE! POLICE!"

Shellz leaped into action by stuffing nine ounces into a bag and looking for a means to get away. Knowing that with all the police action out in front, there was no chance he could slip past them. So he opened the back door cautiously, peeked out, and seeing that it was clear, he ran through the left path and caught up with The Associates playing ball with a couple of dudes.

Back on the lone corner of The View, the police had Bealz and Karma handcuffed and stashed in different squad cars, their windows rolled up.

But fate was not on the side of the police this day. Not only was the Cutlass found to be clean, but so were the names of Jacob Malone and Sharelle Robinson. Finding no warrants outstanding on either of them, both were reluctantly uncuffed and released, but not without a warning from Ramsey, the lead officer, whose white skin was bright red.

"Mr. Malone and Ms. Robinson, if I find out that you two are dealing drugs down here on Crestview, I promise that by the time you two get out of prison, your great grandchildren will be grandparents," Ramsey ranted in a harsh tone, pushing Bealz up against his green unmarked squad car. "Now get your black ass outta my face," Ramsey added angrily, mushing Bealz in the back of the head.

Using his shirt to wipe droplets of Ramsey's spit from his face, Bealz pushed his way out from the circle of the twelve all— white officers, scrunching up his face from the stinking smell of the various after—shave lotions from the different officers.

Moments later, navigating the Cutlass through the undecorated obstacles of police vehicles, Karma asked in a concerned tone, "You good?" She was carefully concentrating on her driving skills in hopes of not bumping another car.

Bealz cracked a sly grin as he watched Ramsey in the passenger's side mirror, waving his hands. He thought about how Jake carried himself when riding to do dirt. Thinking to himself that they may have bugged the car, Bealz thought it best to watch what was said. "It's all good, we got some cars to go clean," he said, staring over at Karma's confused look. He placed his left pointer finger against his outwardly—pushed lips indicating silence. Suddenly his cell phone rang- He checked the Caller ID before pressing the button that shut the power off.

Jap

Bealz pointed out the route to Karma that got them home in four minutes. As soon as he got out of the Cutlass, he made two calls; the first went to Shellz.

"Damn, Bealz, is everything straight?" Shellz inquired, sounding extremely troubled.

Very composed, Bealz responded, "Man, crackers know something. What I don't know. But I'm going to dump the Cutlass after I change clothes."

"What? let me buy it!"

"Nah man, those cops spent almost an hour in that car. Man, it's probably bugged."

"Yeah you probably right. Did they say anything about me or the crib?"

"Nah I don't know what they said or asked Karma, but I definitely didn't do shit but give 'em my driver's license. For now go put the sodas on ice, lay low until tomorrow and give Phil two hundred dollars. Later!"

"Yeah — yeah."

Bealz spoke briefly to Pudding who had been standing on the porch from the time the Cutlass had first arrived. She could tell by Bealz's demeanor that something was wrong but she chose not to ask any questions because he wasn't her man nor had they ever slept together. He told her that he'd see her later and entered the apartment,

Bealz placed his second call to Jake, letting him know what had gone down and that he was going to trade his car in. Jake told him that that was a grown man's decision.

Their call was short and sweet. Because he still had half a kilo of cocaine and three ounces of Mexican Mud, Bealz didn't need to re—up on any drugs.

Bealz and Karma shared their separate experiences when they were questioned by the police. Both stated that silence was their only response and that was that. Bealz told Karma to call a couple of car lots for something in the nineties with a good motor and a reasonable price.

While Karma was doing as requested, Bealz headed upstairs, going into his room, closing the door behind him. He went into the closet, slid his urban garments that hung on hangers to the side, then kneeled down on one knee. He began to work his black safe's combination.

"Thirty—six left, twelve right, two" he said loudly to himself.

Inside of the safe that was the size of a small refrigerator were stacks upon stacks of drug money that Bealz had been stashing.

Bealz took nine thousand dollar stacks, removed the rubber bands that held the money together, then began stuffing the deep pockets of his Red Monkey denim jeans with the bills until his pockets were bulging out like Buffy's ass in some tight Boy shorts.

Next, digging through his dresser drawer, he pulled out a neatly folded crisp wife beater. He snatched off the tee shirt that had Ramsey's dried up spit on it and threw it on the floor. Bealz tossed the wife beater over his left shoulder, then with his head held up high he skipped down the steps.

Seeing Karma on the phone, he gave her a hand gesture. Shortly thereafter they were taking what would most likely be their last ride in the Cutlass.

Two hours later... ...

The sun was almost at its brightest, putting the city streets on baking status. Even the tip of the skyscrapers in uptown Charlotte had what appeared to be a thick haze of heat—wave rotating around the well— built structures. In a futile effort to warn the city's residents, the local news stations were reporting that because the heat index had reached a dangerous level, it was best to stay indoors to be safe, drink plenty of water, and make sure that older family members were checked on.

There was a huge buzz floating around within Unique Designs. Two females were gossipping with Vanilla about the latest money go—getters in the dope game. Although he sported a third leg, to all the females he was just another one of the girls.

Vanilla was just about to give the "girl you heard?" low down when he interrupted himself. "Oh, girl! That's my song!" Vanilla blurted, hearing the '50s song "Many Men" begin to play on his portable CD/radio that was perched between his hair products. As he began to dance and drop it like it's hot, the all—

female twenty—something customers and workers present began to cheer him on. "Many men wish dick on me — Lord, I will drink some mo' — I sure will be a hoe," he sang, remixing '50s lyrics. What was most surprising was that even wearing a tight pair of pink Baby Phat capris and heels, Vanilla didn't fall during his spin moves. When the song ended, he dabbed at the line of sweat that had built up around his thin penciled in eye brows with his right forearm.

Looking back at him, "Boy, yo ass is crazy," BlueBerry, his female client said, sitting in his chair with her legs crossed.

Paying little attention to her co—worker and his clients' conversations, Tiff continued to style her customer's hair. But when the name Bealz spilled from the lips of one of Vanilla's clients, Tiff tuned in and was very attentive to both the client's looks and words.

CHAPTER TEN

3:15 P.M.

It was almost time for places like the DMV to close but luckily for them, Karma and Bealz had been standing in line since one o'clock. Indeed, Bealz had done as he had promised and had sold the Cutlass two hours earlier. He and Karma were at the DMV desperately trying to get tags to the vehicles that Bealz had purchased.

Parked outside the DMV office were a two—toned burgandy and silver '95 Chevy Hitop conversion van and an '87 powder white box Chevy Caprice classic. Bealz put his name as owner of the Chevy and Karma graced the title of the van with her Jane Hancock. In all, Bealz paid six thousand dollars for both rides: twenty five hundred for the van and thirty five hundred for the Chevy classic.

Bealz had taken the time to remove his rims, woofers and amps from the Cutlass before he sold it. The young dude that purchased the Cutlass figured that fifteen hundred dollars was a steal.

Bealz checked the clock on the wall for the time, deciding that he needed to place a call. He knew that with his position in line, he'd ultimately be seen by the Asian female DMV clerk.

"Hold my spot down. I'll be right back," he told Karma loudly enough so that people behind them could hear him clearly.

As he walked towards the restroom he gave the other nine other customers waiting in line his killer stare.

When Bealz emerged five minutes later, Karma was at the desk signing forms. He then looked on as the clerk passed a metal tag to Karma over the counter.

"Next," the Asian woman uttered in her soft sounding Korean accent.

Bealz stepped up to the counter and slid the proper papers across to the clerk accompanied by a generous smile. It didn't take long to comply with the necessary requirements of the State's rules. In minutes the Chevy's title was stamped and safely in Jacob Malone's name.

Immediately after attaching the proper tags to the van and Chevy, Bealz drove the van, with Karma following in the Chevy, to a Pep Boys on Freedom Drive. After he described the job he wanted and paid for it, three workers removed the rims from the van and placed them on the Chevy. By 6:55 P.M., Bealz was watching the Chevy being pulled out of Pep Boys shocks and struts department. Karma had been long gone so he quietly celebrated the Chevy's new look by himself.

On account of the size of the four—door hoopties, with the air shocks and twenty—four inch rims, the Chevy easily outshined the Cutlass. Where the Olds had a 350 engine beneath the hood, the Chevy boasted a refined 455 big block and had only 70,000 miles. Where the Olds had regular black soft—cushioned seats that were fading on the head rest, the Chevy interior was leather the color of peanut butter, not to mention the thick beige carpet minus the burns that covered the floorboards and the unscratched wood grain steering wheel and dashboard. To top it off, the roof's exterior was a thick half—a—vinyl that matched the color of the interior.

"Boy, dat muh—fuck's nasty," the slender white guy with the freckles exclaimed.

"Yeah. Now I gots to get my system hooked up," Bealz replied stroking his six thick fizzy French braids.

The freckle—faced Pep Boys worker looked around to see if his boss was watching since the boss wasn't in sight, he tugged on Bealz's arm and motioned for him to walk around to the rear end of the Chevy.

The dude whispered, "I get off at 7:30." Peering over the Chevy he added, "I can hook up your system after I get off.'

"Oh yeah?" Bealz replied, giving him a quizzical stare, seeing the serious look in the guy's eyes, Bealz agreed, especially after finding out that the guy, whose nickname was Freckles lived only six minutes from Pep Boys.

Sure enough, after Bealz had copped a high tech CD changer and radio from Radio Shack, by nine p.m. Freckles had performed the system transformation inside a single car garage. Aside from making the Chevy system sound like thunder, Bealz also found out that Freckles had connections to various weapons and ammunition.

The two continued with their conversation for another hour over some Kush that Freckles had purchased from a dude at work. They couldn't crank up the car's system because even though the modest home belonging to Freckle's mother was on the left third from a stop sign, the neighbors had already been complaining about the army of people who visited Freckles daily.

Bealz eased out of the wooden garage and stopped briefly at the end of the paved driveway to exchange contact numbers with Freckles with a promise to do more business with him in the future. As the Chevy idled in the driveway while the two men talked, the car's high powered cam and the low sounding baseline from the four 12—inch woofers in the trunk sent deep vibrations throughout seven of the twelve nearby homes.

Freckles watched the car ease out onto the street and cruise proudly all the way to the stop sign, admiring his work as the rattling trunk disturbed the night.

Around the same time, up around Independence Boulevard where an assortment of car lots, department stores and other businesses operated, a sports bar called Admissions was filling up with its regular patrons. In the parking lot outside Admissions a group of undesirables was parlaying. With a bowling alley and a movie theater next to the sports bar and its position behind TGI Friday's the scene was a brewing pot of trouble.

Shellz and The Associates were parked three spaces over from a group of five whose attire was dipped in all red. Between the heavy cloud of smoke in the STS blurring their vision, and the blasting of the music, Shellz and The Associates failed to notice a sinister—looking blacked—out van, meaning paint, with limo tinted windows, slowly approaching from the rear, its side sliding door already slightly ajar revealing two masked men bearing SKS assault rifled with thirty round magazines. With one lying on his stomach and the other straddling him, they were ready to fire.

In the rear of the STS, three of The Associates, Flip, who sat on the passenger side, Lynx in the middle, and Duck on the right, were trying to stop laughing at a joke Shellz had told when it happened. A gunshot rang out.

POP! Of course, the bullet shattered Shellz's rear window, sending Flip's brains onto the back of Banga's neck. POP! POP! The second shots were more rapid, hitting Lynx in the neck. Reacting out of shock, she sat up right into the line of fire of a high—powered rifle shell which entered the back of her skull, passing through her forehead, then travelling through and shattering the sunroof.

"Oh, shit! Shit! Shit!" Duck and Shellz continued to yell. But Banga, gun in hand, opened the door and fired rapidly over the Caddy's trunk at the slowly passing van. Three of the boys in red weren't as lucky as their two associates who had taken off running.

Shellz looked down at Lynx, her lifeless body sprawled over the gear shift drenched in blood from the fatal head and neck wounds. Duck was crying hysterically at the sight of Flip propped against the window, blood gushing form his wounds.

Banga snatched the Caddy's rear door and caught Flip's lifeless body while wrenching the pistol from his grasp. "It's gon' be all right," Banga kept protesting with a trembling voice to an unhearing Flip while cradling him in his arms.

Aware of the wail of approaching sirens, Shellz yelled at Banga,

"Police comin'! Get outta here! I got this!" It was as if Banga was in a dazed state and didn't hear Shellz. "BANGA!" Shellz shouted, finally catching Banga's evil gaze. "Go 'head on ... if you stay, you gonna get locked up! Now go! And take Duck wit' you!"

Covered in his friend's blood, Banga laid Flip down and recovered his pistol. To their advantage, all the bystanders had scattered as soon as the shooting started, making their escapes by car and foot. This was a scene no one wanted any part of, except for two hood chicks in an old model Acura Legend who had witnessed the whole incident as it unfolded and waited to see what would happen next. No stranger to such violence, they identified with their predicament and in a show of empathy offered Banga and Duck a ride — away from the carnage, away from the clutches of the police — providing them an opportunity to maintain their freedom, at least for another day.

Shellz didn't have a chance to call Karma or Bealz before the drones of police cars could weave their way through the multiple fleeing vehicles. Shellz did manage to discard the half—ounce of weed he had by tossing it beneath a car that was ten feet away.

A number of police cruisers converged upon the scene at the same time, all coming to a screeching halt. Officers jumped out of the squad cars with their service guns drawn and ordered Shellz, covered in blood from both Lynx and Flip, to lay on his stomach, his hands behind his head. From his prone position on the ground, Shellz looked directly into Flip's open but vacant eyes from where he laid on the opposite side of the car.

8810 Legacy Park Drive — Colonial Grand At Legacy Park Apartment Homes — to say the least a luxurious place to live. A twenty—one seat movie theater, billiards room, gourmet Java bar, a spa and an elegant pool were but a few of the amenities offered in this community comprised primarily of executives and ex—professionals of the highest jobs that one can hold.

Inside Apartment A—3, on the third wing which overlooked the beautiful, lush trees and meticulously landscaped grounds, and in the distance a picture—postcard view of the city skyline, the head of the Robinson family, Jamil, a retired neurosurgeon, was giving his daughter another of his frequent tongue lashings about life. But Karma sat on her parent's French—made furniture watching the 52—inch Plasma TV screen, paying little attention, as usual. Karma's gorgeous mother, Alicia, was holding Karma's hand, whispering her pleas for Karma to listen but it was no use; their every word went' in one ear and out the other.

The Robinsons had been married for over twenty years and were disappointed that their daughter didn't attempt to take advantage of her Letters of Acceptance from Grambling State or Wake Forest. Actually, this was the first time in thirteen months that the upstanding parents even got a chance to see their daughter. Jamil did, however, keep Karma's credit card and bank account up to par. Jamil loved his youngest daughter, although unaware of what she was involved in.

Karma's medium—sized but very toned father was tired of being ignored. He grabbed his Money Market newspaper from the coffee table and placing it under his left arm pit, he jumped up from his favorite seat in the house and stormed off, mumbling beneath his breath.

"It's okay. You know how your father is," Alicia said sympathetically, patting her daughter's hand in an assuring manner.

Not breaking eye contact with the colorful Plasma screen, Karma was going to respond but a breaking news segment interrupted her train of thought;

"Breaking news ...! With a special news bulletin, here's Amy Politician.

"Thanks, Bill," the attractive blonde news reporter said into a microphone as she stood several feet away from a long line of yellow crime—scene tape. "Moments ago some heavily armed gunmen with assault rifles fired more than fifty rounds at some college students who were wearing their red school colors. Of the five, three had been shot and were pronounced dead on the scene by the coroner's office. But if you look behind me to the far right," she paused and pointed as the camera panned to the scene of the carnage, "... at that Cadillac STS that's been riddled with bullets, two innocent passengers in that car were killed by the reckless assault. There appear to be no witnesses and no motive for the shootings has been announced. The names of the victims are being withheld pending family..."

Alicia changed the channel with her remote in an attempt to get Karma's attention. Instead Karma leaped to her feet and grabbed her small handbag. "Wait a minute! Where are you going?" Alicia demanded.

Karma's voice was choked. "I—I just got to go, Mama." she said, shaking her head.

As Karma headed for the door, Alicia reached out and grabbed her daughter's arm but -she wasn't strong enough to hold on. The younger female Robinson jerked free of her mother's grasp which made her stumble. Helplessly, Alicia watched her daughter throw open the front door and rush out, slamming the door behind her. Alicia plopped down on the sofa, throwing an arm over her forehead. As she closed her eyes, a flood of tears cascaded down her face.

'I wonder where I went wrong,' Alicia thought to herself about her wayward daughter.

"ANSWER THE FUCKIN' PHONE, SHELLZ!" Bealz yelled with frustration into his phone that had failed to connect for the third time in a row. Pacing along the sidewalk in front of a Mighty Midgets convenience store on Beatties Ford Road, cell phone in hand, he muttered, "Where could that nigga be? He better be fuckin' dead ... that's all I got to say!" He stopped his pacing and leaned back against the front fender of his car, his head bowed, rubbing his eyes with the thumb and forefinger of his left hand, fighting the recurrence of that now—familiar sensation of losing control. With his assailant's back to the blinding summer sun, Bealz found himself having to squint as the assassin screw faced Bealz and shouted obscenities, demanding Bealz move his ass and give up the drug money. Bealz felt his body tensing into a prolonged flinch as he watched his killer's finger squeeze on the trigger that would fire a bullet into Bealz's brain the way it was aimed. Just before he pulled the trigger the assailant launched another tirade of obscenities.

"You nuttin' but a low—life mutha—fucka," the bum was saying, the sound of his voice filtering into Bealz's consciousness. "You all uppity, won't spare a dollah to help a brotha out," the man wearing several layers of ragged clothes ranted as he waved filthy hands in front of Bealz. "Sons of bitches like you think you too good — you watch yo ass, your day is coming."

The ringing of his cell phone returned Bealz to full consciousness. Watching the old man limp away empty—handed, still muttering curses under his breath, Bealz barked into his phone without checking the Caller ID display, "Sup, Fam?"

Bealz was assaulted by Karma's frantic voice, barely recognizable, "Bealz, something happened to Shellz!"

Bealz had never heard that kind of fear in Karma's voice before, so he instinctively knew something drastic must have happened. He quickly hopped into his car while he listened to whatever Karma knew of the circumstances regarding Shellz. But

Jap

the next call Bealz received was from Jake who also sounded more troubled than Bealz could ever remember.

CHAPTER ELEVEN

All things considered, Shellz was fine, unlike Lynx and Flip. After it was determined that Shellz hadn't suffered any serious injury, investigators took him downtown for questioning. While the cops did believe that Shellz had not fired any pistol, their main objective was to get him to reveal whose pistol left the eight shell casings found on the ground beside the STS. Shellz told them that he was too busy ducking to see who was shooting.

Shellz quickly grew tired of sitting at the metal table in the cramped interrogation room under the light that hung above his head. Their next question was a trick question.

"Well ..." began the Caucasian lead detective blue dress slacks, white button—down dress shirt and blue tie. "So, while the shooting continued, you crawled over Ms. ..." she paused, checking her notes, "... Mystery Odel, opened the passenger door and helped Mr. Nelson Waldo who was in the backseat, and laid him on the ground . .' Finally finished, she removed her glasses and softly laid them on her yellow writing pad.

"Look here, baby girl, that's what you said. I was duckin' when whoever was fuckin' buckin'," Shellz replied in a sarcastic tone of voice accompanied by a chuckle.

The red on the face of the lead investigator, Detective 1st Grade Sharon Bucannon, told it all: she was furious. She rose stiffly from her seated position, gathered her belongings and along with another officer, stormed out, leaving Shellz to sit there for another two hours.

Being treated like this was no sweat for Shellz. He had served eighteen months in state prison before he turned nineteen. All they had on him this time was the half ounce of skunk they found stuffed inside his boxers, and being in the wrong place at the wrong time, that was it.

By five—thirty the next morning, at last Shellz was freed on bond. He stood outside in the back of the jail for a minute, taking his time to admire the fog that circulated around the castle—like shapes at the top of the Bank of America building. While his neck was still stretched and his head tilted backwards, his moment of observation was interrupted by the loud honk of a car. He glanced over at the four cars that were parked in line up North Calweld Street. From his position, his eyes fixated on the hands that were waving frantically from the passenger seat of a crispy—looking Chevy. Without hesitation, he skipped over and jumped in.

"Sup, baby boy," Shellz said, grinning, inspecting the car's interior.

Bealz extended his hands in greeting over his right shoulder but Shellz had to finish kissing on Karma's cheek before he accepted Bealz's outstretched hand. Bealz then put the car in gear and eased around the dark SUV with the blinking tail lights that was parked in front of them, inches from the curb.

"Here, fire this up, Bro," Karma said, passing Shellz a blunt.

Bealz spoke above the music of Charlotte's hottest rapper, G Monte's the song being How Dirty Is The South. "Is everything a'ight?" he asked, cutting his eyes in the rearview mirror at the smoke billowing from Shellz's mouth.

In front of answering Bealz's question, Shellz took a long drag off of the blunt. Looking down at his blood—stained clothing, he relived the screams, the sounds of bullets whistling past his head, and the dreadful sounds of bullets ripping through the flesh of both Lynx and Flip's bodies.

"Man, some Niggas just started lettin' dem life—takers fly," Shellz described, passing the blunt to Karma. "I don't know if y'all know but both Flip and Lynx are dead."

An eerie silence filtered through the car. They rode through another three lights before Bealz broke the stillness.

"Dead . . . ," Bealz utter in total disbelief. "Damn, that's fucked up."

By Alliance rules, since the apparent accidental shooting claimed the lives of two of The Associates, no more need to be spoken about the tragedy. Accordingly, Shellz did not have to reveal all of the ommitted details that Bealz and Karma knew nothing about definition, ALLIANCE RULES.

"Where did you get tha' whip from," Shellz inquired. Leaning over, he placed his left elbow on the armrest of the rear seat.

Jap

"Oh, man — this used car lot off Wilkerson Boulevard. And we copped a conversion van, too. Ain't that right, Karma?" Shellz watched Karma nod in agreement. "Shit, I got to get my Caddy fixed up tomorrow." Hearing Karma and Bealz sigh, "Ahh, fuck y' all," Shellz joked, as everyone laughed, the somber mood lightened.

When 7 a.m. rolled around, the liquid elements of Mother Nature were drenching the city streets. The rain was coming down so hard that even seeing your hand in front of your face was almost impossible. It was expected that no pedestrians would be braving the storm but not even a stray dog could be seen out roaming around. The only traffic moving were vehicles that safely drove six car lengths behind each other.

But fifty feet away from a basketball court, three people in a van strained to see who sat at a table beneath the rain shed. Even with the van's wiper blades working furiously, it was still difficult for the van's passengers to recognize the figure. From time to time, the female driver let out deep sighs.

"Blow the horn; that's him ..."

"Shellz, how the fuck do you know?" Bealz inquired from his place on the passenger seat.

Shellz took it upon himself to reach up over Karma in the driver's seat and flicker the van's lights while repeatedly blowing the horn.

"Get 'cho ass off me, Boy," Karma complained, pushing him back.

"Look, look" Bealz interjected, pointing his finger.

Whoever it was had risen from the table and step by sluggish step was slowly headed in the van's direction. What bothered the van's occupants was the shiny object barely discernible being held at the person's right side.

"That's him ..." Shellz said. Opening the rear side door, he yelled out, "You Banga, it's Shellz."

Banga lowered his head, squinting his wet eyes as rain poured off of the rim of his black fitted baseball cap. Each step he took looked like he was wading through a small creek of water.

"Climb in here and get out of the rain," advised Shellz in a harsh but concerned tone.

Banga's black Enyce hi—top sneakers made a squishy sound when he stepped into the van. His facial and body language were killer—driven. Sitting directly behind the driver's seat, Shellz tapped lightly on Banga's arm to get his attention. Making sure that neither Bealz nor Karma was watching, Shellz then briefly returned Banga's sinister gaze with a wink of his right eye.

"You heard 'bout Flip and Lynx getting shot and killed yesterday?" Shellz announced, breaking the silence. The remark was an attempt to throw off Karma and Bealz.

Bealz glanced back at Banga. "You ain't know?" he inquired, looking stunned.

There was no reaction from Banga, however; his demeanor didn't change. From being drenched in the rain for so long, it was difficult to tell if the beads of water came from his eyes or the tattooed tear drops beneath his eyes.

In a low sounding villainous voice, Banga responded, "Yeah, I heard. An' Imma kill those who are responsible." He paused, then shifted his head in Shellz's direction. "And that's on my dead Mama," he completed with a deep curve in his eyebrows Apparently Banga had remembered Shellz telling him how The Alliance played by "no speak, no seen" code which was sacred. And like a TRUE SOLDIER, Banga kept his mouth shut.

In the meantime, Role Call was being conducted for a special unit on the fourth floor of Police Headquarters. The leading agent, a black man named Rodney Macmall who had been hand—picked a year before to lead the investigation, stood in front of twenty—five officers and agents from different branches of law enforcement. Young and slim, Rodney, or Hot— Rod as some called him, was good at blending in with the urban world which he and his female undercover partner, Leslie Smith, were preparing to address the assembly when Sharon Bucannon entered the room, a video in hand. She whispered something into Rodney's ear and when he nodded for her to proceed, she faced her colleagues.

"Good morning," she addressed the group, offering a half—smile.

"Morning!" the group responded simultaneously in a monotone.

"I'm sure that you all know about the shooting that took place outside of Admissions, off Independence." Seeing head nods, she plunged ahead. "Well, the driver of the Cadillac," she paused and held up an enlarged photo of Shellz, "... stated that he didn't know who left the .45 caliber shell casings beside his car. But after an initial forensics report combined with the small traces of gunpowder residue which were found on the passenger side floor board and upper door extremities of the Cadillac, we have enough evidence to build a case against Mr. Shelton Davis."

Silence.

Leslie Smith studied the picture of Shellz that Sharon had stuck on the board beneath the pictures of Major League. It then dawned on her where she'd seen Shellz before.

"I've seen him plenty of times and I firmly believe that he is also dealing drugs," the female undercover officer said, staring at Sharon.

"That's good," Sharon softly spoke while placing a video tape into a VCR that sat on a stand beneath a TV set. "As you'll see in this surveillance tape that I just recovered from the parking lot camera of the Sporting Goods store adjacent to Admissions which shows that Mr. Davis lied to me about what he knows." She gave a hand signal to Rodney and when he hit the switch to kill the lights, she pressed "play" on the VCR.

In the ensuing seven—minute video, the squad was treated to the entire parking lot fiasco, all the way up to the horrible images of the killing spree initiated by the assailants in the dark colored van. When Rodney turned the lights back on, the faces of the officers were ashen with rage and shock.

"You got the video, what's the problem?" one officer inquired loudly from the back of the room.

Jap

Sharon responded, "Good question ... the problem is that although the video captured the shootings, the images of the perpetrators in the van and the persons who exited Mr. Davis's car cannot be seen clearly enough to make out and identify. And the heat's on ... word from the DA's office is that these killers are to taken off the city streets immediately, as well as Ms. Tillman."

Rodney picked up on that last name. "Oh, we got Sandra Tillman in the bag already. Even though San, Ms. Hicks, is a big fish, we're holding out for her connect who is a great white shark," Rodney said with confidence, pointing a ruler at the pictures of San, Milky, and Gramz.

Sharon took it upon herself to add the picture of Shellz, placing it next to San. All the officers carefully scrutinized the images of the people in the photos. In their minds, the four individuals were a pox on the Queen City, and even their own community, THE HOOD.

Later that evening, Bealz and Jake were seated outside of Special Treats which was nestled amongst an exuberant array of sidewalk cafes, colorful storefronts, and opulent upscale homes. They were discussing the recent turn of events when the sexy young waitress brought their order. "Enjoy your drinks. If you need me, just give a holla'," the red—headed waitress exclaimed. "All right, Ginger," Jake replied, matching her smile. As soon as she scooted to another table, his smile disappeared and he turned his attention back to Bealz. "Look, son, I know that you wanna help Shelton but if I was you, I'd distance myself from him," he warned, offering a mysterious stare.

Known for its exotic mixed drinks and cuisine, Bealz had ordered some kind of Hawaiian Blue concoction. Listening to Jake but glancing around at the mostly Caucasian customers, he took a sip and lowered the glass.

"Nah. Shellz is my man," he told Jake without making eye contact.

Jake shook his head. "Man, you guys are like your father and I were. We used to be in all kinds of riff—raff, only most of time it was me getting Malone out of a sticky situation," he said, chuckling softly.

Weary of Jake's old war stories, Bealz failed to appreciate the humor. He glanced up at the huge clock on the glass tower of the restaurant. Damn, it's 6:45, Bealz thought silently. Not only was he weary of Jake's continuous reminiscing, the instrumental classical music that oozed from the Cafe's outside speakers were working on his last nerve.

"Jake," Bealz said, interrupting Jake's story, "I hear ya, but I'ma look out for Shellz and 'specially 'Relle," he protested. "They're my people."

Jake knew nothing about how The Alliance worked, nor about the involvement and dirty work of 'Relle. He'd only seen Shellz three times and Karma once. "Okay, son, do it your way," Jake acquiesced, guzzling his Cocola Smoothy. "Ginger!" he summoned, waving his hand. "But I do need someone to drive the Navigator to pick up some special visitors to our fair city."

Jap

Bealz watched Jake reward Ginger with a hefty tip, grabbed his drink and finish off the remaining liquid. Jake stood up but Bealz was taking his time, basking in the unfamiliar environment.

"Well, just think about what I said," Jake said, cracking a grin.

Bealz just sat there, closely watching Jake as he faded into the background of flowing cars and milling people. Mumbling out loud to himself, Bealz bragged, "Drivin' no fuckin' cab. I'm a dope boy. For the love of money, got to make that money in————" The ringing of his cell phone interrupted his reverie.

"Wha's happening," Bealz answered, cutting off the lyrics to Bone Thugs N Harmony.

"Damn, stranger. You been duckin' me?

Bealz immediately picked up on the soft voice.

"Oh. "Sup, Tiff?" -

Since the two hadn't spoken to each other in a couple of days, they agreed to hang out later.

CHAPTER TWELVE

On the day of the mourning, hundreds packed the Funeral Home off of Stateville Avenue. Most of the younger crowd that were shedding tears over Flip's body had gone to school with him. Flip laid in his white casket looking like he was in a peaceful sleep. Since he loved Ralph Lauren, The Alliance not only draped his body in Polo's newest line of clothing, but they also footed the bill for his funeral, especially since his mother showed no emotion over the death of her son. Not surprisingly, everybody was there except for Stephanie, Flip's crack head mother.

When the last person was about to walk away from Flip's casket, Banga rose from his seat and excused himself past The Alliance who were seated next to him. He slowly made his way up to the casket to get one last look at Flip. Standing over the casket, he silently bid farewell to his friend, not wanting it to be over. Finally one of the funeral directors approached and told him that the casket needed to be closed. Banga removed a red bandanna from his rear pocket, leaned over and kissed Flip's forehead.

"I promise I'ma kill 'dose Niggaz for you, My Nigga," he whispered, placing the bandanna across Flip's chest. He stepped back and looked away. When he heard the casket close, a tear fell to the floor from his left eye.

As The Alliance witnessed Banga's whole painful episode, they all felt like Banga had passed into The Alliance family. Given that, Lynx's family didn't want anything to do with Banga, and Duck went to live in Atlanta with his father. The Alliance knew that Banga was in the streets alone, although it wasn't as if he'd never been in that situation. But since Banga's grandmother's sugar made her ill, "The Alliance adopted Banga, streetly.

Twenty—four hours later

By four p.m., the day was beautiful and the skies were light blue and clear. The temperature had topped out at eighty—five degrees and everybody was out washing their cars or buying an outfit for the evening's excursion.

But outside a packed North Tryon Car Wash, Major League were sitting inside of San's gray two—door Denali truck blazing erb watching a dude outside washing her truck by hand. The song "Moments in Love" had San's head lowered and her eyes closed.

Suddenly she peered up at the movie "New Jack City" that played on a monitor inside of the sun visor above her head. She sucked her teeth at G Money as he looked through a fish tank holding a crack pipe as he talked on the phone with Nino Brown. Gramz was riding shotgun directly behind San. He waved off the blunt that Milky was trying to pass him from the driver's seat. Gramz couldn't stand how San kept dipping her nose into a sandwich bag of powdered cocaine.

"Boy, I can't feel my lips," San joked, patting her hand around her mouth.

"You need to chill, San. All you've been doing lately is snorting coke," Gramz cautioned.

San closed and tied her bag of powder into a knot. She rolled her neck around three times. While Gramz took the time to wipe the face of his iced out Jacob, when he looked up he was staring down the barrel of San's chrome Desert Eagle. Stretching his eyes, "San, wha' the fuck are you doing?" Gramz questioned harshly.

"Fam, you police!" San snarled, her finger on the trigger. The sound of the hose that a man was using struck against the wheel base of the SUV. The cat saw what was transpiring through the lightly tinted window. He decided that he wouldn't be a witness to a murder and took off running.

Gramz showed no fear. He tilted his head to the side, "No, I ain't no police," he responded, bitterness heavy in his voice. As San eased the pistol's barrel away from his face, Gramz had been reaching for his hidden trey—pound—seven, but changed his mind.

"What we gonna do 'bout all of 'dem suds," Milky said, pointing at the hood.

San twisted around and stared into the dark colored designer frames that Gramz had slipped on.

"Take 'dem glasses off," she demanded, her face a mask of hatred. "Don't ever comment on what San does. I run this ship," she stated through clench teeth. "We clear ... ?" she added. Gramz saw the nose of the pistol slowly return to his cranium.

"Yeah we clear," he mumbled.

117

"Good, good." She nodded then and eventually went back to snorting coke.

One hour ahead of eight p.m., within Apartment 140 Dr. Dre's Chronic 2001 was blaring from the Sony house speakers. Bealz sat on the floor in front of the couch between Karma's legs. His head leaned to the side as he patiently waited for her to finalize his last zigzag braid. Since her hands were oily from the grease, he passed the blunt over his shoulder and held it between her lips. After she took three deep drags, she exhaled a cloud of smoke that floated halfway across the living room.

"Okay, I'm finished," she made known, seductively studying his neck—line that led to his bare back.

He jumped up, headed to the square mirror on the wall by the 2Pac painting. On the contrary to his white Sean Jean boxer's brief showing, he made no attempt to pull up his black baggy Red Monkey jeans. He smiled as he checked out the designs that went in many directions all over his head.

"Girl, you did the damn thang," he praised contentedly, grinning.

"Shit, you need to get your wig done every two weeks instead of every two months," she joked, slowly passing by him swinging her hips enticingly. With her Apple Bottom jeans and pink snug—fitting shirt that displayed both the word "Sexy" and her protruding nipples, she knew that there was no way Bealz could resist her sexiness.

But contrary to those facts, Bealz's mind was on his date with Tiff. Updated from his break—up with Coneka, Bealz only had sex three times, all of which were oral, twice from strippers and one by Lorraine. He had believed that he and Pudding would've eventually become more than friends, but Pudding's constant nagging that he should quit his street dealings, on top of her not giving any indications of giving up the skins had Bealz backing away from anything but a friendship with Pudding. He did continue to smoke blunts with her sister and buy ice cream and pizza for her nieces.

"How do I look?" Bealz questioned, holding his arms out. He wasn't sure how to interpret Karma's somber reaction. "Well ...?"

"You look all right," she shot back sarcastically while dialing Shellz's number on her cell phone. When Shellz answered, "Hey, Shellz! So what you and Banga have in mind ..."

Waiting for Shellz to finish describing Club Bliss, she glanced over at Bealz pulling on his white Red Monkey tee over his form—fitting wife beater. "Club Bliss, huh? Well, I'll be up to get y'all around ten thirty." She signed off and returned her cell to her black Burkin purse.

Bealz kneeled down to position the bottom hem of his pants behind the tongue of his black silver—tongued retro Jordans. He then stood up and fixed his pants so that they would droop over his shoes. He intently watched Karma storm up the stairs mumbling something under her breath. He smirked, grabbed a box of White Owls from the kitchen table, then headed for the door.

"Karma, I'll see you later," he yelled. Hearing her simple "Yeah" reply made him chuckle. When he made it outside, he sat briefly in the Chevy just staring at the silhouette of Pudding's figure standing in the breezeway of the darkened apartment. Damn, that chick is nosey, he thought to himself as he started the vehicle and drove off.

Bealz honked the horn as he passed some hustlers that were gathered around Rob's Convenience Store on West Trade. Passing six streets, he approached the corner of Beatties Ford Road and the campus of Johnson C. Smith University. While waiting for the light to change, he removed an already rolled blunt from the White Owl box. Although the light had turned green, he had to wait for the six Smith Summer School students to pass through the Rozzels Ferry—Beatties Ford intersection. He lit the blunt with the cigarette lighter and dashed through the intersection in the nick—of—time before the light turned red again. During the next couple of minutes he managed to contact Tiff and they agreed to meet up at the AMC Movie Theater off South Boulevard.

By eleven p.m., most of the city's hot spots buzzing. Enjoyment to suit most everybody was available between both strip and dance clubs, bars, hotels, and crack spots. Everyone was out and about dressed in their finest apparel, on the prowl for someone to spend the night with. Even the jackboys were hunting down their easiest prey. For this Saturday night, the city was on fire.

Hidden between a few oversized oak trees, Club Bliss was smashing Club Enchantment, its competition up the street. The glowing florescent green light bulbs behind the letters CB shined brightly above the club's roof. The Club could hold a maximum of two hundred people and its extensively cemented parking lot easily accommodated them all. Luckily for this Southeast part of Charlotte, the neighboring apartments, homes and local businesses were heavily patrolled by two different police precincts.

Inside the club the monarch of several crews was on point to the others' every move. With eighty percent of the clubgoers high on some type of drug or liquor, there was no telling how it would affect their behavior when it was all said and done. Every time the DJ played a different selection, especially rap music, the patrons sunk deeper into a trouble—making mentality.

Suddenly the rap song "We Ready" by Pastor Troy interrupted the calmer mood that had been established by J—Lo's "I'm Real" feat JaRule. The male clubgoers along with their cliques shoved their way to the dance floor, turning it into a shoving match. Fifteen huge bouncers bum—rushed the dance floor and as a result several young men were expelled from Club Bliss.

Shellz happened to be returning from the restroom when by chance he bumped into someone. "Excuse me," he apologized, staring at the person's medallion that had the letters ML encrusted in diamonds.

"Don't worry 'bout it, partner," the dude shot back.

Shellz stood there as the dude turned back to the two female chicks who had previously captured the stranger's attention. Shellz was trying to figure out where he had seen the stranger before, until the louder of the two chicks blurted out the stranger's name.

"Milky, you so nasty," she protested loudly over the music. Shellz knew right away Milky was the dude driving the Escalade for the mannish—looking bitch outside of the hair salon. He scurried through the throngs of patrons until he made it to the table where Karma and Banga were waiting. Banga immediately sense something was wrong by Shellz's disturbed expression.

Shellz's empty words and intent gaze across the Club made Karma and Banga join his stare. Their eyes fixated on a table beneath a circulation of white, red, and blue lights. Shellz didn't shed light on his target of interest. To discharge the demented thoughts of both Banga and Karma, Shellz grabbed the gold bottle of Ace of Spade from the table and filled each glass to the rim.

"Let's drink up," he suggested enthusiastically, smirking. Again he peered at the same table where he'd witnessed several chicks dancing all over a seated San. He found himself repulsed by her male— acting antics, her legs spread, her head nodding.

Without warning, the DJ started to shout out a few select VIP names to the packed Club over the Usher—Ludicris song called 'Yeah.' He finished with, "Oh—oh—oh ... there's San and her Major League squad from all over ... what up, Big Tyyymmme?"

Shellz nodded, studying the velour—suit—wearing mannish bitch with Nigga Swagga's identity. Closing his eyes and slipping into a self— induced heavenly trance state, Shellz quickly revisited that incident outside the Unique Designs salon, their encounter with San and her boys. When he opened his eyes, both Karma and Banga were staring at him.

"What's the deal, big bruh?" Banga asked, smoking a hyped—up Black N Mile.

Shellz, stone—faced, didn't utter a response.

"I know it has somethin' to do wit' that big bitch San that crossed you and Bealz's path outside the salon," Karma announced confidently.

For the next hour, all three Alliance members kept a sharp eye on the clique that called itself Major League.

Then The Alliance quietly exited the Club unnoticed.

1 A.M.

Vehicles, some packed with people, stretched across both ends of Sugar Creek in hopes of getting served in The Cook—Out Restaurant's drive—through. An eclectic mix of music played at various decimal levels coated the night—time skies. Well—known women and hustlers jockeyed to be seen by sticking their heads out of car windows, reminiscent of the scene on Crenshaw right out of Boyz N The Hood. Police were eight deep standing outside of the Cook—Out's parking lot, all white officers.

Jap

Tiff and Bealz had seen 'Man of the House' starring Tommy Lee Jones at the CinePlex and afterwards she followed him in her car to the Motel 6 off of Clanton Road where Bealz parked his car and joined Tiff in her brown four—door Honda Accord.

Because Tiff had cautioned Bealz that she didn't like the smell of smoke, Bealz had smoked three blunts in his own car before hooking up with her. The first one he had lit up by JCSU, another when he sat outside the movie theater, and finally one while he was driving to get the room. He told Tiff that the only reason he rented a room was to spend some quality time with her alone, but she didn't believe him.

With the Honda Accord trapped in a traffic jam on the Sugar Creek bridge, Bealz quickly grew tired of Tiff's complaints about her job at the Unique salon and her mixed slow jam CD. However, he adored her cream Donna Karan form—fitting sweater dress that stopped at mid—thigh, not to mention her black Jimmy Choo stilettos with the cream letters JC rotating the toes of the boots.

"This shit is fucking ridiculous." Bealz complained, staring around at the traffic.

"How's bout going to the bowling alley?"

"Bowling!" Shockingly he: repeated her words.

"Yeah, we can get something to eat and watch people sing karaoke."

"Don't no Niggas sing karaoke."

Tiff looked over her left shoulder and as soon as the opportunity presented itself, she made an illegal U—turn.

"Ahh ... if you would've been on the outside lane, you

"Made that turn," she interrupted. "Boy, please. I'm like that."

He glanced intently at the sparkling earrings that she was wearing. He had sacred thoughts about rummaging his hands through her hair that was pulled into a pony—tail.

"What's on ya mind. Jacob?" she inquired, cutting her eyes from him back to the road.

"What do you mean ... I ain't said nothing."

Coming to a stop behind three cars at the intersection of North Tryon and Sugar Creek gave her time to look Bealz in the face. She smiled and without looking selected number seven on her factory CD player. The song My Boo by Alicia Keys feat Usher began to play at a low volume.

"Jacob. you didn't have to say nothing for me to read your naughty thoughts," she asserted, softly mashing on the gas pedal to make her left turn. Bealz sat back contemplating what she had just said, which happened to be true. Indeed he knew that he would try his hand if she gave him a small window of opportunity to climb through.

After finding a parking spot near the entrance to the bowling alley, they exited the Honda. Bealz walked close behind Tiff and couldn't keep his eyes off the clearly visible black thongs that led from just below the small of her back into the crack of her ass.

Inside people of all ages roamed about. Some were purchasing a pair of bowling shoes at the desk. Others, a mix of Black, White, Asian, and Spanish families and their friends were cheering for each other as they bowled.

"STRIKE!" was the word shouted from different bowling lanes. "Pickup the spare, baby ... come on!" was the other phrase heard most often over the continuous play of the Rave—sounding music.

It was the first visit to a bowling alley for Bealz so he was surprised when they made their way back to where the bar was located and found a Black man crooning one of Marvin Gaye's songs on the karaoke machine. He noticed how cats like himself were enjoying the scene just as much as the ladies were. He pointed out an empty table next to the wall above pool table number six. Hoping to impress Tiff, he pulled out her chair for her in a gentleman's gesture.

"Thank you," she said, blushing. The nod of his head was good enough for her.

Bealz flagged down the waitress who happened to be a Sista named Alice. After receiving the pleasant smile that Alice had for him, he knew that he'd tip her big. He and Tiff ordered hot wings and two Cokes, since she was a non—drinker, and Bealz treated himself to a Corona and Blue Motorcycle.

Two guys, a Black and an Asian, took to the Karaoke machine, their song of choice being 'Brick House' by the Commodores. The crowd, comprised mostly of females, showed their appreciation by clapping and singing along with the off—key singing. When even Tiff joined in the merrymaking, Bealz decided to get rid of his Blue drink. When the dudes finished singing they were treated to loud whistles and applause.

As soon as the noise began to abate, Bealz made his plea. "So, Ms. Tiff, this is our third time chillin' together ..." He paused, took another sip, then continued. "So you do hair by day and janitor duties at the Train Station by night."

Tiff rolled her neck. "That's 'Environmental Service,' not janitor," she corrected indignantly, making him laugh. "And you run a detail service and about to he driving a cab for Destination," she countered.

"Yeah," he lied without hesitation, quickly saying, "Here comes Alice," to change the subject.

Alice removed a big red basket of wings from her round tray that she balanced with her left hand as she placed them along with their drinks on the table. "Holla, if y'all need me," she invited, leaving another killer smile as she turned away.

Watching Bealz tear into the wings, "Damn, Jacob!" Tiff blurted. "No prayer?"

"Ump mmmh." he mumbled with a mouth full of food.

It didn't take more than ten to twelve minutes for the basket of thirty wings to disappear. Tiff had eaten only six and all the others were annihilated by Bealz.

"Had enough?" she probed, watching him guzzle down his Corona. She interpreted his glassy eyes as a sign of being high and tipsy. "Let me get you back to your car."

"I'm good," he slurred, waving his hand at Alice and placing fifty dollars on the table. Thirty was for the food and beverages; the rest went to Alice.

Tiff couldn't believe that he had ordered another Corona. It wasn't like she'd never seen someone act like Bealz was acting. She'd just never been on a date with someone that was high off a narcotic drug. She didn't really know what to expect as she led their way out of the bowling alley, Bealz still carrying his beer. Before she unlocked her door, she stared across the roof of her car at him.

"You can't drink in my car. I ain't going to jail for your bullshit." she said in no uncertain terms, her anger growing.

"Chill," he urged trying to soothe her agitation.

She shook her head in disbelief as she watched him drain the beer bottle dry. She then gasped at the smashing sound the bottle made when he tossed it ten feet away to an isolated spot in the parking lot. Seeing people making their way towards them, she unlocked the car doors.

"Get in," she urged him.

Before the five people could make it to the Honda, Tiff sped away. She angrily cut the music completely off. As she concentrated on the road, she felt Bealz hand caress her inner thigh and she slapped it away.

"Just what the hell is wrong with you?" she snapped.

"Ain't shit wrong wit me," his words slurred together as he spoke. "You the one dat act all high an muh—fuckin' mighty," he continued "... every time I make a lil move, you get real defensive. Walkin'round like Tyra Banks wit' ya tight clothes and fat ass enticing a Nigga. So what da fuck is wrong wit' you?" he blanked.

Calmly she responded, "So what ... just because we've been out a couple of times, I'm supposed to sleep with you?" Clearing her throat she continued, "Only reason I even called you was because I thought I saw something different in you."

"Like what?"

"You didn't have the dope—boy appearance." She paused to let her statement sink in. "That's all that I attract is dope—boys, and that's all I see go to prison. My last boyfriend did construction and our relationship was great until I walked in on him cheating."

"Well, maybe she was satisfyin' ya man."

"Jacob ... he was satisfying my man."

Bealz flash her a phony smile. "I'ma be honest wit you. I ain't had no pussy in months." Hearing her smack her lips he added, "I'm serious. I've been grinding away to make money doing odd jobs here and there." he lied.

"Jacob you're so loose with the word pussy like it's a piece of meat. I know it must be the alcohol talking for you. I think you are cute and I'd like to continue to see you. But I refuse to be belittled and treated like some bitch that sleeps around with every Tom, Dick, and Harry."

Finally, after exiting and crossing the bridge of the Clanton Road exit, Tiff safely made it back to the motel and pulled up behind Bealz's car. She kept the motor running. Bealz glanced over at her and was about to speak but was silenced by her eyes. He exited her car and casually strolled around to the driver's side. "Damn, can a Nigga at least get some sugar," he said, cracking a stupid grin. To his disappointment, he had to settle f or planting a wet one where she pointed — on her cheek.

"Bye," she sang, pulling away.

While navigating the flat card in the slot to unlock the door to his room, Bealz watched three different couples enter different rooms. He muttered to himself, "Damn, I wouldn't mind spending time wit those two chick that were flirting entering room 150 .. ." He closed the door behind him and fell face—first onto the bed.

5:30 A.M.

Bealz had slept only three hours but was up before the break of dawn and had travelled back to Belvadere. Re caught Too Bad and numerous customers hunting frantically for Boy. He went into the apartment and returned with four bundles which he got rid of in under forty—five minutes. He made sure they knew that this was a one—time thing, and that they should go up the street to The View if they wanted The Alliance's dope.

Bealz started back towards the house when he saw Pudding standing in the door, waving with a wicked grin on her face. He stuffed his money in his pocket, nodded at her and kept it moving. Rearing a sound of a slow—passing car, he parted the curtains slightly and peering out noted two blue and white police cars coupled with Pudding who'd from day one constantly complained about drug—dealers. In Bealz's book, that only meant one thing: either Pudding was a Snitch or an undercover police agent.

Re ran upstairs and silently entered Karma's room. She was asleep, her purple satin sheets exposing her pink thongs and ass cheeks. He tiptoed over and tapped her on her shoulders.

"Karma." he whispered.

"Huh?" she mumbled.

He shook her shoulder and helplessly watched her ass jiggle like it had Jello implants. "Wake up." He waited for her slow rotation and once they made eye—contact again, he spoke, "We got to move. I don't trust our neighbor."

"Wha'." she uttered, repeatedly squeezing her eye—lids together to unfog her dazed sight.

His mouth began to water from seeing her hardened brown nipples and ripe—looking titties. To wake her up he walked over and separated the curtains that allowed the morning sun that had crept into the sky to lighten up her room. Karma let out a deep frustrated—sounding gasp, and was angered when he blocked her from planting her head beneath the sheets. They tugged at the sheets against each other until she knew she had no fighting chance. He tickled her feet which caused her to snicker and kick at his hands.

"Quit playin', BealzI Damn!" she playfully complained.

He sat down at the foot of her bed, pulling her feet onto his lap and beginning to peel the old pink paint from her toenails. She went ahead and filled him in on the details of their findings at The Club about San. Considering the significance of what she was telling him, he told her that to show his appreciation she'd be going shopping and getting a pedicure. Before getting up he sucked on three of her toes, drawing moans from her, and kissed the bottom of her feet.

"Get dressed," he said, then left her room.

"Teasin' me," she complained to herself, throwing her pillow at the door that had closed behind Bealz.

CHAPTER THIRTEEN

Two days later The Alliance was back grinding nonstop. Bealz was considering driving the Navi Cab for Jake to transport his heroin. The Alliance had obtained full cooperation from several other residents in The View, as long as The Alliance helped them with their bills. So not only did they operate out of Phil's crib, they were able to cook up and mix in one house, duck the police in another house, and count, stash, and keep their daily earnings in a minister's crib. Bealz had started to sell ounces of coke for nine five to strangers and nine to those he knew.

The Alliance was inside the brick house that sat next to the hill that led up the basketball court. The owner had given them a key and permission to use the house.

Inside, a picture of Jesus Christ hung over the front door. The burnt orange curtains that drug the floor didn't match the flower print furniture. A small TV with pliers clamped onto the knobs sat on top of an old model 8—track radio set.

The Alliance knew that the chubby, balding minister McCrae loved the Lord, church, moolah, and young girls.

Karma sat beside Bealz on the couch, listening to Shellz suggesting that they expand Alliance business up and down The Ford. Banga sat on the floor rolling blunts, his legs beneath the coffee table.

"What's wrong with The View, we got junkies coming from Small Wood, Belvadere, and parts of the other side of Rozzells' Ferry," Bealz brought up.

Pacing the floor Shellz responded, "Man, you know it's major bread around Pitts Drive, Celia, Fairmount. and Cummings Avenue. These cats that called themselves Seven The Hard Way ... man, you know, uh ...

"Javelle White and his brother Ramone from Cummings Avenue," Karma added.

Seven The Hard Way consisted of the brothers, J—Slim, Cornell, Will, a stripper, and a chick named Slim Golden. They were implicated in a twelve count indictment which included Racketeering, Murder, and Cocaine Conspiracy. But due to the misconduct of the police department and DA, only Javelle was convicted. Taking a lesser charge of Money Laundering, he was sentenced to five years which he was serving at LSCI, Butner, NC.

"Okay, I know who you're talkin' 'bout," Bealz said, patting Karma's knee. "Fire up the blunt," he insisted.

'Shit, it's money in Lake View too," Banga glady interjected. "That cat Trips brought up here name Lil Gas cops at least three ounces every other day."

"Lil Gas, fuck kind of nickname is that? What the Nigga do, fart all day?" Bealz joked.

"Nah, they said he'll gas yo ass up wit' hot balls. And his man, named Smoke, dem Niggas got heart," Banga said with respect.

"Well, y'all — watch dem Niggaz. Fuck around and they'll set yo ass up," Bealz cautioned,

The Alliance spoke briefly about Bizzo who hadn't been in rehab a month and got locked up for smoking crack in the rehab's restroom. So Bealz thought it would be best if they washed their hands of him. But Bealz did keep his word by dropping money off for Lette. He even managed to avoid Lette's constant sexual advances not because of Bizzo but because she told him that she wanted him to hit her raw,

In the meantime, the gossip machine in Unique Designs was in high gear. Vanilla had just finished describing in detail an intimate encounter he'd had with his boyfriend POG. Afterwards, when he made the mistake of barging into San's office without knocking, he was in for a shock.

"Oh, I'm sorry," Vanilla apologized in light sissy tone, turning his head towards the Plasma TV screen which was playing the movie 'Good Fellas' with the volume muted.

"Nah, come on in and watch me work," San demanded, standing between the spread legs of Tracks as she fucked her with a long black dildo.

It was a scene to behold: San had Tracks spread—eagled on her back on the desk, Tracks' denim skirt hoisted and bunched around her waist. San's black cargo shorts with the deep pockets were down around her ankles covering her black Polo sandals. She had the bottom of her white tee with the Polo letters in black emblazoned across the front folded up and held in place with her chin.

Jap

Tracks' moans were muffled by San's hand. A white sports bra held San's small titties in place. But as always San was being careless with her snort bag of powder that laid beside Tracks' head. If it wasn't for Tracks' tight halter top, her titties would have been everywhere.

"I hear ya, Baby," San urged thrusting the dildo into Tracks' throbbing pussy with reckless wantonness. Moments later San brought Tracks to an exploding orgasm.

Although Vanilla was a funny boy, watching the live porn gave him an arousal. There was no way to hide his bulge inside his tight denim jeans. He did his best to adjust his manhood so it wasn't so obvious but San and Tracks had already picked up on it. "Nah, you sissy—ass Nigga. I see your dick print," San teased, unstrapping the dildo which measured nine inches long and two inches thick that she called "The Punisher."

Vanilla managed to dodge the dildo when San rudely tossed it to him. "Uh—uh, girl — dat's nasty!" he said, frowning. Drawing giggles from both San and Tracks made Vanilla feel better and more confident. "Just let me buy a half gram of snort," he begged, struggling to get his hand into his tight pockets.

"I knew your skinny ass snorted by the way you can't be still," Tracks admonished, using some baby wipes to clean herself. San motioned for Vanilla to approach her, holding the opened bag of powder. She stuck it under Vanilla's nose. "Go 'head, snort some."

"Nah, I don't snort ... but a couple of my customers do and they always ask can I get them s————"

Vanilla's explanation was interrupted by the cold steel of San's blue steel 357 snubnose pressed against his forehead. San snickered at the jarring of Vanilla's mouth.

"Nigga, you barged in on me," San said through clenched teeth. "Now if you don't take a hit of this pure coke, I'ma rearrange your brain cells," she promised, snarling.

Vanilla cut his eyes at her Cattier diamond bracelet and since he didn't see a tremble, he started to sweat. From growing up in North Charlotte he'd seen plenty of shootings but he'd never been at the wrong end of a gun barrel. He had always been told that if a shooter didn't show nervousness, more than likely that person wouldn't think twice to pull the trigger. Also, the phrase BULLETS HAVE NO EYES cleared any thoughts that clouded his judgment.

"Okay, San girl ... please lust get that pistol out of my face," he pleaded, feeling more comfortable when San's screw—face gradually changed to a smile. "What do I 'pose to do?"

San stuck the pistol in her back pocket. She pulled a torn— off piece of folded match—book corner from her back pocket and dipped the folded part into the bag. Vanilla eyed the small pile of white powered substance and took a deep breath.

"Press one side of your nostril and inhale," San explained, holding the coke directly under Vanilla's nose.

When Vanilla followed her instruction, inhaling deeply, he felt such an unbelievable rush that he thought his brain had frozen. He staggered over to a chair and plopped down. Even as his head drifted back he could still hear the girls laughing. The drug gave him a feeling of instant euphoria. "Hmm," he uttered as blood trickled from his nose over the cocaine residue.

San eyed Vanilla a half gram into a brown paper towel. She fed Tracks a good amount of powder then treated herself to a mind blowing pile of blow. An unwarranted backhand from Tracks brought Vanilla back down to earth.

Wiping his nose, Vanilla sat up looking confused, like he wasn't sure of his surroundings. "What's that?" he questioned of what San held out to him.

"Here, you can have this. Whatever you do, don't tell your customers where you get ya coke from. If you do, I promise I'll kill you," San assured with a cold stare.

Vanilla made San think that he wasn't coherent but true bill he was high but he hadn't lost his sanity in the process. He stuck the paper towel into his was pocket, thanked San, and exited the office.

"Oh hell no, that Nigga Mickey tried to justify fuckin' den strippers," the bucktoothed beautician with the red hair named Marylin alleged to an attentive and noisy crowd of women.

"Girl, you trippin," Tiff responded, suppressing her giggles while taking notice of how Vanilla's behavior and model strut had changed. She met him in his booth and could tell by how he kept repeatedly sniffing that he'd been hitting the blow.

"Vanilla."

Nothing. No response. He just kept searching through his large Gucci bag.

"Vanilla, you hear me?"

"What, Tiff? What?" he replied, wiping his nose inside the fold of his arm.

"You been snorting coke?"

"Gurl, whachu mean?" he replied, his lips poked out. "Ain't nobody high."

From her brief stint in medical school, Tiff knew when one's pupils dilated it was a sign of someone high on drugs.

"Damn! I see the coke residue around the outer base of your nose," she explained, grabbing hold of his arm. She heard San's voice as she exited her office and turned in that direction. She watched San's display of dominance as she strutted towards the exit, tapping a dildo into the left palm of her hand. Tiff was startled when San suddenly turned back and stuck her head into where she and Vanilla were standing.

"Yes?" Tiff said in a snappy tone.

San drug her words, "Ahhh, Tiff, you need to give me that pussy and quit playin'."

"Keep your hands off me San, I'm ain't playin' neither."

Some of Unique Designs' customers heard the commotion and started doing what women do, be NOSY. They watched San get right up in Tiff's face and was surprised when Tiff didn't back down. Without warning San stole a kiss from an unreceptive Tiff and in turn got slapped.

Jap

"Woooo," in unison the customers boosted. Tracks cut between the two, pointing her finger in Tiff's face insinuating that she could be fired. A defiant Tiff gave Tracks a tongue lashing.

"That's it! You're fired!" Tracks shouted, frowning.

"No, no, she ain't fired. This was all my fault," San interceded. "I didn't have no bidness touching Tiff's fat ass."

Everyone was shocked at San's surprising apology, but none more so than Tiff. "I hope you'll forgive me, Tiff," San said, speaking with what appeared to be genuine remorse.

Tiff glanced down at San's outstretched hand, rolled her eyes and then accepted the hand of the dominant but penitent salon owner.

In minutes, San had left and things inside of Unique Designs returned to normal.

San had come to realize that Tiff could have sued her and the salon for sexual harassment among other things, so she decided with her coke— addled brain that she had too much to lose fucking with Tiff. Besides that she was fucking seventy—five percent of the strippers who worked in INSATIONS. Other than money, coke, and power, San had all the free pussy that she wanted at the touch of a dial.

Tiff wasn't slow by a long shot. She knew that San was going to try her hand in the near future. Almost as soon a she got hired she befriended Marylin AKA Lynn. Tiff took pleasure in Lynn's giving her the low—down on what San liked, which was none other than money, coke, dominance, and eating pussy, not necessarily in that order. So in order not to be blind—sided, Tiff sometimes hung out with Lynn.

Tracks didn't care because in her eyes San could do no wrong. As long as San paid for their shop and house, and kept her in the most expensive clothing, San could do whatever. She even allowed San to fuck other hitches at the home they shared in Hampshire Hills. Besides, she knew where all of San's safes were, even the one in the salon's office where they had recently counted out over two hundred thousand dollars. But Tracks knew that if San got locked up, she'd move on to the next big baller.

CHAPTER FOURTEEN

Thursday evening the male Alliance members were blowing trees and listening to loud rap music when Karma came through the front door laden down with shopping bags. She had been out all day and what she had on showed that she'd been shopping and not just for groceries. She laid the bags on the floor and they separated themselves.

Her shoes were black, six inch stilettos that laced up from the front but stopped beneath her toned calf muscles. The bottom part of her ass cheeks couldn't be hidden by the short pair of tight Gucci booty shorts she wore. Her Gucci shirt looked like a bra which had no chance of hiding her stomach or her new sparkling navel ring. Her hair was a mass of huge curls and a light lip gloss coated her lips.

"Damn, Karma," Shellz blurted.

"Shorty you like that," Banga complemented.

Karma stood in front of Bealz and cleared her throat.

"What?" Bealz asked.

"Well, how do I look?"

"Shit, you look like Karma, now move."

Karma smacked her lips and took three of the five bags up to her bedroom. Before Shellz and Banga were headed out the door, they told Bealz that he was crazy.

He looked up at Shellz. "Man, we trying to get money. Look at these bullshit South Pole jeans and Air Force ones. We ain't out spending money on Gators and shit. If I wanted to wear that shit, I'd be a model."

"Okay, Bealz, man ... whatever," Shellz reacted, slamming the door so hard that the 140 sign fell to the ground.

Bealz ran to the window and peeked out, waiting for Shellz Cadillac to pull away from the curb. He then stuck a mixed slow jam CD in the entertainment system. He cut the volume up loud enough so that the music could be heard upstairs. He peeled out of his shirt and let it fall to the fifth step. His left sneaker came off and tumbled down two stairs. His other shoe came off and balanced on the top step.

When he reached Karma's bedroom, all he had on was his boxers. Placing his ear next to the space between the door and the wall, he could hear Karma's sniffles through breaks in R Kelly's song 'Keep It On the Down Low.' He twisted the door knob slightly, pushed the door open and saw that she was lying on her bed face down.

Karma suddenly felt someone bite down on her right shoulder. She gasped and turned over quickly, surprised to see it was Bealz.

"Don't pl——," was all she could moan when his head lowered to her navel. His hands roamed all between her legs. "Don't play, B———" This time he interrupted her by losing and pulling her shorts and thongs down all together. She felt his hands grip her hips, lift her body up, and his tongue roll over her clit from left to right.

To accommodate his access, she spread her legs and held onto the heels of her shoes. She was able to look down and see his eyes looking over her neatly shaven line of pubic hair. "Oh God," she moaned, squeezing her ass cheeks together. "Oh, Bealz, I'm 'bout to cum ..." Her head swung violently. "Ewwww," she panted, loosening the ties on her shirt, freeing her breasts.

Even as her cream surged into his mouth, he kept on treating her pussy like it was the best thing he ever tasted. Without breaking a stride he licked up the middle of her stomach, circled around both of her titties, up the middle of her neck, her chin, and finally her lips, enabling her to taste and savor her own juices.

As their tongues performed a routine dance, she reached down, grasped his stiff dick and guided him into her compliant love canal. She rose to meet his thrusts that caused sounds of pleasure to echo off her bedroom walls. He could feel her pussy muscles clench around his dick each time he tugged at her taut nipples. With every thrust he looked into her eyes for a reaction.

It became a fuck—fest as they stuck each other's fingers into their mouths. In one swift motion he turned over and she was atop him. Looking up at her he could see her breasts bobbling on course like a routine, her physique glistening. She looked like a goddess, her passion unleashed.

"Give it to me, baby," she begged, her eyes drench with lust.

At that moment, outside the apartment, Shellz was running up the sidewalk. He waved at Pudding as he said to no one in particular, "Hold up, I forgot something."

Noticing that the front door was unlocked, Shellz just walked in and immediately heard the music playing. He looked at the blunt in the ashtray that Bealz hadn't finished. Pausing and looking around, he noticed Bealz's sneaker sitting on the steps that led upstairs. He was intrigued by the scene.

Shellz followed the trail of clothing, tiptoeing up the stairs. The closer he got to his old room, the better Karma's moans could be heard. Nearing her bedroom, he noticed that the door was partly ajar. He peeked around the edge of the door and tilted his head in disbelief at the sight of Karma being fucked furiously from the back by Bealz. Shellz heard her plainly moan, "Oh, baby!"

Shellz quietly backed away from the door and quietly retreated back down the steps, thoroughly pissed. As he made his way to the front door he was protesting out loud, "Dirty Muh-fucker! I knew those two have been fucking behind my back." He was still muttering to himself as he ran to his car, jumped in and slammed the door. "Dirty muh—fucker"

"Wha's wrong, Shellz," Banga asked, clearly concerned.

Starting the car, Shellz mumbled, "Oh, nuttin'." He cut a wheel driving away.

Karma was looking back at Bealz over her right shoulder. He had her succulent ass cheeks spread, his thrust was long and fired with raw passion. He pounded away at her now swollen pussy.

Beads of sweat rolled off the small of her back, down her side and onto her bed. She felt like her insides had shattered. "I'm 'bout to cum," Bealz announced, which was music to her ears.

"Cum, baby! You killing this pussy," she pleaded, her toes curled.

"hmp—hmp hmp," he muttered, hitting her with slow strokes.

"Yes, baby! Yes! Nut in me!"

"Here I cum ... ah! Ah, ah—ahhhhhh . .

"I feel it, baby! I feel it!" she cried, crumpling down to his hairless chest and jerking body.

Their skin drenched in sweat, they were gasping to catch their breath. "What now?"

He gently caressed the small of her back, up to her hair, and continued to plant soft kisses on her lips and cheek region.

"Well ... it's been a long time coming. Problem is we need to tell Shellz. But look ..."He paused, tilted her head with his right hand and gazed deeply into her beautiful eyes. "Business over pleasure. The Alliance and money comes first." He saw her nod in agreement and kissed her forehead.

Staring at the ceiling, catching their breath, both shortly dozed off.

Hours Later — 12:47 A.M.

"How many do you want?" Shellz asked a short slender male crackhead.

"All I got is seven dollars," the crackhead replied, biting on his bottom lip.

Banga sat on Phil's porch serving crack to a friend while keeping a watchful eye on Shellz who had snatched the crackhead's seven dollars.

"Come on, Shellz. Gimme my money back," the crackhead pleaded.

Shellz pushed the crackhead to the ground and was ready to stomp the fragile defenseless man, but somehow the guy rolled to his feet and ran up the hill towards the basketball before Shells could do any real damage. Shells walked over the small embankment strutting like the world was his. He removed the half a blunt from his ear and placed it between his lips. With the blunt hanging from the side of his mouth, he told Phil, "Give me a light."

"Boy, it's cluckin' out here," Banga happily evaluated, counting his earnings.

"Man, I'm going to the strip club ... you going wit' me?"
Banga looked from his money to Shellz, then back to his money.

"Nah, I'ma get this scratch."

"Fuck it then, stay here. Take fuckin' chances while Bealz lay up fucking."

Banga and Phil watched Shellz trot over to The Minister's house, jump into his Caddy and drive away at a high rate of speed. "What's wrong with him?" Phil asked, putting his hands in the back pockets of his cut—off jeans.

"I don't know but I'm not trusting dat Nigga right now," Banga explained, hitting speed dial on his cell phone and saying no time, "Yo, Bealz ... we got a problem ...." and proceeded to give Bealz the low down.

Along North Davidson Street, four businesses competed with each other. In reality, all of them could feed off each other. Sharp Sticks Pool Room sat beside a tattoo parlor and fifty feet away on the corner was a Dominos Pizza. However, the problem that all black businesses shared wasn't the North Charlotte neighborhood or their proximity to the Highland Mills Loft Apartments that their businesses were surrounded by. It was the strip club, The Naughty Spot that stole most of their customers and drove away the rest.

The owners of The Naughty Spot were Dominicans who were reputed to be hustling more than exotic ladies. The club had three levels, the most shocking part was the bar that slowly rotated around the middle of the club but which could also be seen from the outside, rotating like some kind of amusement part ride. Thick bullet—proof glass protected the male bartenders and from the street it was a magnificent sight.

At any given time, an assortment of German, European, and the cheaper American—made luxury and exotic vehicles were parked as if on display in front of the club. Six armed guards patrolled the club's exterior and protected the female parking attendants. Only special friends of the owners got their vehicles parked in the front of the club; the strippers, staff and most of the customers parked in the huge parking lot at the rear. Shellz was a well—known customer who paid heavy dividends, especially when a stripper fulfilled his sexual desires. He was greeted by two strippers after he paid the discounted fifteen dollar door charge. He placed his arms around the sexy strippers. Fondling the exposed breasts of the flirting ladies, he scanned the room through the dim blue lights and recognized someone he knew.

Removing his arms, he said, "I'ma catch y'all sexy ladies later," letting them down easy. He then caught up with one of the waitresses who wore a thong and stilettos. "Let me get a shot of Louie XIII," he told her, slipping her three fifty dollar bills. The shot he purchased cost a hundred and twenty five dollars. It was nothing for Shellz to blow a G in a strip club, and he was just getting started.

He tapped the high yellow waitress on her ass and headed to a table centered ten feet from the stage. Taking his seat, he lit up a hyped Black N Mile that would possibly fuel the four blunts that he'd smoked. He pumped his fist to G 'Montes Strip Club Anthem, 'Let Me See You Shake Somethin' Girl,' all the while checking out the various strippers teasing dudes with lap dances and the five ladies performing on the sectagon stage.

A white petite stripper leaned over and whispered into his ear, "Can I get a dance?"

"Nah, Ma ... but if you go get her ... " he pointed, "... to take me to the VIP Room .. ." He paused, peeled a crisp twenty from his wad of cash, "... it will earn you this."

"That's all?" The stripper tried unsuccessfully to snatch the twenty dollar bill.

"Do what I said first."

She wasted no time interrupting the dancer Shellz requested. The girl in question glanced over at Shellz and gingerly smiled. She walked carefully across the stage, the lights in the black glass floor matching her every step. She slapped the wandering hands of several guys holding money off her ass. With no hesitation she straddled the lap of Shellz and began gyrating her ass to the beat of the music.

"What's up, big spender?" she cooed lustfully, her lips inches from his.

"Nah Blue ... ," wrapping his hands around her ass cheeks. "I'm here on business," he added, savoring the smell of the cherry lifesaver in her mouth.

"Ahh boy, you ain't trying to move up in the game," she teased, licking his chin.

"I'm serious ... you swear you got a connect unless you was lying," he charged, watching her lean back and give him a serious stare as she poked out her lips. He continued, "Well, tell your connect I need half a bird in four days."

"Okay, I'll tell her."

"Her?!" he repeated, wearing a shocked gaze.

"Yeah, her. Niggas ain't the only muh—fuckas gettin' paid," she protested sarcastically.

"Now come on ... take me to the VIP Room so I can fuck ya brains out."

"How much you gonna give me?"

"The usual two hundred," he assured, grabbing his drink. He allowed her to drag him through all of the hating stares. He did catch a stripper who the DJ called Pineapple kept staring at him.

Jap

CHAPTER FIFTEEN

Saturday — 12 Noon

The sun was out and shining brightly over the City. Directly across from the right side of the county jail, regular customers were routinely collecting their clothing from SuperDuper Dry Cleaners.

The salt—and—pepper—haired male behind the counter wearing a plaid shirt and brown pants was taking the customers' payments while his chubby dark—skinned female co—worker gathered people's clothing from the circulating machine. SuperDuper had been serving in this same area for the past fifteen years. Doctors, lawyers, common working folks and even some police officers were its reliable customers.

In the rear of SuperDuper picked up their drug shipments. Surrounded by two females seated in a black lazy—boy, San directed the traffic, distributing small to large quantities of Cocaine to her various levels of buyers. San needed the space in order to move the extra shipment of coke that she received from Ortiz. Not including the normal five kilos that she usually purchased, San had an additional ten kilos at seventeen five apiece. That was the Ruiz brothers' price; San's price started at twenty two thousand.

"Handle Rockboy's order," San commanded Grams while continuing to attend to her tender chicks that were dressed in white two—piece bikinis and heels.

San was smart. Her Aunt Betsy and Cousin Houston were the managers and handled the cleaners whenever they felt like it. All San had to do was break them off a little bread and she could do her business. So with her aunt and uncle out front, San sat back, only occasionally peering at the closed circuit TV monitor watching the traffic entering the cleaners. She'd been dealing her weight like this for six months. She should've been filthy rich, but she spent the cash as fast as she made it, some of it going to take care of several family members. But mostly she's got this snorting habit. She snorted Cocaine at tmes from sun up to sun down.

Grams returned from outside holding two McDonald's bags, both filled with San's money. He tossed the bags on the table where Milky had the counting machine working overtime. Monica stood watch by the gray exit door holding an assault rifle. Conscientiously Monica routinely glanced at the outside traffic through the door's square window.

For the past couple of hours, the heavy vehicle traffic luckily went unnoticed by the police cruisers that went to and from the county jail. Even one of San's buyers, a young dude named Squirt, with eighteen ounces in his backpack caught a city bus only steps from the jailhouse doors.

The Gonzallas brothers supplied only four people in Charlotte with their product. San was out to prove that she was their best hustler. She was to meet up with Ortiz later that night at a gathering he was hosting. For the special occasion, San had sent Tracks and Vanilla to pick her out an expensive suit. She also had them stop at Jewelz, a store that specialized in creating medallions and other jewelry that sparkled. San had ordered a custom piece be made for herself and Jewelz had contacted her the day before that it had been completed and ready to be picked up.

*　　*　　*　　*　　*

Karma stared into her full—length mirror on the front of her closet door. She had her head positioned so she could see the rear of her denim low riding Azzara Capris. Her top was hot pink with spaghetti strings tied across the back. The word 'SEXY' cut across her chest and couldn't hide her protruding nipples. She had a small Burkin purse and matching shoes, both with pink designs. Bealz popped up in her doorway, staring in admiration at Karma's stacked physique.

"See anything that you like?" she asked, smiling, her hands sliding invitingly over her curvaceous hips, waistline, and breasts. He answered by flicking his tongue.

"You crazy." She giggled.

Bealz went downstairs. He stepped at the open front door and stared through the glass screen—door. He shielded his eyes briefly from the three—thirty sunlight that shone inside the apartment. He then went outside to inspect the waxing job that Trips had done on his Box Chevy.

"That muh—fucka clean," he said to himself.

"Damn, wha's up, stranger," Pudding shouted from her porch. Karma's room was above the front of the apartment. Just when he was about to go downstairs, she heard Bealz conversing with Pudding. She peeked through the curtain and sure enough she caught Pudding's playful touchy feely acts.

"Ahh Pudding, you full of shit. We went out a couple of time and you wouldn't give the kid a peck on the cheek," Bealz complained.

"Ewww," Pudding squealed, punching him in the shoulder. "I wanted you all to me, and you a sneaky ass dog," she joked.

Bealz snickered, but it only lasted a second before Karma flew outside in a rush. "Bealz, I'ma go handle that call me when you ready," she encouraged, laying a kiss on his cheek while giving Pudding a threatening glare at the same time.

As Karma's enticing walk disappeared into the Chevy, Bealz and Pudding were both surprised at her antics. Karma started the Chevy and after finding Tha Dogg Pounds, Dogg Food Cd, the song 'Bomb Azz" baseline disturbed the peace.

Pudding waited until she could no longer see the Chevy's taillights, then questioned, "What's wrong wit ya girl?"

"Don't know, but she ain't my girl. We're really good friends," he made clear, leaving Pudding outside. Soon as he made it to his couch his cell phone rang. "To, Banga— what up?"

"Yo Bealz. I need to talk to you 'bout some real shit."
Bealz sat up. "Go 'head, speak to me, dawg," he urged.

"Face talk."

"A' ight."

Bealz had a bad feeling.

Knock—knock!

He looked up to see Pudding's smiling face staring through the glass screen—door, he motioned for her to enter, puzzled as to why she closed the door as she did. "What's up?" he asked, watching her mess with his entertainment center.

Suddenly, Changing Faces' song 'Stroke You Up' began playing at a soft volume.

"Quit ya bullshit, Pudding," he cautioned as he watched her start to dance seductively to the beat of the music. Then without warning she removed the straps from her shoulders causing her Prada mini summer skirt to fall to the floor. His eyes looked as if a ghost had sat in his lap. He licked his lips at her nakedness as he pulled down his pants and boxers. He grinned at her surprised gaze at his rigid dick.

Pudding stepped her black pumps out of the skirt bunched at her feet. She sashayed over to Bealz, placed her left foot on the couch, grabbed the back of his head and pulled herself on top of him. Bealz inhaled the fresh scent of her shaved pussy. Sensing her body beginning to lower, he held his rigid organ with one hand and with the other guided her by her plump ass. Feeding him her orange—sized titties, "Ahhh," she moaned, feeling the tip of his dick penetrate her moist pussy. "Oh, Bealz, that dick's big ... Unghh," she grunted from his light thrust.

A ray of sunlight peeked through a tear in the curtain, and so did Karma. For a couple of minutes she watched Pudding struggle, but ride Bealz's dick like a semi—pro. Seething, she instinctively reached in her purse for her pistol but remembered that it was at the bottom of the Catawba River.

"I knew I shouldn't have come back yet," Karma thought silently.

Twenty five minutes later, Pudding slouched on the couch with her legs wide open. Her pussy throbbed, not to mention the discomfort of Bealz's nut oozing from her pussy. Bealz returned from upstairs with a warm soapy rag and kneeled between her legs.

"Wait, wait," she murmured, grabbing his hand that held the rag. Both of them heard the sound from outside of a car door slamming. Bealz jumped to his feet, ran over and peeked out through the curtain.

"Oh, shit! Here comes Karma," he said fearfully, rushing a naked Pudding through the kitchen. He allowed her to quickly slip on her skirt before closing the door behind her. He darted back into the living room which smelled of sex. As the front door opened, he was spraying a lemon— scented citrus spray over the couch as well as other places.

"Sup," he said.

Karma fanned her hand through the stuffy smell of lemon. "I smell butt," she uttered, flipping her lips in front of her nose.

He looked around like rats were running around the floor "Butt? Girl, you trippin'," he retorted, trying to throw her off.

Jap

"Mmm Hmmm," she shot back. "So what are you gonna do tonight?"

"I ...'

Knock—knock

He cursed, "Who da fuck is it?"

"Dis Banga," a voice shouted back beyond the closed door.

"Come in," Karma yelled, cutting off the stereo system.

Banga entered dressed in his usual all black urban gear. He bumped fist with Bealz, threw his head up at Karma, then took a seat across from the Capo.

"Talk to me, Baby Boy," Bealz said, splitting a Chocolate Philly down the middle.

Banga interlocked his fingers stroking his little bit of chin hair repeatedly with his thumbs. "Yo man I'ma team playa, feel me?" Seeing Bealz nod his approval, he continued, "Ya boy Shellz talkin' about buying his own work."

"That's good. All Alliance members are free to sell their own shit." He paused to sprinkle the Kind Bud weed into the cigar. "You too, soldier," he added, smirking.

Banga checked the understanding look that stretched across Karma's face. "Nah, Bealz ... he talkin' 'bout rubbin' shoulder wit' Lil Gas and a new connect," he made clear.

Banga's words kept reverberating in the heads of Bealz and Karma. Alliance rules were not to speak of the Untold unless betrayal is involved.

Bealz licked the blunt together, lit the ass—end of the cigar, and from his deep drags the blunt lit up like Rudolph the Red—nosed Reindeer. Karma saw the hurt in Bealz's face.

'That Nigga knows that I wacked that sucker at that strip Joint,' she silently thought.

'I can't let that chump live; he know I was the one that busted my gun.' Banga thought to himself.

Four days went by and The friendship between Shellz and Bealz had dwindled to a point where they barely called each other. Their trust for one another was like a pencil with no eraser. Bealz had been hitting the block in The View real hard. Banga's choice, he rode with Bealz. Karma had already sketched out Shellz's demise if it reached that point. So whenever Bealz and crew showed up in The View, Shellz would leave.

Shellz had just hung up from talking with the front desk clerk of the Microtel off Sugar Creek. He had told the lady at the front desk he'd be down to pay for another night. He and BlueBerry were laid up full as a tic after devouring their McDonald's breakfast. He stared at the ten thousand five hundred dollars that was piled on the bed against the wall.

BlueBerry's dark skin to glowed. Her thick braided weave with the blue highlights was still intact after all that fucking she and Shellz had done. She was laying on her stomach ass naked with her legs spread, laughing as she watched a Jamie Fox Show rerun on BET. The wiggling of her thick flawless thighs caused her Juicy ass to shudder involuntarily. Her titties were big enough that if needed she could suck them herself.

Jap

Feeling Shellz's toes brush against her pussy, she looked back at him with an agitated stare. "Damn ... what?"

The tone of her response caused his temper to flare. "Don't fuckin' what me ," he said. "Call, the bitch."

"O—kaaay," she replied, holding a long sigh. Shellz blazed up a blunt while she dialed the Connect's number.

"Hello," Blue spoke into the phone. "I know it's early but..."

She was interrupted by something said by the Connect. "Den I feel ya — he's my people. Hold on .. ." BlueBerry placed her hand over the receiver, and whispered to Shellz, "You got eleven—five?"

"Eleven—five . . .!" Let me speak to her," he suggested as he reached for the phone.

"Boy, are you crazy?" BlueBerry uttered panicky, then remembered how much they had counted. Back into the phone she continued, "Girl, he got ten stacks. Put the rest on my face ... uh huh, I'll make sure that you get the rest ... you will." Blue grinned at whatever the Connect's response was. "Okay, tell him in one hour, in front of Big Lots by North Park Mall ... A'ight gurl wit' yo' freaky ass ... Bye—bye."

CHAPTER SIXTEEN

The following day, around 2 P.M. Bealz tailed Freckles and his very talkative chubby white friend with the long stringy hair. The three of them blended in with the customers, avoiding the attention of Pep Boys shift managers through the rush of work. They walked into the heart of the room that held the hundreds of new tires. Freckles had Chubby stand watch by the room's entry. Bealz stood back while Freckles reached between a stack of eight tires.

"Here, hold this," Freckles said, reaching his arm back.

Bealz studied the black .357 revolver that he'd taken from Freckles grasp. The first was made by Smith & Wesson, the second, a 9mm, was nickel plated and made by Remington. He stuck the .357 into his waistband and covered it with his huge all black tee. He backed up so that Freckles wouldn't fall and destroy the infra—red off the top of the chrome .45 automatic.

"This bitch here will not miss if ya aim on, "Freckles assured, snickering.

"How much?" Bealz inquired in a serious tone.

"Give me four hundred seventy five dollars,' Freckles answered, handing over the foe—fifth.

To get the pistols out to the van, Freckles hid them in a tool box on wheels. He even chatted with the unsuspecting manager and stayed cool.

A short time later Bealz shook Freckles' hand through the passenger side window. And just like that, The Alliance was strapped.

Bealz handed Banga the nine. Karma, behind the wheel didn't take her focus off the road when the .357 was tossed onto her lap. Banga kissed the nine, then pulled from beneath his lap a black .380, playfully crossing the pistols like two swords.

"We ready," Bealz said with a murderous stare. "I got another order a S and AK ... two street sweepers and two boot pistols," he added with a sadistic tone in his voice.

"Yo Bealz ... If dat Nigga Shellz gonna continue to get money outside of The Alliance, we need to run him away from The View," Banga suggested.

"He's right," Karma agreed as her left hand stroked the pistol. Collectively, Bealz and Banga had been out—selling Shellz, especially with Bealz copping two birds and a big eighth of heroin. The Alliance had the biggest bags of crack and although The View was hot, it was booming.

Shellz could have been up to a Bird, but he had to spend money everyday on whatever. He and BlueBerry were now living in different motels on and about the Sugar Creek, North Tryon area.

"We'll see, as long as Shellz ain't on no takeover shit." Bealz paused and stared out at a baby waving at him from the backseat of a late model Toyota. "He's okay," he ended, smiling at the baby.

* * * * * * * * *

"Gurl, a bitch ain't changing," Vanilla defended himself, standing in front of his booth's round mirror, applying gel to his sideburns.

"Bitch, yes you is," Tiff shot back confidently from her own booth.

Unique's female customers mostly sided with Vanilla because he kept it real. Carrie approached Vanilla's booth. "Hey, can you cut off my loose ends?" she asked, smiling.

He heaved a deep sigh, dabbed his drooling nose. "I guess sooooo." he dragged.

A deep vibration from outside rattled the salon's mirrors, interrupting the hair dressers working. All at once everyone's attention was on San's pimp—strut up the walkway. Milky's head could be seen nodding from the driver's seat of the Escalade behind her. Small clouds of weed smoke escaped the SUV's downed window. A burnt—orange '91 Fleetwood Brougham occupied by three females pulled in next to the Escalade. The driver of the Caddy got out and climbed into the backseat of the Escalade. Whatever took place was fast because the female exited the SUV quickly with a nervous stare.

A little later inside the salon Sans, Tracks, and Vanilla exited the office with their mouths twitching. But Vanilla seemed to be in the worst shape, unable to hide the loud grinding noise his teeth were making. Tiff could only shake her head at her buddy Vanilla's antics. San kissed Tracks, made eye—contact with Tiff and a gave her a wink, then stuffed the money she was holding into the pockets of her Coogi shorts

After San had left, Tiff scolded Vanilla about fucking with The Devil, her name for San.

By nightfall the police had run all the hustlers away from Belvedere's money blocks. Only Smokers roamed the streets. They lurked inside the doorways of various apartment buildings for the dopeboys but their attempts to score were unsuccessful. At three hours before midnight, this urban region known for crack—sales looked uncharacteristically like a ghost town. Infrequent gusts of wind shuffled discarded wrappers, beer cans and cigarette butts around the neighborhood.

Bealz headed back to the apartment after scoring a half—ounce of weed from Tuson. He turned Trips away, telling him that if he wanted drugs, he needed to go up the Street to The View. Trip's always begging," Bealz complained to Banga and Karma. Karma smelled the bag of Chronic that Bealz tossed to her. She gave him a nod of approval.

"Shit, let's smoke somethin'," Banga suggested, preparing a Chocolate Philly blunt.

"This is how we do ... we make moves." He is interrupted by the ring tone of his cell phone. Putting the phone to his ear, Bealz speaks, "Yo" Hearing what the caller was telling him, Bealz's face morphed into a look of pure hatred. "I'll be there in a minute."

"What's up?" Banga inquired standing.

"That was Phil letting me know that Shellz, some chick named BlueBerry and Lil Gas has ran him away from his crib."

"Let's go."

"No. Karma, you stay here, we got this. Let's bounce, Banga."

Karma ran to the window and watched the van speed off. She continued rolling the blunt and finishing it, turned on some slow music before lighting it up. She figured after getting high she'd go shower and treat Bealz real nice when he returned.

The van tore around the corner of The View in a matter of minutes. They chose to park at a set of apartments situated by the basket ball court. Bealz and Banga secured their weapons, climbed out of the van, and trotted down the path that led to The View.

Crouching down between some thick brush and uncut grass, the two were concealed but had a bird's—eye view of Phil's house. The front porch was dark but the red tips of something being smoked was easily detected.

"Look, there goes Shellz's punk ass — let's do this!" Banga whispered sternly. He made a move to go but was held back by Bealz's strong grasp of his arm. "What?"

Bealz pointed and Banga peered in the direction of his point. A short dude emerged from the side of Phil's house accompanied by a familiar female crack—head.

"That's Lil Gas," Banga introduced, easing the safety off the 9mm."

"You ready?" Bealz questioned. Seeing Banga nod, Bealz continued. "We gon' see where Shellz's head is at, if he ain't talking right we gon' bust all dey ass," he said with determination.

"Loyalty Reigns, my Nigga." Banga spat.

The stage was set his former partners who Shellz had told Lil Gas about, suddenly emerged from the dark shadows of the path. Watching what at first had to look like an apparition in a frightening nightmare, BlueBerry handed Shellz the same foe—fifth that Banga had used outside of Admissions, a pistol that he'd promised to get rid of.

Shellz and Lil Gas cautiously met Bealz and Banga at the breach of Phil's driveway. BtueBerry leaned against the pillar of the house, watching intently as the men sized each other up. Lil Gas was the shortest of the four, but rugged—looking, especially with the scar that led down his left arm.

Shellz spoke first. "Sup, Beaiz?"

"Ain't shit. Dawg ... what's up wit' ya man? He ain't part of The Alliance?"

"No, but he's selling for me, so no more should be said." Shellz paused, looked in the direction that Bealz and Banga came from. "Where's Karma?"

"She chilun' ... Sup wit' you runnin' Phil away from da crib?" Bealz questioned.

"That Nig———"

"Ain't nobody talkin' to you, Dawg." Banga straightened, pointing his finger in the face of Lil Gas.

"Man, if Phil said that, he's lyin'," Shellz insisted. "He's been gone all day."

Bealz started thinking to himself that perhaps Shellz was right. Little did Bealz know that while he was trying to get to the bottom of things, major trouble was brewing back at his apartment. Karma was totally unaware that a lone intruder had crept through the back door of Apartment 140. The dark—colored trespasser with nappy shoulder—length dreadlocks, quietly approached the couch where Karma was napping. As he silently and menacingly neared her, he secured his black gloves and adjusted the stocking cap which masked his face.

Sensing danger, Karma's eyes suddenly began to flutter open but was slammed in the head with pistol by the 235 pound, five foot ten inch intruder before she could react. The initial blow rendered Karma unconscious, but he kept striking her, causing her blood to spray and splatter the living room walls. He continued to viciously pummel her face with the butt of his pistol for another ten seconds before he ceased his merciless assault.

Breathing with a heavy rasp from the exertion and the overabundance of adrenaline, he was forced to pause to catch his breath. Looking down at his victim, he nearly wretched at the brutality of his work and what was left of Karma's face. He lifted the stocking cap and spit the bile that was forming in his mouth.

He rolled her body off the couch onto the floor, leaving her laying there face down. He was ignorant of the crunch of her teeth under his feet as he stepped over her body, teeth were shattered by the savage blows.

After catching his breath, the intruder hurried upstairs and directly into Bealz's room. Snatching all the drawers out of the dresser and finding nothing, he started in on the closet. After sliding Bealz's clothing to the side, he found what he was looking for. When he struggled to lift the safe, he realized it must be bolted to the floor.

"Shit!" he cursed, striking the top of the safe with his fist.

Looking around in frustration, he noticed the dozens of Air Jordan, Air Force 1, and Timberland shoe boxes stacked neatly against the wall of the closet. He looked closer to read the size of the shoes.

"Shit, I wear a nine—and—a—half," he told himself, grinning. He lifted the lid of a Timberland shoe box. "BINGO!" he shouted, seeing that it was stuffed full of cash.

Downstairs, before vacating the premises, he looked around at the devastation of his savage attack and noticed the PlayStation 2 game console that was lying on the floor a couple of feet from Karma's body. He decided to steal that as well before bolting back out the same way he had entered.

Outside, an accomplice was waiting in a hot red Ford 150. He jumped in and they calmly drove away.

Unbeknownst to the intruder, Pudding had heard the grunting sounds through the thin apartment walls and had assumed they were the sounds Bealz and Karma made fucking. But as she saw the suspicious—looking truck drive out of the unit's rear parking lot, she immediately opened the screen door and peeked out. She wave at Trips as he headed across the street. Giving in to curiosity, she looked through the tear in Bealz's curtains and her eyes fixated on Karma's body laying in a pool of blood. Terrified and in a panic, she rushed back into her empty apartment and dialed 9—1—1. Her next call was to Bealz.

"Sup, Puddin'?" Bealz answered as he sat opposite Shellz on Phil's porch.

In her panic, she could barely choke out her words. "S—s—something h—happened to Karma . .

"What!" he shouted, leaping to his feet. Pausing momentarily to listen, he uttered, and pressed the button to disconnect as he took off like a bat out of hell to where the van was parked.

"Sup, Bealz?" Shellz asked, trying to catch up with him.

"Something happened to Karma."

Shellz heard what Bealz had said and from his former partner's demeanor he knew something was dreadfully wrong. He told Lil Gas to stay put, snatched BlueBerry's arm and ran over to the Minister's driveway. Lil Gas watched in consternation as Shellz's STS cut a wheel and peel up Crestview Drive.

In minutes both the van and the STS were tearing up West Trade. But the throngs of nosey neighbors, emergency vehicles and police cars forced them to park on the next block and sprint the rest of the way to Apartment 140.

Bealz lost it when he saw the paramedics working furiously on Karma as they wheeled her on a gurney to a waiting ambulance. Shellz and Banga had to physically restrain Bealz when an officer tried to question him.

"Fuck you, motherfucking Cracka," Bealz yelled angrily through tears of rage as he struggled from the grasp of his two friends.

Pudding ran up to them. "She's gonna be okay," she said, her eyes oozing concern. Wiping a tear from his cheek with the hem of her tee shirt, she added, "They're taking her to Carolinc Medical."

Responding without hesitation, "Yo, Bealz, I'll drive," Shellz said, taking note of Bealz's venomous glare. "Come on, Dawg, Karma's my friend, too," he pleaded, holding his arms at his side. After a silent, eerie ride, Shellz drove up to the hospital's emergency entrance. Before the car stopped moving, Bealz jumped out and rushed through the doors. Shellz instructed BlueBerry to find a place to park the car as he jumped out and quickly followed Bealz inside.

After speaking with a receptionist, Bealz and company were told they'd have to wait for a doctor for a status report on Karma, and directed them to a waiting area which was semi—packed with a few kids screaming their lungs out. The constant paging heard from the overhead speakers and the sounds from the vending machines played havoc with those who already suffered headaches.

Bealz sat with the back of his head tilted against wall. Even with his eyes closed he blindly envisioned the torture Karma must have suffered. 'Someone's gonna pay,' he thought to himself. 'Someone's gonna pay.' That was the only thought that could calm him enough to sit and wait word on Karma's condition.

CHAPTER SEVENTEEN

In Room 134 of The Knights Inn Motel, located off of Statesville Avenue, the two culprits who had caused Karma's misfortune were celebrating their clean getaway. They had passed off the stolen Ford to one of the many crackheads that roam Statesville Avenue.

The mastermind of the home invasion sat on the edge of the room's single bed thumbing through the measly ninety—two hundred dollars, still wearing the gloves that he'd never taken off. Looking on from his seated position by the room's round table, his partner inquired "Yo, how much Imma get," as he took a drag of his Newport, exhaled smoke creating a mushroom around his dreadlocks.

"Who name the room in?" the Mastermind questioned, stacking the money back into the shoe box.

"Uh .. ," he hesitated, closed his eyes to retrieve the woman's name from his foggy memory banks. Finally remembering, "Oh, Momoney," he exclaimed, and opened his eyes looking right into the wrong end of the barrel of the gun that he had used on Karma. Suddenly terrified, the cigarette fell from his trembling lips. "Man. what's the de———"

Bang!

The gunshot disrupted the dreadlock's word. As his body remained motionless in the chair, his brains slid down the flowered curtains and onto the air conditioning unit, then rapidly discolored the gray carpet.

The Mastermind turned killer calmly peeked through the splattered curtains. In the parking lot, the flash of headlights from a parked car could be seen. He then exited the room, being careful to close the door behind him, nodded politely at a passing couple carrying a six—pack of beer to their own rented room.

Within seconds, the Mastermind and his loyal female accomplice drove away Scott—free, he and his partner's plan executed without a hitch. Now it was time to move on to the next phase.

* * * * * *

Approaching the fifth hour of the waiting game, the black, medium— built doctor entered the hospital's waiting room. "Ms. Robinson's family?" he called out.

"Here," Bealz and another older gentleman accompanied by a fine lady responded simultaneously. Bealz and the man approached the doctor but gave each other inquisitive stares.
"I'm her father and this is her mother . . ." Maintaining unwavering eye contact with Bealz, he continued, "I'on know who he is ... but my name is Jamil Robinson, and I don't want someone that I don't know around me, my wife and daughter," rolling his eyes at Bealz and company.

As Bealz's jaw muscles tightened involuntarily, and venom bled from his eyes, he restrained the impulse to strangle Jamil and continued to stroke his goatee instead. The anger flowing through his veins escalated as he helplessly watched the Robinsons follow the doctor into another room. When sudden shrill screams electrified the room, Bealz closed his eyes and prayed for Karma, aware that the screams belonged to Karma's mama.

"Uh ... Mr. Jacob Malone?"

Bealz opened his eyes and looked up into the face of an officer holding a note pad. "I'm officer Timbell."

Shellz shoved BlueBerry's hands from the fold of his arm and stood up quickly. "Man, y'all fuckin' wit' him ... His girl is in theta fighting for her life .."

"Nah, let's hear what the fuck you got to say, Pig," Bealz said. The officer motioned for five other officers that were waiting a couple feet away. They gathered around Bealz to provide assistance to their fellow officer in case trouble erupted.

"Now as I was about to say, are you and your boys beefing with other drug dealers? We're thinking maybe fuckin' up your girl was some kind of retaliation." He paused, awaiting a response from Bealz. Getting none, he continued, "I mean, first y'all dealt drugs from Apartment 140, then y'all moved your drug dealing to a home up the street on Crestview." Seeing Bealz's fleeting look of surprise, "Oh, you thought we didn't know?" Timbell continued, flashing a phony smile.

"Am I under arrest?" Bealz inquired, his face expressionless. Timbell's smile got bigger. "No ... not yet." Getting up close to Bealz's left ear, he whispered, "If I were you ... Bealz! I'd sell weed and break up The Alliance." Rising and looking down at Bealz, Timbell gave Bealz a wink before turning and walking calmly away, motioning with a slight nod of his head for the other officers to follow.

Bealz cut his eyes at Timbell's back and hatefully watched the pigs disappear. His arms folded, Shellz inquired, "What dem crackas say?" Rising from his seat, Bealz just shook his head. "Yo, man where you goin?" Shellz asked watching Bealz walk off. Banga got up to follow Bealz, bumping into Shellz as he brushed by.

Shellz was about to react to the rudeness when he felt BlueBerry at his side. Her lips near his ear, she offered comfort. "Fuck dem, Baby I'm wit' you all the way," she cooed, caressing his ear lobe.

Shellz felt the vibration of his cell phone. He offered a half—smile at BlueBerry as he retrieved the phone from his pocket and read the display screen. It read""I'M READY!"

Unfazed by Jamil's action, Bealz caught up with the doctor and explained that Karma was his girlfriend. Sympathizing with Bealz, the doctor informed him that if Karma lived she'd be blind in her left eye. In graphic detail, withholding nothing, he described how Karma was beaten within an inch of her life. He went on to say that eleven of her front teeth were gone and that Karma's face was so battered that her scars would be evident the rest of her life.

Despite his pleas, there was no way Bealz would be permitted to see Karma. In the first place, as they explained, she was heavily sedated to quell the pain from her surgeries. And secondly, because the police were determined to be the first to talk to her as soon as she was conscious, the Special Investigative Unit had a police officer stationed outside her door to guard against any unauthorized entry.

Since Bealz was definitely not "authorized," he and Banga caught a ride in a Destinations Cab. All the way home Bealz remained silent and motionless, except for undoing a couple of his frizzy braids. When the cab pulled up, to his surprise they found Pudding still up and faithfully keeping watch over his apartment, in view of the busted front and backdoor locks.

Entering the apartment, Bealz could see that Karma's blood had dried but its remains were still visible from what were pools on the couch and the floor. Strips of yellow police tape were coiled in a medium sized ball around the living room. The residue from a black powdery substance remained indicating that the police had done a thorough fingerprinting job.

To Bealz's surprise, even though it was apparent someone had trashed his bedroom, he found his safe still intact. He was a little disappointed that his Timberland box filled with his vacation money was gone, but when he opened the safe, was relieved to find that the seventy—five thousand was still safe, sound, and crispy looking.

"Yo, Bealz!" Banga hollered from downstairs, his voice strained with urgency.

Bealz reach mid—stair and shook his head at Trips. "Not right now," he said.

"Nah, Bealz, you got to hear this," Banga insisted, giving a looping hand gesture for Bealz to hurry up.

"Sup, Trips?"

"I was telling Banga that I walked right past LJ." Confused, Bealz inquired, "Who the fuck is LJ?"

"You know LJ from Lakeview. He's partners with ... uh, uh ... Lil Gas."

Banga and Bealz gave each other a surprised stare and both nodded. "Here, this is for you."

"One hundred dollars! Thanks, Bealz ... sell me a half eight."

"Ain't shit here. Go up to The View. I think Shellz up there."

"Nah, I'm a go 'round the corner," Trips said happily.

Banga waited until Trips had walked out before complaining. "Man, Bealz, why'd you tell him to go spend wit' doze Niggas? We need to go blow their fuckin' brains out. I know Shellz and Lil Gas had something to do wit' dis shit," he expressed with hatred in his voice. "Fuck we waitin' on?"

"Waitin' for 'em to slip up, 'den we gon' kill 'em," Bealz explained. He turned to Banga with a cold stare and added, "If Karma die, I'ma personally send God two Niggas earlier than his planned schedule."

Bealz's cold—blooded smirk gave chills to an ordinarily stoic Banga.

Silently, Bealz thought to himself, 'Phil must be in with Shellz., but why cross me, and hurt Karma?'

Hours later the midday news had informed its viewers of the City's overnight violence. Channel 3 was the only one that ventured into the heart of Belvedere with their cameras rolling and the audacity to show images of the exterior of Bealz's apartment and a good shot of his car.

Meantime, in another part of the City, behind closed doors a clandestine meeting was underway. "I think we need to go ahead and arrest Sandra," Det. Leslie Smith insisted to her superior. She looked at her partner Rodney, and was disappointed by his argumentative demeanor.

Det. Smith looked back at the chubby black Acting Lieutenant who sat behind her desk rocking in her chair, and smiled to herself about how much Lt. Webber resembled Shirley from the TV show 'What's Happening?' gap teeth and all.

"Lt. Webber, with all due respect, Detective Smith doesn't understand how close ..." MacMall paused, pumped his closed fist twice, then continued, "... I am."

As Rodney and Leslie bickered amongst themselves, Lt. Webber pinched a piece of butterscotch candy from the bowl on her desk, slipped it into her fresh cup of coffee, then stirred it with a white plastic spoon. She cautiously ventured a tiny sip and sensing that the coffee was too hot, she blew over the all black, unsweetened brew. She cut her eyes at the pictures of her two kids that sat behind her name plate on her desk. "Y'all acting like two kids," she blurted with frustration. "I assigned y'all to this case," she admitted, placing her brewed drink down. "Now if y'all can't handle the business at hand ... someone else will be taking over,"she concluded.

Rodney reached over, placed his hand on Leslie's shoulder and batted his eyes like a woman would do. "Com on, trust me. Please? Pretty please, Les, please?" he begged.

Leslie jerked her shoulder away from his hand. "Okay, boy," she agreed, unable to hold her grin.

He stood up. "Well, it's done. In sixty days we'll have Sandra and Major League behind bars," he exclaimed with a jovial smile. The meeting over, Leslie and Rodney turned to leave.

"Don't let me down," Lt. Webber shouted to the exiting agents.

2 P.M.

There was still no word on Karma's condition. Without revealing their suspicions, Bealz and Banga took turns selling crack with Shellz and Lil Gas. Customers were coming from all directions spending money and females from time to time swapped sexual favors with Banga and Lil Gas for crack rocks.

After a while it seemed that no one wanted to buy product from Shellz. The crack fiends complained that his crack burnt like a candle and tasted like Combat. It was a known fact that a Combat taste would tarnish your reputation.

"Fuck you mean, it won't burn?" Shellz shouted to a male fiend.

Shakily holding in his left hand what he'd copped from Shellz, "See? Look at it."

Bealz looked on with his large Afro picked out, Polo shades covering his eyes and his wife beater laying across his left shoulder, he sucked his teeth at the blatant disrespect Shellz showed by knocking the fiend to the ground. He stood up when he saw Banga and Lil Gas running towards Phil's house like they were in rescue mode.

"Whoa .. hol'up," Bealz said, leaping to the ground from the porch. "Let 'im up, Shellz," he protested, helping the fiend to his feet. "Here." Bealz handed the fiend two dimes.

"Good look, Bealz," the fiend thanked. He eyed the bags as he walked away, scratching his butt through his cut—off jeans.

Since Shellz had explained that Phil hadn't been seen, Bealz was convinced that Phil had something to hide. Lil Gas nudged Shellz's arm in a silent suggestion that he should make Bealz aware that he ain't the boss. Shellz nodded in agreement and crossed over the small embankment that led across Phil's front lawn to the porch.

"Yo, Bealz, you got you and I got me," Shellz said in a low, raspy tone.

Bealz ran his hand over his tattooed dogs and exhaled, "You right, Fam."

Banga interjected while faking his smile, "Shellz, it's all good, we still boys, let's get money."

"Don't forget about me," Lil Gas intoned with a hint of jealousy.

They all shared a superficial laugh.

The Next Morning 8 A.M.

Ring—ring!

Politely answering her office phone, "Detective Buccannon."

"Ahh, yes ... This is Detective Abraham Soles from the Fulton County Atlanta Police Department."

"Good morning, Detective Soles. How can I help you?" she responded, tapping a pencil on her desk.

"I have a man that contacted me about a shooting that happened in Charlotte not too long ago. The man said that his son confided in him. Not only was his conscience bothering him, but his son said that he was having nightmares about his two friends ..."

"Waldo and Odel," she interjected, interrupting his unfinished sentence.

The two veteran detectives shared information. Sharon told Soles that she had an active ongoing investigation into the alleged drug dealings of Shelton Davis, as well as the shooting. The call lasted seven minutes, concluding with Sharon assuring that she'd look out for Marvin Goods a.k.a. Duck, if he agrees to spill the beans.

Not even two hours later, San too received an alarming call from Qrtiz.

"Whoa — Ortiz! I can't understand you," Sans said, wiping cold from her eyes.

"One of dour boyz come by da rest—urant talkin''bout dou sent him," Ortiz said in deep Spanish accent.

"What! I ain't sent nobody nowhere," San replied with fury. "What's his name?"

Ortiz explained that he didn't know his name but told San that he'd seen him with her before. Describing him to her was all she needed.

"Don't worry, Ortiz. He won't be bothering you or I any more," she assured him.

Click.

San woke up both BlueBerry and Monica, made them take a shower with her and then they all got dressed. San sent messages throughout her Major League clique. She hit each member with the phrase, "IT'S SHOWTYME!"

CHAPTER EIGHTEEN

Nearing 5 P.M.
Sunny — 82 Degrees

Up Beatties Ford Road, in the vicinity of three well known spots, The Mother House of Prayer Church, West Charlotte High School, and Cummings Avenue, aside from the other places of businesses and eateries it was the well—packed car wash named Four Men and A Van that kept the makings of a car show. Dudes were either waiting to get their cars washed or they'd already had their vehicles cleaned and were trying to get their stunt on. Even the females were just hanging around, hoping to attract the attention of some ballers.

As always, the police had to make their presence known by telling the owner of the car wash to keep the noise down. Sometimes the police would catch customers of the detailing service participating in some kind of illegal activity which would result in a one—way ride to jail.

"Girl, you know I got that fire dick," a short stocky dude bragged to a girl leaning up against a wine—colored Lexus that sat on 22—inch chrome Asantis. He was wearing some colorful Polo shorts, white tee showcasing the Polo emblem, and white Forces with no socks.

"Ahh, Nigga, you ain't been by the strip club lately," she retorted, turning around, hoping that her scantily clad body would entice him. In mid— turn her attention was captured, along with everybody else's, by the thunderous baseline of an approaching car that was six car lengths beyond Lassalle Street. The car's music was clearly heard, but its description was being hidden by a huge red Pepsi truck.

The stocky dude had lost the battle for the stripper's attention to the earth—shaking sound system of the box Chevy now coming into view.

"That's Bealz!" she announced with excitement as she waited for the car to come to a stop in the parking lot of the car wash. She straightened up her clothes before she approached the rear of Bealz's car. She inspected the rim's interior, even the rattle of the trunk. She peeked through the window and saw Bealz rolling a blunt. She tapped lightly on the window but the volume of the music prevented him from hearing. So she strolled seductively around to the driver's window. She jumped back when he rolled the window down without looking at her.

"Sup, Neka?" Bealz spoke, sealing the blunt with the saliva from his tongue.

"Damn, Bealz, you doing it big, ain't ya," she said being nosy, slyly grinning.

"I ain't doing shit big," he replied, sharply cutting his eyes at her.

Watching the smoke rise from his mouth made her want to hit the blunt. She figured that he'd think about all the great sex that they used to have and offer her a seat in his car and a hit of the blunt. But minutes later, with the blunt halfway gone and minimal words passed, Coneka became impatient. She folded her arms and began to pout, especially hearing 2Pacs'"Wonder Why They Call You Bitch' play on Bealz's stereo system.

"Damn, Jacob Malone," she said with hatred in her voice. "I gave you your first piece of pussy."

He offered no response, just kept smoking and toying with the volume of his car's CD player.

She finally became irate. "Nigga, you had that bitch whip my ass a————"

"Hold the fuck up," Bealz shouted, cutting her off. He placed the blunt into the ashtray and continued, "You was the one fucking around wit' some Nigga named Coley." He paused, giving her an evil gaze before he went on. "... who to this day I ain't seen, so don't come at me with that bullshit."

Ignoring Coneka's tears, Bealz turned his head in the direction of a little cutie who was about to walk past his car. He tooted the Chevy's horn.

Coneka took offense to the high yellow girl approaching his car. Just as the long—haired stranger got within two feet of the driver's window of Bealz's car, Coneka held her left hand out in front of the girl's face.

"Neka, what you doing?," Bealz questioned raising up in the driver's seat.

Coneka stuck her head halfway through the downed window. "Jacob, everyone makes mistakes . ." She hesitated, trying her best to contain the mist building up in her eyes, but lost the fight. She took a deep breath. "Look at what happened at your apartment and your business has been in all the news. Streets talking 'bout somebody put a hit out on you and Relle got hurt." She shook her head, saying, "Shit comes back on you."

Even though Bealz didn't stop Coneka from walking away, her words kept echoing in his head, "Shit comes back on you."

"Sup, Baby Girl?" Bealz said to the newcomer. Politely introducing himself, "My name's Jacob."

"My name is Princess .. ." she announced, looking around for Coneka. "Ya girl ain't gonna steal on me is she?"

They both shared a laugh and proceeded to get to know each other a little better.

*   *   *   *   *

The song 'Keep on Moving' had Vanilla putting on a dance show for the customers of Unique Designs. This time he had his portable CD/radio on his shoulder like the old days.

"Vanilla, you makin' a spectacle out of yourself," Tiff teased, snickering.

"Here comes San," Carrie yelled, ushering herself to her post. Everybody quickly resumed work. Tracks helped by switching the TV to a news station. San, Milky, and Grams entered, smelling like a pound of weed. San motioned for Tracks and Vanilla to meet her in the office. Tiff hated San and San's snarling face indicated the reverse was also true. San peeked in everyone's face, sucked her teeth, then entered her office slamming the door closed behind her.

Jap

Since Tiff didn't have a customer, she sat down and watched the news, startled by what was being covered. Reporter Liz Sawyer was doing a remote broadcast live from The Knights Inn where a body was being rolled out of a room. A yellow sheet concealed the man's remains from the crowd, most of them the motel's guests, who stood around gawking. Liz went on to report that the victim had apparently been found by a motel employee.

"These Negros crazy out here," blurted a female client who had been watching the same news broadcast.

Tiff responded, "Things will get a lot worse before it gets better." Her blank expression turned into a smile. "At least that's what my grandma always told me," she chuckled.

In the privacy of her office, San had been giving those present a lecture about honesty. Tracks sat on her lap and like everyone else, was waiting for San to pass the powder. The only one that didn't toot cocaine was Milky whose preferences were weed and ecstacy.

When the powder was finally passed around, San noticed how Vanilla's eyes twinkled when he took a snort.

"Come over here, Vanilla. Come get your faggot ass a good snort." San patted Tracks ass. "Baby, get up," San demanded. Leaning forward, she poured about a gram of coke on her desk top. "Nah, sissy, no match book corner, stick ya nose in the pile," she commanded.

It didn't register until after Vanilla had inhaled half of the gram that this was his first time snorting in front of people other than San and Tracks.

"Shit, Grams, why you bullshittin'? Vanilla's been moving a big eighth of coke in weight every other day for me," San bragged, snorting the remnant of coke that Vanilla failed to consume. She continued, "Vanilla might be taking a Nigga's position in Major League. Would you like that, Vanilla?" she asked. Seeing Vanilla's nose bleeding as he nodded his head in agreement, she added, "It's a well—known fact that if a Nigga ain't capable of his must—have production ..." She paused, intently staring at everyone but Vanilla to drive her point home, "get rid of ya ass." Her ensuing giggle was nothing if not sinister.

"Gurl, I hear that," Vanilla offered his two cents worth of comment, repeatedly snapping his fingers and his hands formulated two circles. "That's why I got rid of POC 'cause that Nigga couldn't satisfy a bitch!" He was unable to suppress giggles of his own behind his clenched fist.

Their conjoined, unrestrained laughter could be heard out in the work area.

Tiff stared at Jacob's number that she had punched into her cell phone. She often reminisced silently about the last time that they had been out on a date. She wanted badly to remind Jacob how her last boyfriend had cheated on her and how much it had hurt. But she couldn't risk Jacob's using her past relationship as a tool to trick her into thinking he cared just to sleep with her. The fact that she felt that Jacob was a dopeboy was a serious negative.

Jap

It just wouldn't sit well with her family if it turned out to be true. Not only was her father, Eddie, totally against law breakers, she too could not afford to be caught up in any bullshit.

Tiff carefully scrutinized Vanilla's demeanor as he emerged from San's office. Behind his back, she rolled her eyes. "Fuck it," she decided, pressing SEND.

"Sup?" she heard him answer.

"Hey, Jacob." She wasn't sure how to respond to his unenthusiastic greeting. "Damn, it's like that, you sounding like you don't wanna talk? Am I getting on your nerves?"

"Nah, but damn, you act so stuck on ya self. A Nigga try to get a little closer into your space, you push me away

"It ain't———"

"Hold up, I'm talkin!" he made clear, cutting her off. "I like affection and you don't give a Nigga none. As I told you the first time that I met you, I ain't no rich Nigga but I'ma true down—to—earth Nigga."

"But I..

"I ain't finished ..." A brief pause. "You telling me that you're afraid of taking me around your family, like I'm ET or something a.." He was glad to hear her say in response that he was right.

"I'm right?" he responded, his gladness mixed with surprise.

"Jacob, I really do like you ... hold on .. ." Tiff walked outside, away from the hair dressers and clients who were intently hanging on to her every word.

Outside on the sidewalk, looking around at nothing in particular but confident she was out of earshot she continued, "Okay, I'm back. What you have to understand is that I've only dated college educated momma's boy type of church—goin' Niggas."

Hearing her giving a warmer explanation, Bealz took it as a sign. 'I got her ass now,' he thought to himself.

"Look, I do understand," Bealz offered.

"I just can't stand to be hurt or risk embarrassing the Talbert name."

"Hey, I won't be no embarrassment but at least you could open up to me some. These past coupla days and weeks have been real hectic for me. You 'member the girl that I brought to the shop? She got hurt bad and is fightin' for her life."

"Yeah, I know."

"How did you know?"

"I saw the whole thing on the news. They keep showing shots of your car sitting outside of some brick apartments. Damn ... what, you don't watch the news?"

"Hell no. I need to start, huh?"

She snickered a reply. "I guess so."

Tiff looked around when she heard the salon's door open and saw San and her crew exiting. She didn't bother to look at San but got out of her way as San headed for her Escalade, Tiff did, however, nod at Grams and couldn't help but notice the troubled look on his face.

Bealz spoke from the phone, "Tiff?"

"Yeah, I'm here. My phone lost reception for a second," she lied.

"How's about hooking up tonight?"

"Hooking up?"

"Girl, get ya head out of the gutter. Damn. I'm talkin''bout goin' out: for drinks or somethin'."

"That's fine, but I wanna take you to a place called 'Man—ife—Stations' pronounced manifestations," she cleared up. "You up for that?"

"Bet, what time?"

She checked the time on her watch. "It's six thirty—five — how's about meeting up at eight sharp?"

"That's fine, but I want you to ride with me this time. I rode with you last time."

Silence.

"Yo, Tiff, stop acting like I'm speaking Spanish."

"I hear you boy. Okay. But you still can't smoke around me."

"Why not?"

"Because my third shift job at the train station always conduct surprise drug tests and I can't afford to lose the job that pays me best."

"Shit, you ain't smokin'."

"Haven't you heard of second—hand smoke, Jacob?"

"Yeah, but you ain't put your first hand on the stuff," he joked, laughing at his own levity.

"Ha ha," she mimicked a laugh. "You better smoke before I get in yo' car. Meet me in the parking lot of the train station. I'll trust leaving my car there."

"Aight. See ya."

"Bye, oh hold! Please, no Air Jordans dress casual." Before he could reply, Tiff hung up. She stared out at the fast—moving traffic on North Tryon Street, then hurried inside to gather her things.

"Bitch, where you goin'?" Vanilla questioned, sliding over to Tiff's booth.

"Out with Jacob," she replied, ignoring the constant smacking of Vanilla's lips. "Not that it's any of your business."

"And you talkin' 'bout me! Jacob, or Bealz, whatever the hell his name is, ain't no my with San," he stated sarcastically, the long nail of his pinky against his bottom lip.

"Whatever," Tiff shot back, turning the palm of her hand in his face. She then walked off, throwing the sway of her succulent ass from left to right making a statement no one could argue with.

"Ewww, no she didn't! Hey. y'all, Tiff gonna get fucked tonight," Vanilla sing—songed, simulating someone getting fucked from behind. "Oh ooo shit," he moaned, drawing gales of laughter. "Damn, I done got myself hot," he added, fanning his hand in front of his face.

CHAPTER NINETEEN

After hearing what Tiff had told him, Bealz reconsidered his decision to drive the Navi taxi, he and Jake had been in serious talks ever since Karma's tragedy. Bealz had been staying at the Redroof Inn off Billy Graham which is within walking distance to both the Waffle Rouse and Prime's Steakhouse Restaurant which also serves an all—you—can—eat buffet. Aside from all the chaos, Bealz's and Banga's plan to deceive Shellz and Lil Gas was working like a charm. And on top of everything else, Bealz now couldn't get enough of Pudding's pudding. They were sexing everyday.

Bealz was looking over his clothes that hung neatly on the hotel room's rack. Of the garments he had brought with him, only two items were casual ready: the black Sean Jean dress slacks, a white shirt, the linen cream—colored Armani pants and a black short sleeve shirt. After selecting the Armani gear, he took out his pair of rare black wing—tipped Gators by Maury. Holding one of the shoes against his attire, he studied the mirror's reflection of the ensemble and smiled his approval.

After showering and getting dressed, he sprayed on Bulgari men's cologne. "It's a good thing I had Pudding braid my hair," he said silently as he turned his head from left to right in front of the mirror.

Before leaving the room, he contacted Banga who was busy selling Crack and Boy, and he checked up on Pudding, telling her that he'd see her later. From the hotel's dresser he collected the four blunts that he'd rolled earlier. Before walking out to meet the world, he checked his appearance once more in the largest of the two mirrors. "I'm good," he bragged before exiting the room, getting into his car and driving away.

*   *   *   *   *

When Lit Gas learned about LJ's demise at the Knights Inn, he was upset. He sat on Phil's porch wondering what the hell had gone wrong. Shellz picked up on Lil Gas's anger and advised him to go home until he cooled off.

Catching a ride with a crackhead, Lil Gas was consoled by his Lake— view brethren. Angry Niggas with itchy trigger fingers were crowded into LJ's mother's home while dozens of others assembled outside the house and even into the street. They wanted answers and Lil Gas wasn't talking, which they understood, considerate of how close he and LJ were and how personal his murder was to LiL Gas.

*   *   *   *   *

Shellz had Blueberry hit up the connect and order half a brick. He was about to move into his own apartment in what had been previously known as Dalton Village. He had saved up some money for furniture and other accessories that he'd need for the apartment. Since Phil had not been seen recently, Shellz had appointed himself in charge of the house only when Bealz wasn't present.

Meantime Tiff was standing by the Line A ticket counter talking to her girlfriend Amaresha when the sound of Bealz's car system interrupted their conversation. Tiff and her friend weren't the only ones who were stretching their eyes to see whose car was causing the uproar.

"Girl, let me go before my date gets me fired on my day off," Tiff said, hurriedly rushing outside.

Bealz put the Chevy's high beams on Tiff. To get a closer look, he quickly got out and waited with the passenger door open. He smiled, then bowed at her beauty.

Tiff was wearing a fitting black short sleeve Chanel dress that stopped at mid—thigh. Her toes dipped into a black pair of Christian Louboutin ankle boots. Her diamond earrings sparkled, matching her choker necklace and the Goody Glitzy Bobby Slides that held her bangs pinned back. The hazel eyelights mascara brought her eye color out to the forefront, accented perfectly by her peach—flavored lip gloss. On her wrist she wore a stylish black watch upon which the silver DKNY emblem was displayed prominently which complimented her black with gold DOONEY & Bourke croc—textured clutch. Bealz just stood there for a moment, his hungry eyes feasting on every morsel of her beauty, leaving him mesmerized.

"Damn, are you gonna let me get in the car, or what?" Tiff asked, awarding his admiration with a blank look.

"Oh. Oh, my bad," he replied, side—stepping to accommodate her entry.

He wasn't surprised when by the time he got back around to his side of the car and got in, the CD player's volume had been turned down.

"Oh, here — let me play something soft," he said, reaching into his CD case. "By the way, you look stunning and your perfume isn't too strong."

"Thanks for noticing," she replied, impressed as well with his outfit which she'd been discreetly checking out. She also approved of his music selection. "Teddy P, huh?" she addressed, smiling.

"Oh yeah ... Come on and go with me ... come on over to my place," he sang behind Teddy's soulful lyrics.

"Oh, you looking handsome in your get—up," she acknowledged. "Jacob, you better buckle up. You know how the police is with that seat belt shit."

"Man, fuck 'dem pigs."

She let out a short sigh. "Don't be so ghetto, and cut the music down a lil bit."

He grinned slyly but his attention had been captured by the vehicle behind him which he was trying to identify without being too obvious. But the sound system's base was so powerful that it was vibrating the rearview mirror, and making out any vehicle proved to be difficult.

Jap

"Which way?" he inquired as he cranked down even more the Sony CD's already lowered volume.

"Thank you. Now do you know where the Residence At Southpark is?" Seeing the dumfounded look on his face, she continued, "Hit I—77, get off on the Tyrola Road exit, head east until we hit Sharon Road, turn left by South Park a———"

"Hold up," he said interrupting her. "Why didn't you just say go to South Park? I'm from Charlotte, ain't never been outta Charlotte, so I know where everyth———"

"Okay," she giggled. "You made your point."

Surprisingly he felt her hand touch his knee. He cut his eyes at her.

"Watch the road before you kill us both," she protested seriously. "Now . . ." she started, but paused. "Where we are going, I hope to change your outlook on life."

"Damn, you make it sound like we're going to heaven ... or worse yet, HELL!" he roared.

"I swear you so silly," she chuckled, removing her hand. "Jacob, after our formal engagement ... I'll know if you're the right one for me," she said with certainty.

"Girl, if I didn't know any better, I'd sear you tryin' to marry a Nigga," he teased, playfully stroking her face beneath her chin. He smiled with silent confidence when she giggled instead of making him remove his hand.

* * * * * * *

Buccannon had just arrived back in Charlotte from her meeting in Atlanta with Detective Knolls, Mr. Good and his son Marvin Good. Even as she drove, she kept glancing at Shelton Davis's mug shot. The whole four hour drive back to Charlotte had been an anxious ride. She felt like her case against Mr. Davis had gotten stronger with Marvin's (Duck) testimony. Even though she knew that Duck was knowingly hiding the identity of the shooter who fired from Shellz's car. "Mr. Davis, with your smart ass," she said to herself, "All I got to do is submit my evidence to the DA and Grand Jury," she summarized.

* * * * * * * * * * *

Man—ife—stations' mirror—tinted glass structure was unbelievably constructed by the best designers in the South. The forty—two hundred square foot building with search lights stuck out like a sore thumb. Even the bigger South Park Mall struggled to compete with Man—ife—stations' business and countless visitors. Perhaps had it not been for the new North Lake Mall, South Park would reign supreme.

Pulling into Man—ife—stations' horse shoe shaped parking lot, Bealz was luckily able to slip into a parking spot near Man—ife—station's entrance. He felt funny parking his older model Chevy between a late— model Range Rover and a big boy Hummer, but he felt comfortable in his trend—setting attire that Karma had bought him and that he was wearing so well. Out of the car, he clutched Tiff's small hand and followed closely, maybe a step, behind. He was mindful of how other males were hugged up and affectionate with their lady friend.

Inside Man—ife—stations countless patrons cheered for a woman on stage with huge dreadlocks and wearing orange African garb. With the help of a live band set up behind her, she spoke as a slow melody began, "For those who don't know, my name is Empathy." Her head drifted slowly from left to right as she continued, "Love is powerful ..." She paused, allowing the man on the cello to let the instrument's strings say hello. "Most deep when its final hour — full — of excitement soft caresses — when he felt — he slowed — me up with his blessings — leaving my head resting — As the poet continued to speak, Bealz carefully studied his surroundings.

Twenty round tables were centered upon the establishment's black marbled floors. Candle—lit tables with soft padded benches encircled both sides of the glass door entries. Waitresses dressed in respectful skirted uniforms took turns serving drinks and passing out real roses. The bartender and owner catered to the patrons wishing to savor the finest exotic aperitif s available in Charlotte.

Bealz was jarred out of his daze by the awaiting sexy waitress. "Oh, yeah," he muttered. "Y'all got any Bulls or Private Stocks?" Bealz couldn't understand why the waitress and Tiff burst into a quiet laughter. "Wha's so funny," he inquired, wrinkling his eyebrows.

Tiff placed her hand on top of his. "Look, Jacob, this ain't the hood . . ." Addressing the waitress, "Excuse my friend; he's not used to this kind of environment. Let me have a Spanish cocktail and give him a Pineapple Red." Sliding the small round scented candle to the side, Tiff cooed, "I'ma teach you, Jacob."

"Alrighty then," the pecan brown—skinned waitress said, smiling. "I'll be right back with your drinks."

Tiff and Bealz turned their attention to the makeshift stage where more artists were taking turns with their spoken words. Bealz took note of the fact that the more Tiff drank, the more submissive her body language became. After six different speakers, the ban played some slow classical jazz music, setting the mood for the slow dancing that began on a large floor behind the stage. Bealz responded to the cue and asked Tiff for a dance.

On the dance floor, Tiff teased with seductive twirls into Bealz's open arms. He pulled her close, caressed her eyes with a lustful stare and tentatively kissed her lips to gauge her reaction. To his delight, he felt her kiss him back, he leaned in and kissed her lips again with the same results. On his third try, with raw passion his tongue searched inside her mouth for a mate. And just like that, the two tasted each other's alcohol flavored saliva. Their kiss became suggestive, both experiencing chills of excitement up their spines. When the kiss was over, she nuzzled her face into his chest and nurtured the throb of his heartbeat. For Bealz, his dick was as hard as stones, but in some strange way he felt that Tiff was Queen of his Ghetto Paradise. Their newly discovered affection for each other continued to build back at their table after their four consecutive dances.

* * * * * * * *

San was seated in the back of her Tahoe sending freaky text messages to BlueBerry and feeding her nose. Milky sat in the driver's seat, rotating a blunt with Grams. The three of them were waiting for the snake in San's organization to be brought up to the forefront. Suddenly they saw some headlights flicker in the distance of a winding trail in a remote part of Kings Mountain. Milky flashed the Tahoe's high beams to signal their whereabouts to the approaching car. Because of how deep they were in this heavily wasteland of forest, paths and fishing holes, all members of Major League knew that someone was in for a very bad day. Everybody exited the Tahoe.

"On my word, y'all clean this Nigga's clock," San instructed with venom in her voice.

"Gotcha," Milky and Grams replied simultaneously, checking again that their pistols were ready for action.

They watched silently as the driver of the other car approached, prodding ahead of him at gunpoint a big dude who was handcuffed and blindfolded. The captive man was pleading for his life. San walked up behind him and nodded at Pug, the silent assassin.

"Shut the fuck up, Nigga," Pug directed, holding a pistol bigger than he was at the much larger captive's head.

"Yeah, TG," San said, walking over to Grams. "I'll blow this Nigga away myself give me your pistol, Grams." Grams handed her his .41 Magnum handgun. She snapped it open, rolled the barrel checking the bullets, closed it back up and aimed it at TG's head. "Take his blindfold off." When Pug did so, TG's eyes became wide as saucers as he looked down the business end of a .41 Magnum's barrel. "You see this shit, TG. This is what happens when you fuck up Major League's rules and regulations."

Hearing the hammer of the powerful hand gun click back, Grams closed his eyes. Instead of the roar of the gunshot, he heard some footsteps shift. He reopened his eyes to behold the shocking sight of pistols brandished by Milky, Pug, and TG pointed at him. He took a step back, almost stumbling, and in a panic shouted, "San, what's the deal?"

San answered, "Nigga, I ain't gotta answer your ass. But since you about to go parlay with the devil I will say that you should've never went to try and cop dope from my connect behind my back." She repeatedly jammed her finger into his forehead.

"What? I ain't done shit! Whoever told you that is lying!"

"Where were you the other day around 4 p.m.?" she questioned. "Quick, Nigga, stop stalling," she admonished, half grinning, her eyebrows knitted.

"I tol' you I went and chilled wit' Momdukes 'cause my brother's baby mamma was over there tryin' to drop my—my nephew's off on her. And since my brother hadn't been home since he got out of jail.

CHAPTER TWENTY

After a bullet from the .41 Magnum permanently interrupted Gram's futile attempt at an explanation, a heavy silence descended upon the group. Since it was Pug's homie TG's first killing, San gave him the honor of beginning Gram's cremation process. After dousing Gram's body with gasoline, he lit a match to it and excitedly watched the body become engulfed in flames. While making their way back to the vehicle that Pug was driving, TG was so hyped up that checking for mistakes was only a distant thought.

Having safely crossed the rugged mountain terrain on their return to civilization, the vehicles driving in tandem finally entered the highway that lead to Charlotte. San called Pug's cell phone.

"'Sup, San?" he answered quickly.

"Good luck, lil' soldier." She paused as she heard a bragging in the bacground about Gram's execution. "Yo, Pug, talk to ya mans, tell him we don't work like dat. What's done is dead and stankin'."

She heard Pug's command away from the phone, "Man, would you shut the fuck up!"

"A'ight, be on stand—by," San said while Pug was still saying his piece. She listened intently to TG brag, still high from the overload of adrenalin amping his system, nicknaming himself T—

Dog like he was Lorenz Tate in Menace To Society. San shook her head and pressed the button disconnecting her call then texted BlueBerry, "Leaving my meeting — go ahead and tell ya boy I'll have that half joint ready."

SEND.

"I got chu', Baby," BlueBerry responded, relaying the message.

*   *   *   *   *   *

Tiff's intoxicated state made it hard for Bealz to chance letting her drive home at the end of their date. He drove at a reasonable speed through the City's streets, taking his time to see if Tiff's intoxication would wear down by the time he reached the train station where she parked her car. As he got within a few blocks, he looked over into her glassy eyes.

"Yo, Tiff... it's about twelve thirty. Let me drive you home." When she spoke, her words were still slurred. "H—Hom—me ... I'm spending the night with you," she made clear while caressing the side of his neck.

He knew that her reply was an ad—lib from the cocktails she had consumed. Nevertheless, he went ahead and took her with him, leaving her car at the train station. By the time he got to his room she was sound asleep. After he unlocked and opened the door to the room, he gently scooped her up, carried her inside and laid her on the bed. To provide for her comfort, he removed her pricey ankle boots then pulled the sheets around her body.

Checking his cell, he saw that he had six missed calls. He returned Banga's call who needed to know which hiding spot the Crack was in. After telling him the location, he rang off and called Pudding, the source of five of the missed calls. He turned the lights off before seeking a more private setting for this call.

"Hello," Pudding spoke in a sexy tone.

"You still up?" he whispered from the bathroom of his hotel room. In an erotic tone she retorted, "Yeah ... lyin' in bed naked, playing in my pussy ... listen."

Hearing the soaking wet sound of her pussy excited Bealz. He stared down at the gradual rise in his crotch area. He could hear her moaning with pleasure and as she put the phone back near her mouth, she let him hear her taste herself by sucking her fingers. That sent Bealz over the sexual edge.

"Leave the door unlocked," he said, peeling off his casual garb so he could change into something more his style.

"I'll be waiting," Pudding replied, hanging up.

When he opened the bathroom door, he was startled to see Tiff's smiling face. She had been listening on the other side of the door. He returned her smile, discreetly placing his hands over the medium—sized lump in his white silk Polo boxers. He could hear the radio on the TV playing at a low volume.

"Going somewhere?" she questioned, holding out both her arms.

"Look, you need to get some" she interrupted him with a barrage of intimate kisses and nibbles on the traps of his neck. As he cleared her feet from the floor, she secured her legs tightly around his waist. She panted, letting herself go to enjoy herself for the first time in nearly ten months. He layed her down, helped her out of her dress, then stared at her fist—sized breasts and hardened nipples.

When he reached for her hot pink thongs, to his dismay she crossed her legs and covered her exposed breasts. He took the pooled tears in her eyes as a sign STOP RAPE CHARGE AHEAD!

"I'm sorry, Jacob," she apologized, unable to stem the flow of tears down her cheeks.

"Oh, don't worry 'bout it," he replied, masking his frustration with a smile.

*　　*　　*　　*　　*　　*

BlueBerry could sense that something was bothering Shellz. She not only got his package at a reasonable price but she had the eighteen ounces on her person. Just as Shellz drove past JCSU campus, she finally took offense to his grumbling.

"Shellz, what's the fucking problem?" she asked, turning her body halfway to him.

"Who was that?" he replied, turning left, driving down into The View.

"Who? Vanilla?"

"No, the muh—fucka Vanilla got the package from in the Tahoe."

BlueBerry pondered his question. She had a decision to make and since she felt safe with Shellz, she answered, "A girl named San."

A mischievous grin covered his face which didn't fade as he drove into the minister's driveway and killed the STS North Star engine.

"Shellz."

"Huh?"

"What? You know her or something?" she asked, clutching his right wrist.

"Nab," he answered quickly. "But maybe you can arrange a meeting with us."

"Maybe ... but San is really territorial."

Both Shellz and BlueBerry were lost in thought, but thoughts that were totally diverse from each other. For BlueBerry, the fear of San's finding out that she had divulged her name to Shellz without permission could prove fatal. But on the flip side, Shellz clearly recalled San, blowing that weed smoke in his face. But he figured, why not align himself with San's get—money squad. Just the thought of surpassing Bealz in the dopegame excited Shellz.

72 Hours Later

Jamil was overjoyed to see his daughter's non-bandaged eye flutter open. He buzzed the nurse for immediate attention. Karma's wired mouth prevented her from speaking. She knew she was in a hospital, but for what she had no idea. After the doctor's examination it was determined that Karma had slight amnesia.

Jamil was upset when a police officer entered his daughter's room with a note pad "Man, my daughter isn't well," he complained angrily, blocking the officer from Karma's bedside.

"Mr. Robinson, I am only following proper procedure," the young slender white office explained.

Jamil got right up in the officer's face and whispered, "Look, forget procedures. I———"

"With all due respect," the officer shot back, disrupting Jamil's sentence. "If it wasn't for the lead officer in this case ..." he hesitated to assure that no one was close enough to hear. With his eyes locked on the doctor who stood over Karma, he continued, "... your daughter would be charged with the hand gun that had the scratched— off serial numbers."

A confused Jamil glanced over at the jumble of tubes attached to his daughter's body and realized it was in her best interest to allow the Law to prevail. With eyes that were starting to mist, he stepped aside.

"Thank you, sir," the officer uttered.

By God's grace, Karma's agonizing torture overshadowed the .357 that was recovered from beneath the pillow of the sofa. Luckily ballistics showed that the hand gun hadn't been used in a crime. All officers who knew about the weapon sided with officer Kirk's decision to destroy the weapon thereby eliminating the possibility of any charges that Karma could have faced when she recovered. Truth be known, however, the police were more concerned with boyfriend, Bealz, than they were with her. The second chapter of Bealz's dealing had been opened, the first being when the cops had him and Karma hemmed up.

1 P.M.

A light drizzle was coating the City streets. Bealz stood outside holding an umbrella which shielded his head from the rain. He listened to Jake's instructions on how to conduct himself when picking up customers. Bealz looked at the rain bead up on the Navigator's eighty percent tinted windows. Smoke from Jake's Cuban cigar escaped through a tiny hole in his clear plastic umbrella. He handed Bealz the keys to the SUV.

"Look, son — this is a lucrative position you are getting. Just look around you," Jake said, puffing on the cigar.

In Bealz's eyes, the other eight cab drivers present not only were racing to steal calls from each other, they also drove standard domestic cabs. "I'm wit' you, Jake. I'ma do my best," he assured while entering the SUV.

Jake stood by the driver's window and was glad that the Lincoln fired up on Bealz second crank. "Now, this baby hasn't been driven in months."

"Where's the meter?" Bealz questioned, almost frantically searching all possible places in the front interior.

"Meter?" Jake laughed. "Son, ain't no meter. Only high level passengers are driven around in this baby," he assured, patting the Lincoln's roof.

"Is that right ..

"Damn, Skippy .. .," Jake again instructed. "Now remember ... you got to open the doors, load and unload any bags or luggage, be polite, don't ask for a tip. Let them award you with one. And most importantly, don't ask any questions." Jake puffed his cigar, blowing a smoke—ring out of his mouth, continuing, "These people who you'll be picking up always tell me what the driver does. That's why Big Ship isn't working for Destinations."

Bealz reached for his buzzing cell phone. It was an unexpected and unlikely text that read:

"SUP, STRANGER I'M READY TO GET THE FUCK OUTTA HERE! COME GET ME. LOVE, KARMA"

"Oh, shit, Jake. I gotta rolll" Bealz blurted happily.

Jake backed up. "Okay, cal————" Sake got ready to say before the Navi sped off. He had to turn away from the gravel the SIN kicked back at him. Driving erratically through the City streets, Bealz tried desperated to reach Karma's cell phone until he reached the hospital 'It After parking, he raced inside, making sure of Karma's room number then ran up five flights of stairs, too impatient to wait for the slow elevator. When he found her room, he stopped, caught his breath, opened the door, and entered. Immediately he noted that there was no way for her to use a telephone.

"Damn, Karma," he said, tearfully staring into her battered face. "Who did this?" he cried, unable to continue his stare into her face, but instead laying his head on her chest.

Tears flowed from her eye and rolled off the right side of her face. Both wept silently. For him to hear her try to mumble words through her sealed mouth was too much for him to bear. He reached up and stroked the soft texture of the hair on her head.

The nurse who Karma had text him quietly entered. "Bealz, Karma wants to leave but I told her it wouldn't be a wise choice," the fairly attractive older black nurse said, smiling.

Bealz wiped his face then turned to face the nurse. "Well, when can she leave?"

"We've told Sharelle that it's gonna be at least another week." The nurse paused while Bealz consoled Karma's struggle and repeated, "Shhhh," to her mumbling. The nurse adored watching him plant soft kisses over her bandages and forehead, and finally turned and left them alone when she too teary—eyed to watch over them any longer.

Minutes later, after pretty much telling Karma how it was going to have to be, she calmed down. When the drugs she'd been administered once again kicked in, she dozed off to sleep. In a chair at her bedside, Bealz also slept.

Friday Morning

In the preceding days, Sharon Buccannon had obtained a warrant for Shelton Davis. Accompanied by a special police unit called SDI, Sharon drove behind a blue van filled with officers of the Drug Interdiction Task Force as they descended upon The View and Phil's house.

Phil's neighbors, some of which were either a part of The Alliance or were on Shellz's payroll, gawked at the cops' every move.

Sharon stood on Phil's porch, frustrated that neither Shellz nor his car were in her clutches. When she looked up from the manila envelope that contained only a short crack pipe and some Brillo, she squinted at the writing on the pillar of the porch that read, THE ALLIANCE. She already knew that Phillip Stokes's house was the dope spot and warrants would be issued for the paraphernalia. But her real objective was no longer just charging Shelton Davis with lying and obstruction of justice about the street shooting, she now intended to build a conspiracy charge against him and the so—called Alliance he ran.

CHAPTER TWENTY-ONE

Moments later, as Sharon and her fifteen colleagues were about to drive off, she thought she recognized someone of interest amongst the crowd of onlookers. She immediately broadcast an alert over her radio and the officers immediately exited the van and quickly contained the crowd to prevent anymore from running off and evading Sharon's scrutiny.

In spite of the vehement racial slurs directed at the officers from The Views' neighbors, Sharon felt confident as she exited her car and made her way through the throng of restless people, her attention focused only on one young man in the crowd. When her practiced quick and professional assessment of the subject determined that the bulge beneath his dark tee shirt might be a weapon, she drew her service pistol and without hesitation gruffly ordered him to the ground. Ten of the SDI team restrained the crowd who were angrily protesting the not—so—delicate handling of their young cohort.

One of the officers retrieved the 9mm Ruger from the young man's waistband. As he went about the business of handcuffing and searching the belligerent young man, Sharon holstered her own weapon and quickly pulled out a pair of latex gloves and slipped them over her hands. She kneeled and carefully picked up the discarded weapon. The serial number had been filed off.

"What a surprise .." she said out-loud a voice laced with sarcasm. She turned to the officer who had searched him. "I-D?"

"Nada," the officer replied shaking his head. "No wallet, just your friendly neighborhood weapon and a lot of attitude."

The subject was struggling violently against his restraints from his prone position on the ground, obviously putting on a show for the unruly crowd whose agitation was increasing. Turning to the incensed captive she uttered, "Okay, Player ... let's get acquainted. What's your name?"

When the only response she got was a pair of dark evil eyes glaring up at her, she shrugged. "Okay, tough guy, we'll do this your way." To the officers, "Give me a hand here with this creep."

Two officers manhandle the struggling young man to his feet. "Hey, wait a minute," he shouts. "You can't ... I din' do nuttin' ... hey, hey get your cracker hands off me ... HEY!"

Sharon gets into his face, "You guys will never learn, will you. It's not nice to be rude to Mother Cop Now stop being such a cry—baby before you get yourself and some your friends hurt." To the officers, "Get him to my car," pointing the way.

She turned her attention to the crowd still having to be kept in check by a dozen of her fellow officers, mindful of the hateful stares and racial slurs thrust at her by some of the more aggressive onlookers. In spite of the crowd's increased hostility, Sharon remained stoic behind her half— smile as she followed the officers and their captive in the direction of her car. She had learned early in her career never let them see you sweat.

Jap

Sometimes that was a challenge in itself. This was one of those times.

The disgruntled youngster was strapped down by the seat belts in the back seat of her official but unmarked sedan. Because she rode alone, her car was not outfitted with the protector glass between the front and back seats since she seldom transported prisoners. She had two of the officers ride with her, one in back with the disgruntled youngster, the other officer in front who immediately started the paperwork on the arrest.

She started the car and sat there waiting for the officers who were doing crowd—control to return to their van and prepare to follow her. She looked in the rear view mirror at the shackled subject. "Hey, they've read you your rights, haven't they?" Receiving the silent treatment from him, "Okay, play hardball ..."

"He was Mirandized while we were dragging him over here," the officer riding shotgun offered without looking up from his paperwork.

Sharon nodded, saw that the van was in position behind her and she eased the sedan forward. Glancing again in the rear view mirror at their captive, she started in with the oldest trick in the book. "It doesn't matter. Shelton already told me that you were the one who fired the shots from his STS," she blatantly lied. She caught his look in the mirror that confirmed she'd hit paydirt. "Brewster, save yourself," she suggested as she expertly navigated through traffic.

Like a true soldier from the streets, besides the steady utterances of vulgar epithets, Brewster Littles, AKA Banga, kept his mouth closed.

*   *   *   *   *   *

Bealz had been spending a lot of time at the hospital ever since Karma's condition had improved. He'd been having a ball driving the Navigator and meeting very interesting people. Behind Jake's back the Navi was being used as a heroin distribution center on wheels. His relationship with Pudding was going exceedingly well and their spontancity never failed to escalate into sexual escapades. That's not to say that his relationship with Tiff didn't have sparks flying as well; it's just that the sparks weren't sexual in nature, but glowed on a more mutually respectful level.

Bealz sat in Karma's room with her mother, Alicia, and Jamil, staring out the huge window at the cars below. Occasionally he snickered politely at Jamil's old corny jokes. He felt his cell phone buzz; the Caller ID read: MINISTER. Bealz excused himself and stepped out of the room.

"Yo, Minister. What's up?"

"The police ran up in Phil's empty house."

Bealz sighed, "Shit. That's good no one was in there."

"Yeah well, before they left they snatched up Banga."

"WHAT?"

"Yeah, they got a pistol off him."

"Okay, thanks. Let me make a couple of calls." Click.

He rushed back into Karma's room, kissed her forehead and whispered, "I'ma see you tomorrow." he nodded at Alicia but ignored Jamil's extended hand as he rushed out of the room.

Cranking up the engine in the Navi, he punched a number which had been pre—programmed into his cell phone.

"Reasonable Bonding," a voice on the phone said.

"Yo Chuck, Bealz — I'ma need for you to go bond my man out of jail." A rocker—looking white bondsman sitting behind a cluttered desk searched for a pencil amongst the litter while asking into the phone, "What's his name and what's the charge?" Jotting notes while listening, he finally repeated what Bealz had said. "Brewster Littles ... and CCW. I got you."

In the Navi, Bealz responded, "A'ight, call me when you get him so I can meet ya'll somewhere."

"Got you, buddy."

Click.

Bealz drove up Kings Drive thinking that if it wasn't one thing, it was another. As always he called Jake who told him that's how life goes, saying also that someone would be needed to be picked up from Douglass International Airport at 3 p.m. meanwhile the Minister briefed Shellz on the situation concerning The View and Banga. Shellz acted like he didn't care since he was at his new apartment in Dalton Village. He had laid out the apartment on an almost spare—no— expense basis. He dubbed the two bedroom, one—and—a—half bath apartment, 'The Pleasure Pad.'

"Blue, how much in the safe?" Shellz yelled, as he sat naked in his black leather recliner, smoking a blunt of kush mixed with Purp while enjoying the sound of the Isley CD playing low on his customized entertainment system. Blue emerged naked from his bedroom, her juicy ass swaying from wall to opposite wall. Her slow strut had her titties simulating her stripper bounce on stage. Shellz had spent considerable cash on her nails, hairdo, and other accessories so she took serious being called his Bottom Bitch.

"I think, not counting the Bird that you gonna cop from San ... it's eighty five hundred in the safe," she said grinning, taking a drag from the blunt that he held between her lips. She didn't release the smoke as she guided her hand down the base of his shaft. "Ahhh shit," he whined, locking into her heated lustful state. His toes curled from feeling her soft bites, her saliva drooling down his stiff dick and coating his balls.

"Shit, I'm a bust ... Ahh," he cautioned as her slurping and experienced tongue—swirl around the head of his dick brought him to the edge. "A——·-— I—I'ma cummin'," he cried, pumping his load into her mouth.

After swallowing his unborn seeds, she licked the excess cum from around her mouth. "Go call San," he demanded with erratic breathing. He looked down at his dick and saw it spew a bit more. "Ày Blue, you left some," he told her, pointing at his medium hard erection.

After she handled business, they went and showered together, then got dressed. This was the day he was going to be formally introduced to San for the first time. He remembered how

Jap

San was dressed the time he and Bealz had the small misunderstanding with her over the parking space. Conscious of the impression he wanted to make on her, he chose some cream Polo shorts to slip into, a money green Polo shirt, and a pair of money green string up Polo slides with no socks. He had Blue attach to his wrists a wide David Yarmin bracelet and Cartier watch with the black face, He sprayed on Sean Jean cologne and topped it off with his gold Gucci frames that accented perfectly his fresh haircut.

"How I look, baby," he asked. "Wait." He placed a blunt in his mouth.

"Blue snickered, "Sexy, baby ... how 'bout me?"

He slapped her ass and enjoyed how her ass seemed like it wasn't ever going to stop shaking. "You wearing Baby Phat ... all that Phat Baby," he teased.

"I swear you so silly."

3:47 P.M.

Bealz had finished unloading the Spanish couple with their luggage that he'd picked up at the aiport. He accepted a fifty dollar tip, thanked them and climbed into the Navi, mission completed. A parking attendant at the uptown Marriott told him to move the SUV. He checked the time on his watch and dialed a number on his phone.

"Reasonable Bonding. Chuck speaking."

"Yo — what's the deal?"

"Who's this?"

"Bealz. Damn, Chuck — what's the hold up?"

"Hold your horses. I'm downstairs waiting on him. Evidently your boy had been in the interrogation room. His bond showed up in the computer an hour ago."

"I see. Well, call me asap? when you get him."

"Gotcha, dawg."

4:53 P.M.

Blue was slowly cruising Applebee's parking lot in the STS looking for San's SUV. Since neither she nor Shellz spotted it, they assumed San was running late. Without warning a black unmarked car pulled in front of them, throwing a brief scare into them. Shellz was prepared to jump and run but hesitated when the dark tinted passenger side window eased down revealing San's sixty thousand dollar smile. Shellz let out a deep sigh. Blue's laugh caused Shellz a flash of anger. "What?" he said. "I knew it was her. You didn't know it was her? I knew it was her."

San motioned for him to approach and directed him into the back seat of the four—door Crown Vic. "I scared your ass, didn't I," San joked, motioning for Milky to drive off.

"Nah," Shellz lied, gazing over at the sissy—looking dude beside him. San pointed, "This is my boy, Milky and beside you is my boy/girl Vanilla."

"Huh uh, girl — you know Vanilla is da shit," Vanilla responded reaching up lightly and tapping the back of San's shoulder.

"Okay, den," Shellz said, nodding at Vanilla but laughing inside at the pink woman's capris Vanilla was wearing.

"So, how'd you meet Porsche?"

Looking confused, Shellz replied, "Who?"

"BlueBerry! Damn you, fucking her and don't know her first name."

"Nah, I thought you asked did I have a Porsche," he replied trying to hide how foolish he felt, especially considering how right San was.

San opened up her snort bag. "You get right?" she asked, holding out the bag.

"Nah." He caught Vanilla's lustful stare at the powder, and explained, "Only weed."

"I feel ya, Bra," Milky blurted, driving into a carwash stall. San cocked her Coogi cap to the side and passed Vanilla the snort bag. She then proceeded to dab at her drooling nose. "Impress me, Shellz, what's most important to you?"

He pondered her question. "Shit, keeping it one hundred and money."

"I like 'dis Nigga," San announced proudly. "Look, I get 'dis shit like water. Vanilla took the spot that my boy Grams had but nobody's seen him in a minute. So Vanilla will be meeting you."

"Betta say it," Vanilla cut in, poking out his twisted mouth. "You got twenty two five ... Nah, fuck it, give me twenty one five." Shellz sent the Taco Bell bag over the front seat to San.

"I ain't gonna count it because Blue never brought any short money that came from you. Bold up ... it look like I've seen you before."

Shellz became nervous, he thought. "Nah, I can't recall seeing you before," he responded, swallowing his spit.

"Well, Sugar, do you like Vanilla?"

Shellz pushed Vanilla's hand off his leg. "No thanks, Playboy."

"Hand him the shit," San commanded Vanilla.

Shellz did not approve of Vanilla's removing two half bricks of powder from the black strap beneath his shirt. He looked at the black ML letters on each of the green plastic that secured the Cocaine.

"ML — what's that?" Shellz inquired, turning each package over. Proudly San replied, "Major League, baby!" She grinned slyly. Shellz had unknowingly aligned himself with a dangerous clique and an investigation that could ultimately earn him a one— way ticket to a federal prison where poor little Vanilla would most certainly become some dude's bitch. San stayed so coked— up that if she saw her father who'd abandoned her after finding out that she was part dyke, she wouldn't recognize him.

6:18 P.M.

Bealz was glad to see Banga finally walking with Chuck. It had been decided that their meeting place was an ice cream parlor on Central Avenue. He paid Chuck and bought him a triple—decker cone before he and Banga went in a separate direction from Chuck.

"Sup? The pistol wasn't stolen, was it?"

"Nah, it was concealed, plus I ain't old enough to have a hand gun. But shit, man, that police bitch Sharon Buccannon talking 'bout Shellz running his mouth, ya dig?" he said, his eyes filled with venom.

"Running his mouth about what?"

Banga didn't say 'Alliance rules' like he was thinking, but instead said, "Shit, I don't know, but she did mention something to the effect of Shellz running his crew called The Alliance."

Bealz almost ran the Navi into a curb when Banga made that last comment. Banga didn't understand Bealz's sly grin.

"Shit, Bealz, I'ma wear mines, what you need to let me do is kill Shellz before I go to court," he suggested with vile in his tone of voice.

Stopped at a red light, Bealz was given the opportunity to look around to appreciate the city's beautiful scenery. Feeling that he wouldn't have any more people to pick up, he torched a blunt with Banga. Their destination was Karma's hospital room, where the next phase of The Alliance was to be formed.

CHAPTER TWENTY-TWO

"Mr. Ice Cream Man — Mr. Ice Cream maaaan — Mister Shellz is the Ice Cream Maaan," Shellz sang along with Master P's classic playing on the house system. He was back at home, standing over the stove turning thirty— six ounces of pure cocaine into forty—four. The kitchen countertop was covered with Arm & Hammer baking soda. A few of the baking soda boxes were laying on the floor empty.

BlueBerry had gotten comfortable. The wifebeater she wore couldn't contain her braless titties. Her black boy booty shorts surprisingly failed to get any attention from Shellz, so she began her cleaning when she received a mysterious text message which she stopped to reply to in secret.

"I'ma cop me a Bird and a half next re—up," Shellz emphasized, grinning greedily.

"That's good, Baby," she shot back with a phony smile.

Knock—knock!

Shellz looked out towards the front door. He killed the power to his house system before walking over and cautiously spying through the door's peep hole.

"Oh shit," he said, releasing a deep sigh.

He opened the door for Lil Gas who still had on the suit he had worn to LJ's funeral. Shellz bumped fists with him, then started back to the kitchen. Without a word being uttered, Lil Gas pulled out his concealed pistol and without warning clubbed Shellz over the head with it. Shellz fell into the kitchen, his head striking the edge of the stove on his way to the floor, knocking him unconscious. Lil Gas then turned his attention to Blue who was screamining hysterically.

"Bitch, shut the fuck up!" he demanded, striking her with the back of his hand.

"Okay, please just don't kill me," she pleaded, holding her hands defensively from her downed position.

Lil Gas calmly began to load the dried cookies of cocaine into a two— handled plastic Harris Teeter bag. He saw that Shellz was coming around so he walked over and stomped his head twice, rendering him back to unconsciousness. Blood from Shellz's head wounds was spreading over the waxed kitchen floor.

"You tell that Nigga Shellz this is for my man L.J. ," he said, double bagging forty—one of the cookies that Shellz had cooked. He stood over Shellz, heaved up as much hawk as he could muster, leaned over and spat in Shellz's face. He aimed the pistol at Blue. "Bitch, I know what strip joint you work at." He smiled knowingly, then quickly left.

Blue crawled over to Shellz, sickened at the sight of the blood leaking from the back of his head. She shook his upper body, "Please, Baby! Wake up!" Shellz could hear her desperate cries but found it difficult to respond. His body was cooperating. "I'ma call 9—1—1," she screamed frantically, trembling as she tried to dial the number.

"Not good!" his mind was registering but he was trying to find where he'd left his voice. Finally he was able to mumble, "No—no!" He struggled to regain his faculties. She stopped her efforts to dial.

"Baby, you need an ambulance."

"No!" he managed to emphasize groggily. "Just help me up." She did her best to help him stand upright, but he was trying to function on legs that felt like spaghetti that he couldn't get to cooperate with his efforts to even balance himself. Helping to stay on his feet Blue said to him, "Look at you, Baby I told you not to call Lil Gas. Are you all right?"

He placed his hand over the huge bump that rose on the back of his head. Blood trickled from a small wound on his forehead but other than that he thought he was okay. Blue went to the refrigerator, trying her best not to take her eyes off Shellz as she removed a tray of ice cubes from the freezer. She grabbed a plastic bag and filled it with ice cubes and applied the pack to his head wound.

"I'ma gonna kill that Nigga," he pledged, still bleeding profusely from the wound on the back of his head. "Go get my cell phone," he ordered, roughly pushing her hands away. "Muh—fucka!" he cursed loudly.

The subsequent talk with Bealz left Shellz with feelings of betrayal when the conversation didn't go in the direction he had expected. Only a conversation with San made him feel better. His impulse to go search for Lil Gas was nipped in the bud when he went outside and found that the tires on his Caddy had been flattened. He started acting like a fool which attracted a small crowd of nosey neighbors. Blue couldn't stand the embarrassment caused by his loud and obnoxious rants of vulgarity, so she retreated back to the apartment, figuring she'd do the only rational thing at the moment, call a cab for Shellz then have Hunter from Hunter's Garage come get Shellz's car.

"9—1—1. How may I direct your call?" the dispatcher answered in a composed tone.

The caller replied nervously, "Please send the police out here to calm this boy down."

"Ma'am, is he armed or threatening you in any kind of way?"

"No! But he's scaring my kids and the neighbors."

"All right ... and this is in the new Dalton Village Apartments? What is his apartment number?"

"C ... Apartment C. Please hurry. I can hear him right outside my apartment, justa rantin' and ravin' Ima 'f raid he's going to hurt someone."

"Okay, Ma'am, units are on their way.

"All right. Thank you."

"Okay, ma'am."

* * * * * * * * *

"That's wha' that sucka gets," Banga said, pushing the 'recline' button on the beige leather passenger seat of Bealz's Navi.

"Yeah" ... Bealz acknowledged. "See, Shellz loves the spot light. He loves to splurge on strippers and a bunch of bullshit." As

Bealz drove carefully out of the hospital's parking lot, he continued. "That's part of what that meeting was about."

The Alliance had been conducting a planning session in Karma's hospital room until her father, mother, and pastor showed up which brought the meeting to an abrupt close. Before leaving Karma's bedside, however, Bealz talked her into going to her parent's house, but only until she recovered. Through her bandages, Karma was able to mumble and drool her protests, but her eyes finally signaled her resignation when they recognized the sincerity in Bealz's eyes, a look which she could never resist. 'What was most shocking was when Jamil thanked Bealz and shook his hand.

Outside, as they approached the vehicles in the parking lot, Bealz offered something to Banga. "What's dis," Banga asked, looking confused. "Keys to the van ... can't you drive?"

"Hell yeah!" he answered proudly, grinning gladly. "Got license?"

"Hell no," his voice lowered into shame.

"Here, take the keys. Just don't ride dirty."

"Shit, man. I ain't going nowhere wit'out a headbuster," he exclaimed.

"Look, you my lil Nigga; it's only you and I now." Bealz extended his arm until his hand rested over the center console arm rest. Banga immediately accepted his firm handshake. "Fuck da bullshit, let's get money ... you wit' me?" Bealz asked.

The traffic light had turned green but they ignored the repeated blares of car horns as they gave honor to this magic moment. "I'm wit ya, Dawg," Banga replied, briefly sharing a dedicated stare with Bealz.

"Loyalty reigns, my Nigga. Loyalty reigns," Bealz repeated.

* * * * * * * *

The sounds of police hammering on the front door of Shellz's apartment brought out the neighbors. Men in blue had congregated around his apartment, paying particular attention to Shellz's Cadillac. When they ran the plate on the STS, the name Shelton Davis was found to be registered as the second leinholder on the car's title.

To add to the gravity of the situation, Detective Sharon Buccannon was on the scene awaiting a search warrant to be signed by a judge, a warrant that would allow a thorough search of Apartment C, regardless of the fact that neither Shellz nor Blue were home. A heavy battering ram already stood at attention on the front porch, ready to do its duty as nearly two dozen officers stood by, ready to enter. Sharon kept checking her watch. She was getting impatient.

Meanwhile, a furious Shellz was a passenger in a Purple Cab Nations as they roamed Lakeview. He'd already dropped BlueBerry at her stripper friend's apartment in the Grier Heights neighborhood. He and the African cab driver were now on a serious hunt, combing every Street in Lil Gas's hood repeatedly.

Suddenly adrenalin shot through Shellz's veins as he shouted at the driver, "Stop! Turn around! I think I spotted who I was looking for!" He peered over his left shoulder out into a dark street by a yellow home.

Without warning: TIC! TIC! TIC—TIC! TIC! BOOM! BOOM!

"Oh shit! Shellz screamed.

"Oh sheeet!" the cab driver yelled in his deep African tone. They both ducked as a hail of bullets shattered the windows of the cab without looking, the driver jammed the gas pedal all the way to the floorboard; the engine screamed, the tires burned rubber. The car reached the corner and it fish—tailed into a parked car and overturned, ejecting the driver. His neck snapped and he was killed instantly.

Dazed, Shellz lifted himself up enough to look through the broken out window on the driver's side and saw several guys running in the direction of the wrecked cab. Acting quickly, he made sure the foe—fifth was ready to fire then braced himself against the steering wheel, raised his arm through the window and fired. BOOM! BOOM! BOOM! BOOM! His hand snapped back with each shot. The smell of gunpowder permeated the atmosphere.

POW! BOOMI BOOM! POW! TIC! TIC! Shellz kept his head ducked as a barrage of shots from the approaching assailants interrupted his offense.

The sounds of police cars suddenly lent their wails to the cacophony of the sounds of violence and death that echoed through the mean streets.

"I got to get the fuck outta here," Shellz said to himself from a huddled position. Attempting to rise, "Ow," he uttered, suddenly feeling a burning sensation in his left hip and left forearm.

Hearing the approaching sirens getting closer, he managed to use the cab's steering wheel as leverage to struggle out of the overturned cab and onto the ground, keeping the body of the cab between him and his assailants. Ignoring his wounds, he ran as fast as he could through the dark neighborhood until he emerged behind a convenience store on Highway Sixteen that sat across from the Honest Rest Inn Motel. Out of breath he paused beside a phone booth, doing his best to hide his bloody injuries from customers going in and out of the store.

Inspecting himself, he realized he'd been grazed by one bullet but another had passed through his hip and he was sure it was lodged in the bone. With his adrenalin subsiding, the excruciating pain was becoming unbearable. Because of the store's bright exterior lights that illuminated the entire area, it was becoming almost impossible to hide the blood oozing from wounds to hands, face and neck caused by flying glass, as well as the gunshot wounds. When he spit it was a mass of bloody phlegm.

"Hey, buddy!" a pot—bellied cigar—smoking white man asked. "You all right?"

"I'm good."

"You sure? I s————"

"Mind your fuckin' business," Shellz shouted, cutting the stranger off.

Shellz realized he was attracting other unwanted stares of curiosity from other customers. He could do little but return their looks with a gaze of pure hatred. Wiping blood from his eyes, he noticed the convenience store's phone being grabbed behind the protective glass.

Shellz took that as a sign to move on and turned to stare across the busy Highway Sixteen, remembering that his partner Brice lived in Creektown, a quiet unpretentious neighborhood that was nearby. All he had to do was get across the highway without being hit by an inattentive motorist.

"SSSSS———" he hissed at ear horns that blared at him as he hobbled his way painfully across the highway.

Stumbling, dazed by the pain, he managed to make his way down the dark steep hill into the Creektown neighborhood. Out of breath, he just barely managed to locate and crawl onto the porch of Brice's small brick home before succumbing to the numb stage of his gunshot wounds which overtook him and he descended into the blackness of unconsciousness.

Around the corner from where Shellz had dropped BlueBerry off, inside Apartment C off Alpha Street, the picture was approaching completion. BlueBerry sat on the arm of the cheaply upholstered couch. Aylah's song 'One In A Million' set the mood as it played from a portable CD player. Other pieces of the plan revealed themselves, adorning the top of an old coffee table, pieces that included eighty—five hundred dollars in cash, Shellz's jewelry and pricey charm, and forty—one ounces of crack.

"You done good, Baby," Lil Gas applauded, turning back and kissing BlueBerry.

"Sure did, girl — you a sneaky ass bitch," Coneka AKA Moberry told her fellow stripper. "Didn't she, Baby," she added, hugging the other mastermind from behind.

Taking a break from counting the money, "Yeah, we all did good," Coley added, gazing across the table at Lil Gas. "This is for L. J., right Gas?"

Lil Gas raised his head, kissed two fingers, pointed at the heavens and responded sincerely, "Yeah, L.J. I hope you ain't mad at us but like B.I.G. said, 'You're Nobody 'Til Somebody Kills You." he nodded his head sadistically.

All four demonic thinkers sang along, "You're Nobody 'Til Somebody Kills You."

"I don't wanna die," Coneka ended, making everyone laugh.

"We need to get that Nigga Bealz, but he's much slicker than Shellz," Coley said, pocketing his share of the money.

Ring—ring.

"Sup, Kato?" Lil Gas spoke, cutting his cell phone off in midring.

"Yo, man, we had to bust at this cab that kept rollin' through. A———"

"What! Is everybody a'ight?"

"Yeah, but the cab driver is dead. The passenger was looking for you."

"What? Why y'all bust on him?"

"Man, that bug—eyed, black ass Nigga tried to pay crackhead Nelson to show him where your mom stayed. I think he got a hot one in his ass. But da Nigga got away ..."

Lil Gas listened intently to Kate's account of the chaos surrounding the shoot—out, every detail, even up to and including the point when the cops covered the cab driver's body with the yellow sheet. Once the call ended, Lil Gas threw his cell phone across the room. He was upset that Shellz had come through his hood. The last thing on Lil Gas's mind was the deceased cab driver.

"Wha's wrong, Baby?" BlueBerry asked Lil Gas, her down— low sexual partner of the past thirteen months.

Lil Gas leaned back with his eyes closed, his right leg nervously twitching at a fast pace. Repeatedly folding and licking his lips amongst his cohort's chatter, Lil Gas stayed in deep thought.

CHAPTER TWENTY-THREE

Early Morning

The View was hot; a squad car routinely made a round every hour. Phil had a warrant out for his arrest for the drug paraphernalia that the cops found in his residence.

Shellz, shot by a .22 revolver, refused to go the hospital. Brice's baby—mama had cleaned out his wounds with Peroxide. What Shellz had believed was a bullet stuck in his bone was merely a piece of glass that had lodged into his hip.

Shellz was not aware that he had a warrant out for his arrest as well. In addition to the charges of Obstruction of Justice and Possession of a Firearm by A Felon, he also landed a new dope charge after further search of his apartment uncovered three ounces of powder and scales.

While Shellz laid up in Brice's house, recovering from his wounds, not only did the police turn his apartment into a scene of strewn clothes and overturned furniture, the police also had the STS towed, confident that Shellz would go all out to locate and recover his vehicle.

A good thing for The Alliance were the people Banga knew around Cox Avenue. Karma laid in her hospital bed watching 'The Price is Right," when two office is abruptly barged in, holding up their shields. Karma released a deep sigh before rolling to her other side, rolling her eyes at the female and slender male officer.

"Ms. Robinson, we're sorry to disturb you, but we need to show you three pictures."

Karma opened her eyes and cued in on the mugshot that the female in the pantsuit held out to her. Karma shook her head no, but the second picture made her eyes protrude. Even though Karma's head shook no, the female officer saw the protecting factor in Karma's eyes.

"Well, Ms. Robinson, we wanted to let you know that the first picture is a man named Fred Wilbur. Mr. Wilbur was apprehended two days ago driving a stolen Ford F—150, the same make and model that a guy named Trops, or Trips, described as the vehicle he saw exiting the parking lot of the apartment where your attack occurred. Mr. Wilbur gave investigators an excellent description of the person who gave him the truck. Further investigation has led us to believe Lawrence Jackson had help from this man..." Buccannon held up another mugshot but didn't disclose his name. "Jackson met a horrible death in a room at the Knights Inn Motel."

Seeing the pain on Karma's face, the officer turned away. Looking at her male partner she said, "Let's go." Then to Karma she added, "I'm leaving you my card ... call me," then left the room, her partner following close behind her.

Hearing the door close, Karma turned over and seized the card from the patient's table by her bed. She read the officer's name, SHARON BUCCANNON. She ripped the card to shreds and dropped the pieces into the trash can. She licked her gums where her teeth used to be, and felt the edges of metal that held her mouth together. She reached up and patted the bandage that covered her eye.

'I'ma kill me a Nigga when I heal,' she thought to herself.

*   *   *   *   *   *   *

11:30 a.m.

Bealz had just finished sexing Pudding in his hotel shower. He now enjoyed the feel of her soft hands applying lotion to his chest and back.

"Why did you cover yourself in all these tattoos," she asked.

His eyes followed her hands down his chest, past his navel, until they reached his manhood inside of his Polo boxers. "You havin' fun?" he asked, staring directly into her soft morning eyes. She licked her lips enticingly, turned her back to him and using her muscles she made her asscheeks jiggle. He slapped her naked ass.

"Ewww," she purred, looking back at him over her shoulder.

"Aight now, aren't you gonna be late for your first class at CPCC?"

"Nah. Why do you say that?"

"Because if you don't ... you better get dressed before I fuck your li'l sexy ass again."

Slipping on her white thongs, then shifting her hips from left to right to pull up her snug House of Derrion denim pants, she looked at him with submissive eyes. "Jacob, what are we?" she asked, sticking her arms into her red Vernon tunic top.

"Wha''chu mean?" he wondered, looking bewildered by her question.

Careful not to mess up her short hairdo, she stretched out the neck of her shirt with both hands and stuck her head through. "What I'ma saying is, are we just fuckin' or ..."

"That's up to you, Pudding," he said, cutting her off. He stared down at his baggy Coogi Passport denim jeans pants leg that partially covered his black Retro 2 Air Jordans.

"Okayyy," she held, sticking her foot into her red Nicholas Kirkwood laced up pumps.

Inspecting himself in the full length mirror, "I mean, I'm single and I'd love to be your Nigga."

"That sounds so ghetto ... I want you to be my man, mines and mines only."

He kissed her glossy lips. "Say no more," he said, tasting her cherry lip gloss again, passionately kissing her.

*   *   *   *   *   *   *

"It's one o'clock and I wanda—way BlueBerry's black ass is," Vanilla inquired, sounding as feminine as he could as he sat in his client's chair, crossing his legs.

"Bitch, you ain't cute," Tiff teased, filing her fingernail at a fast pace.

"Who! Girl don't hate partic———"

Vanilla's reply was interrupted by a deep sound that penetrated Unique's walls. The salon's glass vibrated and hair stylists caught their supplies that had begun to fall from their shelves. Tracks and Carrie rushed to the window to see if it was storming but the sun was shining. Minute by minute the sound got louder and deeper.

"Damn, somebody shit's banging," Tracks said, looking back at her workers. Abruptly a white Chevy appeared and stopped behind Tiff's Beamer. When the driver's door opened, smoke bellowed out. The driver exited the car and headed directly towards the entrance to the salon, strutting slowly like he didn't have a care in the world. The ladies inside of the salon revered his swaggerful strut, especially Tiff. When he opened the salon's door, the ceiling fans and air conditioning system picked up the aroma. Tiff rushed him outsideand spoke her mind.

"Damn, Jacob ... is it because we haven't slept together," she offered, frowning. His eyes lowered to her camel—toe print that shouted 'can you see me?' between her legs. Prepared to tell the truth, "Nah, it ain't about sex," he straight—faced lied instead.

"Well, what is it then?"

"First off, you scared to take me around your family. A——"

"But ..."

"Hush up. I'm talking," he demanded, pulling away from her grasp. "You grown. If your pops don't like me, it's your decision." He cared less about her lowering her head. "Look, I work hard. I'm driving a cab and making good money. I have needs. I'm human."

"So that's it, you wanna meet my family?"

"Among other things."

"How about this c———" she started but was interrupted.

"Yo Bealz, come get the phone," Banga shouted, standing outside the car on one foot. He saw Bealz raise one finger in response. "Nah, Baby Boy, dis shit urgent," he protested, shaking Bealz's cell phone.

"Look, I gotta go handle this. I'll call you later."

"Jacob, every time you say that, it be a week before I see or hear from you."

"I'ma call you, I promise," he repeated, kissing her cheek. Tiff watched the man of her dreams scurry off to his car. She wanted desperately to reveal her true feelings to him. She waved good—bye, and in disbelief watched him back the Chevy up until cars on North Tryon Street layed on their horns, angered by the Chevy that cut in front of them. Tiff released a grateful sigh when she saw that no accident had occurred.

Bealz drove erratically, fortunate that he didn't attract a traffic cop. He raced for the highway ramp off Sugar Creek. It seemed only minutes that it took him to drive up to Brice's apartment.

He and Banga walked past Brice's angry barking rednose pitbull that was tied to a tree in the front yard. Brice met them at the door and gave Bealz a chest bump hug. Brice and Banga's head nod and fist bump introduction was short.

Bealz saw how Shellz layed on the funny colored brown couch. Before speaking, he and Shellz's former road dawgs shared an intense stare—down. Banga stood behind Bealz by the fish tank containing dirty water.

"Who shot you, Dawg," Bealz inquired, tilting his head.

Jap

"I don't know.. ." Shellz answered, struggling to sit up. "Ahhh," he groaned," Man, dat Nigga Lil Gas stuck me up yesterday, and flattened my tires," he told, sucking his teeth.

"Yeah, dat's some hoe—ass shit," Brice protested, showing his three top gold fronts. He tightened his do—rag and sat down, grabbing his game sole controller and resuming his game.

Shellz explained over the sounds of the Madden football game that Banga had joined Brice in playing. He let it be known that he didn't know who'd shot him. But under no circumstances did he speak of the dead cab driver. Little did Shellz know his name was circulating around the police force.

Never load a pistol bare—handed, an Alliance rule that he'd forgotten.

"I'ma be a'ight. I was hoping that I could borrow five stacks from you."

"Yo Shellz, although I didn't entertain your phone call yesterday, I still got love for you. Only reason I'm here 'cause someone had shot you .." Bealz paused, retrieved a stack of money from his pocket and handed Shellz what he'd asked for. He then motioned for Banga, "Let's roll," he said, without looking back or acknowledging Shellz's thanks.

Shortly, the Chevy rolled out of Creektown.

In the meantime, Officer Buccannon sat in an interrogation room with a terrified inmate. He wore an orange oversized Mecklenburg County jump— suit, listening intently to how much time his charges carried The inmate lit up his ninth cigarette,

240

making a big deal of blowing out the match and discarding it with the other cigarette butts and ashes that overflowed from the small metal ashtray that sat on the square table between him and his interrogator. In spite of his attempted bravado, his fear intensified as he continued to listen to Buccannon's promises of taking his freedom. She topped the threats off by swearing to place the inmate's name in a cocaine conspiracy, an automatic enhancement that meant even more time facing him.

Buccannon finished her spiel, then sat there in silence staring at him intently, hoping that her serious threats, stern silent demeanor, and the constant tapping of her pen on the blank yellow pad would break his reserve and entice him to cooperate and talk. When the inmate took a long, dramatic drag of his cigarette, he failed to notice the length of the ashes until they fell into his lap, a dead giveaway of the fear he was trying to mask. His lips were white and crusty. All he knew for sure was that he wanted his freedom and a hit of crack, not necessarily in that order.

Buccannon turned and looked at her fellow interrogator, a male officer who remained silent throughout the interrogation, simply there as a witness. "Let's go," Buccannon said to him. "We'll let Mr. Parks rot in prison," she threatened in a hateful tone of voice.

As Buccannon abruptly stood and turned to the door, Parks suddenly blurted, "Okay, okay." His eyes blinking rapidly, he crossed his legs and leaned back in his chair. Looking up at

Buccannon, "Now you promise that I won't go to prison?" he asked, holding the short cigarette close to his lips.

Bucannon sighed leisurely and smiled. "That's up to you. If you tell the truth, everything you know, and it checks out, then we'll see what we can do for you."

Inmate Parks started talking. In halfway detail he implicated those involved with dealing dope at his 2235 residence. In five minutes he had managed to help make Buccannon's conspiracy case against Shelton Davis, aka Shellz, and Omar Gaston, Jr., aka Lil Gas. Pleased with Parks' admission, she gave him another cigarette, praising him for the admirable deed for the City of Charlotte.

As she continued to write down what he'd told her, she casually asked where he'd been living. Parks admitted that he crashed at the homes of several crack smokers around the corner from The View. As Buccannon continued to furiously jot her notes, Parks started to say something but paused; it dawned on him that he could offer a serious revelation that just might work mightily in his favor with this woman, since she held his fate in her hands, or rather in the notes she was writing. He thumped some ashes in the ashtray, blew smoke up towards the light that hung over the table and looked intently at the top of Buccannon's head. Parks turned and looked momentarily at the officer who was witnessing the interrogation and received his empty stare in return. Parks glanced in the direction of the one—way glass, then back at Buccannon. His eyes betrayed the myriad of thoughts that were going through his head as he silently evaluated the information he was tempted to lay on the table. Through second—guessing himself, without warning he just opened up.

"You know that girl who was badly beaten in that apartment in Belvedere?"

Buccannon's head shot up, her hand stopped writing. Giving him her full attention, she said, "What about it?"

"Yeah, a Nigga named Coley paid me to get Jacob away from his apartment, that apartment there in Belvedere so Coley and some cat named L.J. could go into the place to jack Jacob's shit off. But what happened was, Jacob's girl was home, which she wasn't supposed to be. Now I'm not sure what happened but I just know that Karma oops," he slapped his hand against his mouth, then correcting himself continued, "I meant that girl, Jacob's girl, was beaten pretty bad."

Although Parks had tried not to reveal too much, it was too late. The damage had been done.

"Thanks, Phil..." Buccannon said, smiling eagerly. "I'll be in touch." She gathered her things and left Parks sitting there at the table, smoking the last cigarette he had given her as he stared at the smoke rising to the ceiling, contemplating his fate.

CHAPTER TWENTY-FOUR

5 P.M.

Bealz was serving heroin to fiends while seated at the rear table of the Church's Fried Chicken located at nearby JCSU. Since all employees of the establishment either smoked crack, did heroin, or both, Bealz had them on his payroll. The runner, "Too Bad", did the directing and was the look—out for any Narcs or the Head Manager who made an appearance only when he felt like showing up.

Too Bad stood by the entrance like a sentry, dressed in street uniform, long pants and shirt — bragging to every junkie about the authenticity of Bealz's dope. To top it off, not only did the long line of heroin users that crowded Churches get their fix, they also got a free two—piece dinner and drink, compliments of Bealz. So the crowd of mostly clean—cut and professional—looking junkies appeared to be regular patrons with normal appetites.

It didn't take long for the Churches crowd and Bealz's bags of heroin to rapidly dwindle away. Looking inside the empty chicken box on the table, Bealz was amazed that he'd gotten rid of ten bundles of heroin in little more than thirty minutes.

Too Bad rushed over and sat across the table from Bealz. "'Sup? You through?" he inquired, his mouth twitching. Disappointed to see Bealz respond in the affirmative by his happy head nods, "Damn, what 'bout me?" he asked, placing his left elbow on the table and vigorously rubbing his forehead with his ashy left hand.

"Come on, Baby — you know I can't forget about you . . ." as he offered a clutched hand, "Spend it wisely."

Too Bad's eyes protruded as he looked at the two one hundred dollar bills Bealz had thrust into his hand. "Good lookin' Dawg. I'm gone," he said. And he was.

Bealz snickered at Too Bad's quick exit. He thanked the two male and female workers before he too exited the fried chicken establishment.

*   *   *   *   *   *   *   *

Thin white clouds streaked through the blue skies. The temperature on this late July day was mild but still a little humid. Acting on a tip, the badly decomposed and charred body of a male had been discovered in the woods. Kings Mountain investigators were trying to determine how long the body had been there, deep in a wooded area. Although the man had died from a gunshot wound, his upper torso was badly burned. His wallet containing his driver's license had been spared, however, which revealed the victim's identity. The only other clues immediately discernible on the scene were a pack of matches with one match missing from the book.

9 P.M.

After being briefed on all the particulars involving the discovery of the man's body, Officers MacMall and Smith were dispatched to the man's home. They descended upon the modest home off Archdale Drive in South Charlotte.

Fifty—two year old Pamela Sams, who resembled Tinica Arnold, was folding clothes when her concentration was disrupted by the sound of bold knocks on the front door. She yelled to her daughter, "Nikki, answer the door. My hands are full here!" She heard Nikki mumble something and then her light footsteps going to the door.

Nikki's scream echoed through the house causing Pamela's blood to run cold. She dropped the towels she was folding, knocking over a neat stack of clothes, responding in a panic to her daughter's frantic screams. Pamela's heart hit the floor when she rushed into the front room to see Nikki on her knees, sobbing hysterically, two officers holding badges standing helplessly by. Pamela's brown eyes immediately misted up.

Silently hoping there had been some kind of drastic mistake, she bravely asked the nearest officer, "Is there a problem?" As soon as she saw her son's old mugshot being held by the female officer, Pamela could no longer hold back the tears. Pointedly she said, "My son's dead, isn't he," and quickly looked away when she saw both officers nod.

The mother of three picked up her one—year—old grandbaby who had waddled up to her, drinking a half bottle of milk. She hugged Corey's son Lil C tightly and wept herself like a baby. The agents felt badly for Pamela but they also had a job to do, questions that needed to be answered. Rodney waited patiently until Pamela's cries subsided before approaching her and gently touching her left shoulder.

"Ms. Sams, do you know who this is?" he asked.

Sharply Pamela cut her eyes at the picture that he was holding. "Don't tell me that San is dead, too," she said through her tears.

"No, ma'am ... we just know that your son hangs out with her, and maybe Ms. Tillman might know who killed your son, is all," Leslie said.

The agents knew from previous experience that mom wasn't going to divulge her dead son's illicit activities, so all they really needed was confirmation that Corey and San were closely connected.

The agents left their business cards with Ms. Sams before excusing themselves, expressing their condolences and departing. Back in their unmarked, Leslie sat looking over the mugshots of San. Grams, and Milky illuminated by overhead interior lights

"You got about six more weeks, Rod," she said, referring to Rodney's deadline.

"I know ... I know" He responded skeptically.

1:05 A.M.

While investigators and local authorities in Greenville. North Carolina were searching for the man who had left fingerprints on the match book cover, Major League had entered a strip club called Irresistibles. Relatively speaking, San's clique was treading unchartered territories.

Jap

Irresistibles sat on the outskirts of Wilmore. It used to be a night— spot called Stoneys until a big dopeboy named Endz bought the place, fixed it up and hired fifteen strippers. Endz's clique not only was bigger than Major League but he was trafficking just as much if not more cocaine than San. Although the two leaders had never been formally introduced they knew of each other.

Endz wore long shoestring dreads with reddish dyed ends that he kept in fresh neat braids. His tattooed name couldn't be missed since the words ENDZ WORLD in blood dripping letters were tattooed on the side of his neck. The ex—high school basketball star had entered the dope game straight out of high school following his mother's tragic death.

Endz sat back inside his glass—enclosed VIP Room, playing Playstation on a 42—inch LCD monitor. In addition to his hired armed security, five of the strippers entertained him and his boys, Lii Rosco, Flame, and Kilo Breed. Bottles of the club's high priced Champagnes had been quenching the men's thirst. Everyone but Endz consumed liquor, weed, and Ecstacy pills. Under no circumstances did Endz drink anything alcoholic, which was why his yellow skin tone kept its complexion and remained bump free. Puberty had yet to allow Endz to grow a full mustache and chin hair but twins Lil Rosco and Flame looked older than their twenty—four years. The brothers already looked like linebackers and they loved to brawl. Kilo Breed hailed from Brooklyn, resembled Mase and swore that he used to hustle on the block with Biggie. All—in—all, Endz and his boys stayed fly, their whips and jewelry spoke for them.

San two—finger saluted a cat she knew named Al as she was leaving the bar. As usual, Milky and Vanilla trailed behind San like little puppies. San had one of her velour sweat pants rolled past her left calf muscle as she moved through the crowd of men and strippers like she owned the place.

Once the DJ announced BlueBerry's appearance on stage, San bobbed her head excitedly to Color Me Badd's song, 'I Wanna Sex UP." The only reason for San's visit to the club was to support BlueBerry's debut. San licked her lips at BlueBerry's skillful dance move as she emerged from behind the pink curtain. San stuck her thumb and pointer finger in her mouth and her short quick whistles could be heard over the song.

Through the dark lights BlueBerry recognized the huge figure of San looming over the congestion of males that crowded the stage. The place went wild when Blue freed her titties, tilted her head, cupped her chocolate twins and licked them with her long tongue. The excited males tossed one—, five—, and ten—dollar bills at her six—inch heels. Their cheers for "MORE!" was answered when she eased her long legs into a precision split, perfectly executed which made it look effortless. She turned on her stomach, arched her back and somehow made her ass cheeks separate, then smack together to the beat of the song. Her massive hips and ass made her yellow thong look nonexistent.

"How much?" one wale yelled lustfully, throwing money at her.

When BlueBerry's time on stage ended, she collected the scattered bills off of the floor, stuck the money into her matching garter belt and went and sat on San's lap. BlueBerry giggled from San's ear— nibbling antics.

Vanilla gushed, "Girl, I'on know how you shake your ass like that on stage."

"Ahh, Vanilla, all these dicks in here? You'd shake your ass too if you could." Blueberry shot back giggling.

Vanilla smacked his lips then expertly covered half of the long straw from his drink.

"Damn, Nigga, you sick," Milky quipped, cringing his face. BlueBerry waved for one of her buddies to come meet San, saying to San, "Meet my friend, MoBerry."

San studied MoBerry's impeccable petite frame with lascivious eyes.

"Girl, turn around and let San see that plump ass," Blue suggested. slapping MoBerry's ass cheeks, making them jiggle.

"Oh, Baby, don't be bashful," San cooed. "How's 'bout you joining me and BlueBerry at a room ... everything on me."

MoBerry shrugged her shoulders

"She'll go — we'll be off in about an hour," Blue explained. She leaned in close enough to hear what San suddenly wanted to know, then answered so only the two of them could hear, "I'on know why Lil Gas did what he did. I spoke to Shellz he say he gone kill Gas," she ended.

A stocky, light brown security guard, clean shaven face and head, approached San's table. "Excuse me... Endz wants to see you," he announced in a deep tone.

San ushered BlueBerry off of her lap and grabbed one of her Coronas from the round table top. "I'll be right back," she said, falling in behind the messenger, taking occasional swigs of her beer as she followed him through the club.

"Right this way," the security guard said, opening the glass entry door to the VIP Room.

San hummed to herself as she intently watched Endz clear out the room. When the last person had left and the closing door latch resounded, with a hand Endz gestured for San to take a seat next to him.

"So you are the great San, huh," Endz said, offering a flute of Champagne to her.

Accepting the Champagne graciously, she took off a little of his exaggeration when she replied, "Nah, bra, I'm San the Boss." Cutting his eyes at her, Endz leaned back and interlocked his fingers. "Well, perhaps two Bosses is better than one, in this case."

"How so?" she shot back, sipping the Champagne.

He took a soft white cloth and wiped off the face of his two toned Frank Muller Presidential watch. "Imagine if you and I link up . . we could run the whole city. I already got my hands in Gastonia, Concord, and Rock Hill. "

"If you puttin' shit down like that, why hook up wit' me?"

"Because your name holds weight in the streets and so does Major League. Imagine if Pac and Biggie would of hooked up. Not only would they have run the rap game, those two Niggas could of built their own army out of the East and West coast."

San got an ear full about Endz's barber shop, detail service, and Untold Record Label that he had started, to which she responded with a series of "mmm hm."

"So wha's really good," he asked, sipping his Tropicana Orange Juice.

"You got any balls?" San retorted.

Her question caused him to choke on a swallow, the liquid he was drinking spewing out of his nose and mouth. She giggled and passed him a cloth napkin so he could contain the juice that dripped from his chin.

"Damn, San," he coughed. "What kind of a question is that," his voice cracking from a combination of lack of air in his windpipe from the onslaught of liquid going down the wrong passage, mixed with a touch of resentment.

"It's a question that if you had asked me, I would of told you no. But I could get you some if a Nigga tried to fuck over me."
The cold tone in San's voice did not escape his attention. It took him a second but he figured out what she had meant. The left side of his face twitched as he grinned snugly, saying, "Let me just say that those who can't speak, can't tell." He leaned in close to San, "When you got loafs on top of loafs of bread ..." he paused.

San followed the direction of Endz's eyes and saw the twins brandishing firearms outside of the VIP Room's thick glass. San smiled. When Endz turned back to face her, he too smiled at the two—shot derringer that she had pointed at him over her right thigh.

"How did you manage to get that in here," he asked with interest, his eye brows knitting into a frown.

"Ain't no tellin', " she said, pointing.

Endz stared in the direction opposite the twins and saw BlueBerry's smiling face and waving hand "Slick girl. You slick as hell," he bragged, stroking his thighs with both hands.

The conversation between the two bosses progressed quickly to a new level of significance and mutual respect, resulting in their decision to seriously consider doing business together.

Their discussion ended with both introducing their workers and just like that a solid bond was formed. San got Endz to understand and appreciate BlueBerry's loyalty, which he respected and promised he wouldn't fire her or order her killed by the twins.

Realizing Endz's fondness for the PlayStation, since Milky knew how to play Madden, San bet Endz a stack a game against Milky. By two forty seven a.m., San was four stacks richer.

Endz ended up closing at three and had the girls entertain Major League and his own clique until five A.M.

CHAPTER TWENTY-FIVE

Sunday 7:30 A.M.

The raspy sounds of a male and female trying to catch their breaths echoed throughout Room 534 of the Best Western Hotel. The smell of sex mixed with sweat saturated the air as freshener. Bealz laid behind Pudding, his throbbing cock still nestled inside her cum—soaked pussy. From second to second the muscles of her vagina involuntarily contracted, the post—orgasm spasms producing droplets of left—over remnants from Bealz's nut sack.

Ring! Ring! ... Ring! Ring!

"You gonna answer that?" she inquired, looking back at him through half—open eyes.

Bealz sighed at the annoyance of the persistent ringing of the hotel phone. He gave one last thrust but his softening dick slipped out. "Dammit, man!" he cursed, turning over. Grabbing the phone, he growled into the receiver, "What?"

"Yo, Bealz, dem girls ran out and I can't find the others."

It was Banga telling him in code that he'd sold out of crack and couldn't find the stash. Bealz explained that he knew of some girls that overlooked Highway Sixteen that stayed by a short round bush.

Taking precautions not to be seen as he walked behind Phil's apartment, Banga followed Bealz's code until he came upon five trees and one lone bush. He dug down by the bush's root and removed some wet soil.

"Got it," Banga said excitedly.

Click.

Bealz scooped Pudding from the bed and carried her into the shower. When they finished cleaning up and had gotten dressed, she tried to get him to go to church but that wasn't happening. Pudding's Dolce & Gabbana white curve—hugging dress was an appetizing sight in Bealz's eyes. But he had other things to do. Following a passionate kiss, she reapplied her bronze—colored lipstick and smiled as she exited the room.

Bealz peeked through the curtain at Pudding's Toyota driving out of the parking lot before he placed a call from his cell phone. "Good Morning," a sultry voice spoken softly was heard answering his call.

"Sup."

"Good morning," she repeated with more enthusiasm.

"Oh ... good morning."

It was Tiff. She and Bealz had been in talks the previous day about his going to church with her. He figured he'd give it a try and inquired about the location of the church she attended.

10:05 .A.M.

Bealz drove into the already crowded parking lot of St. Paul Ministries Church off Park Road. He smiled at a family who crossed in front of his car. He noticed how the father of the family was dressed which made Bealz feel underdressed.

'I look like I could be dressed to go clubbing,' he thought to himself, looking down at his Coogi sweater short sleeve, cream

Polo slacks, and black slip—and—slide round—toed leather Mauris. 'Damn, I can't get jiggy wit''dis shit,' he muttered jokingly, his head bowed as he was deciding whether or not to go through with his pledge to attend church with Tiff.

When he lifted his head he froze when he saw a woman headed in his direction, looking sexy as anyone can imagine. "Holy shit," he uttered out loud, quickly turning his head in all directions. Seeing no way to avoid the inevitable, he sighed and rolled down his window. "Hey," his voice expressing surprise at seeing her.

"I'm glad you decided to come."

Thinking quick, he retorted, "Nah, I, ahh ... brought you an extra hotel key," hoping she wouldn't question his avoidance of the truth and the way he was nervously scanning the parking lot to his right, then back to Pudding, then to his left and back to her.

She studied his frantic gestures momentarily before taking the key. Trying valiantly to mask her disappointment, she kissed him and then walked away towards the entrance of the church.

"No, no, no..." he repeated, striking the steering wheel with his fist. Hoping that Tiff had told him the wrong church, he rolled through the parking lot, praying that he would not see her Beamer. Just as he was passing the last rows of vehicles, a green tree air freshener hanging from a rearview mirror caught his eye. He rubbed his hand firmly over his forehead as he drove slowly by Tiff's Beamer. Without second guessing himself, he quickly exited the parking lot and drove off, thinking that perhaps Tiff and Pudding didn't know each other. 'Yeah, 'dat's it,' he told himself as he checked his rearview mirror.

The church's congregation was clapping, some stood, lending their voices to their choir's soulful number. The pews were filled. Up front older ladies' big colorful hats rocked back and forth. The leading female usher showed Pudding to her usual seat. Pudding excused herself as she made her way to the middle of the row. She sat down and joyfully embraced her first cousin Tiff.

"Girl, my friend guy is supposed to be coming. I guess he's running a little late."

"My boyfriend just came to drop off a key," Pudding said. "Those men just don't like church, do they." Both giggled before joining the others in the singing of the hymn.

*   *   *   *   *   * *

Rather than joining Banga, Bealz met up with Jake at Shoney's off of Tyvola. He filled his plate with scrambled eggs, grits, and bacon. Over breakfast, the two discussed everything from Karma, to the cab company, to Shellz, to Bealz's close call at St. Paul's. Jake advised him to tighten up his network before his structure began to crumble. Bealz felt his cell phone buzz. The display on the Caller ID read, TIFF.

"Excuse me, Jake," he said, then into the phone, "Hey Tiff." "What happened to you? My father wanted to meet you. And he doesn't like liars," she softly blasted.

"I had car troubles."

"Jacob, that's bull ... and you, you expect me to give myself to you? I———"

"Hold the fuck up," he interjected in a serious but composed tone. "I don't do church. Only time I get to see you is when you're ready." He glanced around at the stares from a couple of Shoney's customers and placed his cell phone against his chest. "Jake, I'll be right back."

Outside of Shoney's, as he started pacing, he continued, "Tiff, I know you ain't used to a Nigga like me. I————"

"But————"

"Let me finish ... I refuse to not be me, if that's what you trying to do, change a Nigga. Let's end our conversation and forget that we ever met. I'mma man wit' needs and you a female and have needs as well. a shame they don't seem to be the same needs. So if we can't come to some kind of compromise, an arrangement that will benefit us both, then let's just cut this bullshit."

Tiff peeked her head out of the ladies restroom. Seeing no one in sight, she replied, "Nigga, if I give you some pussy and you cheat on me, I'ma kill your ass. And I know what it takes to get away with murder. So later on tonight, I need to see you. For now, I'ma lie to my father and hope that he'll forgive you later on."

Bealz finished letting her rant, then calmly responded, "Now you hear this: I am the one who wears the pants, so if any ass— kickin' and killin' happens, it's gonna be by my hands. Do I make myself clear?"

While waiting for her reply, he could hear her heavy breathing through the phone. "I hear you," she responded in a defeated tone. "Let me get back upstairs. Bye."

"Bye."

Jake grabbed his glass of orange juice from the table after Bealz tripped from running, but caught his balance. He complained to Bealz "Your manners" then took a gulp of his drink. "Man, this chick I've been trying to hit is now talkin' my language," Bealz expressed with gladness, showing his pearly whites.

Jake folded his lips, shook his head. "What about this Pudding girl?"

Bealz waved his hand at Jake as if to say he wasn't worried about Pudding.

"Well, what about Sharelle?"

Hearing Karma's government jogged Bealz's memory. Quickly he revisited in his mind Karma's love—making faces and her beautiful untarnished body, and especially the uncaring look she made when the bullet from her gun saved his life months ago. Bealz could still see the blood gushing from Angeleo's head and the thick stream that led up to the tip of his Air Force sneakers.

'Damn , Karma ...' he thought to himself.

"Where you going?" Jake asked. -

"I'll call you later," Bealz answered as he left Jake's table. A few minutes later Bealz was driving towards Carolina Medical from South Boulevard. He called Karma's nurse's station and was told that she'd gone home. His eyes glued to the road and traffic, he carefully texted Karma's cell phone ... -

Karma sat up in her bed and became animated when she read the text from Bealz that came through: KARMA IM SORRY I AINT BEEN TO SEE YOU. I WISH I HAD YOUR PARENTS ADDRESS. I LOVE AND MISS YOU MUCH. SINCERELY, BEALZ. PS U DA QUEEN OF THE ALLIANCE.

Tears trickled down Karma's cheek as she immediately texted him back Bealz stood by watching the numbers turn on the Super Unleaded pump at the BP Gas Station when his phone buzzed. As he removed the nozzle from the Chevy, he read Karma's text: DAMN DAWG A BITCH MOUTH AINT GON B WIRED 4EVER. BY DA WAY, A COP NAME BUCCANNON PAID ME A VISIT DA OTHER MORNING WITH TWO MUGSHOTS. ONE WAS A NIGGA NAMED FRED WILBUR WHO GOT CAUGHT IN A RED TRUCK. DA OTHER ONE I RECOGNIZED FROM BEING WITH SHELLZ AND LIL GAS, A NIGGA NAMED L.J. WHO WAS KILLED IN A MOTEL ROOM. DA SAME NIGGA THAT I GOT A GOOD LOOK AT BEFORE HE STRUCK ME. I PLAYED THE AMNESIA TRICK TO THE DOCTORS. BUT AFTER THE NIGGA FINISHED SLAMMING ME, I SEEN HIS FACE AFTER HE LIFTED HIS MASK, THINKING I WAS OUT COLD. IMA TOUGH BITCH, EVEN AS THE BLOOD FILLED MY EYES AND BEFORE I PASSED OUT I SEEN THIS NIGGAZ FACE PLAIN AS DAY. FACT IS I DIDN'T PASS OUT UNTIL THE NIGGA ROLLED ME TO THE FLOOR. SO SOAK UP WHAT TM DOUCHING. PS 8810 LEGACY

PARK DR, APT A3 COME WHEN YOU WANT FUCK FAMIL HA HA, LOVE KARMA.

Bealz pulled away from the gas station, his anger shooting his blood pressure into overdrive. As much as he hated to believe it, it looked more and more like Shellz was behind Karma's injuries. If that was so, Shellz had to die.

Before long, the Chevy made it to Cox Avenue, a one—way street of run—down drug—infested homes and brick apartments. This strip of heroin and crack trafficking laid on the other side of Rozzels Ferry Road. Still, Cox Avenue was in close proximity to Belvedere Apartments and The View.

Bealz had praised Ranga for turning The Alliance on to this strip which had turned out to be a hidden gold mine. Since The View was lava hot, the two Alliance males slipped into the fold with the few Niggas that hustled on Cox. A fat dude named Jughead ran a liquor house that sat across the Street from the apartment that a female crackhead named Renee allowed The Alliance to commandeer. Renee's apartment was furnished with odds and ends that someone had discarded by a dumpster. Her kitchen sink constantly dripped over dirty dishes. The rail was missing from the staircase that led upstairs. The bathroom's filthy sink, tub, and toilet stool had huge dirty rust rings. The apartment indeed had been run down over the years, but all the drug users knew and liked Renee.

The most unpredictable fact about Apartment One's situation was Renee herself. She had an amazingly petite frame. Her pecan—brown skin tone matched her mascara that she used to lighten her facial appearance. She only had one missing tooth on the side of the bottom row and she kept her hair cut short. Finally, Renee, an ex—cheerleader, wore the most skimpy outfits that showed the most skin. At first glance there was no way of telling that she, at twenty—four, was the mother of four kids that her mother took to Alabama to raise.

"How much you tryin' to spend? Quit stallin'," Banga cautioned a slim crackhead with a large afro.

The bumpy—faced man recounted his money and added an old school trick. "I got seventeen dollars."

Banga had already peeped game. He snatched the wrinkled bills from the man's hands, then counted as he flipped each bill, "Five, seven, nine, ten, eleven, twelve, thirteen ... where's the other four?" he asked, giving the man a sinister look, aware that crack had the man's brains fried Banga too had some added tricks. He looked past the man's shoulders up the street. "Man down," he signaled. Once the man's head turned in the direction of Banga's eyes, Banga cleared the man's feet from the ground with a powerful punch reminiscent of D—Bo in the flick 'Friday.' Banga enjoyed hearing the other hustlers brag on him stealing a helpless man.

"You Banga, wha's up?" Bealz came to the man's rescue, helping him to his feet. "You a'ight?" he asked the man, brushing dirt from the crackhead's back.

"Ima — I — Ima a'ight, ma just a lil short. N—my name's N—meatman." he introduced himself, extending his ashy hand out to Bealz. His eyes looked nervously in all directions.

"OK, Meatman," Bealz replied, firmly shaking the man's frail hand. "Banga, hand me three dimes."

Banga retrieved a sack of crack rocks from the crack of his ass. He opened the clear plastic sandwich bag and handed Bealz three bags. Bealz turned and gave the man the drugs, bumped fist with him, then watched him run away.

"Say, we need to talk," Bealz said to Banga in a serious tone and motioned for Banga to follow him.

"Yo Chop, I'll be right back," Banga told a cat with whom he'd gone to school.

"A'ight my Nig," Chop shot back, crouching down by a green Dumpster shooting dice with a handful of other hustlers.

Renee opened the door for Banga and Bealz. As she spoke a greeting, she sprayed some perfume on her neck and wrist before running upstairs. To the surprise of The Alliance, she had cleaned up and the smell of boiling link sausages electrified their empty stomachs.

Banga sat on the arm of the worn couch, listening closely to Bealz's talk about what Karma's text message implied. Banga's anger showed from his-repeated pounds on the sofa's already weak arm. Beaiz shushed him and pointed towards the ceiling to where Renee could have been all ears. Bealz tilted his head back, vigorously stroking his goatee, his eyes closed, deep in thought.

Jap

Gradually Bealz lowered his head and gave Banga an ice cold stare. "We gonna bait Shellz up. If he lies, we gon' spill his brains," Bealz whispered.

CHAPTER TWENTY-SIX

Later on that very day, when Pamela informed him about Corey, Coley was unable to contain his grief or keep in check the tears that streamed down his face. Coneka's attempts to console him failed. All he appreciated was hearing Lii Gas offer to help him seek revenge for Corey's death. Neither Lil Gas nor Coneka had understood the magnitude of their affection in relationship he and Corey had shared.

True, Coley and Corey both had the last name of Sams, and although they were cousins, they had been raised as brothers. When Coley was five years old, Pamela's sister, Melanie, had dropped him off at Pamela's place one weekend and never returned or called. Thirteen years later, on a fateful winter night, Melanie's body surfaced beside a dark Greensboro Road. Her raped and battered body traumatized Coley, catapulting him deeper into a life of crime.

Coley had an idea who might be behind Corey's murder, the same person who he used to hustle for around nine and a half months previously. He used to be this person's right hand man until her accusations caused his ouster from Major League.

"Yo man ... San killed Corey, or had him killed," he accused, interrupting the inane chatter between Coneka and Lil Gas.

"Shit, BlueBerry and I could've done that bitch at the room early this morning. Why wait? Blue knows where San's major stash house is in Hidden Valley. Let's run up in that bitch tonight," Coneka suggested, massaging Coley's shoulders.

"Nah, we gonna stick to the plan...." Coley insisted. Blue supposed to make plan A "A'ight, you know I'ma fuck da shit out of you later," he cautioned. Blue made a 'whatever' face. "You promise?"

"Damn ri———'1 Click.

Shellz looked at his cell phone, unsure if she hung up or they just had a bad connection. He told the cab driver to hold up while he went inside Hunter's Garage to see how much it'd cost to have his car towed. He could see his dusty Cadillac amongst the hundreds of vehicles secured within the garage's fence.

The two white gentlemen inside the office gave Shellz suspicious stares. Judging from their reactions after learning his government name, it was obvious to Shellz that the garage had been instructed to alert the police if the owner of that Cadillac made an appearance.

"I'll be right back," Shellz said, and dashed out of the office, ignoring the tobacco—spitters.

The redneck with the longest, thickest beard stayed on the phone describing the Yellow Cab, its tag number, and the direction it was headed. Hunters was located in North Charlotte where there were heavy police patrols, but the cab was long gone by the time the first squad car descended upon the towing garage.

Shellz got out of the cab at the Burger King off North Tryon Street. After ordering a Number Two, ten minutes later he was getting into a Checkers Cab. Shellz sat in the back seat of the taxi, stewing as he thought about the fact that he'd let Lil Gas into his circle only to have him play Shellz like a sucker. To add to the indignity, he'd been shot, his car was fucked up, and he'd been unable to return to his apartment. Now here he was being forced to over—pay another foreign taxi driver for transportation.

'Ain't this a bitch — I shoulda stayed down wit' Bealz,' Shellz thought.

The taxi driver brought the cab to a stop at the Sugar Creek, North Tryon traffic light. Suddenly a sound vibrated the cab's interior and Shellz's head pivoted to determine the source of the rumbling. Quickly determining that it was the sound system from an adjacent blue Suburban sitting on 24" rims that was causing the ruckus, he smiled at the smoke that emerged from the driver's mouth as his head nodded to the beat of the thunder.

As the light turned green, Shellz had a thought: since San owned the salon up the street, that's where he'd go to chill for a minute, thinking maybe he'd pull some chick at the same time.

"Yo — stop up the street at Unique Designs," he instructed the cab's driver.

"Ahh, yes, dem ho's be up dere deep, my man," the Jamaican driver responded in heavy Island accent. "Do jou blaze dat gunga mon."

"I jou mon, I jou," Shellz replied, mocking the foreigner, grinning.

Both men giggled.

Shellz quit laughing when he saw the driver hold up an ounce of skunk. "Shit, stop at the stoe blaze somethin'," he suggested excitedly.

It was fortunate for Shellz that he had switched cabs and cab companies. The police had the Yellow Cab and its driver hemmed up. The driver didn't hesitate to tell where he had picked Shellz up where he was dropped off. In moments law enforcements from different divisions hit Burger King and Brice's crib. There was nothing the employees of Burger King could tell the police except that they thought the man they were looking for ordered a Number Two special.

But outside Brice's crib, officers had set up a surveillance perimeter to be on the alert for any sign of activity in or around Brice's crib, surveillance which was easily hidden by the small wooded area surrounding the house. Thirty minutes later the surveillance paid off when Brice was observed exiting the house to feed his dog.

Without warning, what appeared to be an army of police officers appeared out of nowhere with their weapons drawn, converging upon the unsuspecting Brice. Brice's pit bull reacted with a growling, snarling fury but was quickly subdued with pepper spray.

Inside Brice's home, although they didn't find Shellz, there was no way they could fail to notice the half—ounce of crack cocaine that Brice had been chopping up. The dope and a .380 automatic pistol were sitting in plain view on the table.

Sitting in the rear of a police car, Brice was furious that the cops had the cuffs on extra tight and he couldn't help but grimace from the intense pain.

Officer Buccannon opened the rear door of the police car and kneeled to make eye contact with Brice as she questioned him.   "You understand you're in a lot of trouble here, Mr. Mills ... trouble that can easily bury you. But if you don't play hardball with me and help me find Shelton, all this trouble can disappear." "How 'bout this ... you suck my dick and we'll call it a day," Brice responded, grinning through clenched teeth.

10:43 P.M.

A distraught Tiff sat at her dining room table, her head bowed, holding a nearly empty crystal wine glass. She looked again at her watch, then reached over and topped off her glass with what was left of the expensive bottle of wine which she had uncorked three hours earlier and carefully set the empty bottle back in its place. The table was otherwise immaculate, replete with fresh flowers and the requisite candle to complement the two perfectly prepared place settings, still undisturbed. Sipping her wine, she stared into the flame of the candle that, along with the soft R&B music playing on her sound system, was to add ambiance to her carefully planned evening of dinner and romance. Almost three hours past the time Tiff and Bealz were supposed to meet and the candle was now little more than hunk of melted wax

Fighting back tears of disappointment and outrage, she pushed herself away from the table, stood up, leaned over and blew out the now pathetic flame, with wine glass in hand, drifted in to her plush living room, now lit by the soft glow from the purple florescence emanating from the fish tank under the 42 inch Plasma television. She took a seat on her soft black French—designed sofa, set her glass on an engraved coaster, and knees together, leaned over and rested her forehead on her fists clenched tightly on her knees.

Twenty minutes later she was roused from her reverie by gentle knocks.

Knock. Knock. Knock.

She rose, straightened her gown and walked stiffly to the door. Opening it, her eyes narrowed into evil slits and without any kind of greeting, started in. "How dare you show up here at…" she paused, looked at her watch, "Eleven something an———"

Tiff's rant was interrupted by Bealz's mouth on hers, his hot determined tongue searching for hers and finding it responsive. She had always found his spontaneous and dominant moves somewhat of a turn— on and this time was no exception. His vehemence quickly extinguished the embers of her fury, igniting in its place flames of passion. Giving up her feeble attempts to resist, she responded by snaking her arms around his neck.

He untied her white see—through silk nightgown, freeing her perky breasts, revealing huge brown nipples that rapidly sprouted. With his free hand he closed the door, shielding their sexual antics from any neighbors that just might happen to pass by her apartment.

Bealz's hot mouth worked its way to her nipples, eliciting cries and moans of unleashed passion. She pulled his shirt over his head, then reached her hands into his pants and wrapped her hands around his throbbing dick.

"Ahhh," she moaned, staring at him with desperate eyes. "Is that for me, Jacob?"

"Just for you, Baby."

"Then give it to me, Jacob," she pleaded, lustfully licking her lips. Rushing, he got naked, enjoying the feeling of the black plush carpet beneath his feet. He maneuvered her white thong panties from her body, quietly studied the neatly—shaven thin line of pubic hair above her pussy before parting its lips. Becoming even more aroused by her pussy sounds of wetness, he planted tender kisses around her sweet— smelling peach—pie.

"Ewwww," she cried, stroking his thick braids. Teasing her, he skimmed his nose between the lips of her vagina and kissed his way back up to her mouth, leaving her breasts wet with his saliva. He then scooped her up in his arms and carried her over to the condo's granite fireplace. He carefully lowered them both to the thick Persian rug while at the same time, using no hands, expertly guided Tiff's eager pussy onto his turgid manhood.

"Ohhhh, Jacob," she moaned, her hot wet pussy slowly adapting to his size. She bit down on her bottom lip to quell the exquisite pleasure—pain, and keep from screaming.

Jap

Seated on his butt with Tiff astride him, her irresistible breasts presented themselves to him in all their glory, and he helped himself with relish, flicking his tongue against each nipple. With his large hands he spread her plump ass cheeks in hopes of making her tight defiant pussy invite him deeper inside her love channel.

She heaved and panted from each of his deep thrusts. He hissed from the pain of her fingernails digging into his back. The deeper relentless thrusts the louder her cries of pleasure as her long pent—up passion was tapped and unleashed. She bit his ear lobe, neck, and muscular shoulder blades in her unrestrained sexual delirium.

The sounds of their passion blended with the music of the mixed R&B CD which she had programmed to repeat so that it never stopped playing. The Luther Vandross song 'I Promise' began to play.

Tiff pleaded, "Wait, Jacob ... stop," but her pleas only made him slow his thrusts, the impact of each stroke registering on her face as she talked in gasps. "I don't like ... to be played wiiiith ... ain't ... gonna be no ... other bitches ... okay?"
Satisfied with his nodding agreement, she shifted her hips in a circular motion. Using his shoulders for leverage, she raised up and then as she lowered against his upper thrust, made her waist and hips rotate, reminiscent of her working a hoola—hoop while pressing her breasts against his attentive and eager face, lips, and tongue.

272

"Fuck me, Baby," she enticed breathlessly. The feeling of her inner walls being stretched was minimally painful but they would always manage to adjust, taking her higher and higher into unexplored ecstasy. Finally, when she felt she could stand it no longer, "Ewwww, 'bout to cum," she exclaimed.

Their sex surrendering to raw animal passion, her pussy clenched his dick tighter and tighter. His adrenaline pumping wildly, his thrusts got harder and his breath shortened as he approached the inevitable explosion..

The lone position that they used had worked like a charm. Seconds later, as their loud sounds of passion echoed through the large condo, in screams of explosive convulsions their love liquids finally mixed together. Bealz roared, climaxing as Tiff panted uncontrollably while holding on to his heaving body for dear life. As their passion slowly subsided, the two lovebirds cuddled with each other on the carpeted floor.

When he returned to normalcy, Bealz began to fully appreciate the elegant set—up of Tiff's condo. "Damn, this place looks like Eddie Murphy's crib in Boomerang," he said, stroking her damp, curly hair. "I need to get me a job at Unique's," he joked, laughing.

She gazed up at him over his chiseled chest. "Jacob, I wasn't gonna bring it up .."

"What?" he asked, peering down into her soulful eyes.

"A dude named Shellz came by the shop today ... and I heard him mention what they call you on the street — Bealz. And that wasn't the first person that I've heard speak the name Bealz ..."

She hesitated, then crawled up his body until she overlooked his face, adding, "A while back some stripper named MoBerry talked to one of San's stripper bitch friends named BlueBerry about you. They didn't know I could hear ..." She held Bealz's expressionless gaze. "I don't fuck with dopeboys Jacob. They always die or end up in pr——— Ahhh," she moaned as Bealz's re—entered her.

"W———" Just that quickly, they were back to sexing.

Just that quickly, they were back to fucking.

Like he had nothing to loose with BlueBerry at his side, Shellz hustled his product in the dark shadows of The View. He didn't know that the police had run up in his apartment and he hadn't taken the time to go check. What he did know was that Brice was in jail being held for Possession with The Intent to Sell, and a firearms charge. He promsied Brice he'd get him out when his bond got lowered.

Shellz was glad that San let him owe her fifteen hundred on a quarter kilo of crack. He had BlueBerry get her name registered at the Microtel Motel off Sunset Road.

From The View's faithful crackheads he learned that Banga and Bealz had relocated to Cox Avenue. Shellz basked for the time being in the awareness that he was the only one with crack down in The View.

The doors and windows to Phil's apartment had been boarded up so BlueBerry sat on the Minister's porch. She held a stash of money in her purse that Shellz had thus far made. And she also held his foe—fifth, the same one used in his shoot—out in Lakeview ... and that wasn't the only shooting.

It's been said that a calm always comes before a storm. In this case, a damn tsunami of bad luck was quickly approaching from all directions.

CHAPTER TWENTY-SEVEN

Three Days Later

Loud cries and sniffles were heard from the scores of family and close friends who were on—hand for Corey Jet Sams' home—going. His crisp white suit blended perfectly with the off—lavender casket adorned with white stuffings. Among the long line of people waiting to get one last glimpse of Corey in his final rest was agent MacMall who had appeared uninvited and unannounced.

Coley sat up front beside Pamela, holding his only son on his lap with one arm and with the other wrapped around Pamela's shoulders, consoling her with comforting pats of his hand.

Nikki, both Corey and Coley's baby mothers along with their children, Pamela's grandkids completed the front row.

Behind the dark sunglasses that masked his swollen eyes, Coley cut a hard glare at San and Milky standing over Corey's body, their hand interlocked behind their backs. He struggled to contain his impulse to pounce on San's head right there and then, but he knew that to do so would destroy the plan that had been set in motion for San and Major League.

San turned and kneeled in front of them, hugging Pamela's neck. "I'm sorry, Ms. Pam. If you need anything. just let me know," she whispered, then turned her attention to Corey.

Their matching lenses hid the true feelings of the two former good friends, emotions that only eyes could reveal. San reached out and patted the head of Coley's son then shook his father's hand. She slipped Coley her cell number with her left hand which boasted her custom—made ring with her initials prominent in baguettes and black diamonds.

"Get at me, Dawg. Let by—gones be by—gones," San spoke sincerely in a hushed tone, showing her sparkling teeth.
"Okay, San - . ." he replied. As she turned towards the exit, he kept a tight grip her on her hand, preventing her from walking away. "Thanks for showing your support," he said, finally releasing her hand. He then bumped fist with Milky but pulled back from the gay—looking dude that followed San and Milky.

A man resembling Bruce Bruce approached the microphone and with a sultry voice started singing "Amazing Grace" a cappella which elicited even more tears and moans of sorrow, raising the roof with mourning inside the Funeral Home.

On her way out, San crossed in front of Lil Gas and pointed her finger at him. She approached him and told him that Shellz owed her money. Lil Gas assured San that he wouldn't fuck with Shellz unless he came at him sideways. She smiled and told Lil Gas to call if he needed to get straight. Then along with her two cronies, Major League made its departure.

*　　*　　*　　*　　*　　*

Friday morning, Bealz delivered his furniture and other belongings in a large U—Haul truck to his new two—bedroom apartment at 220 Alpha Mill Lane, which was within walking distance to Uptown. His top floor apartment offered dramatic views of the skyline. Other luxury features included eleven foot ceilings, eleven—foot oversized windows, interior exposed brick walls, a kitchen island, an elevator, and an outdoor fireplace on his roof—top terrace. The beige wall—to—wall carpeting was plush and had no dirt markings. Other available luxury amenities for the building's occupants included high—speed Internet, a spa and gym billiards, a bar and a DVD theater room.

Jake, Banga, and Bealz moved all of the heavy stuff while Pudding helped out with the smaller items. She had an attitude because Bealz wouldn't allow her to move in with him. He stressed to her the importance of maintaining separate residences.

"Pudding. I already help you, and I'll continue to help you if you wanna move away from Belvadere." he said, holding her hand. "So find yourself a place if you want . . ." he paused, pointed towards the floor of his apartment, "Just not here, okay?" He cupped her chin, smiled, then planted a kiss on her poked out lip.

She smacked her lips. "Okay," she sighed her agreement between smooches.

In the meantime, in a meeting place downtown, roll call for two dozen investigative officers and regular uniformed police wasn't going so well. Agents MacMall and Smith stood in front of their colleagues expressing the urgency of ridding the city streets of Major League, with Detective Buccannon insisting that arresting Mr. Shelton Davis was just as important.

Behind the three presiding officers, all the players of Major League were displayed prominently in red Magic Marker on a white board. On another board, written in blue Magic Marker were the names Shelton Davis, Omar Gaston. Brewster Littles, Phillip Parks, and Angie Horton AKA BlueBerry, underneath the heading THE ALLIANCE which had been underlined twice.

Also present to support Detective Buccannon were Officer Timbell, and, all the way from Fulton County, Detective Abrahms.

Detective Buccannon stepped in front of Agent MacMall. "I respect the work of Rodney and Leslie and the effort they've put into the Major League investigation. But the problem is .. ." she turned around and gestured for both agents to step aside and pointed a long wooden ruler at the two names who were the leaders of their respective cliques. "Ms. Tillman is the big fish of all the guppies on this board ... but Mr. Davis is also doing it big," she explained, adding. "My CI" she pointed the ruler... "Mr. Parks, gave me confirmation about the conspiracy involving Sharelle Robinson's beating, which one Lawrence Jackson, now deceased, had been hired to do by ..." she paused, wrote down another name, "... Coley Sams. Now Mr. Sams also used to work for Ms. Tillman. Corey Sams, not to be confused with Coley. was just buried and I'd be willing to bet next month's pay that Coley, because the two of them were as close as brothers, will seek revenge for Corey's murder. And isn't it ironic that not only were each of the bodies burned, but the victims all had some connection with Ms. Tillman. Now Mr. Davis, too, has been around some deadly shootings,

Jap

"Why don't you go arrest him, then?" Agent Smith interrupted, holding her flipped up palms out in front of her.

"Yeah, put his face on TV, someone will call in," Agent MacMall added, dabbing his runny nose.

"Because if he sees his picture on TV, he'll go underground for sure. Mr. Davis already has several warrants out for him, and he's already skipped a court appearance for a weed charge. People like Mr. Davis will eventually slip up, do something silly. I think we just make a sweep. Out of all these people someone will snitch." Detective Buccannon finished, her hands resting on her waist.

Outbursts of different opinions rippled through the classroom—sized meeting place.

"All right, all right!" Lt. Webber shouted, placing her Styrofoam cup of coffee on the table. "I agree with Detective Buccannon. Agent MacMall, how much longer before you have enough on her to arrest Ms. Tillman."

"About two—and-half weeks." he replied, dabbing his draining nostrils. "Sorry, I got a slight cold."

"All right then," Webber said, staring at the calendar. "That means Tuesday, September the 21st. Major League crumbles. Meantime, Detective Buccannon, I'm going to grant you extra units to hunt down Mr. Davis."

All three leaders of the two investigations shared a brief smile before everyone began leaving the room to go their separate ways.

The Next Day ...

The police had Shellz shuffling around to different motels in his attempt to stay a step ahead of them. His attorney had finally caught up with him on his cell phone, informing Shellz about the multiple warrants that he had out for his arrest.

Shellz reached out to Bealz but was told he had problems of his own. By that evening, through various wheeling and dealing, Shellz had San's fifteen hundred dollars for her. San told him to meet her at Irresistables at eleven—thirty.

6:05 P.M.

When Bealz had finished with his shift he stopped at a car wash. As he was vacuuming out the Lincoln Navigator, he started getting calls from heroin customers informing him that he had a rack of customers waiting for him in Churches Chicken, So he hurriedly completed the vacuuming and drove away from the silver vacuum pumps, rushing up Freedom Drive. It was only a matter of moments before he rolled through Tusckasegee Road, making a turn that would lead him over some railroad tracks and up State Street. Just as he was about to turn into the Churches Chicken parking lot, something didn't feel right to him.

"What the fuck?" Bealz asked himself out loud, seeing no one inside Churches, nor were there any cars in the parking lot. With his identity concealed from the outside by the smoke tint that he had added to the Navigator, Bealz drove on by and into a car wash that sat directly across from Family Dollars. After closer examination of his surrounding he peeped Too Bad in the backseat of a green unmarked vehicle. Luckily for Bealz, Too Bad had never seen Bealz driving the orange Navigator.

Bealz eased the SUV into a slanted position in the third stall of the car wash, from all appearances just another vehicle amongst the others there being cleaned. As he sat unseen, watching Too Bad nervously light up a cigarette, Bealz gave a beggar who approached two dollars, never taking his eyes off Too Bad. He took note of the fact that the unmarked vehicle was occupied by two people, with a red—headed woman doing all the talking while waving her finger as if she was giving Too Bad directions.

The more Bealz surveyed the parking lot, which also accommodated a A&P Super Market and a dry cleaners, the more certain vehicles and one white van stood out. To him there were just too many white people apparent on this violent urban side of town. Since Cox Avenue and Churches were within walking distance, Bealz phoned Banga.

"Bealz! Wha' up, Baby," he barked quickly, laid back with his dick down Renee's throat.

"Yo, man, have Too Bad been up to the spot?"

"Yeah. D—Dat nigga done spent a ball thirty wit' da lil nigga Slugga — I got him workin' for me." Banga covered his mouth as he exploded into Renee's mouth.

"Well, I'ma lookin' at this nigga right now takin' up space in the backseat of a vice car."

Banga replied breathlessly, "That nigga Slugga sup———"

"Not Slugga!" Bealz said, cutting Banga off. "I'm talkin''bout Too Bad."

"What?" Banga leaped to his feet, struggling to free his limp dick from Renee's clutches. "Man, fuck dis, Bealz — we ain't gon' let no base head fuck us up."

"I feel ya, Dawg .. hol' up. Too Bad is getting out of the car," Bealz reported as he slouched further down on the soft beige leather, continuing to peer over the steering wheel at Too Bad crossing the street. "Look, shut shit down for now," he ordered, frowning, not sure what to make of what he's seen.

"Gotcha. You straight, Dawg?"

"Yeah, I'm good ... holla."

"One ..

The gun was suddenly right in Bealz's face. Without a word being said, Bealz saw the gunman's finger tightening, ready to fire the kill—shot right into Bealz's forehead.

Bealz's eyes blinked at the sound of the fatal gunshot, but instead of feeling the impact, he saw his assassin's head explode. Instinctively Bealz moved to shield himself from the resulting splatter of blood and cascade of skin fragments bone and brain matter while his mind clearly registered the sound of the dead man's pistol when it slipped from his lifeless hands and clattered to the ground.

Bealz heard the voice of his savior. "You all right?"

Wiping bloody gunk from around his eyes. Bealz blinked repeatedly and frowned as the bright afternoon sun shining in his eyes prevented him from seeing anything but the silhouette of a shadowy face. Like a magnet, however, Bealz's' eyes were drawn in disbelief to the shiny gold police badge that was attached to the shirt of the rescuer who had stepped out of nowhere.

"W—Who are you?" Bealz questioned as his eyes cut momentarily to the prone body on the ground, then to the loaded pistol, then back to the shiny gold badge. He felt the urge to move but somehow couldn't force himself to.

"You must learn to ask the right questions," the gunman answered in a deep voice. ". . . you know who I am..." the voice continued. ". . . There is none so blind as those who look but don't see."

Bealz was trying to clear his head, to think, trying to be his usual glib self, but his thoughts remained garbled. "What the hell is that supposed to mean?"

A quiet, almost taunting laugh assaulted his senses when Bealz found his eyes were rooted lustfully on the perfectly formed 34D—sized breasts to which the gold badge was attached. "... But now you know too much already," the voice droned on as Bealz's eyes were drawn to his rescuer's gun, still smoking, as it rose to take aim at his head. "Say your prayers, Bealz..." And Bealz could do nothing but close his eyes.

The blast of the horn from a passing Escalade startled Bealz's eyes open. Looking quickly around, his mind snapped into gear when he realized that tension and exhaustion had caused him to doze momentarily, and that same dream loitered in his semi—consciousness, waiting for any sign of drowsiness so it could commandeer his thoughts and invoke terror with its disturbing implications.

His mind once again focused, Bealz saw that he was in somewhat of a tight spot since some of the other suspicious—looking vehicles he was watching had commenced mobilization in the area. Where he was positioned he managed to lose sight of Too Bad so he started the SUV and slowly drove from his observation post beneath the roof of the stall. Just past the Ice House, he spotted Too Bad on foot. "Snitching—ass nigga." Bealz cursed to himself out loud as he continued to watch Too Bad pass Dudles Beauty College. Seconds later, as expected, he watched Too Bad and two regular heroin customers descend upon Churches Chicken property.

Having seen all he needed to see. Bealz drove off undetected in the opposite direction, past Bojangles. then exited onto the Interstate I— 77.

Sometime later, after Bealz had spent some time driving and thinking, he drove through the double gates of the fence around the Destinations Cab Company garage. He followed Jake around, watching him replace some batteries in a few cabs. Bealz finally confided to Jake about what had taken place, but quickly grew tired of Jake's constant repeats.

"Okay...Jake, I heard you," he said, firing up a Black N Mile Cigar.

"Look, son, I'm only tryin' to help you. Man, those streets are"

Jap

"I know — wicked and greasy," Bealz interrupted, finishing up Jake's sentence.

Jake removed his gold—framed reading glasses, placed his right hand on Bealz's left shoulder, and said. "What you need to do is save your money and invest in something lucrative."

"Why don't you turn me on to your connect?"

Jake's face turned to stone- his eyebrows knitted. "I would but you'd have to show me your growth. Only then will I even consider the introduction."

Bealz grinned and turned to head back to the SUV. "I got cha', Jake. You'll see."

Jake watched his boy drive back out through the double gates. "Son, you ain't ready," he said to himself, still hearing the SUV's factory system blaring.

Hours later Bealz had been home, changed clothes and vehicles. He drove the Chevy to Pudding's apartment, meeting Trips upon exiting the car Bealz got a kick out of Trips' new— but—old—school damage outfit and dirty white Chuck Taylors.

"Yo Bealz, Ion know what chu laughing at, Dis is da shit," Trips said, ignoring Bealz's constant giggles. "Man you straight? I got thirty—five dollars."

"Nah man — you got to go up to Cox," Bealz replied, pointing.

"Shit man — dat's seven to ten minute walk. I'd rather walk up to The View but ya man Shellz got the police searching for him."

Suddenly Bealz was interested. "For what?" Bealz inquired, walking back towards Trips.

Trips explained, "I wasn't sure but I understood from the streets that Shellz was a wanted man." But Bealz already knew that much from the previous panic calls he'd received from Shellz. Trips slapped skins with Bealz and sped away toward the circle of hustlers that stood outside of Smallwood Grocery.

Pudding stepped outside wearing a flirtatious, peach, form—fitting cocktail dress, its plunging neckline exposing a little cleavage. On her feet she wore matching Jimmy Choo peep—toe pumps. Her hair was in a stylish wrap that showed off her Marni hoop—horn earrings. Her wrist was adorned with a Dragon Silver Cuff, and her Lips were wet—looking, compliments of Mini Moonbeam. She turned around to let Bealz got a good look, but it was someone from a passing car that whistled.

Both Pudding and Bealz giggled.

"Damn, Baby, I think I'm underdressed," Bealz said, hugging Pudding tightly. Palming her ass, he could feel her soft cheeks through her thongs.

"Stop! You gonna wrinkle my dress," she chided, pulling away from him. "Me an' Tanya are going out. Her husband is keeping the girls."

"Damn ... you sure just you and her are going out," he questioned, following her into the apartment, hoisting her skirt and sliding her thongs to the side, with no resistance offered from her.

Jap

"Yeah, now stop — I don't have the time ... ahhhh," she moaned, after Bealz forced his hard dick into her from behind, "Boy, you nasty," she said, pushing back against his thrust. "Unn, unn ...SSSS agh." she looked back at him while parting her legs farther.

Fifteen minutes later, her insides milked and her dress wrinkled, both rested on the couch.

CHAPTER TWENTY-EIGHT

11 P.M.

Irresistibles had an extra large crowd of dudes throwing money at the dancers. Some of the more rude men had to be escorted out for disorderly conduct inside the strip club. The song 'Hot in Here' had the girls shaking their asses like there was no tomorrow. All the men wore their jewels, some of which were real and others fake, but they all glittered with the help of the green and red florescent lights.

Major League entered with VIP status. With San leading, she two— finger saluted those who spoke. Her walk had an extra dip, a white towel wrapped around her shoulders. She wore a pair of Gucci frames with the lightly tinted lenses. Her left Sean Jean velour pant leg was rolled up just below her knee, which showed off her hi—top Gucci two strap shoes. Conspicuously missing was her chain and ML medallion. She knew the Jack Boys would be out and she didn't want to chance getting robbed.

Endz caught up with her and told her to bring Major League into the VIP lounge.

On this night, Milky had a little sexy redbone at his side, and for the first time, Vanilla had POC with him. He held POCs hand, even though he was two inches and thirty pounds heavier. POC's mixed Puerto Rican and black bloodline had the strippers on his jock. To complement his medium build, POC boasted fine black hair and soft light brown complexion, set off by a thin mustache and shaved down the middle beard. Two diamonds sparkled in his ear, and he wore a black silk button down, cream pants, and black leather Polo shoes with the tassel. Now whether or not the owner of the hand holding POC's whose outfit included some tight Baby Phat apparel, would set off a light in the strippers' heads, remained to be seen.

BlueBerry entered the Stripper—filled VIP room, pranced past her co—workers and leaped into San's lap. The two shared a short giggle and a few smooches before Blue handed San fifteen hundred dollars.

"Wha's this," San questioned, looking confused.

"That's from Shellz ... he said he wouldn't be able to make it." Half—grinning, San responded, "Well, that's more pussy for me," nibbling on Blue's neck.

"Girl, you crazy," Blue laughed.

At the same time, on a road called White Plains, two men exited a dark colored sedan that they had parked in front of a home. The men, dressed in black clothes, walked quietly a couple of blocks past where they had parked undetected by any neighbors. One of the men kneeled as if to tie his shoe but instead was looking around to make sure the coast was clear. Sensing it was all clear, the two moved quickly towards the rear of a home. Ordinarily the house's motion sensors would have switched exterior lights on to detect the intruders, but someone had disarmed the all—important ADT alarm system.

Inside, lights throughout the house burned brightly. A television in the bedroom was still playing while the lone occupant slept.

Donning black ski—masks and latex gloves, the two intruders worked vigorously for five minutes to pry the back door open. The shorter of the two who was a pro at breaking into cars finally got the door unlocked with a credit card. His accomplice, who'd been in the home several times previously headed towards the sound of the television.

"Shh," he gestured, peeking through the open bedroom door at the person prone motionless on the bed. He approached the unsuspecting sleeper with his revolver aimed and snatched the silk sheets from the sleeping woman, exposing her nakedness.

He stifled her screams by shoving his pistol into her mouth clearing several of her teeth. She gagged on the long barrel. Blood oozing from her mouth dripped off her chin and down onto her perfectly—shaped breasts. Tears gushed from her eyes and her deep sniffles made it seem like she was desperately trying to catch her breath. The tallest gunman sushed her, promising that he would kill her if she didn't give him the dope and the money. She cut her eyes at the shortest gunman who had his weapon turn sideways at her head. He pulled his pistol from her mouth and her broken teeth fell to the bed. Her body shook, her trembling fingers touched her sore mouth and gums. Withdrawing bloody hands from her mouth, despite the short gunman's use of profanity, she led them to the hidden wall safe.

Working the safe's combination, she protested in a frightened tone, "Do y'all know who y'all's robbing."

"Yeah, bitch, we know ... I used to work for the bitch," he replied. Becoming infuriated at her stalling, he struck her, the blood spewing from the open gash in the rear of her head painting the walk—in closet.

"Okay, okay," she cried, sprawled on the floor, covering her wound with her left hand.

Within moments, the intruders had the female lying on the floor with her hands and feet bound, her mouth gagged. The intruders stuffed two of San's Louis Vuitton bags with her money and three kilos of powder.

"Monica, I'm sorry," the gunman apologized, standing over her with his weapon aimed at the floor.

Monica, San's live—in girlfriend at 1312 Snow White Drive, fearfully stared up at the gunman as he removed his mask. Her eyes opened wider in recognition. As he raised the pistol, she mumbled his name just before the bullet entered her head. Thick blood flowed from her nose, open mouth, and the exit wound in the side of her head.

"Let's bounce, Coley," Lil Gas insisted, pulling on his accomplice's left arm.

In the wee hours on Cox Avenue, Bealz and Banga were still grinding. Since the other Street hustlers decided to go out clubbing, The Alliance members preferred to earn money. They made their dimes extra big and paid runners who came from surrounding hoods to all the way up Beatties Ford Road. With what seemed like every other crack sale, Banga would enter Jughead's crowded liquor house and emerge with a shot of Hen and had the brown cognac guzzled in seconds.

Bealz kept his eyes on Banga's staggering walk. "Yo, Banga." he shouted, gesturing Banga with his finger.

"Sup, Baby Boy," Banga slurred, leaning against the broken down Toyota pick—up.

"Man, you need to slow up on ya drinking, Dawg," Bealz suggested, handing a customer three dime bags.

Banga sucked his teeth. His face screwed up, he turned his drink upside down draining the last of the fluid, he crumbled the clear plastic cup then tossed it in the street. As he ran his hand over his face, he could make out the approaching figure of a man. He pulled his pistol from his back pocket, met the man twenty feet from where he and Bealz were posted. "Sup, Dawg,?" he snarled, keeping his pistol concealed behind his back.

"Not much. Can I get four for thirty five?"

"Sure," Banga replied. As the man took his time recounting his money, Banga suddenly and without warning lashed out against the man's forehead with the pistol. He followed the man's body to the ground, striking the man repeatedly about the face and head area.

"What's up wit' ya man?" a male crack head runner asked Bealz pointing.

Bealz looked over and in the light from the street lamps could see Banga's brutal beating on someone's down and helpless body. He leaped from the pickup truck's hood, ran over and tackled Banga from atop the man.

"Fuck you doing, Man?" Bealz questioned, struggling to contain the larger much stronger youngster.

"Man, fuck dat Nigga, Bealz ... fuck him," he shouted, still trying to get back to his victim who sounded like he was strangling on his own blood.

It took a couple more dudes and Renee to subdue Bangs and rush him into Renee's apartment. Attending to the victim who was unrecognizable through all the blood, Bealz was relieved to hear the man speak. Grabbing a rag someone had handed him, Bealz wiped enough of the blood away from the man's face that he could be identified. Any remorse he felt for the victim quickly disappeared when he recognized Too Bad.

"Yo, Bealz, what's the deal?" Too Bad inquired, struggling to his feet.

"Bad, man, ain't nobody fucking wit' you," Bealz answered, walking away from Too Bad leaving his questions unanswered.
Bealz knew that in all likelihood Banga would have to pay for assaulting an informant but that's the price one has to pay for SNITCHING!

Bealz entered Renee's apartment. To his delight Banga was calmly seated with his pistol in his lap. No words about the assault were spoken. The Alliance men began to count their nightly earnings, which was disrupted by frantic knocks on the door. Banga clutched his gun as Bealz stuffed uncounted money in one pocket and Renee peeked out through her curtain.

"It's Foxy, y'all calm down," she said.

Bealz told Renee to delay opening the door while he and Banga gathered things from the coffee table. Renee waited until the men ran upstairs before opening the door. The men heard Foxy speak about Too Bad telling her that someone had beaten him but he didn't know his attacker's indentity.

Bealz let out a deep sigh. "Damn ... Man, I'm sleepy as hell. I'm glad that Too B————"

"Man, Bealz fuck Too Bad .. fuck Shellz ... fuck all den Niggaz," Banga interjected, angrily overturning the chair that he was sitting on. "Man, before I leave these streets, I'ma leave me some Niggaz stankin'," he kissed his right pointer, and middle finger. "That's my good word." He lowered his hand from where he believed Flip rested, seriously holding shocked gaze.

Dawn — San's residence

An unsuspecting San exited her Tahoe, accompanied by Milky. Opening the front door, they were immediately confronted with the sight of foot prints marring the wall—to—wall carpeting. Milky stunned, stared at the stains. "That looks like .."

San already had her weapon drawn, frantic. "Son of a ——— MONICA!" No response.

Followed closely by Milky, his weapon drawn as well, San stepped gingerly on tiptoe following the trail of bloody footprints which led directly to San's bedroom. She stopped at the door and yelled out Monica's name once more. In the resonating silence, she took a deep breath, looked around quickly at Milky, then eased the door open cautiously.

Stepping inside they could immediately see Monica's bloody body. A quick survey of the room revealed San's safe standing open, the stash spot cleaned out.

"Mutha Fucka rob me," San whispered, defiantly holding her pistol outward.

"What about her?" Milky asked, staring down Monica's body lying in the pool of blood.

San walked over and kicked Monica's lifeless body. "Fuck her. The bitch should've been on point," she shouted, putting her gun away and pulling out her cell phone, punching a speed—dial button.

San caught BlueBerry and gave her the 4—1—1 about Monica's slaying and the rip—off, sharing her suspicion that Shellz was behind the carnage since nothing like this had happened until Shellz learned of the spot. BlueBerry confirmed that Shellz was acting strange when they spoke and he gave her San's fifteen hundred dollars. When San declared in no uncertain terms that Shellz was a dead man walking, BlueBerry promised to help set her boyfriend up. When their call ended, San and Milky quickly made an inspection of the place to make sure no drugs were left around before dialing 9—1—1.

A legion of squad cars from the North Division Police, accompanied by a number of medical vehicles and personnel and unmarked investigator sedans descended upon 1312, disrupting the peace of the early morning. Throngs of curious neighbors ventured out and milled about, many still in their robes and night clothes, discussing the unfamiliar commotion being caused by all the flashing lights and horde of uniformed officers running rampant through their ordinarily quiet street. Some of the neighbors began to complain about the disregard shown by the officers who parked disrespectfully on their manicured lawns. Added to the clamor was the annoying barking of neighborhood dogs as they too voiced their displeasure at the disturbance.

A ripple of relief spread through the two large crowds of onlookers that had assembled behind the yellow tape around San's house when they witnessed San, their mysterious, rude neighbor, followed closely by Milky, both being escorted out in handcuffs. Murmurs of "Good riddance" could be heard before their sudden gasp when the Coroner rolled out a body stuffed in a black bag and deposited it in a white van parked on the lawn in.

Sitting in the back of separate squad cars, both San and Milky shouted slurs at the onlookers. San did the most taunting. Several people watched in disgust as San's spit rolled down the rear passenger's window.

10:45 A.M.

San sat across from two uniforms and a plain clothes investigator in the small interrogation room. She lit a cigarette and defiantly blew smoke across the square metal table into Investigator Chump's face. San smiled into the huge reflector glass, the only window in the room. On the other side of the one—

way glass Agents MacMall and Smith stared back impassively as they listened through the speaker system and made notes of San's evasive answers.

"This is some bullshit," Agent Smith flatly stated, shaking her head. "Why don't we go ahead and pull, the plug on Ms. Tillman's smart ass now, before someone else is killed."

Watching her in silence Agent MacMall crossed his legs, adjusting his body to a more comfortable position, and stifled a secretive half— grin.

Around Noon

Bealz reclined on the couch with his feet crossed, watching Pudding waltz around the room in a blue thong and wife beater preparing lunch. He was texting back and forth with Karma, updating her on all the new moves The Alliance was making and his recent discoveries. He smiled as he read Kana's text, "GOTTA GO GET THESE WIRES TOOK OUT OF MY MOUTH. TELL PUDDING I SAID HELLO — LOVE, KARMA."

Bealz responded with, "GOTCHA HOPE TO SEE YOU SOON." He placed the cell phone on the glass coffee table and gave Pudding's spacious hips lustful stares as each cheek bobbled with her every step.

CHAPTER TWENTY-NINE

Just days before the scheduled big bust, Detective Buccannon received an anonymous call, the voice implicating Shellz in the murder of Monica Luiz Alvera. Thus far into the investigation of her murder, no one had been arrested and San had not made good on her promise to kill Shellz. San knew she'd be implicated by any revenge plots if she acted impulsively so she waited patiently while she made her plans.

Meanwhile, inside an interrogation room of the Pitt County Detention Center (PCDC), Terrance Gilton aka TG was spewing every 'profane word and invective known to man, denouncing the stolen car charge to the two uniform officers present. When the door opened, TG turned his attention to the red—headed female wearing a suit who strode through. The two officers who had been interrogating TG backed against the room's gray painted walls, deferring to the woman's confidant entrance. TG laughed at the ziplock plastic bag the smiling redhead was holding up which contained a book of matches.

"Fuck is that," TG inquired, leaning back, interlocking his fingers behind his head. "We going to light some candles?"

"Mr. Gilton, you're in bigger trouble than you know. You have the right to remain sil————"

"Yeah, yeah. Blah, blah," he interrupted, taunting her with flicks of his tongue.

"Mr. Gilton, I seriously advise you to help yourself here. I have the authority to make your stolen car case disappear on the condition you tell me all about the Corey Sams murder." She saw how his face straightened when she mentioned murder.

TG cued in on her gold name plate that was pinned onto the collar of her coat. "Uh, Ms. Buccannon, I don't know what the fuck dem matches for," he said, pointing at the plastic bag, "Or what da fuck murder you're talking 'bout. Now just like the dismissal of the case I had in Durham, this stolen car case will be dismi—"

"Hey!" she raised her voice, cutting him off. "The body you burned in a wooded area of Kings Mountain."

Agents MacMall and Smith entered the room, jarring TG out of his daze. The picture of one of Corey's mugshots seemed to contribute to T.G.'s deflated demeanor. He lowered his head as the words "death penalty" echoed through his consciousness.

Two hours into his interrogation, confronted with the telling evidence, Agent Smith recognized TG's defeated emotional state and laying a hand on MacMall's shoulder, said to TO. "Mr. Gilton, you're in a tough spot here, I realize, but your best bet, in fact your only bet, is to make it easy on yourself ... this isn't going to go away, and neither are we, but help us out a little and I promise to go to bat for you with the prosecutor."

For the next forty—five minutes, not only did TG implicate his childhood friend Pug, who had enlisted his involvement in the murder, but he also described how San had tricked Gramz into believing that he, Pug, was supposed to be killed, and not Gramz.

Feeling they had enough evidence now against San and Major League, the jailer was summoned and the interrogators all watched with contented smiles as the black youngster with twister plaits was being escorted back to his cell.

"I'm going to have the Greenville Police Department pick up Mr. Gibson to bring him in for questioning," Agent Smith said, turning the volume on her walkie talkie up.

"The guy called Pug?" Agent MacMall asked.

"The one and only ..." Agent Smith responded over her shoulder as she hurriedly exited the room.

Agent MacMall laid out a recent picture of San's smiling face, taken inside of a local Charlotte night club. He drew his finger around her eyes and nose which he'd seen too many times. "I've finally got your ass," he whispered to himself.

*   *   *   *   *   *   *   *

In the Navigator, Bealz was about to turn into the parking lot of an upscale restaurant off Park Road to meet Pudding for lunch. Thinking he was being paranoid or delusional, he thought he recognized Tiff's Beamer parked near the front of the establishment.

Paranoid or not, he decided to drive on by, pounding his right thigh three times in frustration. The church might have been coincidental, but this was too much. He dialed Pudding's cell phone as he stared up at the clear blue skies, silently praying. On the third ring, Pudding finally answered. "Hey, Baby — where are you?"

"Damn, Baby, I got to take the Navigator to Jiffy Lube. It's leaking oil," he lied.

"Okay — guess I'll see you later," she replied disappointedly as she watched Tiff emerge from the restroom, stabbing at a stain on her canary yellow Chanel skirt with a monogrammed hankie. "All right, Baby. I'll make it up to you. Bye."

She was ready to express her love when she heard the dial tone.

Tiff sat down. "Sup cuz? Why tha long face?"

Brushing off the fact she'd been stood up, she responded, "Oh. nothing." She smiled, grabbed a menu, "So what are you gonna order ... let me guess. Fried chicken," she teased.

"You betta say it," Tiff responded, waving her hand to get the waiter's attention.

The two first cousins shared a giggle.

Bealz approached the juncture of Tyvola and South Boulevard. Silently he justified his unfaithful and unjust betrayal that he'd done behind the backs of both Tiff and Pudding.

Since he wasn't going to be joining his girl for lunch and had several bags of heroin in a hidden compartment, he redialed a few of his faithful customers numbers instructing them to meet him at the car wash off Freedom Drive, willing to battle through midday rush hour traffic to help quell the sickness of nine dope fiends.

As he drove up Freedom Dr., he looked over and unexpectedly recognized a familiar face standing outside of McDonalds, talking on a cell phone. Bealz looked over his left shoulder, put on his left turn signal light, then with the help of an accommodating motorist, safely moved into the turning lane. He waited until a break in the oncoming traffic enabled him to make his turn. In seconds he'd pulled in front of the car that the person of interest was about to pull out in. Bealz blew the horn, catching the driver of the black '96 Chevy Impala by surprise. Bealz threw his fist up then leaped from the SUV.

"Wha's up, Bizzo — when you get out?" Bealz inquired, chest—bump— hugging the man, smiling.

"Oh, man — like a week ago," Bizzo replied, hiding his lie behind an insincere grin. "Man, inside the County I heard that you and Shellz had done fell out. And I heard about Karma. Wha's the deal? I got myself together, ya feel me?" he said. Pointing at the Chevy sitting on factory rims, he added, "Me and Lette are sharing the payments."

Bealz nodded, "Put my number in your phone," he said, waiting for Bizzo to pull out his cell. "It's 704—953—0017. Now what's your digits?" Bealz inquired, wondering why Bizzo was acting so apprehensive about divulging his numbers, and taking note of the way Bizzo's eyes kept nervously darting back and forth. Bealz assumed Bizzo was still getting high.

"704—953—2727," Bizzo finally replied, looking everywhere but in Bealz's eyes.

"A'ight man, I'ma get at you."

Bizzo waited until Bealz climbed back into his SUV before he yelled out, "Yo tell Karma I'm praying for her."

Bealz grinned, threw a peace sign over his left shoulder, then drove away.

By nightfall, Bealz and Banga were steadily grinding with other hustlers whose quality and quantity were no match for The Alliance. Two of the seven other dope boys made a wise decision and affiliated themselves with The Alliance brethren especially in view of Banga's display of violence over what he'd do to anyone who shorted him or disrespected his rigid, inflexible Street rules of engagement.

Bealz stood in Jugheads yard talking sports with him when a crack head approached wanting two dimes of crack. Bealz took Jughead's nod of approval and accepted the junkie's money, directing the fiend towards a folded bottle cap on the side of the road by a sewage drain. After the crack fiend complied and brought Bealz the cap, Bealz banded the chubby toothless man his purchase, closed the cap, then tossed it back near the drain, he and Jughead then resumed their conversation.

As fiends of both heroin and crack suddenly began to flood the strip, Jughead's liquor house customers started to navigate through the congestion of foot traffic and motor vehicles on Cox Avenue. From time to time a police squad car would roll through. If the crowd was thick enough, or made any suspicious moves, the officers would alight and search certain individuals and then inspected the surrounding grounds for any sign of the dealers' stashes.

Bealz had two male crack heads wearing small Radio Shack earpiece headset transmitters on point as look—outs, corner to corner, whenever they weren't off hitting their own crack pipes.

In different areas of the strip, especially in the murky points, anything could be seen at any particular time. Bealz had excused himself and walked behind a vacant apartment to take a leak when he stumbled upon a hustler getting a blow—job from a female. He quickly turned away and jumped a chain link fence into another back yard to drain his snake. Unseen, however, a female mixed breed dog nursing her young pups beneath the house regarded Bealz as a threat. The angry dog came out growling and approached slowly with thick drool hanging from her mouth. Bealz retreated in a panic. Feeling the jagged edges of the fence, he managed to leap over it just before the dog charged. His shoelace got caught up, violently slamming him onto the dirt ground strewn with broken glass. He grunted in pain, opening his eyes and from his upside down position, sighting the dealer now sexing the female from behind.

"You a'ight Bealz?" the man asked, hitting his sex partner with a quick thrust.

"Yeah, I'm good," Bealz answered, struggling to his feet. Wincing from the pain from the cuts on his hands, he was unable to brush the dirt from his clothes because of the blood oozing from the cuts.

Making his way to Renee's apartment created a stir from more than a few people as he passed. "No, I 'ain't get beat up," he kept insisting.

With a little help from Banga, Bealz finally made it to Renee's sanctuary where Renee treated his cuts with peroxide and placed three bandages over the more serious cuts.

"Damn, my Nig, real Nigga's overlook those nicks," Banga jokingly mocked Bealz's hissing noise, and both laughed.

Sunday 10 P.M.

Shellz was glad to be out on the town. He rode shotgun with Milky and Pug, headed towards club Vague. Passing through a dark wide spot on the road that was surrounded by a few trees and modest homes, Shellz happened to read the Rea Road sign and recollected the torment that a professional football player had put his then pregnant girlfriend and unborn child through, when she had been shot and eventually succumbed to her injuries.

On top of that, Shellz developed an uneasy feeling when the short driver wearing the do—rag kept glancing back at him in the rear view mirror.

"Puffin' on lie, hoping that it gets me high, got a Nigga going crazy," Milky's ring tone on his cell phone sang out. "San — wha's up?" he answered, expelling weed smoke from his mouth. Shellz grabbed the blunt from Milky's hands, intent on decoding Milky's conversation.

"Yeah, he's chillin' wit' us, blowin' da best chronic ... on point, da girls are full . . . "Milky paused to let San talk, then answered, "Ahh, thangs gonna go smoothly, da bitches promise to distribute enough head," Milky giggled. "We'll be there in ten minutes. Blink the lights so that we'll be able to locate you ... yeah, yeah."

Click.

He turned and took the blunt from Shellz, then passed it to Pug. What Major League and Shellz wasn't aware of was that BlueBerry was secretly playing both fields. She already had San believing her loyalty to her but with sexual favors she had control of Shellz's mind as well. BlueBerry on the other hand, had confided to Shellz that San thought that he was the one that broke into 1312 and was responsible for Monica's death.

So as Pug drove off into a remote and unpopulated neighborhood, close to the city's outer limits, Shellz removed his foe—fifth from his waistband. Shellz waited until the opportune time when Pug pulled to the side of the road by a wooded area, dimly lit, by widely spaced street lights.

"I gotta piss. I'll be right back," Pug said, exiting the vehicle. Shellz watched Pug disappear into the woods and looked back at the headlights of another vehicle slowly approaching from the rear, "Have y'all found out who robbed the spot?" Shellz asked.

He caught a glimpse of Pug emerging holding a dark object, then Milky's smiling face, at the same time hearing the squeal of the brakes from the approaching vehicle. Making a snap decision, Shellz hoisted the pistol.

"BOOM! BOOM! Shellz's hand jerked upwards, firing two shots into Milky's head, sending his body sprawling forward and his common sense distributed unevenly against the car's dashboard and windshield.

BOOM! BOOM! BOOM! ... BOOM! BOOM!

Pug kneeled down, letting his 9mm sing at Shellz, while at the same time, from over the opened door of her Tahoe which San had stopped near the back of the stolen car, three feet of fire emerged from San's AK— 47 which had been outfitted with shell catchers.

San let a rapid succession of bullets fly from the hundred round drum, most of which ripped through the trunk, shattered window and all the way through the death car. For the second time Shellz found himself in the backseat of a car ducking bullets and flying glass. He wiped Milky's blood from his face.

From twenty feet away, Pug continued to fire his pistol at Shellz from behind a tree. While San continued her violent onslaught against Shellz. "You dead Nigga," she shouted from her position, now crouched behind the Tahoe. She yelled, "Come on, Pug!" She kept Shellz at bay with rifle fire that lit up the night skies like the Fourth of July as Pug made his way to the SUV.

POP! POP! POP! POP! POP! POP! San continued to fire as she calmly walked back to the driver's seat. She paused and passed the warm rifle to Pug.

As Pug released another succession of rapid shots at the stolen '87 Nissan, Shellz laid low on the floorboards, ducking the hail of bullets that pierced the car's metal. He felt the back of the sedan drop as the bullets flattened the tires. Hearing the SUV's squealing tires, he chanced a peep over the carnage caused by the shell casings. Seeing the SUV's headlights swaying side to side as whoever was steering struggled to control it in reverse, Shellz jumped out of the car, firing at the SUV with the few remaining shells.

Shellz stared through the darkness at the receding still as the Tahoe's driver regained control, made a turn, then faded into the night. It was only by the grace of God that Shellz hadn't gotten shot. He rushed over to see blood flowing from different areas of Milky's Coogi velour outfit.

In the distance he could hear the wailing sounds of sirens. He looked around frantically for somewhere to run. Through the trees he spotted a sliver of light and started running in its direction.

Finally emerging from the wooded area, he was relieved to approach a well—lit part of South Boulevard, several yards from the James & Martin Freeway, and Pineville's county line.

Approaching a couple of convenience stores Shellz tried to act normal as a line of police emergency vehicles rushed past him, their flashing blue lights temporarily modifying the surroundings. He turned to see a city bus headed in his direction. Spotting the bus stop sign a few yards away, he trotted over to it and waited for the bus.

Boarding, the bus driver inquired about the blood that trickled from his right ear Shellz ignored the inquiry, covered his neck, paid his fare and proceeded to a seat. He wasn't concerned about the pistol because his oversized black tee and black pants disguised the bulge. He cut his eyes at a few passengers, patting his pockets in search of his cell phone. It was missing.

Jap

"Fuck!" he cursed out loud, pounding his fist against the window of the bus.

"Hey, buddy, calm down," the bus driver cautioned over the loudspeaker, Shellz threw his hand up and prayed that he'd lost his cell phone in his dash through the woods.

CHAPTER THIRTY

San drove up Woodlawn erratically, cursing, repeatedly striking the dashboard and stabbing a finger at Pug to emphasize her point. Pug sat low in the passenger seat, quietly watching the hampered traffic as he felt the adrenalin rush from the attack on Shellz slowly subside. The potent stench of exploded gunpowder from the warm AK—47 propped between his legs prompted him to lower the passenger window a few inches with his right hand. His left still gripped the other pistol snuggled on his lap, the slide still locked back from being empty.

San was spewing invectives, complaining that Milky's untimely death left Major League in its most vulnerable state. Pug cut his eyes at the mist of spit from San's nonstop jabbering mouth, illuminated sporadically by the headlights from passing vehicles beamed into the Tahoe.

"Let me call this bitch," San said suddenly,. Gripping the steering wheel with her left hand, she held her cell phone in an elevated position with her right hand and hit speed dial.

On the other end, BlueBerry reluctantly picked up when she saw on the Caller ID who it was.

"Hey San, what's up?" BlueBerry asked, breathlessly suppressing her moans as Lil Gas worked his oral magic on her.

"If dat Nigga Shellz ain't in jail, I want you to set his ass up for me, girl?" San demanded harshly.

311

"Okay, baby, what happened," she inquired, staring down into Lil Gas's beady eyes locking onto hers as he looked up at her from between her legs. In her state of ecstasy, BlueBerry only half—listened to San describe what had just taken place, quivering from the expert teasing of Lil Gas's veteran tongue on her swollen clit. When she felt herself about to explode, she hoisted her legs into a "V' shape to give Lil Gas extra leverage.

"SAN, I GOT CHU," she shouted into the phone, throwing it aside to unleash her moans and release her climax juice into his mouth. In the SUV, San looked at her phone in disbelief as she protested, "This bitch hung up on me!" Turning and looking at her passenger, "Pug, I'ma need you 24/7 until 'dis shit blows over. You know that, don'cha?"

Pug nodded, "I got you, Homie," he replied, still looking out the window as he stroked his trimmed—up thick beard.

Meantime, in the aftermath of the deadly gun battle that had just taken place, a mixture of blue and red lights from Charlotte's squadron of elite emergency vehicles cast a foreboding radiance over the mélange of medical and law enforcement personnel that encompassed the slumped, bullet—ridden corpse in the stolen vehicle. Aside from the endless squawks from the walkie—talkies and the wail of an occasional siren in the distance, the crime scene along the stretch of desolate road was relatively quiet.

One of several officers searching for evidence and collecting shell casings from the embankment that led into the woods suddenly heard the muted sound of a cell phone's musical ring tone. He flashed his flashlight along the ground towards the sound. Through a small patch of weeds he spotted the phone's green LCD light just as the ringing ceased.

"I got something," he yelled out.

He waited until others had gathered around him, then with latex covering his hands, he picked up the cell phone with two fingers. Turning it over carefully, he read out loud the name of the missed caller.

"BlueBerry?" he said, looking around with a look that asked silently if the name meant anything to anyone.

The supervising officer, an older black man, stocky build, shook his head then offered, "Here," as he held open an oversized clear plastic bag. As the young officer deposited the cell phone carefully into the bag, the senior officer nodded. "Good work, son."

A legion of officers had already been dispersed to conduct an exhaustive search for suspects involved in the shooting. Unbeknownst to the officers, one of the subjects of the intense manhunt was seated in a McDonald's near the intersection of Remount Road and South Boulevard.

Nervously, Shellz picked at the hot fries of his Number Two. Staring transfixed at nothing in particular, he reflected on the fact that up to this point in his life he had been lucky not to have been killed or locked up. Suddenly reminding himself of the critical situation he was in, he snapped out of his reverie and looked around for anything out of the usual. In particular he studied every car that entered McDonald's parking lot, hoping that the cab he'd called for would arrive sooner than later.

As he sipped his sweet tea through a straw, his eyes caught those of a man seated at another table who had been staring at Shellz over his opened Charlotte Observer newspaper, but who looked quickly away.

Shellz took the expression of fear he'd immediately read in the man's eyes as a foreboding, especially when he saw the stranger signal for the black, stocky, balding manager.

Shellz rose from his seat, took his tray of half—eaten food to the wastebasket located in the rear between the bathroom and exit when he heard the three bleats of a car horn from parking lot. Without risking a look back, Shellz bolted from the restaurant to the waiting cab.

As they drove away, Shellz caught a glimpse of the white, mid— to late—forties customer inside McDonald's pointing out to the manager the picture in the paper of one Shelton Davis AKA Shellz, underneath which the caption in bold letters read ARMED AND DANGEROUS.

The manager quickly shuffled over to the restaurant's phone and dialed 9—1—1. Within minutes several police cruisers, some from the murder scene, converged open the fast food restaurant, momentarily blocking all exits. Inside, investigators followed the manager into the office and on the restaurant's security video tape, closely viewed the somewhat -distorted recording of Shellz ordering his food and flirting with the female cashier.

Immediately after being informed by the manager that Shellz had been picked up by a cab that took off in the direction of uptown, an APB was issued for any two—toned light blue and orange cab in a five to eight mile radius.

Shellz sat in the back seat of the cab being driven by a Jamaican sporting a serious dreadlocks. Somewhat relaxed, Shellz silently thanked God for being alive. He tapped his fingers on his right leg to the beat of the Reggae music the driver had blasting on his CD player. The music was interrupted by the cab's two— way radio as the dispatcher alerted the driver of an emergency and instructing him to contact local law enforcement immediately. The driver of the cab, who bore an uncanny resemblance to Bob Marley, looked back and briefly held Shellz's intimidating gaze.

"Hey mon' - it's not me problem what you do," he said in a deep Jamaican accent, "but tif you ton't hurry up and get where you are going ta, PoPo gonna be on our ass real soon," he cautioned.

Shellz let out a sigh of relief that the driver did not bitch up. "Drop me off on Fifth Street," Shellz said, staring at the lights shining on the two huge Panther heads outside of the Stadium. Shellz had only one opportunity of evasion available and hoped he wouldn't be turned away. The cab driver did as directed. Shellz paid him, then hopped out on Fifth Street.

In the small neighborhood that sat off in the cut, he approached an apartment that had four units down and an upstairs apartment. Shellz ran up the flight of stairs and softly tapped on the door of Apartment.

C. Putting his ear to the door, he could hear someone on the inside of the apartment shushing a crying child, muffled talking and then footsteps that sounded like they were headed towards him. He retreated a step just as the door opened.

Shellz met Lette's eyes over the brass security chain that prevented the door from opening all the way. -

"Lette, hey, can I call a fr———"

"Hold on," Lette responded, closing the door in his face. Shellz heard the verbal sounds of a heated argument between Lette and some male and wondered who she had in the apartment. To Shellz's knowledge, her man Bizzo was still locked up.

Shellz heard the jingle of the brass security chain being removed, then the door was re—opened to reveal Bizzo blocking the doorway, a pistol in his left hand being held behind his back.

Shellz gave Bizzo surprised and apologetic half—grin.

"Sup, Babe Boy — when did you get out?" Shellz questioned, squinting his eyes and extending his hand greeting to Bizzo.

"Not long — 'bout a week an sumpin'," Bizzo answered. Sensing no threat, he shoved the pistol into his left rear pocket and shook Shellz's extended hand, stepping aside to invite Shellz's entry.

"Damn, Babe Boy, your face is all over the tube."

"Yeah, I figured," Shellz responded, staring at the pricey furniture and TV that had replaced the older model Zenith. "You and Lette done moved up"

"Have a seat, my Nigga ... yeah, she was in a wreck and got a lil cheese. This shit is from a rental store. I know Bealz told you about the Impala that he seen me in."

"Bealz? Nah Dog, dat Nigga won't reach out to a Nigga. Man, this lil Nigga named Gas stuck me for forty summin' ounces. Then his homeboys in Lakeview tried to assassinate a Nigga. Now I'm beefin' wit' a bitch named San .."

"San!" Bizzo shockingly repeated, sitting up from his money—green leather sofa.

"Yeah, man. You know her?"

"Who doesn't that bitch is gettin' that gwap," he grinned mischievously. Bizzo leaned back when he saw Shellz pull out his pistol.

"I ain't got no bullets and thirty five hundred dollars in my pocket," Shellz explained, making it sound like a cry—nut for help "I'll help you, Dawg," Bizzo said with his closed fist extended to Shellz.

The two went over plans for a hide—out and a place to set up shop as Shellz's picture and all of his info continued to dominate every local news telecast. He had become the Most Wanted Man in the Queen City, especially after the police linked him to the shooting through his fingerprints on the bullet casings the police found in the backseat of the Nissan. Though ballistics hadn't been completed, investigators and police felt the bullets that went into Milky's head came from Shellz's .45 caliber.

9 A.M.

Exhausted, after having pulled an all—nighter with Banga, Bealz lounged in a recliner, his feet propped up, still wired as he looked over the currency stacked on his glass coffee table. He'd been home for only an hour and thirty of the sixty minutes he and Karma had been texting back and forth. Besides sharing information about Shell's misfortune, Bealz was relieved to learn that Karma had her dental work completed. Although she was anxious to get back into the fold, Bealz had to quell her enthusiasm, advising her that the time wasn't right.

Hanging up, Bealz grabbed his universal remote control and turned on his home entertainment system. After cranking up Biggie's 'Life After Death' CD, he nodded his head to Notorious Thugs, then enjoyed a blunt of Kush. As smoke curled from his mouth into his nose, he answered his cell phone.

"Good morning, Jacob," a soft voice said.

"Hey, Tiff. You up early. Wha's happenin'?"

"I be at work early every morning ... uh, can you turn that music down ... thank you. Now are we still on?"

"On? On for what?" he replied, cutting her off.

She heaved a sigh. "Dinner at SA'MORES remember?"

318

Playing it off, he recovered, "Girl, you kno' I was kidding I remember. What time ...?"

"How's about seven o'clock?"

"Sounds good. I'll pick you up at six—thirty." There were sound of multiple voices in her background put him on alert.

"Alright, Baby. Bye."

"Yeah—yeah," he said, frowning. Click.

Meantime, in another part of the city, Detective Buccannon stood in front of her peers, heatedly reminded them of the importance of finding Shelton Davis. Even Agents MacMall and Smith agreed with Buccannon's raves, although Smith continued to pressure MacMall about arresting Sandra Tillman.

In the field, an additional unit of officers and two other divisions were called in to join the manhunt for Shellz. Pug's name was added to the pursuit, having been identified from his fingerprints found on shell casings left behind in both the Nissan and on the grassy side of the road.

*　　*　　*　　*　　*　　*　　*

Bealz peeked out of his eleven—foot windows at the city's skyline highlighted by the morning sun. He had his wife—beater tucked into his faded baggy Sean Jean pants, the gold emblem on the buckle displayed prominently on his Gucci belt. His pant legs overlapped his crisp white Air Force Ones, the outfit completed with a white and dark blue wide—spaced Pique Polo three button short sleeve shirt. He checked his blacked out Movado time piece on his left arm, picked up his keys and made his way to the door.

Outside, he cut his eyes at the Chevy but went to the Navigator instead. Opening the door of the SUV and climbing in, he started the engine, adjusted the AC, and replaced The Games CD for a mixed R&B, cutting the volume to a comfortable level. He grabbed the two—way radio from its holster on the passenger seat, then cut his eyes once more at his Chevy as he put the Navigator in gear.

As he drove out of the parking lot of the huge complex, he spoke into the broadcast device, "Good mornin', this is Bealz from Destination's special transpo and I'm ready to work."

Seconds later, a response. "Hey, Son — at controls this morning. Wifey's at the doctor."

"Sup, Jake. If you don't have no calls for me, I'ma go steal some calls," he joked.

"No, you ain't. In twenty minutes a couple at the Embassy Suites will be waiting for you. Take them wherever they wanna go ... big tippers."

"That's a big ten—foe, roger that, over and out," Bealz joked, replacing the two—way in its holster. Pulling down the sun visor, he caught and donned his Gucci shades.

On his way to the hotel, Bealz stopped and filled up the gas tank. Thirty minutes later he was holding the door open for his two female passengers, a chunky blonde and a very attractive brunette. Once seated, the brunette spoke for both of them, and in a flirtatious Spanish accent requested a visit to North Lake Mall, then a freaky store. As he drove away from the Embassy Suites, he was only half— listening to the ladies discussing a modeling show while he thought about his plans for the evening.

"Hey, driver — what's your name?" The brunette asked.

Before answering, he glanced at her in the mirror, amazed at how much she resembled Penelope Cruz and allowing his mind to wrap around her Spanish accent. Finally, "My name's Jacob, but everyone calls me Bealz."

"Bealz?" the chunky blond with her hair in a bun said, squinching up her face.

"Yes, ma'am, Bealz," he repeated. Stopped at a red light, he was able to look back at them both. "It's a nickname that I earned in Junior High School, and it stuck with me."

"Well, my name is Montella Giles," the nicer of the two said.

"And this is my friend, the famed designer Artillia Alverez."

"Charmed, I'm sure," Artillia said, rolling her eyes.

"If you don't give a fuck about a bitch, then you rollin' wit' the Row."

The conversation was interrupted by the ringing of Bealz's cell phone. Bealz struggled to drive and answer it before the ring tone sounded again.

"Back with the on ———"

He pushed the hands—free and answered in mid—ring, "Hello."

Over the hands—free speaker, "Wha's up, My Nig? It's clucking over here," Banga reported on the crack—sells.

Bealz cut the cell phone's volume down but after seeing in the rearview mirror Artillia's face turning bright red, he knew it was too late — the damage had been done.

"Yo man, I'ma call you later," Bealz said, disconnecting the call.

Montella leaned up between the driver and passenger seat, "Hey, that's my song — turn it up," she proclaimed, singing along to Vanessa Williams's song 'Dreaming.'

As the music played, both Bealz and Montella ignored Artillia's constant sighs. Three hours and several stops later, Bealz was finally back at the Embassy Suites. Having just helped the ladies tote their dry cleaned garments and shopping bags inside, he ambled back to Navigator sticking the cab fare they'd paid him in one pocket and his hundred and fifty dollar tip in the other. He decided to go shopping for an outfit that was sure to impress Tiff.

After plotting a short route, he proceeded to a shop known to offer finest tailor—made clothes, suits, and shoes in the city. Once there he allowed the tailor to take his measurements to assure a custom fit. It wasn't long before Bealz was standing in front of a full—length mirror, navel—gazing his outfit. A pair of navy blue Ralph Lauren pants and striped button down Ralph Lauren shirt complemented a pair of blueberry square bloc Maury Gators. He smiled at himself then quickly changed back into his outfit, paid for his clothes, and left, humming.

On the way home he called Pudding and was able to convince her that he and Banga were headed to Rock Hill, South Carolina, on business, although it was a lie. Back home, he took his shower, got dressed, sprayed on his Sean Jean cologne, then armed with pre-rolled weed—laced blunts inside a chocolate Philly box, he headed out to pick up Tiff. He drove the Navigator just in case anyone recognized the Chevy.

CHAPTER THIRTY-ONE

San and Pug sat inside Irresistibles watching the ladies prepare for the night's activities. Ordinarily they would be anticipating the approaching festivities with enthusiasm, but they were in no mood for celebration on this particular night.

Earlier San had had to face up to the fact that only forty seven thousand dollars remained in her possession, and considering the fact that she was a hundred and fifty thousand in the hole due to some product she'd received on consignment, San's mood was dark. She had one ace left up her sleeve and she was ready to play it.

And at that moment, her ace walked through the door. San stood when Endz and his crew made their entrance with no less grandeur than Moses parting the Red Sea. Immediately spotting San, Endz motioned for her to follow him, which she did.

In his VIP room, San commented on Endz's Now & Later colored Air Force Ones, "Sup, Playa — nice kicks. So what chu want a bitch to do?"

Endz pulled a Cuban Cigar from his designer shirt pocket and bit off the end. Before speaking, he lit the cigar and puffed on it three times.

Leaning back, he finally spoke, "I think ya girl BlueBerry's tryin' to get me robbed."

San retreated, opening and closing her legs. "Nah ... Blue?... Hell, Nah .."

"Look, she swore she had a Nigga named Lil Gas and Coley would be needing to cop big after they got rid of three Birds. She told me not to mention it to you, but tha' shit don't add up right." He paused to take a deep drag from the cigar, then continued, "I like you, and I hope that together we can take over the city. It's fucked up 'bout your clique being snubbed out. But me and . . ." he hesitated, pointed at his clique that stood guard outside the glass, staring in at them with menace. "... My boys believe in loyalty. Feel me?"

San dropped her head in resignation, now that all the pieces were fitting together in her mind. Quietly she admitted to herself. This whole time it was BlueBerry, Lil Gas, and it was Coley who went to see her connect and not Grams. Damn, it was Coley and Lil Gas that robbed me. The bitch even played me and Shellz against each other. I should've known how insistent Blue was trying to get me to kill Shellz.

Endz had been watching her intently as she went through her emotional changes. Finally thumping ashes into the tray, he asked, "San, you a' ight?"

She snickered. "Yeah, my Nigga. I'm good ... I'll do whatever I got to do."

San read Endz's lips say "Kill BlueBerry."

With no hesitation, San whispered back, "I got 'chu."

Sa'More's restaurant was a wooded enclave of luxury overlooking Lake Norman. Inside, crystal light fixtures hung from the twenty—foot ceilings, their sparkle reflecting in the black marble floors. An orchestra reminding Bealz of the one on the Titanic played soft classical music. Chefs rolled grills up to the tables and cooked patron's food right in front of them.

Bealz and Tiff were seated at a table ten feet from the wet bar. Over glasses of Champagne they gave each other flirtatious stares. He couldn't stop staring at the plunging neckline of her short peach mini— dress. He leaned back and peeped beneath the table at her sexy black lace with pink engraving platform pumps. Blushing, she asked, "What?"

He shook his head. "Oh, nothing," he replied. In a special sparkle of light he was able to capture her keen features. "Tiff, you're truly beautiful," he admitted. Making her smile he added, "Or is it this wine?"

She poked her lips out and turned her head sideways. "Don't zhate."

They giggled.

Following their expensive meal, they sat in the SUV and watched the waves of water wash up on the rocks. Bealz had the old Keith Sweat Song making the unpractical moment last forever. He stared out at a woman playfully riding on a man's back. Abruptly a feeling and the fresh scent of Tiff's pink thongs tickled his right cheek. He turned to catch her opened legs and the moist sound of her fingers stroking her clit.

"Tiff, wha' you doin'." he inquired, knitting his eye brows but simultaneously pulling out his swelling dick. He looked around and saw others exiting the crowded restaurant towards the parking lot preparing for departure.

"Oh — shit," he said, feeling Tiff's warm mouth swallow half of his dick. He placed his right hand on the back of her curly—do. Switching hands, he began to play in her wet vagina, separating her labia with two fingers.

"Damn, girl ... Oh, shit," he mumbled as he pressed the lever on the side of the seat, reclining it as far as it would go. He could feel her slobber dribble down over his nut sack.

"I got to fuck you now," he protested.

She flicked her expert tongue against the head of his dick, then removed her mouth from his slippery shaft and threw her left leg over his lap, mounting him backwards. In the driver's seat, Tiff braced herself by the steering wheel as she reached between her legs and grabbed his dick. She held it steady as she lowered herself onto the throbbing shaft, her murmurs filling the SUV. Hissing from his upward thrust, she made noises like her breath was being taken away.

She looked around at Bealz over her left shoulder and in the light of the full moon he could see a twinkle in her eye. She under cuffed the steering wheel, making it like she was doing pull—ups off then back down on his shaft. They pleaded with each other for leniency as they both approached their peak of rapture.

Little did either of them know that in the midst of their sexual acrobatics, Bealz had accidentally depressed the number two on the speed— dial of his cell phone which was in his pocket.

Jap

The sound bites of their entire sexual tryst was broadcast through the airways to ears that were always open.

During the entire ride to the drop—off point to Tiff's crib, Bealz enjoyed her special lip service and swallowing technique. A couple of times on the way he almost wrecked the SUV before he was able to regain control.

Finally parked in front of her crib, she closed her eyes, "Give me some sugar," she pleaded, poking out her lips. She felt him kiss her cheek. "Damn ... oh, now you can't kiss me, huh."

"Not tonight, no sir," he responded. "I'll kiss you tomorrow."

After completing their good—byes, he waited for her to enter her building before driving off into the night.

Bealz retrieved his cell phone, cut on the interior light and was surprised to displayed on the screen, "last caller." He pressed the recall button and was shocked when Pudding's name popped up.

"Oh, shit. I wonder when . . ,".

"Hello," she answered calmly.

"Hey, Baby. I'm just gettin' back."

"Bealz, come on now. I heard you fucking some bitch." He continued to listen to Pudding's shit—talking.

He grew tired of Pudding's yapping, "Hold up, okay I fucked another girl you wanna break up with me, do so," he shouted into the phone. He heard only heavy breathing on her end. "... Well?"

"Is it okay if I fuck another Nigga?"

"It's your pussy, we'll still be friends and I'll still fuck you."
Who tha fuck you think you is, Sweet Dick Malone or somethin'?
Nigga, fuck you wit' yo lame ass"

"Fuck me? Fu————"   Click.

Bealz considered calling Pudding back but then thought better of it. Momentarily, he pulled up in the small parking lot outside of Renee's apartment. He tugged his dress shirt from his inside his pants and let his wife— beater show after he unbottuned his shirt. He approached Banga, and, ignoring his jokes, seized the lit up blunt from his hand. Other hustlers gathered around to greet Bealz. Bangs told Bealz that Bizzo and Shellz had been by looking for him. Banga claimed something was fishy about their demeanor.

"Whose turn is it," one hustler yelled from Jughead's yard. "He got fifty dollars."

Banga pointed to a tall youngster that had half of his afro out. "Kato, it's on you, Dawg."

Bealz watched Kato repeatedly pull up his droopy baggy denim jeans as he approached the male crack—head. "How is the Nigga gone bail on the police wit' his pants hanging off his ass."

Banga shrugged his shoulders. "Dat Nigga hustles hard. He's buying a Big every other day. Yo, you know NeeNee is my lil woman now."

Acting surprised, "You bullshitting."

"Nah, Dawg — I'm dead ass. She's trying to stop smoking, I'ma get her tooth fixed and hopefully I'll get at least one of her kids. Bealz extended his hand. "Good luck, my Dawg," he congratulated.

Bealz ended up buying some wings from Jughead's, fed the whole block, and knocked out on Renee's couch.

* * * * * * *

The morning sunrise was casting its rays over the city. Shellz rode in Bizzo's Impala with the passenger seat reclined just enough for him to look over the car door. The two men were in deep discussion about making a transition into North Charlotte's cocaine and crack trade. Bizzo pulled into a store to get gas while inside Shellz search for a napkin in the glovebox. Just when he was about to close it, a receipt from Duke Power caught his attention. Upon closer inspection of the yellow slip, Shellz read the name Coley Sams. He looked up to see Bizzo making his way out of the store, so he shoved the receipt into his pocket.

Shellz wondered to himself where he had heard the name Coley from. Then it hit him. "That's who Coneka was fucking with behind Bealz's back." Shellz said above a whisper, pretending to be changing the CD.

Bizzo finished pumping gas and climbed into the car. "Man, dat chick inside always be tryin' a Nigga," he said, bumping fist with Shellz, chuckling.

Shellz lit up some smoke as he thanked Bizzo for helping him. Shellz requested to be taken to his hotel room to get some sleep. Bizzo outlined the moves they'd make later on that day and Shellz agreed. The whole ride to the hotel, the men seemed to revitalize the old Alliance days in Belvedere. The minute the

Impala pulled into the Days Inn, Shellz yawned, shook hands with Bizzo, then headed into his room.

Even as Bizzo drove away, he was contacting Lil Gas, informing his partner in crime of the latest developments.

Shellz prayed that Bealz would answer the phone

Bealz's eye popped open on the third ring, picked it up and saw Days Inn on the Caller ID. "Hello, who dis," he spoke in a groggy morning voice. Hearing the urgency in Shellz's voice, he sat up. "What you say?"

"Man, don't you remember the Nigga's name who Coneka used to fuck wit' ?"

"Yeah. Some Nigga name Coley .. so what? Fuck her an' him."

"Look, man — I'm a loyal dude, man, believe me. What's Bizzo's real name?"

"Bobby somet———"

"Nah, bra — his name is Coley Sams."

"What!" Bealz said, leaping to his feet from Renee's couch, catching Banga' s attention.

Shellz updated Bealz on how he had learned Bizzo's real name. Through additional discussion, the two came to the conclusion that Bizzo must've just left from seeing Coneka that night when he gave the ride on Frazier Street that avoided arrest. Bealz commented to the fact that when Coneka and Bizzo wasn't around at times, they must've been at a room together.

Silence...

Jap

"Oh, now I feel like Biz and Coneka musta been behind the break in. Think about it! Who knew about the safe and knew how easy it was getting in the back door," Bealz said.

"That's right, man. You remember that time that we left the apartment keys in the crib and Bizzo got into the back door so easy," Shellz brought to light.

"Yeah, yeah, I remember, smart dirty mu—fuckas. Hol'—up, wasn't that Nigga Grams's real name .

"Corey Sams."

"That's why Bizzo used to say he used to be on, he might of used to work for San."

"Well, man, I ain't gon' hold you up. I just wanted to let you know wha' da deal is."

"Hold up, bra, I appreciate your thoroughness, man. Shellz, you my dude. I know you in some deep shit. I'ma help you out financially, bra — dat's my word. But I do want you to help me trap Bizzo or Coley, wha' evva da fuck his name is ... an' dat bitch Coneka."

"I got chu, Dawg. I suppose to meet up with him later on."

"Good, play it off, make him think you down wit' whatever."

"Gotcha, if I don't get caught first I'ma help you out," Shellz looked towards the door, hearing someone yell room—service. "Yo, man — someone's at the door. I'll call you back later," he whispered.

"A'ight one."

"One."

Shellz got up, crept over to the door and looked out of the peep hole. He saw an Hispanic female maid's head barely overlooking her cart. Too quickly, he opened the door.

"Get down, mother fucka! Police!" the maid yelled, aiming her service revolver in his face. She was quickly joined by at least fifty other screaming officers who had exited several neighboring rooms.

Outmanned and out—gunned, Shellz dropped to the floor.

CHAPTER THIRTY-TWO

A Few Seconds Earlier

Her back against the wall adjacent to Shellz's motel room, Detective Buccannon nodded her head at the short, stocky Hispanic woman in the maid's uniform, a janitorial cart between the maid and the door. The woman acknowledged Buccannon's nod before speaking.

With a heavy Hispanic accent, "Maid service."

A moment's hush then the rattle of a security chain being removed. The door opened. Before Shellz can react, the policewoman dressed in a maid's uniform had pointed a handgun at his face.

"Police, don't move!"

In the same instant, Detective Buccannon stepped around, steadying her service revolver.

Amid shouts of "Don't move, Mutha Fucka," officers suddenly appeared from behind parked cars and from adjacent rooms where they'd hidden themselves.

Twisting his head and looking up, all Shellz could see was the mass of law enforcement professionals sporting enough fire power to start another world war, every weapon locked, loaded, and aimed at his prone figure in front of the motel room door.

He closed his eyes — in his mind it was as if everything had shifted into slow motion, the shouts fading so that the command

"Put your hands behind your back," shouted by a strong female voice, seemed to come from some place far away.

Shellz felt himself smile.

This time the command was more of a threatening scream. "I said put your hands behind your back, NOW!"

Shellz's hand moved slowly from beneath his stomach ... gripping a pistol.

"GUN!! GUN!!"

The atmosphere exploded with what sounded like an arsenal of weapons discharging. Detective Buccannon had jumped to the side as she fired her weapon, her left hand shielding her face from the mist of Shellz's flesh, blood and brain fragments that mixed with burnt gun smoke to contaminate the atmosphere outside Shellz's motel room door.

Buccannon held her hand up, a signal for the officers to cease fire. As the air cleared, she surveyed the carnage with obvious dismay that was left of Shellz's body which continued to jerk as blood poured from his numerous wounds and from his mouth and nose, his clothing smoldering from the heat of bullets fired at close range. Laying on his side, his left thumb and pointer shaped like an "L," his eyes were only able to focus the legs of his assailants and on the slow—moving traffic from Sunset Road beyond the parking lot, his last visual image being of what appeared in his daze to be Bizzo and Lil Gas driving by in the Impala, waving their hands.

Detective Buccannon kicked the gun away from Shellz's body and leaned against the rail, her smoking gun held at her side pointed at the ground, the intensity of the moment having drained her completely of energy. She watched with dead eyes as an officer went through the futile exercise of checking for a pulse. He looked up at Buccannon and gestured confirmation of what the detective already knew, that Shelton Davis was indeed dead. Detective Buccannon made no effort to hide her disappointment which misted her eyes.

The appearance of Bizzo and Lil Gas driving by the scene of Shellz's take—down told the whole story. In the forty—five minutes from the time Bizzo had dropped Shellz off at the motel, Buzzo had picked up Lil Gas from Lakeview and one of them alerted the cops of Shellz's whereabouts. With Lil Gas in the car, Bizzo hurried back to the Days Inn just in time to be slowly driving by in the Impala to witness Shellz's violent death.

CALCULATED SETUP

Within the hour, news choppers crowded the blue skies, each one frantic to capture sound bites of the horrific scene for their live coverage. Ultimately, regular programming was interrupted for "'breaking news." Images of the bloody white sheet covering his body in front of his motel room with a small photo of Shellz in the upper right hand corner of the screen, dominated the air waves for hours.

The army of TV news reporters who had converged upon the scene were kept at bay in the parking lot of the nearby Circle K convenience store along with their cameras and satellite trucks.

They jockeyed for position and scrambled for interviews with the eye witnesses, guests of the Days Inn who were more than willing to share details of the mayhem. The killing of one of the city's most wanted was big news and most were anxious to be part of it. Bealz was getting into the SUV when a text from Karma came through on his cell phone: TURN A TV TO CHANNEL 9 — URGENT! RIGHT NOW!

Bealz closed the Navi's door and ran back into Renee's apartment. Ignoring Banga's curiosity, Bealz grabbed the remote and snapped on the TV, letting what was on the screen answer any question either of them might have had. Seeing his friend's face with the word DEAD beneath it left him in a state of shock, his eyes misting up. Standing with his mouth agape, he was speechless as he caught a repeat of Shellz's death and the details from interviews with eye witnesses.

As if in a trance, Bealz eased himself down on the couch, disturbed by the news anchors alleging that Shellz might have been involved in other murders. Upset, he threw his cell phone at the TV. It shattered when it hit the floor. Bealz buried his face in his hands as memories of Shellz's jokes echoed through his mind. Banga approached from behind Bealz and placed hands of consolation on Bealz's shoulder in an attempt to comfort his anguished mentor. Sniffles from the kitchen betrayed the impact Shellz's death had on Renee as well.

"My Nigga, they killed him." Banga stated dryly while eyeing Renee leaning over the kitchen sink.

Bealz sighed and ran his left hand once over his face. "Damn, Shellz," he barked angrily.

"What's next?" Banga questioned angrily, retrieving the pieces of Bealz's shattered cell phone and handing them to him. "Well, I'ma contact this broad ... an' we gone set Coley and dat bitch Coneka up wit' me," he spoke with rage and resentment.

Banga bumped fist with Bealz. Renee's emotional sniffles, the only sound in the silence that hung heavily in the house, were interrupted by the action noise of a 9mm pistol Banga had pulled from his back pocket. Bealz traced his goatee with his left hand, held the pieces of his cell phone with his right, nodded affirmation to Banga, and strode from the apartment.

*   *   *   *   *   *   *

Her head down, writing furiously, Detective Buccannon sat on the front seat of her white unmarked squad car on the perimeter of the yellow— taped crime scene, oblivious to the beehive of investigative and medical activity which could be seen beyond her. She had the car windows up, the AC blowing on high, and KISS FM 102 playing loudly on the radio in an attempt to blot out the distraction of the helicopters that hovered and the various personnel rushing to and fro by her vehicle.

She held Shellz's cell phone in her left hand and was jotting down names and numbers extracted from its memory on a yellow legal pad. From the several dozen she had listed, she had circled in red the names or nicknames of Major League, BlueBerry, Bizzo,

Lil Gas, Banga, and the last one who had spoken to Shellz moments before his death — Bealz.

Detective Buccannon had already relayed the cell number for Major League to Agents MacMall and Smith. MacMall had assured Bucannon that San had eight days left on the street, no more. He remained resolute in his determination to delay any action against Major League in spite of the intense pressure from his colleague to move immediately.

2:20 P.M.

Bealz drove into the parking lot of his complex. He expelled a tired breath at the sight of Pudding's car parked next to his Chevy. He grabbed a new cell phone from its Radio Shack box and disconnected it from the charger. As he exited the SUV, he saw Pudding sitting in her car waiting for him, an uneasy look upon her face. He approached her car and noticed the heaving of her chest as she battled her emotions.

"Sup .. how long have you been out here?" he inquired, folding his arms, unresponsive to the tears that began to cascade down her cheeks. "Look, I don————"

"I'm pregnant," she blurted tearfully.

Bealz opened the door of her car, kneeled, laid his bag on the ground and pulled her into a tight embrace. Through his tender smooch and caress he began uttering soothing words in her ear.

Neither paid much notice of the parking lot security vehicle which coasted to a stop near them, the yellow caution light on top of the car flashing. "Is everything all right?" the slim black security guard asked.

Bealz looked back over his left shoulder. "I'm having a baby, Dell." he proudly declared, feeling goose bumps rise on the back of his neck.

"Congratulations," the security guard responded before driving away and leaving them to their moment.

Not much later, inside Bealz's apartment, the sounds of lovemaking and Bobby Brown's song 'I Wanna Rock With You' echoed. Bealz's heart— pounding thrusts and the constant swivel of Pudding's head seemed to eclipse the emotional impact of Shellz's death. As both arrived at the explosive sexual pinnacle, her body trembled and he roared from the intensity of the moment.

Shifting her hips as her inner muscles contracted, she snickered at Bealz's pleas for her to quit.

Trying to catch his breath, his member relaxing inside her honeycomb, "What we gonna name him?"

Her fingers moved lovingly up his sweaty back as she responded, equally breathless, "You mean her ... I like Cindy Shameka Malone."

"Well, if it's a boy ... Xavier Jadon Ezekila Malone."

"Damn, is there enough room for all of those names———" She suddenly caught her breath from Bealz's unexpected thrust. "Stop boy. I feel your limpness," she teased, grinning stupidly. "Shay, Jaylin, Japlin, Talencia, why don't you."

"Ain't No Place I'd Rather Be Then Chillin Wit————"

His 2Pac ringtone cut into the mood. Bealz grabbed the cell phone from the lamp stand, checked the Caller ID on the new phone he'd copped from Radio Shack on his way from Renee's, and spoke into the handset.

"Yo, Jake ... 'sup — you heard about ————"

"Yeah, son, I heard about Shelton. I'm sorry 'bout your friend."

"I'ma pay for his funeral. I didn't go to the hospital because I know it's crawling with cops."

"Good. Listen, I need to talk to you about something serious." Bealz's attention was diverted by two knocks at the door which sidetracked his conversation with Jake. "A'ight, Jake — gotta go. I'll see you later."

Bealz slipped on a pair of black gym shorts and walked barefooted to the door. Since he wasn't expecting anyone, he cautiously checked for the identity of the visitor through the peep—hole but breathed a sigh of relief when he saw it was Dell, the security guard.

Bealz quickly opened the door but before he could speak Dell grabbed his arm and pulled him into the hallway. Silently Dell gestured Bealz to close the door as he looked up and down both sides of the brick corridor.

"Dell, man, wha' da flick wrong wit' you, Dawg?" Bealz questioned, scowling.

"Man, it's a fine chick outside in a red Beamer question your whereabouts."

Up until this time, Bealz had been careful not to allow Tiff anywhere near his apartment.

"Oh, shit ... tell her I'm not home ... whatever you do, don't let her in."

"I got chu, Dawg. I'm like Mike Epps top flight muthafuckin' security," he pledged, pointing to his flashlight and gold badge.

Downstairs, Tiff was standing just outside the front door rummaging through her purse like she was looking for her card that permits entry for tenants. A gullible female tenant walked up and judging by the quality of Tiff's dress and speech had no reason to question her credibility and allowed her to gain access.

Once inside, Tiff had a problem — she didn't know the floor Bealz lived on or his apartment number. She waited by the elevator and when she heard the bell sound, she stood against the wall as the door opened. She saw Dell exit but when he went in the opposite direction, she was able to slip unnoticed onto the elevator. With only three floor buttons to choose, she selected the top floor.

On the third floor, she encountered a male tenant taking out his trash and made up a story about someone running into Bealz's Chevy.

Tiff smiled when he pointed out Bealz's apartment.

In his bathroom, Bealz' toyed with Pudding's naked ass. He especially enjoyed its jiggle as she climbed into the shower. He stood for a moment watching his reflection in the mirror and was about to join her when he heard another knock on the door.

"I'll be right back," he said, watching the steam from the hot water rise over the glass shower stall. "Don't go nowhere," he teased as he closed the bathroom door behind him. He was still a few steps from the front door when he yelled, "Dell, wha' did I — ——" Throwing open the door, he stood there with his mouth ajar, shocked to see Tiff standing there. Recovering quickly, he managed to block her entrance, keeping her in the hallway.

"What are you doing here? I told you on my time," he said nervously, closing the apartment door behind him.

"I know, Jacob." Giving him a look that could be described as a cross between suspicion and accusation, she added, "You got company or somethin'?"

"Naw, just respect me. You wouldn't approve of me sneaking up on you now, would you."

"I'm sorry, you right," she agreed, lowering her head contritely. "You heard about that boy the police shot?"

"Yeah — that used to be my main man ... but look, I'ma see you later, okay?" He leaned over and kissed her. "Now get up outta here before my neighbors think that we're arguing."

"Okay, call me later. I wanna see you," she said, walking away, hips swaying in all directions. She looked back at him and smiled as the elevator doors opened and she stepped inside.

Bealz released a sigh of relief as he stood and watched the closed doors of the elevator momentarily.

His adrenalin still pumping from his scary encounter with Tiff, he channeled the energy making passionate love to Pudding in the hot steamy shower.   Much later, the two got dressed and separated, each going in different directions.

8 P.M.

San, Pug, Tracks, and Vanilla were the sole occupants in the salon. Pug was the only one smoking weed while the rest fed their noses from the ounce of powder on the office desk.

Heating a commotion at the locked front door, Tracks went to investigate and returned escorting BlueBerry who lost no time strutting her stuff up to San. When she leaned over to kiss San, her white thongs were exposed underneath her midnight blue sequined mini—skirt.

Knowing exactly what she was doing and what was showing as a result of what she was doing, BlueBerry coyly offered an insincere "Ooops," while making no attempt whatsoever to cover her exposed privates.

"Girl, you silly. You want a toot?" San inquired with a devious grin that failed to mask evil intentions BlueBerry might have noticed if she had been paying attention.

"Sure. A bitch needs one before I go to work," BlueBerry replied, laying her purse on the desktop.

Just as BlueBerry stuck her nose in the powder, San clubbed her over the head with the butt of her Desert Eagle. Blood from BlueBerry's nose splattered, spotting the cocaine and staining Vanilla's pink top.

Vanilla jumped back like he'd been slapped. "Oh hell no bitch!! Ms is Loui," Vanilla complained desperately, wiping at the stains with a napkin, oblivious to BlueBerry's condition.

BlueBerry was crumpled on the floor, holding her left hand over her nose. "San — Baby, what's wrong? What I do?" she shrieked fearfully, in her dazed state oblivious to the fact that her breasts had inadvertently freed themselves from her small top.

"Bitch, it was your funky ass that had me robbed!" San accused harshly, following up with a vicious kick in the mouth with her black Timberland boots, knocking out three of BlueBerry's teeth.

It was Vanilla's first time to see San in action and he cringed at each savage stomp to BlueBerry's head. BlueBerry's grunts ceased after the second stomp to her face and her body jerked like someone having a seizure. San ceased her brutal assault and took a seat behind her desk, out of breath. She scooped up the damaged part of the cocaine and threw it on BlueBerry's body before taking a snort from the untainted powder.

"Pug, handle that," San ordered, sticking her finger into the powder, then into her mouth.

Pug got up and stood over BlueBerry, his .357 aimed at BlueBerry's head, he coldly pulled the trigger six times before leaning down and whispering, "Bitch, that could've been your ass." Pug looked back at Vanilla, who was showing a boyish grin but whose face had drained of blood. "Quit trippin'," Pug added, opening his hand that held the pistol's hollow point bullets.

Vanilla was the only one not smiling, instead doing some soul— searching as he watched San and Pug unceremoniously drag an unconscious BlueBerry out of the office. Vanilla had enjoyed doing hair. getting high, and even selling cocaine, but he had no stomach for what he'd just witnessed.

San and Pug stuffed BlueBerry into her rental car. Pug drove it with San close behind to a dark and deserted spot above North Tryon's car wash where they dumped BlueBerry's battered body. They then proceeded to the Plantations Restaurant off the Plaza where they abandoned her car.

BlueBerry wasn't dead, but she was in bad shape. Fifteen minutes after they had thrown her out onto the street, an anonymous 9—1—1 caller reported seeing a half—naked woman laying in the street, unsure if she was dead or alive.

By the time San and Pug had made their way back to the salon, Tracks had cleaned up the blood but with no help from Vanilla. Tracks told San that Vanilla had voiced concern about BlueBerry's beating.

San approached Vanilla and laid her pistol on the desk then barked at him, intense and foreboding anger in her voice. "Sissy ass Nigga, you in 'dis shit wit' us ..." She paused and pressed a finger against Vanilla's powdery nose. "Don't bitch up on me now."

"I ain't scared," he replied, feeling something cold press against the back of his head.

"Den wha' da fuck up," Pug said in a forceful tone, holding his pistol to Vanilla's head with the hammer cocked back. "And Nigga, this time it ain't empty," he added, holding his open free hand in front of Vanilla's face.

"Vanilla, you know what happens to bitches?" San asked with venom in her voice. San took a seat as she watched Vanilla shake his head. San nodded at Pug, then snickered as Pug's powerful backhand to Vanilla's face sent him sprawling to the floor. Vanilla immediately drew himself up into a fetal position. "Now, fag—ass Nigga, you down? Or will the next be a bullet that's sure to alter your thinking?"

Vanilla removed trembling hands from his face. "I'm down, I'm down," he muttered, keeping his anger and frustration in check.

Tracks was laughing her ass off until San's next comment changed her mood. "Matter fact, Vanilla, I wanna watch you fuck Tracks, right here and now. Pull ya dick out."

"WHAT!" Tracks and Vanilla exclaimed in unison as Pug burst into a laughing fit.

"Chile, I ain't got no rubber," Vanilla blurted, poking out his lips, scooting up into a sitting position and crossing his arms. San opened a drawer in her desk, retrieved two condoms and threw them onto the table. "Now fuck," she ordered.

Wanting no part of this scene, Pug said, "Man, I'ma go watch a movie." Leaving the office, he stopped at the plasma screen out by the front area. As he selected the DVD "Belly" from the rack, he snickered hearing Tracks' painful moans. "Damn faggot killin' da bitch," he joked out loud to himself.

Pug started the movie and blazed up a blunt of Dro, but instead of becoming engrossed in the film he found himself failing to suppress the nagging thought that his days on the streets were going to be cut short ... unless he killed TG.

CHAPTER THIRTY-THREE

A heavy black tarp protected the mourners from the rain. About a hundred and twenty or so, mostly strippers, had attended the funeral to pay their last respects to Shellz and had proceeded to the cemetery for the burial.

Pudding sat up front between Bealz and Banga, watching as an enlarged picture of Shellz, encased in a gold frame, was lowered into the ground atop his white casket. Smoked frame designer shades concealed the identity of the other two Alliance members in attendance.

On the opposite side of Bealz sat Karma, a pair of Prada designer shades covering her eyes.

The Alliance discreetly but intensely focused their attention on the man in the black suit, his tight hand clasped to his left wrist, who served as a pall bearer: one Coley AKA Bizzo. The Alliance couldn't help but notice Coley's repressed smile behind his solemn demeanor during the entire funeral procession.

In the past couple of days leading up to the funeral, Bealz and Banga had allowed Bizzo to hang out with them. Totally unaware that Shellz had informed Bealz of his true identity, Bizzo acted with smug confidence. Bealz's plan was working like a charm.

Karma refused to let her damaged and discolored left eye and long scar that traversed the- left side of her face, or the hard—to—recognize false teeth, keep her away. She was back in the thick of things and was thrilled about Pudding's pregnancy.

On the other hand, Pudding wasn't too thrilled about Karma having a bedroom in her man's apartment. But since that's how things were before she met Bealz, Pudding was not going to contest his decision.

Meanwhile, the NAACP and Civil Rights activists were coming down hard on Detective Buccannon and eight other officers over the fifteen shots that were fired into Shellz's body. An internal investigation revealed that the officers had indeed feared for their lives when Shellz made an offensive move with his weapon. Additionally, the pistol Shellz had pulled from his jeans proved to have been one used in other shootings, including the murder of Milton "Milky" Harton. In spite of the public outcry, two days after the investigation was completed, the Chief of Police issued a statement that the shooting was indeed justified and the officers were cleared of any wrong doing.

Seventeen hours after BlueBerry's surgery, she awoke finding herself handcuffed to her hospital bed railing. A mere forty eight hours later, a short time before Shellz's funeral, she was okayed to be released from the hospital into custody.

BlueBerry was hit with a cocaine charge because of the drugs that were found in Shellz's apartment, since her ID was in close proximity of the drugs. Detective Buccannon, who had officially arrested her, came down hard on her, promising her that she would remain in custody unless she could raise the outrageously high bond set for her, which would be unlikely because more serious charges were pending and would be filed as well. Bottom line was, BlueBerry wouldn't see daylight for a long time, if ever, unless she agreed to assist in their apprehension of Omar "Lil Gas" Gaston and Coley Sams.

BlueBerry had no choice; to save herself, she was placed in protective custody as she began detailing her dealings with Major League, Pug, and Vanilla.

Twenty Four Hours Later - Sugar Creek Road 2: 30 A.M.

The city's clubs had closed and with nowhere else to go3 dozens of partiers milled about outside the 24—hour RaceTrack Convenience Store/Gas Station, some huddled in groups, others in vehicles. It was through this melee that a shiny black Nissan carefully threaded its way, Renee at the wheel. A couple of days earlier, in exchange for a few bags of crack rocks, Banga had acquired the use of the black Nissan Altima for the funeral. In their neighborhood cops didn't even need probable cause to pull someone over and hassle them, and since Banga's license had been suspended again, to be safe Renee was appointed the designated driver.

With Banga as her passenger, Renee navigated the black Nissan through the congregation in the parking lot at the RaceTrack which was so crowded she had to park quite a ways from the entrance. Banga exited the car and was approaching the store's entrance when he overheard three dudes bragging to some females about the shooting at Admissions.

Jap

When Banga returned to the Nissan a few minutes later with a bag of goodies, he told Renee to circle the store. It didn't take him long to spot a very familiar van parked at the rear of the establishment, unoccupied.

Banga sat for a moment staring at the van, then selected number two on the CD mix. Turning to Renee he asked, "Look here — you my bottom bitch, ain't you?"

Renee's dark brown eyes narrowed as she noticed the pistol he had placed on his lap She looked from the pistol then back at Banga who was nodding his head to the JayZ & Slim Shady song, "Renegade."

"I got your back," she declared, offering an insincere smile.

"Good. This is what I want you to do ..."

The Altima trailed the van for a few minutes at a close but safe distance. The three black males in the van dressed in different oversized jerseys were unaware that they were being surveilled.

Inside the van, the passenger in the front seat, Slim, accused the rear passenger, named Trouble, of hiding his weapon that had been placed beneath his seat. The driver, Vin, exited off Sugar Creek onto the off ramp. He too was missing his .380.

"I ain't got neither of you Nigga's pistols," Trouble protested, as he fired up a Newport.

Suddenly Vin's attention was diverted by the Altima that had pulled up alongside them and, matching their speed, drove side—

by—side. The Altima's interior light was on which revealed the female driver playing between her parted legs.

"Oh shit — look at 'dis bitch," Vin exclaimed, quickly rolling down the window of the van.

Vin's cohorts joined in the excitement as both the van and the Altima decreased their speed.

"Yo, baby — what's up, you need some help," Trouble yelled over head.

"I'm hoping to get fucked," she replied. "Follow me."

The van fell in behind her as the Altima sped up and shortly exited the highway at the LaSalle Street exit. In tandem, the vehicles proceeded up Lasalle and when they reached Beatties Ford, made a left turn.

"Trouble, find my pistol and quit playin' — you know how deez Beatties Ford Road Niggas is," Slim protested, frantically searching beneath the passenger seat.

Before long, both vehicles made their way down a dark dirt road behind North West Middle School. Only the barest minimum of light glowed from three different street poles that were forty feet apart from each other. The vehicles came to rest just above Coleman's, a park which only had four basketball goals, a grill beneath a rain shed, monkey bars, and sliding boards.

Vin killed the van's engine turning on the interior lights to help locate his pistol. He glanced in the rear view mirror and screamed, "Oh shit, look out!" as the foreboding figure of Banga rose silently from his hiding place in the rear of the van, his weapon extended in front of him. In his panic, the driver was scrambling for the door handles without looking.

"Man, wha' da fuck wrong wit' you scary ass Nigga," Trouble questioned, still scrunched down on his knees searching the floor boards and beneath the rear of the front seats for the pistols.

"Don't none of you Niggas move," Banga demanded, his pistol aimed at the back of Trouble's head. "Ain't dis somethin'," he smiled.

Renee snatched open the driver's door, "Dis shit ain't no fuckin' game," she protested.

Banga had donned latex gloves; his eyes wickedly pierced the darkness. "I got time for only one question, only one answer. 4hich one of you Niggas pulled the trigga from this van outside of Admissions?"

"I don' kno' wha' you tal————" POW!

Banga's arm twitched as the .380 distributed Trouble's wits, his body blown onto the floorboard as the stench of gunpowder filled the van.

"Now I won't ask again," Banga assured, ignoring the frantic pleas from Vin.

"Man, it was Slim's idea," Vin tearfully snitched, looking down at brain matter oozing from Trouble's wound. "Please don't kill me, Dawg." Tears splashed from his terror—filled eyes.

"I ain't no bitch ass Nigga," Slim fearlessly spat screw facing Banga's approach from the rear.

Banga told Slim to open his mouth but in the process of crawling from the back to the front, tripped over Trouble's leg causing him to momentarily lose his grip on the pistol. Seizing his opportunity, Slim recovered and grabbed the gun as Vin grabbed Renee and giggled.

"Now muh—fucka," Slim shouted, aiming the pistol at Banga, "You want an answer? I done it ... I pulled the trigger, me and Trouble. You satisfied? Now that you've killed my Nigga, first I'ma fuck 'dis bitch, kill her, then kill you, Nigga." From the menace in his eyes, there was no question that he meant every word.

"Yo, Slim — aren't you missing a 9mm?" Banga questioned, half—grinning, a chill in his voice.

CLICK! CLICK! CLICK! CLICK! CLICK! Slim removed the empty magazine from the .380.

"Now will you open your mouth," Banga teased. "Never mind!" POW! POW!

The passenger window shattered from the bullets that exited Slim's head. Being inside the van muffled the blast. Vin released Renee in horror as he watched Slim's head lay against the passenger door, his eyes wide open, his blood and brain matter racing in streaks down the right corner of the windshield.

"Man, please don't kill me," yin pleaded. Squeezing his eye—lids together, he folded his hands together like in a praying position. "Please, Dawg — I'm sorry."

"Chill. You ain't done shit to me and you just was wit' da wrong Niggas," Banga said, opening the side door so he could exit the van.

Banga continued to talk to Vin about hanging with the wrong people as he stepped out onto the moist ground. Renee had meanwhile retrieved the pistol she had concealed in the rear waistband of her beige Dolce & Gabbana jeans. While Vin was busy wiping his tears, Renee gripped the pistol with both hands as she raised the barrel to within an inch of his head. Renee's hands trembled slightly as did her finger that tightened on the hair—trigger of the weapon. She closed her eyes. POW! Her hand jerked upward. She opened her eyes in time to see Vin's body falling towards her.

"Oh shit," she said, quickly backing away from the plump driver's body as it fell to the ground, making a sound like someone had body—slammed him. She lowered the smoking gun with her right hand and with the other she covered her mouth.

"Let's go, baby," Banga said, easing into the Altima.

If they'd had a phony tag, no eye witnesses, and a tightly sealed alibi, all victims in the van would have remained alive; perhaps in jail for the murders outside of Admissions, but alive. Their lack of diligence no longer mattered.

During the entire ride to the apartment Banga was hyped, repeatedly pumping his clenched fist to the gangster rap music that played. Sporadically he waved his pistol out in front of his body as he rapped along with different rappers. He praised a quiet, trembling Renee for how she handled business.

"Baby, I ain't never killed nobody," she said apprehensively, turning right on Rozzelles Ferry Road.

"Turn right at the next Street, Baby," he instructed and she immediately clicked on her right turn blinker. Banga continued, "Look

Just keep quiet. I'ma get rid of da pistol an——— oh, shit ... keep straight, no! Turn left here!" he cautioned in a panic, pointing. With her right turn indicator blinking, Renee swerved sharply to the left, attracting the attention of a squad car. Automatically suspicious of anyone cruising the neighborhood at such a late hour, the erratic move by Renee clinched it; the squad car was in quick pursuit.

Seeing the blue lights behind them, Banga shouted, "Yo, turn up into Smallwood and tell the police that you was giving a hitchhiker a ride."

The blaring sounds of the squad car's siren penetrated the hush of the night. Inside the patrol car, the officer radioed for assistance. Rounding a corner, the patrolman brought the car to a screeching halt as he witnessed the passenger from the Altima bolt from the slowing vehicle. The officer didn't have time to chase the passenger who had disappeared into the darkness, so with his service weapon drawn he charged the vehicle and ordered the female driver to the ground. When Renee quickly did as he commanded, he dropped his six foot one, one hundred and ninety pound weight onto her back. Several law enforcement vehicles descended upon the scene, their sirens still wailing and their blue lights decorating the neighbors' homes. Handcuffs were slapped on Renee's wrists extra tight. "i am' do nothing," Renee protested, grimacing in pain from the cuffs and the pressure of the officer's knees on her spine.

"Who da fuck ran from your vehicle?" the officer demanded. With his flashlight he pointed the other officers in the direction the escapee had run.

"I got some specs of blood over here," one officer searching the Altima proclaimed.

A disgruntled Renee was lifted roughly by the muscular black officer who had apprehended her, shuffled to his squad car and placed in the rear before he returned to check out the blood drippings. Sensing foul play, he radioed for the crime lab.

The crime lab van showed up about forty minutes later. The technicians took prints and blood samples were gathered but no evidence of a crime was discovered. Since they had no reason to hold her, and she had no wants or warrants outstanding, Renee was released, but not without a stern warning from her captor. "Ms. Renee Murphy, listen very carefully to what I'm tellin' you. I know where you stay. You better hope nothin' comes from the blood samples, or I promise that I'll lock your ass up. Don't think I won't. You're getting a pass for the minute, but I'm going to be looking for any excuse to take you down."

Although her purse which contained her Driver's License was returned, the Altima was towed and impounded and to add insult to injury, the black officer, named Austin, ordered her to find another way home.

Renee walked up Rozzelles Ferry Road with her arms folded, clearly upset. She kept thinking that one of the few barking dogs would emerge from the dark street corners and attack her. The words of the black officer kept resounding in her head. She shook her head in disgust as the faces of her kids flashed before her eyes. It seemed to her like it took an eternity to make her way home in the foreboding darkness.

When she got within thirty feet of the safety and comfort of her apartment, she was shocked to see Banga leaning through the downed window of a car making a crack sale. Upset, she waited for him to complete the transaction, her hands on her hips.

When Banga turned around and saw her, "Oh, hey, Baby," he said, grinning. Re reached for her but when she turned and started to walk away, he was taken aback by her unresponsive demeanor. "Wha's wrong?" he asked, following her with his arms stretched out.

"This is some bullshit. I 'on need 'dis trou. .." her voice trailed off as she entered the apartment.

"Yo, Banga, what's wron' wit ya girl," a chubby hustler named KB asked.

Banga smacked his lips. "Nan, shut your fat—ass up," he replied, as he entered the apartment behind Renee.

Renee spat as she cut her eyes angrily, "Nigga, you left blood in the fucking car. Those cops had a fucking crime lab come out and go over it ..." She tried to avoid his roaming hands but to no avail. In no time at all, she was offering no resistance as he sexed her right there on the cold wooden living room floor.

Jap

Eight Thirty A.M.

Bealz placed a call.

"Sup Bealz," Banga answered in a deep groggy voice.

"Yo, man, you heard 'bout da bodies found behind North West School?"

"What bodies? Nah, my Nig .."

"Man, call me when you get up."

"A' ight."

Click.

Bealz felt like a pimp, sharing breakfast with two women both of whom he'd had sex with. He cut his eyes at Karma's lips as she chewed her bacon, then at Pudding gulping her orange juice. The silence around the circular glass table was unnerving.

"Pudding, what time do your classes start?"

Pudding flashed a bogus smile, took another sip of her juice, dabbed the corners of her mouth then replied with a hint of defiance in her voice, "Ten thirty."

Karma huffed sexily, excused herself from the table and with an enticing swivel of her hips disappeared down the hallway to her room.

Pudding closed her eyes, exhaled and slowly allowed them to flutter open. She reached across the table, placed her hand on Bealz's left forearm and inquired, wrong with her?"

His eyes locked on hers. In a silent internal battle he shrugged his shoulders. Unable to keep her voice steady, "Well, you need to have a talk with her."

"About what?" Karma blurted, emerging from her room dressed in a tank top, lime green Baby Phat sweats and white Air Max trimmed in lime green.

Pudding took a deep responsive breath, "Nah, I'm just tellin' hint to make sure everything's okay."

"You see this shit," Karma shot back, pointing to her eye and scar. Pudding swallowed her spit at Karma's sinister look. "Ain't shit all right," Karma continued, folding her bottom lip.

Pudding's nervousness subsided once Bealz stepped between them. "A'ight now, that's enough," he shouted, looking from Karma to Pudding. "Don't start 'dis bullshit ... Karma, Pudding knows how close we are. Now I want y'all two to hug," he suggested, his eyebrows lunged upwards expectantly. The two ladies eyed each other with suspicion, but then softened and deferred to his request, embracing.

"Now that's better ... 'We Are Fam—i—ly," he sang, clapping his hands.

They all shared a laugh.

CHAPTER THIRTY-FOUR

Bealz was seated at a picnic table outside of Destination's headquarters talking with Jake.

"How's Karma?" Jake inquired.

"She's good. Matter of fact, I just dropped her off on Cox Avenue on the way over here, right after we dropped Pudding off at school for her 10:30 class." He wondered how long Jake was going to continue with the small talk and get to whatever the important thing was Jake wanted to see him about.

"Bealz, you remember me ..." he paused, rose up from the picnic table and looked off into the distance, thinking, choosing his words carefully.. Taking a deep breath, "Okay, the thing is, I need to confide in you about something." He held his right pointer finger out, "But only if you promise not to interrupt and hear me out." He watched Bealz promise with a nod of his head. "For openers, there's something you need to see." Jake handed Bealz a legal—sized envelope. As Bealz studied the envelope and then went about opening the flap, Jake continued, "Now you remember when I took you to the doctor, you were about thirteen?"

"Yeah, I think so," Bealz replied. He removed a sheet of paper from the envelope upon which DEPARTMENT OF SOCIAL SERVICES was displayed prominently across the top of the paper as its letter—head. Bealz cued in on the following line: IN THE CASE INVOLVING THE PATERNITY TEST OF JACOB MALONE, IT

HAS BEEN DETERMINED WITH 99.99% CERTAINTY THAT JAXE
WILSON IS THE FATHER.

As the information assaulted his senses, trying not to drown
in the flood of emotions. His eyes starting to mist up, Bealz looked
up at Jake then back to the paper several times, making no
attempt to stem the stream of tears. He listened attentively, half—
numb with shock, as Jake explained to him that Malone Senior
had never treated Londa right and so she and Jake had carried on
a three—year relationship behind Malone Senior's back.
Finally, Bealz wiped his eyes and took a deep breath, turning his
neck slowly back and forth.

"I hope you understand ... I've been wanting to tell you for a
long time," Jake said, taking a seat and awaiting Bealz's response.
"So that's why you started calling me son." Bitterness crept into
Bealz's tone and his face became a scowl as Jake nodded his head
in affirmation. "Are there any more secrets ... Pops?" Bealz added
sarcastically.

Jake looked at Bealz in silence monetarily, as if trying to
make up his mind about saying anything else. Instead of
acknowledging Bealz's question, he pulled out his cell phone and
dialed a number.

An Hispanic accent answered on the third ring. "Hello, Jake,
mi amigo."

"Hello, my friend. I need for you to make that meeting
happen."

"Cuando?"

"Today."

"Seguro, my friend, I' 11 see you in a couple of hours."

"Gotcha ... and ... thanks."

"Por nada. It is my pleasure."

Click.

Two Hours Later

Bealz followed Jake into a Mexican eatery where they were escorted to an office in the rear a few feet from the noisy kitchen. Jake tapped twice on the black door. It was opened by a short Mexican man sporting a thick mustache and wearing a cowboy hat and boots who looked vaguely familiar to Bealz. The man shook Jake's hand enthusiastically, then turned to Bealz who Jake introduced as his son.

"Mucho gusto, me amigo," the man replied as he cheerfully directed them to the two huge leather chairs facing the wooden desk. As he was taking a seat, Bealz's memory kicked in to recall picking him up the Hispanic man at the airport.

"May I offer you some refreshment?" their host asked as he took a seat behind the massive desk and took out a huge cigar. Before they could respond.

Knock! Knock!

"Vente," the Hispanic man yelled as he lit fire to the cigar.

"Sup, Ortiz," San said as she entered, but stopped dead in her tracks when she saw the men in the leather seats turn in her direction. She knew who Jake was and recognized Bealz from their encounter in the parking lot of her salon and wondered what he was doing here.

"Shut da door, San," Ortiz ordered, blowing a big ring of smoke into the air. Sake rose to his feet as he watched San's cut to him accusingly. "Bealz

The look on Bealz's face betrayed his bewilderment.

"I don't know how to handle this except just say it. Son, this is your sister," Jake introduced San.

Both Bealz and San heard the words but were unable to wrap their minds around the announcement. The siblings silently held each other's shocked gaze. His head was still spinning about learning about Jake and being hit with this disclose now had Bealz's head spinning.

Jake utilized their stunned silence to proceed to apologize to San for not accepting her gay lifestyle, explaining to Bealz that the only reason he had always maintained the lie that his son accidently shot himself had a lot to do with the fact he was so firmly against San's preference for women, as unfair as his behavior might have been.

San was animated in her response. "Daddy, I ain't heard from you in a minute," she cried. "I tried to reach out to you ... and now you do this?" San said, gesturing with her right hand at Bealz. "Okay, so I'm human, an' I ain't perfect," she added in a quivering voice as she tried to maintain her sense of coolness but having difficulty seeing through the tears that she was unable to contain.

"Ain't this some shit . . ." Bealz stated jokingly, crying vainly to relieve the heaviness of the moment with a false sense of levity. "Dis some underground Maury Povich shit."

A tense silence ensued.

The maxim BLOOD IS THICKER THAT WATER proved its profundity for the next thirty five minutes. A spirit of forgiveness prevailed. Bealz and San even ended up laughing about their initial run—in outside of her salon.

San informed the men that her lawyer assured her that although she had been under investigation; the authorities had nothing concrete on her. Ortiz and Jake promised that if she were to get locked up, they had her back. Bealz echoed the sentiment with a promise to help his sister out if a push came to a shove.

Bealz walked San outside to her rented white Range Rover. Waiting in the SUV's passenger seat, Pug buzzed the window down to exhaust some of the accumulated weed smoke as San introduced Bealz as her brother.

In the next ten minutes while leaning against the SUV and watching the restaurant's patrons coming and going, the siblings shared information, catching each other up on the most recent developments concerning Coley, Lil Gas, Tiff, BlueBerry, and Shellz. In the process, they discovered that in some weird way, San and Bealz thought a lot like Jake, but were just more devious. Finally, Bealz and San exchanged numbers and embraced. As Bealz opened the door for her, once again they collectively, along with Pug, vowed extreme vengeance and retaliation against Coley and crew.

When Bealz returned to the office, another Spanish gentleman dressed in a gray Armani suit, eyes veiled behind dark designer frames, was waiting. He stood at least six—one and weight about two hundred and forty pounds. A thick but neatly trimmed mustache complemented a bald head. His expressionless face revealed nothing.

Ortiz did all the talking, pacing the floor while explaining that someone had to replace San and Bealz had been nominated.
Before accepting that role, Bealz learned where Jake had been copping his cocaine. Jake cautioned Bealz that he would be in the advanced form of the drug game, a position that was no place for amateurs. Bealz assured them that he was more than ready.

The stoic Spanish man finally broke his silence. "Ser honesto Siempre es la Mejor polica, ser fiel es todo," he said in a mellow Spanish lilt.

"Bealz had a confused look on his face. "What'd he say?"

As Ortiz was about to answer, he was silenced by the uplifted finger of his Spanish cohort which sported a huge diamond ring.

"Honor is de best policy ... loyalty is everything." The taller Spanish man spoke in a plain, calm demeanor, his serious face continuing to show lack of any emotion or expression.

Bealz kept his face directed at the Spanish gentleman but cut his eyes at Jake who stared down at his fingernails. "So what is your name?" he asked, turning back to lock eyes with the Spaniard.

"Budda," he answered.

"Like the weed ... Budda," Bealz teased. Getting absolutely no response from Budda at Bealz's nervous attempt at levity, the smile slowly disappeared from Bealz's face. "Can't you take a joke?"

"Look, son th——"

"I got this, Jake," Budda interposed. "Let me decide what's funny. Now get out!" he shouted.

Bealz rose to his feet to depart. At the door he stopped and turned back, perplexed about why Jake laughed along with the Spaniard. "What's so funny?' he questioned in a snappy tone.

"The look on your face," Budda said, pointing with one hand, covering his stomach with the other.

"Oh, I see ... that was a joke," Bealz said, returning and sitting down.

"Of course. You remember the ladies that you helped pick out this suit?" Budda asked, running his hands over the sleeves of the jacket.

Bealz decided not to mention what he remembered about how Artillia had been totally against that same suit that he'd suggested Montella purchase for her boyfriend. He just smiled while stroking the hair on his chin. "So ... they weren't famed designers?"

Budda and Ortiz laughed so hard that their faces turned colors. All laugh finally subsiding, Budda responded, "Montella Ruiz Gonzallas ... a designer."

"Oh, Gonzallas ... she told me her name was Montella Giles."

"Giles? Man, our sister is a great actor," Ortiz offered, straightening the big hat on his head.

Budda explained that Jake had been a great asset to his business in the Charlotte and surrounding area. Furthermore, he swore how easy it had been to haul kilos and pick up a quarter million from a cleaners without the driver's knowledge, even though the cleaners was adjacent to the Mecklenburg County Jail. Again Bealz revisited his memory of Montella emerging from the cleaners with a Louis Vuitton two—handled tote bag and a few dry cleaned items neatly covered with plastic on a hanger.

"San has made my organization a lot of money, but was never met me in person."

"Yo, Bealz. I just saw Pudding with a dude coming out of the police station."

"What!"

"Yeah, Dawg. I was just leaving my lawyer's office 'bout my gun case. She didn't see me but I saw her. That's my word," Banga said with confidence.

"A'ight ... I'ma see you in a bit."

From Bealz's sudden silence, Jake knew something about that phone call had unsettled him. Jake waited until he drove into Bealz's complex parking lot before addressing any concern. Parking and killing the engine, he turned to his son. "Is something ailin' you?" he asked, gazing over at Bealz's lowered head.

Avoiding eye contact he responded in a low whisper, "Nah, everything's all right," before opening the door and exiting the car.

Jake restarted the engine and called after him, "Call me ... and your sister." He heard Bealz okay his suggestion, then watched his son enter the glass door to his apartment complex.

Bealz chose to take the stairs instead of the elevator to his own apartment to give himself time to think. Step by step he tried to entertain thoughts that Banga probably was mistaken about seeing Pudding. Regarding his relationship with Pudding, he'd grown to believe they were a perfect couple. During his walk up the cement stairwell, he mulled over finding out that Jake was his father and San was his half—sister.

"Look, son. I had my reasons for lying to you about my son killing himself. And I had my reason for not telling you about me being your father." He paused as he slowed behind a truck approaching a red traffic light. "But I have no more reason to keep anything from you or to distort the truth. It was hard staying away from Sandra especially after her mother, Wanda died, then Londa up and disappearing. Psychologically, I was drained. But I knew I had to raise you. Now I didn't want you to deal drugs but you were raised around it and made your own mind up."

"Green light," Bealz blurted, thinking about all the times he'd seen Malone Senior nodding out, his works dangling from his arms. Yeah this shit's crazy. Silently he thought, "I always wished you were my Daddy, and now that I kno' you are, it seems funny.

"Look, you can call me Jake. Daddy ain't nuttin' but a word."

"I got a sister," Bealz said, just above a whisper.

Over and over he tried to make sense of the past few hours, shaking his head as he entered his apartment, encountering Karma's alluring stare and the strong odor of marijuana.

She sat on the couch with her toned legs crossed, wearing a pink over—sized tee shirt and black gladiator sandals. Nodding her head to the Art of Noise song, Moments in Love that played at a comfortable volume on his entertainment system. Bealz watched her slowly rise from her seated position and licked his lips at the sight of her hips shifting from her catwalk approach.

He took a drag from the blunt that she placed between his lips and exhaled a cloud of smoke into her face. She then stuck the lit up part in her mouth, pulled him close, and engulfed his open mouth with a funnel cloud of weed smoke. After taking in as much smoke as his lungs could handle, he inhaled some up his nose, then began to cough uncontrollably. She giggled at the drool that fell from his mouth.

Abruptly Pudding entered through the front door, disrupting their moment. Pudding walked over and tossed her purse on the granite countertop by the kitchen.

"Sup," Bealz said, approaching her with the blunt in hand. "Nothing. I just had a long day," Pudding replied, loosening the bun on her head and letting her hair fall.

"Hit dis," he suggested.

"You kno' I don't smoke," she replied, shaking her head.

"Let's go, Karma," he said, heading towards the door.

Jap

"Where you going?" Pudding questioned, only to be answered by the slamming of the door behind Karma and Bealz. "What did I do?" Pudding screamed through the door, slapping her purse to the floor, scattering its contents, cluttering the floor with items such as her license, lipstick ... and a badge.

CHAPTER THIRTY-FIVE

Since Jake was having the Navigator serviced, Karma drove the Chevy as she listened to Bealz describe his day's findings. He sat so low in the passenger seat that only the top of his head could be seen from outside.

Karma looked up at the overcast sky. "It's finna pour down," she said, making a right turn on Remount Road.

Bealz stared out the window at a man holding a little boy in his arms at a city bus stop. It reminded him of the times when Jake waited with him at a school bus stop.

After they grabbed a quick bite to eat at Wendys, Karma weaved the Chevy through the six thirty crack—head customers on Cox Avenue.

Returning to Renee's apartment, Bealz had Karma back the car into the spot in front of Renee's unit. He told her to sit still, then exited the car. He moved towards Banga and five other hustlers who had gathered around the front end of a gold Honda Accord. He stared at two men having a disagreement in Jughead's front yard. More importantly he wondered who the three strangers were that lounged around a black late model Lexus that sat on chrome rims next door to the Liquor House.

"Bealz, we got some intruders and doze Niggas been selling dope," Banga explained.

"Is dat right. Where dem Niggaz from?" Bealz inquired, screw facing one of the men.

"Dey from Florida," one of the other hustlers responded, pointing out the Lexus tag.

During the sometimes heated debate over whether or not they should take action on Banga's suggestion to run the strangers from Cox grounds, the light precipitation turned into a downpour.

Seeking cover from the rain, Bealz shouted to Banga, "Let me holla at you in the crib.

Karma fixedly observed the light gray shade over the cornea in her left eye. Then she traced the scar on the side of her face with her left hand. She flinched when Bealz tapped on the window. Following the direction of his hand gesture, she extracted the keys from the ignition, exited the car and followed Bealz into the apartment.

"Hey, Renee," Bealz spoke, taking up position on the new but used wine—colored leather sofa.

"Sup, girl you alright?" Karma inquired, sitting on the arm of the love seat where Renee was sitting.

Bealz and Karma accepted Renee's silence and her fidgeting fingers as a sign.

Banga ordered Renee upstairs. He waited until he heard the squeaky sound in the upstair's hallway followed by the slam of their bedroom door before he spoke "Go 'head, Dawg dat girl's crazy. It's her monthly" he lied.

Karma knew better because Renee wouldn't have worn some cream sweats if she was bleeding.

"Look here, I found out that Jake is my daddy," Bealz calmly announced.

"That's good, Dawg," Banga happily acknowledged.

"Yeah ... but how 'bout San of Major League?"

"Oh, yeah — that bull—dagging bitch," Banga interrupted, firing up a blunt and taking a seat on the sofa.

"Turns out, she's Jake's daughter, my sista."

Banga coughed harshly as a puff of smoke escaped his mouth prematurely. He banged his clenched left fist on his chest to curb his cough. "Go 'head, my Nigga. I gotta hear this," he said, wiping his watery eyes with the back of his hand.

By degrees Bealz brought Banga up to speed, then outlined their plan to wreck vengeance on Bizzo and Lil Gas. When Banga was finally brought current, Bealz made a call to Bizzo. They agreed to hit Mother's Pool Room off South Boulevard.

A Little After 11 P.M.

Banga led three of the old Alliance members into the crowded pool room, with Bealz trailing the pack. They acknowledged those who showed them love.

Since all of the eight pool tables in the front nearest the bar were occupied by a mixture of men and women, the group proceeded to the rear where a smaller group of people were playing pool. They took up refuge at a table with four stools which sat next to a window that was covered by opened blinds. A thick—set coffee—brown female waitress scratched through her weave that was highlighted with pink streaks, then asked for their order.

"Yeah, baby girl, lemme have a round of Hennessy and thirty hot wings," Banga ordered. Clearing his throat and with flirtatious eyes, he continued, "And, uh, maybe ya phone number." His smile quickly faded when the waitress's lips curved and she strode away, hips reluctantly swaying from side to side. "Damn, baby girl got ass but ain't dat cute and she tryin' to diss a Nigga," he referenced with distress.

"Damn, Skippy, bitch playin' hard to get," Bizzo implied, rolling a Black-N-Mild cigar between his clasped hands. "And she's a fucking waiter," he added with a short snicker.

Bealz exhibited puckered brows across his dissatisfied stare. He momentarily held a matching gaze with Karma. Finally, after getting their drinks, they accepted table nine, selected four sticks and proceeded to play teams. It didn't take long for Bealz and Karma to whip them in the best two out of three.

2 A.M.

As the Chevy wandered aimlessly through the rain—slicked streets of the city, the group inside continued to blow weed. To throw Bizzo off, Shellz's name was never mentioned. The casual chat over the low playing music was essentially about the rebuilding of The Alliance.

2:15 A.M.

Bizzo was dropped off at his place. The consensus among the remaining members was that they had Bizzo completely faked out. Bealz contacted San and speaking in code assured his older sibling that the ruse was secure and affective.

In the next thirty—six hours, two things were about to take place: Bizzo's supposed demise, and San's removal from the city's street at the hands of the Feds.

Bealz had been spending more time with his father and sister but less time with Pudding. He'd even spent the night at Tiff's apartment, leaving Pudding at his apartment with Karma and her weed smoking.

Bizzo felt a little wary about the new spot that they agreed to pump out of in North Charlotte. So he had Lil Gas waiting, strapped up nearby in an abandoned apartment on Eighteenth Street. Bizzo felt more secure when Bealz decided to ride in the Impala unaccompanied, leaving Banga and Karma behind on Cox. Around ten thirty, after a business meeting with Freckles, Bealz was scooped up by Bizzo from Renee's apartment. The two old acquaintances spoke of old times. Bizzo was about to turn into North Charlotte when Bealz told him instead to proceed to the Cherry Community. Bizzo questioned the change of plans but Bealz explained that they needed to go pick up Haley who rented the house in North Charlotte.

The Impala took an alternate route past Presbyterian Hospital and shortly entered Cherry from the rear of Baxter Street. Once Bizzo drove around the corner by a flashing yellow caution light, Bealz told him to turn left and park in front of the gray house that sat across from a small pool hall. Several winos kept the exterior and the interior of Lolita's pool hall busy.

Checking over his shoulders, Bizzo vigilantly inquired as he gripped the steering wheel tightly, "Where is she?"

"Roll the window down. There she is," Bealz replied, pointing his finger at a fairly mixed—looking woman that seemed to be walking towards a payphone. "Yo, Haley," he shouted, capturing her attention. "Dis Bealz." He made himself known at the same time liking the look of this respectable neighborhood.

The high—yellow woman ran across the street and climbed into the backseat of the Impala. Bizzo had rotated the knob that produced a brighter interior light and turned to see her face more clearly. He smiled when he saw her stunning features, small mouth, long hair, and hips that spread against the car's leather. Once she gave a small account about the other hustler's earnings, he happily drove off. Little did Bealz know that Lil Gas had been listening to the entire exchange through Bizzo's cell phone that was in his shirt pocket.

"So now we're headed to Eighteenth Street," Bizzo spoke loud and clear.

"Yeah, baby," Haley answered, sticking her head out of the downed window for air.

In the driver's door mirror, Bizzo stared at Lob's hair blowing in the breeze from the opened window. He thought she looked pristine, like a princess. "Baby girl, you got a man?" he inquired kittenishly, smiling.

"Nah. These Niggas out here ain't 'bout that ... dey BI."

"My man Bizzo is a real Nigga," Bealz stated in a respectful tone.

"Oh yeah?"

Bizzo was taken aback by Haley's functional hands that reached over his shoulders and into his black Roca Wear tee—shirt. He cut his eyes at Bealz with a 'what—you—gonna—do' look. When Bizzo felt her teeth softly bite into his right ear lobe, he felt his shaft swelling. He quickly switched hands on the steering wheel and made an attempt to control his inner being.

"Yo Dawg, we'll be there in a minute," Bealz cautioned. He checked his cell phone and feigned discovery of a dead batter. "Yo, let me use ya cell phone. My shit's dead," he fabricated.

"A'ight ... hol'up baby girl," Bizzo demanded, removing his cell phone from his shirt pocket while at the same time killing the connection with Lil Gas so their conspiracy wouldn't be discovered. He handed Bealz the phone, telling Haley "Proceed, baby girl," thinking with the wrong head.

Bealz made a bogus call and pretended that he was talking to Pudding.

Before long Bizzo drove into the heart of the infamous North Charlotte neighborhood. In size there was no telling how many square miles this rugged urban part of the city stretched. Each street they rolled through was packed with street people of all description. Three liquor houses were live and jumping with activity on Parson, Seventeenth, and Pilgrim Streets. In certain areas, Mecklenburg's boys in blue harassed the most uncompromising brothers. A few people standing at the edge of streets clustered around perimeters of yards in front of local crack spots, tried to flag down the Impala as well as other passing vehicles.

Shortly, Bizzo was relieved to see the Eighteenth Street sign ahead. "Finally," he said. "Eighteenth Street."

"Seventeenth Street ... I live around on North Davison," Lob protested.

"Bold the fuck up," Bealz blanked. "You told me Eighteenth Street. Yo Biz — 'dis bitch might be tryin' to set us up," he accused, turning and facing her with knitted eye brows.

Without warning Bealz lunged into the back seat, wildly swinging at her. Haley's frantic screams made Bizzo pull over by Cornelius Pool, a broken down van, and a shadowy road. He put the car in park and yelled for Bealz to chill, but once he knew his pleas were to no avail, Bizzo exited the car, opened the back door, and attempted to pull Bealz from atop Haley. Then Bizzo heard Bealz call him Coley.

"Wha' you say?" Bizzo questioned. Standing back up, he was surprised to be greeted by the smiling faces of Bealz and with his attention temporarily averted, he didn't hear or notice the two people exit the dark—colored van with a white cloth hanging from the driver's door handle.

Bizzo reached for his pistol.

"Don't do it," Coley heard a familiar mellow voice warn. Hearing the unmistakable sound of two pistols being cocked, he relunctantly raised his hands. His eyes cued in on Bealz handing Haley some money as she exited the Impala. He heard Bealz thank not Haley, but Princess.

Princess, the same girl who Bealz had met at the car wash on Beatties Ford Road who Bealz had secretly been sleeping with and hanging out with since that day. Listening to Bealz's intructions, she hopped in the driver's seat and drove off.

Bizzo's pistol was removed from his waistband and his hands were bound by silver duct tape. Once he was finally forced into the van, Bealz introduced Bizzo to his sister, San, who sat on the rear seat smiling triumphantly. Bizzo realized the familiar voice had come from Banga who was in the driver's seat. The other, who completed the four, was the short and deadly Pug, who sat in the passenger seat.

"Hey, Coley. Wha's up, my Nig ..." San jokingly said, leaning up to the middle row seat where Coley had been seated by himself. "Nigga, you rob me, kill Monica and thought you'd get away wit' it?" Feeling ignored, she struck him with her Desert Eagle, dislocating his jaw and rendering him into a state of oblivion. As his body gradually slumped to the floor board, San wiped his blood from her hand and the pistol on the plush black cushion seat. "Lil Bra, make that call."

"Gotcha," Bealz responded from the row that was directly behind the driver and passenger seat. He scrolled through Bizzo's cell phone, found Coneka's number and dialed it, disguising his voice when she picked up.

"He—l—---way ————yo————.

"I can't hear, you breakin' up," Coneka responded, prone on her hotel bed pressing one left finger in her ear.

With his mouth utilizing a stuttering and broken technique, he generated a gasping sound from deep in his throat as he continued. "Me—et mmme ... at Free——dom Pa———"

"Freedom Park ... I got chu," she responded excitedly.

Bealz killed the phone call and looked behind him at Bizzo. Frequent flashes of street lights shone inside the van enabling Bealz to eyeball the sprawled body that rocked on the floor board from the motion of the van. They managed to cruise through the city streets unnoticed, failing even to draw the attention of a squad car they'd pulled up beside.

During the ride, the siblings had time to discuss their Uncle Ed, their mothers, Londa and Wanda, who used to be best friends, and of course, their father.

The van came to a rest on a remote stretch of road near the motel where the police had killed Shellz. Banga drove off the road into a wooded area adjacent to several ponds that were used by local fishermen.

Everyone exited the van. Banga and Pug grabbed the barely conscious Bizzo by his ankles, dragging him from the floor board. His body made a thud when it hit the ground. To get his full attention, San lit a lighter and held it against his finger. In a millisecond, Bizzo screamed and shouted out obscenities, but since his hands were tightly bound behind his back, he ceased struggling but continued cursing and kicking his legs.

"Be still, Nigga," San demanded, kicking him in his stomach which drew a grunt of pain. Her next three kicks made blood spew from his mouth.

Coley and Bizzo made a last ditch effort to be defiant. Lying on his stomach he twisted his head and cut his eyes at the quartet that surrounded him. "It was me behind the robbery at your crib, Bealz." He came short of spitting blood at Bealz's feet. "It was me who robbed 1312 and killed Monica. Yeah, I made San and Shellz beef. So what! Shit bitch, you killed my cousin Grams for nothin'. I———!" he shouted with abhorrence in his voice, "——— mastermined it all ..." He paused as he saw Pug aim a sawed—off .410 at his head. "Hey, I'll see y'all in hell a———" BOOM!

The powerful, illegal shotgun with black electrical tape wrapped around the handle, jerked upward. Pug casually blew the lingering smoke from the tip of the barrel. The black Dickies outfits and Air Force One tennis shoes worn by the youngsters were splashed generously with Bizzo's brain—matter spillage, but no one seemed to mind. Jokingly, Pug began to crip walk, eliciting a nervous chuckle from the others.

San and Bealz retreated back inside the vehicle and watched while Banga attended to the final act of retribution: pouring gasoline over Bizzo's mutilated upper torso. He set a match to the inflammable fluid, setting Bizzo's entire body afire. He then ran to the van, started the engine, and while driving away he watched in the mirror as Bizzo's body, engulfed in flames, burned itself into an eternity of hell.

Jap

Around the same time, Coneka sat impatiently in a gray sports car parked in the lot of the park, constantly looking at the clock display on her dash while diligently watching for Bizzo's Impala to appear. She blew cigarette smoke out of her downed window and watched the smoke disappear into the star—laced skies. Suddenly she took notice of a red dot that appeared on the dashboard, then moved to her hand and arm. Her eyes widened at the realization of what it was, but before she could react, her head opened like a squished tomato. A second later, the sound of a rifle blast echoed through the night. Coneka never heard the blast. Coneka would never hear anything again. Coneka was dead.

CHAPTER THIRTY-SIX

In eerie close—up, as if a movie in slow motion, Karma watched through the magnified scope of a bolt action Reminton .308 Model 700 as the cigarette drifted from Coneka's lifeless hand, making a burst of tiny sparks as it hit the ground outside the sports car. Although Karma was at least a hundred yards away, with the rifle propped on the Impala's door, through the scope it was if she was standing next to Coneka. She held the rifle in place momentarily, finally exhaling, her finger moving from the trigger. Emotionally spent, her deadly mission was completed.

Princess had no idea after leaving the Impala in the parking lot of the ParkNShops grocery store off North Tryon, leaving the keys tucked away behind the driver's side visor that Karma was picking up the vehicle. However, it would have made little difference if she had known. Princess had agreed to setting Bizzo up; setting up a dopeboy to be robbed was not something she hadn't done before.

At dawn's first light over the city a few hours later, local fire departments responded to reports of two smoldering vehicles, one a van and the other a '96 model Chevy Impala.

Simultaneously, as two joggers prepared for their morning jogging routine with requisite stretching exercises, one of the white females glimpsed what appeared to be a thick liquid trailing down the door of a Mitsubishi sports car. Her curiosity aroused, over the objections of her running partner, she stepped closer to investigate. In the early morning light, she wasn't sure of what she was seeing as she approached the vehicle for a closer look. When it dawned upon her what it was, her hands flew to her mouth in a futile attempt to supress the screams when she realized that the liquid was blood and that it was splattered generously over the entire interior of the small vehicle, and it came from the barely—recognizable woman whose remains were sprawled grotesquely over the gear—shift.

Not far away, Lil Gas had passed out from waiting on Bizzo. He struggled to his feet from the old couch that he slept on, stretched and without paying much attention, walked outside. Temporarily blinded by the glare of the morning sun rays, he covered his eyes. Eyes shut tight, he took a couple of deep breaths. When he removed his hand from his eyes, what he blinked into focus was the shocking sight of a group of hateful—looking North Charlotte dope boys surrounding him.

"Who you, Dawg? An' wha' da fuck you doin' in dere," a tall stocky dude in baggy clothes and wearing a baseball cap cocked sideways questioned, brandishing a firearm.

"Yeah, Nigga. Who you?" another shorter dark—skinned dude with short plaits angrily backed up his home boy's confrontation, menacingly extending a black machete towards Lil Gas's neck.

Holding his hands outward in an attempted plea, Lil Gas replied, "Nah, man, I was waiting on Haley." His face paled with fear and his stomach knotted when the bigger dude, along with seven others, aimed various weapons at him.

"What!"

"Nigga, she sent you over here to rob one of us ... not again," the big dude declared.

Thirty minutes later, as the police broadcast band sizzled with preparations for the arrest of San, the conmiunications were interrupted with the report of a shooting victim in the vicinity of the seventeen hundred block of North Charlotte. The dispatcher added that the unidentified caller claimed that the unknown black male victim was apparently dead.

9:30 A.M.

A clean—shaven off—duty police officer stood in line at a convenience store with a box of doughnuts and a cold soft drink waiting to check out. Dressed in regular street clothes, the officer heard someone reciting some explicit rap verses out loud. The officer briefly looked back and saw a short boyish—looking black male doing the rapping. Even with a black do—rag covering the top of the boy's head and pulled down to just above his eye brows, the observant officer nevertheless recognized him from the BOL (Be On Lookout) notices. The quick—thinking officer calmly set his goodies down and eased his service weapon from its holster that was concealed under his loosely fitting shirt, and ordered the rapper to the floor. Staring into the business end of a service revolver, the young man knew better than to resist, but on the floor he immediately barked up at the officer, "Fuck is your problem?"

"Mr. Trevin Gibron, you are under arrest," the officer stated. Yelling to a surprised clerk, he ordered, "Hey, dial 9—1—1 and tell the dispatcher that Officer Spasshole needs assistance." Officer Spasshole read Pug his rights before methodically searching his pockets and removing a hotel card. Within minutes multiple units converged upon the BP gas station off Freedom Drive.

In conference with an arriving supervisor, consensus was that the hotel key discovered on Pug's person was to a guest room at the Ramada Inn that sat off the highway up the street.

Pug continued to be interrogated in the back seat of a police cruiser, but like a true soldier, he remained silent. Fifteen minutes later, Agents MacMall and Smith rolled up. Although they were unable to get any kind of response from Pug, they left him with a shocked look on his face.

Forty minutes later, as San waited for Pug's arrival, she received a distress call on her cell phone from Vanilla complaining that he was unable to get into the salon, informing her that Tracks hadn't showed up and most of the hair designers had left promising they'd return around noon. San kept him on the line while she tried in vain to reach Tracks by way of the hotel's phone. San then told Vanilla to come to Room 238 of the Ramada Inn off Freedom Drive.

Fifteen minutes later, San heard a knock on her hotel door. She peeked out and identified Vanilla before she opened the door.

"Damn, girl, lemme get a hit of dat," Vanilla said, staring at the bag of cocaine that sat beneath the lamp shade on the bedside nightstand inches from San's huge pistol.

"Go 'head," San replied, handing Vanilla the key and retiring to the restroom. Washing her hands, she looked up in paralyzing fear to see in the mirror the hotel door burst open and a multitude of officers rushing in, their weapons locked, loaded, and aimed. Responding to the officers shouted demands, both San and Vanilla dropped face down onto the floor's burgandy carpet.

Lt. Weber spoke first. "Ms.. Sandra Tillman, someone has something to tell you,"

"Fuck you. Can't nobody tell me shit," San defiantly responded, looking at Vanilla's chin resting on the carpet. Suddenly, as if in some kind of diabolical nightmare, San watched Vanilla's head turn in her direction and meet her gaze.

"Sandra Tillman, leader of Major League," Vanilla said, his voice gradually changing into a deeper, more manly tone as he rose slowly to his feet. "You have the right to remain silent. If you give up that right, every————"

"Wha' da fuck, Nigga! You police?" San shot back, interrupting Vanilla. "How Vanilla, how?"

"First off, the name is MacMall, not Vanilla Agent Rodney MacMall." Brushing lint from his tight jeans, he produced his gold badge with a sly grin. "And second of all, you're under arrest, Ms. Tillman."

Jap

"Good job," Webber said, patting MacMall on his shoulders.

San was escorted out of the room in shackles and forced to run a gauntlet along the curious stares from other hotel guests. When she was placed into the rear of a squad car, she got another shocking surprise when she looked up and saw who the agent was who was driving the car.

"Hey, San," Agent Smith offered a light greeting through the glass partition, smiling into the mirror at San's face frozen in disbelief.

San's usual arrogance was nowhere in evidence as she was driven downtown. However, regardless of the consequences, San refused to be taken into the interrogation room of the police department, insisting that they take her across the street directly into the jailhouse.

After appearing before the magistrate who read the charges to her, charges which included Conspiracy to Murder, Cocaine Conspiracy, Assault, Money Laundering, Racketeering, and Queen Pen charge, she was ordered held without bail.

When San entered the phone area she spotted Pug in a glass cell wearing an orange jump suit. She looked around and and also saw Tracks sobbing in a cell with other women. She too was wearing an orange jump suit. San walked past them to one of the unused phones and placed a call.

"Sup?," Bealz answered, interrupting his lunch at Nikki's Restaurant off Beatties Ford Road.

"Lil Bra, dis San. Den Pigs got me locked up."

"What!" he responded, dropping the sweet tea straw from his lips.

"Yeah, man, the Feds got me," she said sorrowfully, looking at the blue band on her wrist.

San asked Bealz to contact their father and Bruce Starks, her high priced lawyer. Just when she was about to tell Bealz something important, she was commanded to get off the phone to dress out. Disobeying the command, she got into a struggle which took three male officers and a female to get the phone from her tight grasp. On the other end of the line, Bealz listened helplessly to his sister's curse words screaming in his ear. He also heard her say something to the affect that "Smith is . . ." before the line went dead.

Bealz paid for his meal and left the restaurant, on the way out giving a few dollars to the beggar who stood outside the place on the sidewalk that led up to Cummings Avenue. He then made the calls that his sister in her desperation had asked him to make.

In the following days, Bealz and Jake showed up faithfully for San's first court date where she was denied a bond hearing.

September 29th — Sunday evening Bealz attended a cook—out that Pudding's uncle was hosting at a modest home in the University area. He spoke to the kids that played in the front yard as he held onto Pudding's hand and was led through the front door. What he failed to see was a car that he knew so well parked near the rear of the long driveway.

Inside the house, as Pudding introduced him to several of the family members, Bealz grinned as he firmly shook the hands of each male. He accepted hugs from Pudding's friendly aunts and female cousins. Once they made it to the huge wood fencet in the back yard, he spoke to Pudding's sister and squinted at the familiar face of the man who sat beside her.

"Sup, Bealz," the man said, grinning while bouncing Tonya's youngest daughter on his lap.

"Bealz, wha' up," Tonya spoke. "This is my husband, Rodney ..." She winked. "Agent Rodney."

"Oh, yeah," Bealz shot back, all the while listening to Pudding yell for someone to come meet him. When Bealz faced the person that Pudding had hailed, he got the shock of his life.

"Baby, this is my favorite cousin, Leslie," Pudding introduced.

"Leslie," Bealz repeated, snarling at the woman he knew as Tiff. Maintaining her composure, "Yes the name is Leslie. Agent Leslie Smith" The deception was finally revealed, the surprise no longer prolonged.

It suddenly dawned on Bealz who San was calling Smith during that initial frantic phone call from jail. In his mind all the pieces were falling into place and it was finally making sense to Bealz. No wonder Tiff always spoke low of people who smoked weed and the dope boys. He too regretfully accepted the fact that his intuition had been right about it being more than coincidence seeing Tiff's car at church and the restaurant. Besides that, Bealz was more concerned that Tiff and Vanilla were both the cause of his sister: facing a life sentence. His thoughts about having a baby by the kin folks of the ones responsible for his sister's troubles, cast a gloom over the marvel of Pudding's carrying his child.

The remainder of the cookout was for the most part uneventful. But later on, Pudding explained that she wanted to stay the night at Tanya's to spend time with her nieces. Bealz had no objection, actually a bit relieved because he wanted to make a last ditch effort to help San out, thinking that perhaps Tiff AKA Leslie could utilize her influence as a federal agent to their advantage.

Subsequently, Bealz invited Tiff over to his apartment to discuss San's predicament, but it didn't take long for lust to raise its fiery head and consumed them.

Afterward some intense love—making, Bealz came to his senses and confessed to Tiff the real reason he'd invited her over. When she asked about a future for them, he assured her that there was no future, that Pudding was having his baby and that the sooner she realized that, the better off they'd both be.

Feeling used, abused, and taken advantage of, the hatred of a woman scorned surfaced and she started screaming at him.

"You think you're some kind of player who can just play a bitch? Is that what you think?"

The more he tried to reason with her, the more outraged she became. With both tempers flaring, a heated argument ensued. She began to pick up anything not nailed down and throw it at the wall, the intensity of her rage increasing until she started striking herself in the face with a clenched fist, discoloring an eye and causing her nose to bleed.

Bealz freaked. Convinced she was crazy, he demanded "Get the fuck out you crazy ass, bitch!"

Ignoring his demands, she howled, "You gonna be one sorry Nigga!" She started ripping her clothing.

"You one crazy bitch, that's what you are," Bealz said, slipping on his boxer shorts. "Now quit playin' and get da fuck outta here before I have to get nasty."

Just as he reached the bedroom door he heard the metallic echo of a pistol being cocked. Looking back at her he saw that she had her service weapon leveled at him. "Now who's crazy," she snarled.

"What? You gonna shoot me, you stupid bitch? How you expect to get away with that, OFFICER?"

"When I tell them how you raped me, that's how, player."

"Quit playin' and get the fuck outta here," he retorted sarcastically. As he reached for the knob of the door,

POW!

His eyes flew shut when a shot rang out and a bullet entered his lower back. Falling to the floor in agony, he turned over and opening his eyes, saw her approaching him with the smoke still smoldering around the barrel of the pistol. The crazed look on her face made it quite clear that if she couldn't have him, no one would.

"What da fuc————?" he managed.

POW!

The pistol bucked as it roared. Bealz grunted as the second shot tore into his lower abdomen.

Tears brimmed in her eyes and she had difficulty holding the revolver steady.

POW!

The third shot from the .38 revolver caught him in his inner thigh. Convinced that he'd bleed to death from the three wounds, Tiff taunted him with the remainder of the bullets, wildly firing two shots into the floor and the last bullet she fired into the painting of Bealz that hung on the wall over his bed.

"You don't play with me," she smirked through her tears as she struck herself again and again, any grip on sanity totally gone. Exhausted, she fell to the floor, releasing the pistol, as in the distance the wailing of sirens could be heard growing louder. She had anticipated that the neighbors would call the police after hearing repeated gunshots.

Abrupty the door flung open and instead of an army of police officers she expected, Leslie stared up from the floor with her mouth agape at what was standing in the doorway.

"Sorry it took so long, Bealz," Karma said, aiming her registered .380 that she had purchased from Hyatt Gun Shop off Wilkerson Boulevard.

"Bitch, you better put that pistol down. I'ma federal agent," Leslie protested, scrambling for her empty pistol.

In her deranged state of mind, somehow it didn't register that she'd fired all the bullets from the revolver and aiming the pistol at Karma, pulled the trigger repeatedly. Time and time again the hammer fell on empty chambers but she just kept on pulling the trigger. Karma, her pistol aimed at the insane woman, cracked a demonic smile. "What!" Leslie snarled, flinging the gun at Karma but hitting the Plasma TV screen instead.

"Ain't it just like a hairdresser to come to a gun fight with an empty gun," Karma said, as she squeezed the trigger of her own loaded pistol. Leslie half—grunted as a bullet hole appeared in the center of her forehead slightly above her manicured eyebrows. Blood trickled down her face, her bulging eyes crossed themselves and she fell face first to the floor.

Rearing a commotion at the door, Karma quickly laid down, keeping the pistol near her, as police burst through the front door.

"Damn, this some movie—type shit," she joked, making an attempt at levity which got a half—smile and a choked chuckle from a barely conscious Bealz before everything went black for him.

EPILOGUE

A Few Months Later

Even though Diana "Tracks" Hicks testified against San, because of Agent Rodney aka "Vanilla" MacMall's extensive drug usage while operating undercover, San's defense team got many of the charges filed against her thrown out of court and the leader of the Major League crime syndicate only received a twelve and a half year Federal Prison sentence. Although Agent MacMall claimed his drug usage was in the line of duty, a means to keep San fooled, because it was an election year, the District Attorney pursued charges against Agent MacMall for violating department policy, proving the DA's "tough on crime" election platform. As part of a plea bargain, in return for her testimony against Agent MacMall, San's sentence was reduced to sixty months. A bitter and disillusioned Rodney MacMall was forced to abandon his law enforcement career.

Ultimately, the testimony against both Pug and San offered by TG and BlueBerry was nullified due to the constant changing of their statements in their desperate attempts to absolve themselves of any wrongdoing. San's high—priced attorney successfully argued that TG acted alone in the murder of Grams for which he received a thirty year sentence. BlueBerry ended up pleading guilty for the crack that was found in Shellz's apartment and received a slap on the wrists of eighteen months in State Prison.

No one was charged with the murder of Milky when ballistics revealed that the bullets that killed him were from Shellz's weapon. The investigation into the murders of both Coneka and Coley continued to be open cases which remained under investigation. The killing of Lil Gas was swept under the proverbial carpet when the pistol retrieved from his dead body resulted in the closing of three previously unsolved murder cases in Charlotte.

The investigation into the circumstances which precipitated the violence inside Bealz's apartment determined that Karma's actions amounted to justifiable homicide and she was cleared of any wrongdoing.

The day before San was to be shipped off to prison, she enjoyed an emotional family visit. Jake laughed long and hard at his daughter, bumping fists with her several times through the thick glass partition, and in turn San laughed at Bealz's newly developed limp. Although Bealz had managed to survive Tiff's gunshots, he was left moving much more slowly than what he was accustomed to and doctors had assured him that although he'd fully recover, his limp would most likely be permanent. He and Karma thought it gave him an air of distinction but San and Jake used the limp to make fun of him.

Bidding her family farewell when visiting hours were up, managed to prove San had a heart after all, even though it was a fact she had worked long and hard to disprove. What heart she did have had become like stone as she was forced to develop the toughness required to not only survive but to excel in the mean streets of Charlotte.

But as her family turned to go, for the first time in memory, her heart softened momentarily. True to her defiant nature, San was quick to mask the unfamiliar mistiness that appeared in her eyes, but not before both Jake and Bealz caught a glimpse of it, a fact neither of them was ever to mention to her or to each other.

In parting, the three again reiterated their love for each other, and San's brother and father promised they'd be there to visit once she got settled. Walking away from them, San didn't even look back, her toughness and don't—fuck—with—me attitude once again very obvious to anyone who happened to see the bull—dyke being escorted out of the visiting room and back to the holding cells.

In her new surroundings San never wanted for anything. Bealz made sure her account stayed full as he continued to dabble in the cocaine and heroin trade on the streets of Charlotte. Through his connect with the Gonzalles brothers, he moved up to dealing in pounds of weed. He and Karma got an apartment together near Uptown at a place called Circle at South End.

Bealz and his baby's mother maintained a good relationship. Pudding forgave his indiscretions, accepting the fact that he was just doing what men do. And besides that, it turned out that Leslie AXA Tiff had been a snake to her cousin more than once and she was just being true to her nature and doing what snakes do. From time to time Bealz and Pudding would continued to have sex together but basically their relationship was limited to preparing for the arrival of their child.

Although the unforgiving streets had nearly claimed each of their lives, the ordeal had earned Bealz, Karma, and Banga the respect Bealz had always coveted for The Alliance. Since their exploits had been played out in the media, they evolved into urban celebrities. Through San, Bealz became tight with Endz and when dropping in at Irresistables, he was treated with VIP respect. On top of it all, in his loyalty to his father, Bealz continued driving the Navigator for Jake.

By all appearances, the turbulence in the lives of Bealz, Karma, and Banga had subsided as they settled into normal routines. But someone else was just as determined that their days were numbered. In another part of the city, Detective Buccannon had all three of their pictures displayed prominently above her desk.

In the course of the detective's ongoing investigations into the city's homicides, a few hair fibers that matched Karma's were found at the murder scene of a dope dealer named Angelo. Although Detective Buccannon didn't have enough evidence for an arrest warrant, she was confident it was just a matter of time.

As for Bealz, Nicolette "Lette" Wilson assured Detective Buccannon that Bealz was the last one with Coley before he turned up dead. That testimony, plus the fact that Bealz's name was found in Coley's cell phone, definitely implicated Bealz in Coley's murder, but again she didn't have enough physical evidence to have him charged ... yet.

Unbeknownst to them, all three were sitting on on a lethal bomb and a determined Detective Buccannon was confident she'd find the match that would ignite the fuse. The fact that no one would talk against The Alliance was the only thing that kept them free.

Loyalty could be a bitch, sometimes a cruel and fickle mistress, but she was what Bealz depended on to stay alive. There was no question about it: in the streets of the Queen City, "LOYALTY REIGNS!"

In the heavy silence of the room lit only by the subtle rays of a setting sun, all that could be heard was the ticking of a clock. Two people sat in shadows across from each other staring at glint of sunlight reflecting off the solitary badge laying face up in the middle of the desk between them.

An unfamiliar male spoke in a voice just above a whisper: "Are you sure this is what you want to do?"

"I have no other choice, It's the way it has to be," Pudding replied.

Neither one reached for the badge.

THE END

RECOMMENDED READING FOR ALL AGES, COLORS AND INTELLECT

FOUNDATION BUILDERS IN A BOOKSTORE NEAR YOU.
"THE TRUTH SHALL NOT ONLY SET YOU FREE, IT GIVES YOU POWER
OVER YOUR SURROUNDINGS!"

Black Robes White Justice *by:*	**Bruce Wright**
Illusions of Justice *by:*	**Lenox Hinds** *(Iowa University)*
The Browder Files *by:*	**Anthony T. Browder**
Bad Blood *(The Tuskegee Experiment) by:*	**James H. Jones**
From Superman to Man *by:*	**J. A. Rogers**
Assata Shakur *by:*	**Assata Shakur**
Stolen Legacy *by:*	**George M.G. James**
Miseducation of the Negro *by:*	**Carter G. Woodson**
They Stole It but You Must Return It *by:*	**Richard Brown**
The Isis Papers *by:*	**Dr. Frances C. Wesling**
The Gnostic Gospels *by:*	**Elaine Pagels**
Possessing the Secrets of Joy *by:*	**Alice Walker**
The Conspiracy To Destroy Black Boys *by:*	**Jwanza Kujufi**
Before Columbus *by:*	**Ivan Van Sertima**
Christianity, Islam and the Negro Race *by:*	**Blyden**
Glory of The Black Race *by:*	**El Jahees**
7 African Arabian Wonders of the World *by:*	**Khalid Mansour**
Blood In My Eye *by:*	**George Jackson**
The Autobiography of Malcolm X *by:*	**Alex Haley & Malcolm X**
The Holy Quran translated *by:*	**Yusuf Ali**

E-books $9.99 www.kobo.com

HOOD WARS by ESCO
ISBN# 978-0-9844071-4-9
Page count: **401** Price Book **$16.99**
Prison order price: **$11.00**

Nina and Toast are two disheartened enemies who vowed to "WARN AND PROTECT" each other over the course of an impending war. Soon, Nina feels betrayed after a rush of slugs nearly claimed her life. She next goes on a manhunt tracking down Toast, revealing her own treacherous behavior to her circle that soon may get her killed!

Toast has too much to worry about than explaining his innocence to Nina. At the moment, he and his "FLUNKIES" are having a transformation of power. Toast must find ways to keep him and his underlings safe from the most monstrous gang in the city. Plus the risk of death ten folds when Toast soldiers have a clash of ideas and a division of loyalty. Plunged into a world were HONOR and RESPECT is cut paper thin, Toast is not going to know who to trust.

Who will be left standing when the smoke clears at the end of this bloody tale of deception, betrayal and survival of the fittest? Will Nina be able to eliminate Toast before her own treacherous past catches up with her? Will toast find sanctuary away from the madness; or will he walk right into the line of fire set up by either friend or foe?

D.D. Ellis explosive novel HOOD WARS is non-stop action, filled with larger than life characters, and will keep you asking "What will happen next?"   It's a must read!!!

FIVE STAR REVIEW
Esco you got one. HOOD WARS truly a great read.
Finally a representation of a writer from Allah Born.
Very entertaining. Keep pushing, we're moving......

GOAT
Albany, New York

E-Books $8.99   www.kobo.com

FALLEN ANGEL by FruitQuan
ISBN# 978-0-9844071-3-2
Page Count **333** Price Book **$15.99**
Prison order price: **$11.00**

From the Brownsville slums of Brooklyn, New York and Los Angeles, California all the way to the Federal Penitentiary, the hourglass is ticking, the streets are watching, and Gangstaz gotta KEEP IT GULLY!

With Albert Anastasia roots and links to the Biggie Smalls vs Tupac rival, Brooklyn's home of the legendary Mike Tyson is saturated with history...... Brownsville has a story to tell.

FIVE STAR REVIEW

Fallen Angel is a story of the games that are played on the streets; some people's reality. The characters in the book remind me of actual people that live & hang in the street of the five boroughs (NYC). I found myself constantly picking up the book to read at every opportunity that I could.

FruitQuan did an excellent job characterizing Hurricane, the main character as well as the others (Mama Maxie, Pale Face etc). Hurricane reminds me of "Midnight" from Sistah Souljah's book "A Coldest Winter Ever". The story is written whereas you know Hurricanes every thought, whether you agree with those thoughts or not. So if you like a book with lots of family love, street hustle, action & fast money this is the book for you."

Crystal
Brooklyn, NY

E-Books $7.99   www.kobo.com

WHAT'S NEXT by Courtney B. Walker
Drama, Pain, Heartache & Betrayal
ISBN# 978-0-9844071-2-5
Page Count **257** Price Book **$12.99**
Prison order price: **$9.00**

The author weaves a dynamic plot showing how one young woman's life undergoes drastic changes with each situation she faces, much of which leads to more pain and heartbreak. The character, Angel Reneé Walker, is unlike other people in the world. She can tell what lies ahead 惘 all the drama, pain, heartache, and betrayal. It all began on the first day of her senior year when her mother's life was taken in a car accident. Since then, her world has turned upside down.

Angel finds herself in difficult situations, while her relationship with her father is at its breaking point. It seems that nothing can go right. She starts to give up on life, on everything. When she meets someone who makes her believe there is still a chance, she feels hopeful again. But like everything else in her life, will this love be destroyed? Angel will be tested when a dark secret shocks her and she finds out that the one person she trusted most in the world was involved in the tragic accident that took her mother's life. Is she destined for a life of despair and betrayal? What's Next reveals all.

FIVE STAR REVIEW

"I recently read "What's Next," and I was amazed. I thought that this book would be a self-help book to help young people deal with the trails of growing up. But I was wrong. It was real talk from the beginning to the end. The young Angel Reneé Walker goes through things that a lot of adults can't handle. She lives, learns and falls down. But most of all, she had to find a way out of the place where people hide to get away. I find that this book is inspirational and just what is needed in today's world for our young people, both guys and girls. Grief comes to us all, but not all of us make it through. The aspect I admire is how she maintains her social standing among her peers."

KAY JOHNSON
Brooklyn, NY

BROOKLYN ICE by Anthony Brewer
ISBN# 978-0-9844071-0-1
Page Count **308** Price Book **$14.99**
Prison order price: **$11.00**

Brooklyn Ice follows its main character Theresa Jones. A Financial Consultant and Attorney; known through academic, corporate and judiciary realms as Ms. Jones. She is known on the streets and by friends as B.G. (short for BabyGirl), and there is only one thing she loves more than her desire to acquire money or her zeal for drama - and that's Joseph Cohen.

Joseph who is cut from the old school cloth of stick up kids use to rob banks, drug dealers and payrolls. He started investing money early on and sent his virgin love to school while he styled under the guise of a Real Estate Agent. That was back in the day, but now, the laid back, more reserved J.C. comes to find his BabyGirl has adopted his old gun slinging ways and combined them with her education and unrelenting Brooklyn ways.

Tempted by millions in diamonds, Joseph has decisions to make. In a time of recession, the Brooklyn bad boys are coming out with hopes Joseph will let Brooklyn do what it has always done - get money. Ride with J.C. or BG; she will not only get you money, but she'll show you how to use it. You decide. But whatever you do, don't get it twisted. The school girl is no longer taking lessons: she's giving them...... There's a new Brooklyn bully. Who would think it's a female?!

FIVE STAR REVIEW

"BROOKLYN ICE by Anthony Brewer is an exciting, breath-taking, fast pace novel to read. This book will have you on the edge of your seat waiting for the next piece of excitement. This book is definitely a page turner. BROOKLYN ICE is packed with plenty of action..."

Barbara Morgan
ATL, Georgia

E-Books **$7.99** www.kobo.com

TERRORIST IN BROOKLYN by Anthony Brewer
Revolutionary or Conspirator
ISBN# 978-0-9844071-1-8
Page Count **272** Price Book **$14.99**
Prison order price: **$11.00**

Terrorism activity has picked up on American soil as a result of the construction of an 80 billion dollar American oil project in Iraq, leaving the Federal Bureau of Investigation with work to do. With Corporate buildings getting blown up, dead bodies appearing out of thin air and the Bureau short on answers all fingers point to Special Agent Black of CTU.

No one ever thought terrorism would be on the door step of Brooklyn residents as victims or practitioners, but what is discover will change Brooklyn forever.

It doesn't help matters when Sheppard's Private Contracting Security Agency (Mercenaries) who served in the Iraq, Afghanistan and Saudi Arabia killing with impunity, have come to America after MOST WANTED terrorist that fled from Iraq seeking refuge in Brooklyn.

Equally alarming are the African American faces with international ties that are popping up as suspects of terrorism. In the midst of Agent Black's investigation, he connects Muslim residents from local Mosques supporting none terrorist. What's worse he finds he is not only a suspect, but a MOST WANTED.

With all eyes on Special Agent Black, he will have to choose between clearing his name when suspected of terrorism activity or making a name for himself by standing for justice against terrorist no matter who the perpetrators......

E-Books $7.99   www.kobo.com

SHOESHINE BOY by Charles Belim
ISBN# 978-0-9844071-6-3
Page count 271 Price Book $14.99
Prison order price: $11.00

The "Shoeshine Boy" saga chronicles events in the life of a young kid growing up in Boston, Massachusetts. At age ten he's given an opportunity to shine shoes in a shine parlor deep within the "Mob" controlled section of Boston's notorious 'North End'. Unbeknownst to him, the shine parlor is a front for illegal betting from horses to the local 'nigga number' in his community of Roxbury.

The experiences and exposure of that Summer will catapult the Shoeshine Boy into being dubbed one of Boston's most infamous 'Common Known and Notorious Thieves.' The Shoeshine Boy story is about his beginning.

"Payin' My Dues", **"Plastic Money"**, and **"Paper Money"** by the same author, will chronicle his rise, fall, and resurrection. Mr. Belim's resurrection as a new urban writer has given his readers a glimpse into the Black Underworld of trickery and deception.

E-Books $9.99 www.kobo.com

LOYALTY REIGNS by Japlin Cureton
ISBN # **978-0-9844071-8-7**
Page Count **413** Price Book **$17.99**
Prison order price: **$11.00**

"Loyalty Reigns" exposes the raw and often ugly truth about survival in a world tainted by jealousy, rivalry, violence, drama and mayhem; disagreements settled only by bullets and blood. The question whose answer determines who lives or dies that day is, "Will Loyalty Reign or will the storms of betrayal make it hail?" Be for warned, it's not a fairy tale or a story for the squeamish or the faint-hearted, but if you're unafraid to be inoculated with a dose of reality, jump into a Destinations Cab and join Jap Cureton for an "adults-only" tour through the unforgiving world where only "Loyalty Reigns," and honor rules.

This story chronicles the act of deception where there are no honor amongst thieves. Where mayhem thrives in a sinful world of MONEY, SEX, and POWER. Decrypt coincidences, coordinated murders, set-ups, perpetrated by Blueberry, and dishonest Agents will test ones quest of LOYALTY REIGNS!

Jap Cureton is presently at work on the second book of the "Loyalty Reigns" trilogy.

E-Books $9.99   www.kobo.com

INDICTED by Lamont Christian
ISBN# **978-0-98440071-7-0**
Page Count **341** Price Book **$16.99**
Prison order price: **$11.00**

They say that there are two sides to every story and to every coin, but what most don't know is that there are two sides to a small section of the city's world renown Island "MANHATTAN". And it all Depends on which side you are on. Harlem always rung louder and there is only one thing that mattered above all and it's that "paper".

In this story of East meets West, the traditional fashion of how the sedative that is excreted from a syringe, through the eye of a needle and finally into the blood stream of heroin hungry veins, causes sides to clash. This eventually places the "self proclaimed king of Harlem" Lavell Collins in direct opposition with the eastside and that inadvertently puts Yvonne, Lavell's girlfriend in a freedom compromising, life altering situation.

INDICTED is a story that illustrates love, lost and the desperation that often justifies the behavior of those residing in Harlem and the various communities that mirror it. Places where addiction consumes the home, demoralizes the people and erodes the spirit. Like the many that came before it, INDICTED gives readers a unique and in depth look at a world where the social, economic mechanics, that has for generations plagued our culture, could be unfair and outright discriminative.

This goes beyond the 2014 version of Romeo & Juliet because it takes place in HARLEM where Lavell and Yvonne have to fight for everything, including the basic liberties such as life and love while fending for one another, even if it's by their own set of rules.

E-Books **$10.99**

www.kobo.com

FANTASY BALL by ADENA
ISBN#**978-0-9844071-9-4**
Page Count **437** Book Price **$17.99**
Prison order price: **$11.00**

ABANDONED 310 MILLION YEARS AGO, IN WHAT IS NOW SOUTHWESTERN PENNSYLVANIA, A GROUP OF BALLS ARE SLOWLY UNEARTHED DEEP IN A FAMILY COAL MINE. THE FIRST TO BE DISCOVERED IS A NINE FOOT TALL YELLOW FANTASY BALL. NEITHER, NASA OR OTHER SCIENTIST CAN IDENTIFY WHAT THE IMPENETRABLE SPHERE IS MADE OF.

WITH NO APPARENT USE OR VALUE, THE OWNER OF THE COAL MINE PLOPS THE BALL DOWN IN HIS BACK YARD FOR HIS 13 YEAR OLD SON TO PLAY ON. YET IT IS THE AUTISTIC NEIGHBOR GIRL WHO USES HER GIFT OF MENTAL TELEPATHY TO OPERATE THE YELLOW SPHERE. SO JOIN CHAD AND VENUS ON THEIR SOMETIMES DANGEROUS, YET ALWAYS THRILLING, ADVENTURES THROUGH TIME AND SPACE IN THE FANTASY BALL. THE FIRST BOOK IN THE SERIES.

JO ANN
"SHE ROSE FROM THE ASHES"
ISBN # **978-0-9844071-5-6**
Page Count: **384** Book Price: **$17.99**
Prison order price: **$11.00**

America, the most powerful country on earth, has produced some of the most prolific families on earth. One such family is the Douglass'. Spawned from England and hardened by the Civil War, the family history is intriguing (mixed heritage) ruthless, and unique. This story entails the first of the mixed heritage, Jo Ann Douglass, and the family members that blazed a burning trail through the civil war era and reconstruction. A taut, suspense filled story in which the protagonist joins the union army passing as a white man, and shares adventures with us as a war hero, feminist, Romantic Heroine, and business woman that happens to become the first black female woman of wealth, all the while harboring a viscous secret.

Travel with me down the pulse pounding, page turning road with
"Jo Ann."

Little known fact; over 250 women enlisted and fought in the civil war for both the Union and Confederacy as men, now comes the story of the only black women to do so!

ORDER FORM

Name:_____

Address:_____

State:_____

Phone# _____

Title(s) purchased:

Send Mail :

New Era Books

1211 Atlantic Ave, Suite 303

Brooklyn, New York 11208

_____

_____ Ship: $2.50

_____ Total $_____

Purchase on line: www.newerabooks.net   or call 347-651-6366

Always include alternative book selection for unavailable books

Book Submissions & Inquiries: newerapublication@aol.com

Free shipping with the purchase of any two books.

PRISON DIRECT

Prison Direct: Family and friends can send New Era books, posters, greeting cards directly to any inmate in State/Federal prison. New Era Books promotes education for this reason we sell books to the prison population at a discounted price. Order Prison Direct through newerabooks.com

Rehabilitation Begins With Education......

www.ingramcontent.com/pod-product-compliance
Lightning Source LLC
Chambersburg PA
CBHW071641260626
47170CB00001B/184